MW00586665

OATHBREAKER

IN THE BLEAK mountains of the Warhammer Old World, the dwarf race fights a bitter battle for survival against its ancient enemies.

In a time before even Sigmar walked the earth the dwarf hold of Karak Varn is overrun by skaven rat-men and its venerable lord, Kadrin Redmane, slain. Thane Uthor vows to reconquer it, paying little thought to the enormity of such a task. Drawing together a force led by mighty heroes from across the realm he ventures into the dark, determined to wrest the flooded hold from skaven, greenskins and the foul terrors of the deeps. How can this band of dwarfs, brave and stalwart as they are, ever hope to triumph against such impossible odds?

More Warhammer adventure from the Black Library

GRUDGE BEARER
by Gav Thorpe

GOTREK & FELIX: THE FIRST OMNIBUS
(Contains the first three Gotrek & Felix novels: *Trollslayer*,
Skavenslayer and *Daemonslayer*)
by William King

GOTREK & FELIX: THE SECOND OMNIBUS
(Contains books four to six in the series: *Dragonslayer*,
Beastslayer and *Vampireslayer*)
by William King

Book 7 – GIANTSLAYER
by William King

Book 8 – ORCSLAYER
by Nathan Long

Book 9 – MANSLAYER
by Nathan Long

GUARDIANS OF THE FOREST
by Graham McNeill

DEFENDERS OF ULTHUAN
by Graham McNeill

MASTERS OF MAGIC
by Chris Wraight

EMPIRE IN CHAOS
by Anthony Reynolds

A WARHAMMER NOVEL

OATHBREAKER

NICK KYME

*For the wisest and oldest longbeard I know. For my guide and
lorekeeper. For grandad.*

A BLACK LIBRARY PUBLICATION

First published in Great Britain in 2008 by
BL Publishing,
Games Workshop Ltd.,
Willow Road, Nottingham,
NG7 2WS, UK

10 9 8 7 6 5 4 3 2 1

Cover illustration by Paul Dainton.
Map by Nuala Kinrade.

© Games Workshop Limited 2008. All rights reserved.

Black Library, the Black Library logo, BL Publishing, Games
Workshop, the Games Workshop logo and all associated marks,
names, characters, illustrations and images from the Warhammer
universe are either ®, TM and/or © Games Workshop Ltd 2000-2008,
variably registered in the UK and other countries around the world.
All rights reserved.

A CIP record for this book is available from the British Library.

ISBN 13: 978 1 84416 543 6
ISBN 10: 1 84416 543 5

Distributed in the US by Simon & Schuster
1230 Avenue of the Americas, New York, NY 10020.

No part of this publication may be reproduced, stored in a retrieval
system, or transmitted in any form or by any means, electronic,
mechanical, photocopying, recording or otherwise, without the prior
permission of the publishers.

This is a work of fiction. All the characters and events portrayed in
this book are fictional, and any resemblance to real people or
incidents is purely coincidental.

See the Black Library on the Internet at
www.blacklibrary.com

Find out more about Games Workshop
and the world of Warhammer at
www.games-workshop.com

CENTURIES BEFORE SIGMAR united the tribes of man and forged the Empire, dwarfs and elves held sway over the Old World.

BENEATH THE MOUNTAINS of this land lies the great realm of the dwarfs. A proud and venerable race, dwarfs have ruled over their subterranean holds for thousands of years. Their kingdom stretches the length and breadth of the Old World and the majesty of their artifice stands boldly for all to see, hewn into the very earth itself.

MINERS AND ENGINEERS beyond compare, dwarfs are expert craftsmen who share a great love of gold, but so do other creatures. Greenskins, ratmen and still deadlier beasts that dwell in the darkest depths of the world regard the riches of the dwarfs with envious eyes.

AT THE HEIGHT of their Golden Age, the dwarfs enjoyed dominion over all that they surveyed but bitter war against the elves and the ravages of earthquakes put paid to this halcyon era. Ruled over by the High King of Karaz-a-Karak, the greatest of their holds, the dwarfs now nurse the bitter memories of defeat, clinging desperately to the last vestiges of their once proud kingdom, striving to protect their rocky borders from enemies above and below the earth.

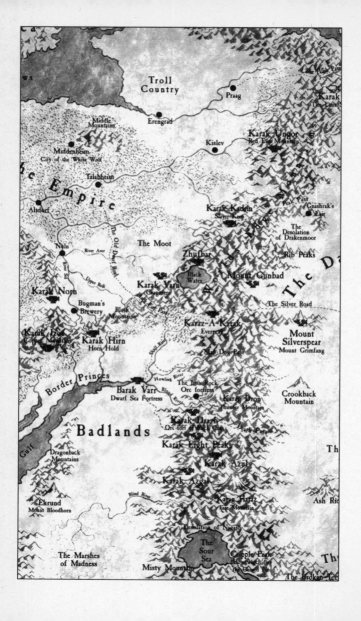

PROLOGUE

RALKAN FLED THROUGH the crumbling ruins of the underdeep, feeling his way frantically along the craggy tunnel. The ancient walls were warm, just like the stagnant air wafting languidly towards him, and dried the dwarf's sodden clothes. The heavy stink of sulphur pricked at his nose, but he ignored it.

Heart pounding, Ralkan risked a quick glance behind him. The tunnel stretched on forever, its vaulted roof creeping higher and higher until it was lost in a firmament of stars. There was nothing else, no monsters following, yet still he fled. Looking ahead again quickly, he didn't see the narrow cleft in the tunnel floor. He stumbled over and fell into it, down deep into the bowels of the earth, all sense of time and space passing away until he was brought thunderously to the ground. A dagger of white heat burned into Ralkan's hand, where the rock had cut a bloody gash into it, and he realised he was back in the very same tunnel.

Struggling to his feet, Ralkan bundled himself around a corner, the nameless fear at his heels driving him. He fell again, tearing his leather jerkin. Muttering an oath to Grungni, he got up. Then, enshrouded by the creeping dark and the waiting silence of the under-deep, he stopped. Breath held painfully in his chest, he felt along the wall again. Not for guidance, for his dwarf eyesight pierced the thick shadow well enough to see, but to try and remember.

As Ralkan's gnarled fingers traced pitted rock and jagged stone they found a runic symbol. It was a massive diagonal cross, with four short lines capping the end of each longer one, so large that it should have been impossible to feel and recognise. But know it, he did.

'Uzkul,' Ralkan muttered. Icy terror gripped his heart as the dwarf discerned its meaning instantly. It was a warning. It also meant something else – he had no memory of this place and with that came a crushing realisation.

He was lost.

Hurrying on further, he saw a wan light up ahead – the flickering flame of some burning brazier or the lambent glow of coals in a hearth hall. He made an oath to Valaya for it to be either. Getting closer to the light, the tunnel opened out and the foul sulphur smell assailing his nostrils grew more pungent. Heat radiated off the walls, without the need for Ralkan to touch them to feel it. By the time he reached the opening from where the light was spreading his clothes were bone dry.

Ralkan stepped tentatively into the corona of light, and gripped the talisman of Valaya around his neck.

'By the everlasting beard of Grungni…' His voice was barely a whisper as he regarded the huge cavern before him and basked in a lustrous aura.

Beyond the threshold of the room there were mountains of gold the likes of which Ralkan had never seen in all his long days. So vast and immeasurable was the hoard that it and the massive cavern appeared to have no end. Before he knew what he was doing, the dwarf had already wandered into the room, stepping into a diffuse shaft of natural light coming from above. Appeasing his desires, Ralkan blundered headlong into the nearest treasure mound, delving gleefully. The heady scent of gold filled his nostrils; the taste of it in the air tingled on his tongue as he immersed himself. Coins and gems spilled freely but as Ralkan dislodged them in his frenzy something else was revealed beneath – a desiccated dwarf head. Ralkan recoiled, and as he did so a different aroma assailed him, overpowering the whiff of gold – the stench of something old, as old as the world, a sentient presence.

Rasping wind emanated from a distant patch of thickening shadow at the back of the grand chamber. No, it wasn't wind… It was something moving slowly, gradually uncoiling, hidden in the dense shadows where the aura of light seemed too afraid to venture.

Running into the chamber was a mistake.

Ralkan's gold lust, which lay in the heart of every dwarf, bled away to nothing. The sound of heavy snorting echoed off the walls. Ralkan would have fled, had his dwarf legs allowed it. Instead he was like a statue, staring at the dark. The sulphur stink came at him again, so strong it made his eyes water, and he was certain he felt warm, wet breath against the back of his head. Whatever lay in those shadows had slipped past the dwarf somehow and was now behind him. The snorting abated, replaced by a deep, resonant sucking.

The eyes to the desiccated head sprang open, defying all laws of nature.

'Flee!' it hissed with decaying breath.

Ralkan turned...

White, blazing heat blinded him. Intense pain surged over the dwarf's body as fire ravaged it, hungrily devouring leather, metal and cloth. It flooded his senses, the nerve endings searing shut until he felt nothing; saw nothing but an empty, beckoning void. Ralkan opened his mouth to scream but fire scorched his throat, sealing it, and stripped the flesh from his bones...

RALKAN AWOKE WITH his gnarled hand covering his mouth to stop from shouting out. He was drenched in sweat despite the cold stone chamber surrounding him. He blinked back tears, a sense memory of the vision, as his eyes adjusted to the dark. He waited a moment, listening intently to the silence... Nothing stirred. Ralkan exhaled his relief but his heart still pounded at the nightmare – no, not a nightmare. It was a portent – a portent of his doom.

ACT ONE
HEARTH AND HOLD

CHAPTER ONE

THE VAST EXPANSE of the Black Water stretched out in the valley below like some infinite obsidian ocean. Dense fog, cooling in the early chill, sat over it like a vaporous white skin. Even at its craggy banks, it did not stir but sat like stygian glass: vast, powerful and forbidding. In truth it was a mighty lake, massively wide and impossibly deep, set in a huge crater that yawned like a giant maw, jutting with rocky teeth. Ribbons of glistening silver fed down through clustered stones and hidden valleys, filling the chasm-like basin of the lake with the melt waters of the surrounding mountains. Its glassy surface belied, in its apparent tranquillity, what dwelled in the Black Water's depths. Rumours persisted of ancient things, alive long before elves and dwarfs came to the Old World, slumbering in the watery dark.

'Varn Drazh,' muttered Halgar Halfhand almost wistfully.

A smile creased the old dwarf's features, near smothered by his immense beard braided into ingots of gold and bronze clasps, as he surveyed the vista laid out before and beyond.

Even standing upon a ridge overlooking the deep basin of the Black Water, rugged plateaus and dense groves of pine scattered amongst the sparse landscape were visible. Wending trails and precarious passes made their way across the rock. Halgar followed one all the way up to the zenith of the mountains. Peaks, jagged spikes of snow-capped rock, weathered by all the ages of the world, raised high like defiant sentinels. This was the spine of the Karaz Ankor, the everlasting realm of the dwarfs, the edge of the world.

Halgar smoothed his thick greying moustache absently, with a hand that had only two fingers and a thumb; the other, replete with all of its digits, rested lightly on the stout axe cinctured at his waist.

'Ever am I impressed by the majesty of the Worlds Edge Mountains,' came the deep voice of Thane Lokki Kraggson beside him, the dwarf's breath misting in the cold morning air.

Halgar frowned. A wisp of brooding cloud scudded across the platinum sky filled with the threat of snow.

'Winter is a time of endings,' he said, dourly.

'The cold will be hard pressed to vent its wrath beneath the earth; we have little to fear from its asperity,' Lokki returned.

Halgar grunted in what could have been amusement.

'Perhaps you are right,' he muttered. 'But that's the thing about endings, lad, you never see them coming.'

'We are close, my old friend,' said Lokki, for want of something more reassuring, and rested his hand, encrusted with rings etched with the royal runes of Karak Izor, upon the longbeard's shoulder.

Halgar turned to his lord, released from his reverie, and clapped his hand upon Lokki's in a gesture of brotherhood. 'Aye, lad,' he said, all trace of his earlier melancholy gone.

There was a strength and wisdom in Halgar's eyes. The old dwarf had seen much, fought many foes and endured more hardships than any other Lokki knew. He was the thane's teacher, instructing him in the ways of his clan and of his hold. It was Halgar that first showed him how to wield axe and hammer, how to form a shield wall and become a link in the impregnable mail of a dwarfen throng. Halgar still wore the same armour of those days; a thick mail coat and metal shoulder guard that displayed his clan-rune, together with a bronze helm banded by silver. The ancient armour was an heirloom, fraught with the attentions of battle. Though it was routinely polished and cleaned, it still bore dark stains of blood – ages old – that would not be removed.

'I for one will be glad of the hospitality of Karak Varn's halls,' said Lokki, walking back from the ridge and through the long grasses, pregnant with dew, to the Old Dwarf Road. They had travelled far, a journey of some several months. First, north from Karak Izor in the Vaults – the Copper Mountain – then they'd taken a barge across the River Sol in the shadow of Karak Hirn, the Horn Hold. Crossing the spiny crags of the Black Mountains had been hard but the narrow, seldom trodden roads had led them to Black Fire Pass.

They'd ventured through the wide gorge stealthily, keen not to attract its denizens, until at last they'd reached the edge of the mammoth lake. Now, just the undulating, boulder strewn foothills of roiling highland stood between them and the hold of Karak Varn.

'The soles of my boots grow thin, as does my appetite for stone bread and kuri,' Lokki complained.

'Bah! This is nothing,' snapped Halgar, his mood darkening abruptly. 'When I was a beardling and Karak Izor in its youth, I trekked from the Copper Mountain all the way to Karak Ungor, curse the grobi swine that infest its halls,' he spat and winced sharply as he got back onto the road, clutching at his chest.

Lokki moved to the longbeard's aid, but Halgar waved him away, snarling.

'Don't fret, 'tis just an itch,' he grumbled, biting back the pain. 'Wretched damp,' he added, muttering, shading his eyes against the slowly rising morning sun.

'Why have you never removed it?' Lokki asked.

Piercing his armour, and embedded deep into Halgar's barrel-like chest, was the tip of a goblin arrow. Its feathered shaft had long since been snapped off, but a short stub of it still remained.

'As a reminder,' returned the longbeard, eyes filling with remembered enmity, 'of the blight of the grobi filth and of the treachery of elves.' With that the longbeard tramped off down the road, leaving his lord in his wake.

'I meant no disrespect, Halgar,' Lokki assured him as they crested another rise.

'When you are as old as me, lad, you'll understand,' said Halgar, softening again. 'It is my final lesson to you,' he added, holding Lokki's gaze. 'Never forget, never forgive.'

Lokki nodded. He knew the tenets of his race all too well, but Halgar drove them home with the conviction of experience.

'Now, let us– ' Halgar stopped and pointed towards a shallow ravine below them, where the road went down into the basin and to the edge of the Black Water. Lokki followed his gaze and saw the wreckage of several ore chests. They were old, the wood warped and overgrown with moss and intertwined by wild gorse, but there could be no mistaking it. It was what lay next to the chests, though, that gave the thane greater pause – skeletons; bones and skulls that could only belong to dwarfs.

Halgar descended down into the ravine, picking his way through rocky outcrops and stout tufts of wild grass, Lokki close behind him. They reached the site of the wreckage in short order.

Grimacing, Halgar crouched down amongst the skeletons. Many still wore their armour, though it was ravaged by time and tarnished beyond repair.

'Picked clean by the creatures of the wild,' said Halgar, inspecting one of the bones. 'They have been gnawed upon,' he added with distaste and sorrow.

'There are more…' Lokki uttered.

Beyond where the two dwarfs were crouched there stretched a windswept highland plain, the fringes edged by shale and shingle from the lake's shore, scattered with more bones.

'Grobi, too,' spat Lokki, throwing down a manky piece of leather as he ranged across the rugged flatland. Skeletons were everywhere, together with more broken ore chests. Predated on by wild beasts, the battle that had unfolded there was scattered far and wide, making it impossible to discern its scale or significance.

'I don't like this,' said Lokki, going to another chest – this one empty, too.

'This was a party headed from Karak Varn,' Halgar muttered, having followed Lokki, running his fingers across old tracks.

'How many?' asked the thane.

'Difficult to say,' murmured Halgar, examining one of the wooden chests more closely. 'Wutroth,' he said to himself, remarking on the rare wood the chest was made from.

Above Lokki, a thick tongue of rock overhanged the grassy plain, blotting out the harsh winter sun. A narrow path, little more than a thin scattering of scree, wound up to it from the ancient battlefield.

'I'm going to try and get a better vantage point,' he said, forging up the pathway, beard buffeting as the wind swept across him.

There upon the rise, Lokki saw the full extent of the battle that had taken place. There were at least a hundred dwarf bodies, twice that number in goblins and orcs, though Grungni knew how many others had been dragged away by the beasts of the foothills to be gnawed upon in caves. There was a large concentration of bones at the edge of the Black Water where Lokki saw Halgar crouched – dwarfs and greenskin. The dwarfs seemed to be arranged in a tight circle, as if they had fallen whilst defending fiercely. Orc skeletons spiralled out from this macabre nexus, likely the remains of those repulsed. The shattered remnants of maybe thirty chests were in evidence, too. Old tracks, made with heavy, booted feet moved away from the site, too large and brutish to be dwarfs. It had not ended well for the warriors of Karak Varn and Lokki muttered an oath.

Returning from the overhanging rock spur, Lokki found Halgar tracing a flame seared rune on one of the chests.

'Gromril,' said the longbeard without looking up, indicating the chest's contents. 'Most likely headed for the High King in Karaz-a-Karak,' he surmised, based upon the direction of what tracks still remained.

'What's that?' asked Lokki, his keen eyes picking out something amidst the carnage in the direct centre of the formation he had espied from above. Around one dwarf skeleton's neck was a talisman. Its chain was tarnished, but the talisman itself remained pristine as the day it was forged. There was a rune marking upon it. Lokki showed it to Halgar. The old dwarf squinted at first then took it from Lokki for a better look.

'It bears the personal rhun of Kadrin Redmane,' he said, looking up at his lord, grim recognition on his face.

'The lord of Karak Varn?' Lokki's tone was similarly dark.

'None other,' said Halgar. 'Doubtless he fell guarding the gromril shipment to Karaz-a-Karak.'

'He must have been dead some time,' said Lokki, 'and yet no word of it has come from Karak Varn.'

Halgar's expression grew very dark.

'Perhaps they were unable to get word to the other holds,' the longbeard suggested. 'I saw no dawi tracks leading from this runk,' he added, indicating the bonestrewn battlefield. 'It is likely the fate of Kadrin Redmane is unknown to his kin.'

Lokki looked down at the dwarf skeleton that had worn the talisman, the remains, it seemed, of Lord Redmane. Its skull had been nearly cleft in twain. A split metal helm lay nearby. He ran his finger, the skin brown and thick like leather, across the wound. 'The blow is jagged and crude,' he said, 'but delivered with force.'

'Urk,' Halgar said, showing his teeth as he ground them.

'I saw their tracks, trailing away from the fight. There was a mighty battle here,' Lokki told him. 'How old do you think these skeletons are?' the thane asked, accepting the talisman of Kadrin Redmane back from Halgar.

The longbeard was about to respond when he sniffed at the air suddenly. 'Do you smell that?' he asked, getting to his feet and unslinging his axe.

A bestial roar echoed from the surrounding rocks. Lokki looked up and felt hot bile rise in his throat. Charging down the east side of the ravine, following the route taken by the two dwarfs, there was a group of five orcs brandishing bloodstained cleavers and crude spears. Seven more emerged from behind a cluster of boulders in the opposite direction, armed with brutish clubs. At least three more came from a second path, across the overhang of the grassy rise, bisecting the route of the other two groups, wielding wooden shields and crude, fat-bladed swords. Decked in filth-stained leather, studded with rusted iron and rings punched through their thick, dark skin, the orcs yelled and bawled as they piled across the flatland.

'They have been watching us,' Lokki realised, on his feet and moving back-to-back with Halgar as he drew his hammer and lifted his shield.

'Aye, lad,' Halgar growled, sniffing contemptuously.

'Never forgive, never forget,' Lokki snarled as the orcs met them.

* * *

UTHOR ALGRIMSON FILLED his lungs with a mighty breath of icy air as he regarded the mist wreathed peaks of the distant Worlds Edge Mountains. Standing in a patch of lowland in the foothills of the mighty range, he worked out the cricks in his back and neck. The sun was just breaking the horizon as he appreciated the view, his home of Karak Kadrin to the far north a distant memory now as the shadow of Zhufbar loomed close to the west, and beyond that Karak Varn.

The wings on the helm the dwarf wore fluttered in a highland breeze, his short cloak disturbed into small fits of movement. The errant wind cleansed him of an otherwise dark mood and committed the desperate plight of his liege-lord and father to the back of his mind.

Below him, down a steep escarpment, the wide, dark shadow of Black Water glistened. He had emerged at its western edge, about halfway down.

'A wondrous sight, is it not?' a voice said from above Uthor. The dwarf, momentarily startled, looked up and saw a balding dwarf with a thick, ruddy beard. He was sat upon a rocky outcrop, overlooking the gargantuan lake. Smoke rings spiralled from the cup of a bone pipe pinched between the thumb and forefinger of his right hand and a strange-looking crossbow rested on his lap. Perched in profile, he wore a stout leather apron over a tunic that bore the rune of Zhufbar.

'Legend tells that the crater was formed by the impact of a meteorite in ages past. Nowadays, the rushing lake waters wash the ore extracted from the mines and turn great water wheels that drive the forge hammers of Zhufbar and Karak Varn,' said the dwarf, and looking over to Uthor added, 'Rorek Flinteye of Zhufbar.'

'Uthor Algrimson of Karak Kadrin,' Uthor responded with a nod, noticing as the dwarf faced him that he wore an eye patch.

Rorek got to his feet and came down from the rocky outcrop. The two dwarfs shook hands heartily. Uthor noticed a ring upon his brethren's finger was inscribed with the crest of a dwarfish craft guild.

'An engineer *and* a tour guide,' he said when he recognised the crest.

'Indeed,' Rorek answered, chewing on the end of his pipe throughout the exchange, seemingly unfazed by Uthor's mild derision directed at his encyclopaedic utterance.

Smiling thinly, Uthor released his grip. Judging by his hands, Rorek could only have been a craftsdwarf, for they were coarse, ingrained with oil and metal shavings, and he smelled like iron.

'You are far from home, Uthor Algrimson,' Rorek said.

'I have been summoned to a council of war by a distant member of my clan, Kadrin Redmane of Karak Varn,' Uthor replied, straightening up. 'There are greenskins around Black Water that seek the taste of my axe,' he added, grinning.

'Then we are brothers in this deed,' said Rorek, 'for I too am headed to Karak Varn.'

'Your crossbow is impressive, brother,' said Uthor, who had never seen its like.

Rorek looked down at the weapon, and cradled it in both hands so that Uthor might see it better. 'It is of my own design,' he boasted proudly.

The crossbow was larger than those wielded by the quarrellers of Karak Kadrin. Uthor was well acquainted with the missile weapon, having used one during the many goblin hunting expeditions he had accompanied his father on. A dark memory sprang unbidden into Uthor's mind as he thought of his liege-lord. He crushed it, instead focusing his attention on the engineer's creation.

It was well made, as was to be expected from the dwarfs of Zhufbar. A small metal crank attached to a circular base was bolted to the stock and its large wooden frame accommodated a heavy looking metal box filled with bolts. Uthor couldn't help but notice a similar looking box attached to the engineer's thick tool belt, but this one contained bound up rope with a stout metal hook at one end.

'It is... *unusual*,' he said.

'I've yet to declare it to the guild,' Rorek admitted.

Uthor was no engineer, but he knew of the traditions established by the Engineers' Guild and of their reluctance to embrace invention. To impress such a device upon the guild could place Rorek's tenure in jeopardy and would likely be met with scorn and disgruntlement.

Before Uthor could say anything of this to the engineer, the sound of clashing steel and the cries of battle carried on the breeze. Words of Khazalid were discernable through the clamour of the distant melee. Rorek's good eye grew wide as he turned towards the source of the commotion. 'Not far,' he said. 'South, just beyond this side of Black Water.'

'Then we had best hurry,' said Uthor, his top lip curling into a feral smile. 'It seems the battle has started without us.'

* * *

GROMRUND OF THE Tallhelm clan, hammerer to the great King Kurgaz of Karak Hirn, and so named because of the mighty ancestral warhelm he wore upon his head, stalked down the Ungdrin road, his companion a few short steps behind him. Great was the subterranean underway of the dwarfs, carved into the rocks in ages past in an effort to connect the many holds of the Worlds Edge Mountains. Runic beacons that could be made to glow, and even blaze, with a single word of Khazalid, the language of the dwarfs, provided guidance and illumination through myriad tunnels that ever since the Time of Woes had become, at least in part, the domain of fell creatures: orcs, goblins and even worse denizens all stalked the ruined passages of the Ungdrin road now.

'The gates of Karak Varn are not far,' said Gromrund, raising a lantern as he noted a runic marker inscribed in one of the ornate columns set along the tunnel walls. Statues of the ancestor gods sat in between them, wrought into the very walls themselves. At their feet were thick stone slabs of grey and tan, rendered into knotted mosaic interweaved with the runes of Karak Varn. 'This way,' said the hammerer and forged off into the darkness.

'Have you ever seen the gilded gates of Barak Varr, my friend?' asked Gromrund's companion, a dwarf who had introduced himself as Hakem, son of Honak, of the clan Honak, bearer of the Honakinn Hammer and heir to the merchant houses of Barak Varr, Sea Gate and Jewel of the West. The longwinded title had failed to impress the hammerer.

'No, but I suspect you are about to describe them to me,' Gromrund replied with gruff disdain.

The two dwarfs had met at a confluence of the Ung-drin road by sheer chance at a point where the subterranean tunnels that linked Karak Hirn and Barak Varr met. Three days they had been travelling together. To Gromrund, it felt like months.

'They rival even the great gates to Karaz-a-Karak in their majesty,' boasted Hakem, 'eclipsing even the Vala-Azrilungol with their beauty. Wrought of iron, inlaid with coruscating jewels that shimmer in the refracted sunlight, each gate bears the likeness of Kings Grund Hurzag and Norgrikk Cragbrow forged into the metal, founders of the Sea Gate and my esteemed ancestors. Bands of thick, lustrous gold filigree mark it in the rhuns of the royal clan of Barak Varr.' The merchant thane's eyes grew misty at the mention of the architectural masterpiece.

'A wonder, I am sure,' remarked the taciturn hammerer, wondering if he could silence his travelling companion with a blow from his great hammer, doubtful that the merchant thane would be missed. Yet in truth, even Gromrund was moved, as all dwarfs were when talk was made of the elder days, but he did his best to hide it.

Hakem's merchant garb was almost as grandiose as his tongue: gilded armour, ringed fingers and a purple velvet tunic spoke of wealth, but nothing of heritage, of honour. Gromrund found such ostensible opulence distasteful and decadent. He knew that the War of Vengeance had hurt the purses and the pride of the merchant thanes of Barak Varr. Now, some four hundred or so years later, trade had ceased with the elves. They needed to establish stronger links with their kin, to garner favour and forge new contracts wherever possible. He could think of no other reason for Hakem to have been summoned. To invite such a dwarf to a council of war seemed incongruous at the very least; at most it was an insult.

The Ungdrin narrowed ahead, the roof had become dislodged and sloped downward sharply, doubtless the result of the earthquakes that had ravaged Karak Varn and all of the Karaz Ankor. It forced the hammerer's mind back to the matter at hand. The damage only affected a short section of the underground tunnel, but Gromrund had to stoop to get his helmeted head, replete with two massive curling horns and the effigy of a bronze boar, through it.

'Why don't you just remove your warhelm, brother?' Hakem offered, just behind him, ducking only slightly as he took off his own jewel-encrusted helmet. Gromrund turned to glare at the Barak Varr dwarf, his face hot with indignation. 'It is an heirloom of my clan,' he snapped. 'That is all you need know. Now, keep to your own business and stay out of mine,' he added, and continued through the tunnel without waiting for Hakem's reply.

Once they had traversed the narrow passage, the Ungdrin opened out again, into a much larger cavern with three portals leading off from it. A great circular bronze plaque set into the floor at the centre of the room bore further runic symbols. It was a *bazrund*, a way marker that indicated they were close to the hold and showed the roads that led to Zhufbar and Karaz-a-Karak.

'I know of heirlooms, kinsdwarf,' said Hakem, seemingly unfazed by the hammerer's outburst as he stepped onto the plaque. 'What say you of this?'

Out of the corner of his eye, stooping over the plaque as he confirmed they were indeed headed in the right direction, Gromrund saw the dwarf hold a rune hammer aloft. So beauteous was it that even he stopped to look at it.

The rune hammer was clearly crafted by a master. It was plainer than Gromrund might have imagined, a simple stone head – inscribed with three runes that glowed dully in the gloom – topped an unadorned haft carved from stout wutroth, studded with fire-rubies. The grip was made from bound leather and a thick thong attached it to Hakem's bejewelled wrist.

'Have you ever witnessed a thing so truly magnificent?' said Hakem, his eyes alight with pride. His immaculately preened black beard bristled, the gemstones set in braid clasps within it glistening with the reflected rune-glow of the hammer.

'It looks a fair weapon,' Gromrund said, feigning his indifference as he turned away again and started walking.

'Fair?' said Hakem, in disbelief. 'It is worth more than the entire wealth of most clans!' he said, brushing down his tunic when he realised some dirt from the narrow tunnel had marred the velvet.

'Why does a merchant have need of such a weapon, anyway?' Gromrund remarked, feigning disinterest.

'*That*,' said Hakem, clearly relishing the moment, 'is *my* business.'

Gromrund snorted, contemptuously.

'Silk-swaddled cur,' the hammerer muttered beneath his breath.

'What did you say?' Hakem asked.

'We're nearly there,' Gromrund lied, a wicked grin ruffling his beard, before Hakem continued to boast of the wealth of the merchant thanes and the house of Honak. They couldn't arrive soon enough.

ROREK WAS GASPING for breath by the time they crested the final rise. Below them, in a narrow ravine a battle was being fought. Two dwarfs, one clearly a thane and carrying an axe and shield; the other much older, a longbeard, similarly armed. They fought back-to-back. Rorek counted nine orcs surrounding them, another six dead at their feet. He watched as one of the greenskins waded in with a reckless spear thrust. The longbeard hacked the haft down whilst the thane reached over his back and stabbed the spike of his axe into the orc's neck, blood fountaining from the wound.

Uthor had seen enough and a wild grin crept across his face as he bellowed, 'Uzkul urk!' and charged into the melee.

One of the orcs, a thickset beast with broad tusks jutting from its slab-like jaw and an iron ring through its nose, turned to face this new threat. There was a flash of silver and the deep, 'thwomping' retort of a blade slicing air. The orc was smashed off its feet and hit the ground before it could throw its spear, an axe embedded in its cranium.

ON THE RIDGE, Rorek watched as Uthor flung his axe end-over-end into the nearest orc. He waded in quickly after it, ducking the savage swing of another greenskin before punching it hard in the face with his leather-gauntleted fist, shattering its nose. He stooped to retrieve his axe, wrenching it free with one hand. More blood spurted from the mortal wound as he did so. Uthor then used the haft to block an overhand cleaver swing from the orc with the shattered nose.

Further down, the thane and the longbeard were still pressed hard by the remaining orcs, one of whom looked like some kind of chieftain. His flesh was much darker than the rest, his body bigger and more muscled, and he wore an antlered leather helmet. He wielded a heavy-looking morning star and pummelled the thane's shield with the crude weapon.

Uthor had dispatched a second orc, the top half of its skull cut off by the keen edge of his axe, the matter within spilling onto the ground. He was breathing hard and two more orcs came at him wielding wicked cleavers and crude, curved blades.

Rorek unslung the crossbow from his side, released the safety catch and turned the crank at the wooden stock. A fusillade of bolts peppered the ravine. One of the orcs was struck in the jaw, a second bolt pierced its neck, and a third pinioned its foot to the ground, though at least four more bolts thundered harmlessly into the ground. The engineer roared with glee, then exhaled sharply as an errant bolt careened off Uthor's winged helmet while a second whistled closely by his ear. The dwarf cursed, scowling at Rorek before dispatching the pin-cushioned orc with his axe and then turning his attention to its unscathed kin.

Thinking better of it, Rorek shoulder his crossbow and drew his hand axe. He'd have to do this the traditional way.

'Kruti-eater!' Uthor snarled at Rorek as the engineer reached him from atop the ridge, disembowelling the second orc, though more were coming to replace it.

'Though it might suit you, I've no desire to wear an eye patch!'

Rorek nodded apologetically, before hacking off another orc's hand at the wrist. Uthor finished it, beheading the creature. 'Stay behind me,' he said, 'and keep that crossbow well harnessed.'

AT THE BASE of the ridge, as he was slowly being crushed beneath his shield under the continued blows of the orc chieftain, Lokki saw the two strangers rushing to their aid.

'Halgar!' he grunted.

The longbeard kicked an orc in the shin, shattering the bone, and cut the greenskin down as it crumpled in pain. 'I see them,' he growled, half-turning to regard his liege-lord as another two orcs demanded his full attention.

'No, old one,' said Lokki, pain spiking up his arm as his shield was pounded incessantly, 'I need a little help.'

Halgar swung his axe in a wild arc, forcing the two orcs in front of him to give ground. He then whirled around and rammed his shoulder into the flat of Lokki's shield, the thane doing the same. 'Push!' he roared.

The blow from the orc chieftain came again, but this time it was met with the force of two angry dwarfs and his morning star was parried aside. Lokki and Halgar followed through, smashing the shield straight into the orc chieftain's body, who staggered backwards, stunned.

Halgar cried out as a spear struck him in the side. It split some of the chain links of his armour and grazed bone, but didn't impale him. Lokki's expression was fraught with concern for the venerable dwarf, but Halgar just bellowed at him.

'Kill the beast!' The longbeard gestured toward the staggering chieftain, before swatting the spear aside and turning back to face his foes.

Lokki did as ordered, swinging his axe around full circle to reaffirm his grip, and lifting his shield to work out some of the pain and stiffness in his shoulder. The orc shook its head, a long drizzle of blood and snot shooting from its ringed nostril as it snorted. It snarled at the advancing dwarf.

'Come on,' Lokki growled, meeting its bestial gaze with his.

UTHOR BATTERED ANOTHER orc with the flat of his axe blade before hacking up into its chin, his face and beard sprayed with greenskin blood as the orc's jaw caved. He shrugged it disdainfully off his blade then hawked and spat on the cooling corpse.

'I count another five, since we joined the fight,' he said to Rorek, who was watching his back.

'I saw at least three more come from the rocks cresting the western ridge,' Rorek returned, 'but they are thinning,' he added, breathing hard.

The two dwarfs had left an impressive trail of greenskin dead in their wake. Another group had emerged from the rocks almost as soon as they had arrived, though, placing themselves between them and the other dwarfs. But with the orc reinforcements dispatched, only a handful remained, and Uthor had a clear route through to their two embattled kin.

The longbeard faced three, while the thane made ready to fight the orc chieftain, wielding his axe and

shield with practiced ease. Two further greenskins –
bigger than the others and more heavily armoured –
stood behind the chieftain, presumably at the orc's bidding. Uthor snorted.

'I'll get to you later,' he muttered and fixed his steely
gaze on the three fighting against the longbeard.

THE ORC CHIEFTAIN facing Lokki was about to commit to
the attack when, as if abruptly aware of its surroundings, it backed off and grunted in its debased language.
Two heavily armoured orcs behind it rushed forward
suddenly and into the thane's path. Behind them, the
chieftain bellowed again, a shrilling cry that ululated in
its throat. Lokki flashed a brief glance over his shoulder
to see the remnants of the orc horde retreating.

The two left alive against Halgar were already running. Three more fled the other two dwarfs making
their way across the flatland, now only a few feet from
Lokki and Halgar. One of the fleeing greenskins was
pitched off its feet, squealing, as an axe 'thunked' into
its back. When Lokki looked back, he saw another two,
together with their chieftain and his bodyguards, making good their escape. They scattered back up the ravine
and into the nearby foothills at the edge of the Old
Dwarf Road. The will of the orcs was broken it seemed
and, by the time it was over, some sixteen greenskin
carcasses littered the ground.

'Filthy urk,' growled Halgar. 'No stomach for a fight,
not like in the old days.'

Lokki decided not to give chase. He doubted Halgar
could keep the pace, despite the longbeard's
undoubted protestations to the contrary, and in truth,
he was weary himself. He wiped blood from a cut on

his brow, caused by a wound he hadn't realised he'd received, and watched as one of their new found allies, a dwarf wearing a winged helmet and bronze armour etched with the runes of Karak Kadrin, wrenched his axe from a greenskin body.

'You have our gratitude, kinsdwarf,' said Lokki, slinging his shield to his back and hitching his axe back to his weapons belt, before proffering his open hand to the axe-wielding dwarf. 'I am Thane Lokki Kraggson of Karak Izor.'

'Of the Vaults,' the axe-wielder said, trying to keep his tone even and without derision. There was some ill feeling between the dwarfs of the Worlds Edge Mountains and those of the other ranges. Exiles, some called them. Others had less pleasant names.

'Yes, of the Vaults,' Halgar returned proudly, daring the stranger's scorn as he stood beside his lord.

'*Gnollengrom*,' the axe-wielder muttered to Halgar, bowing deeply. Rising again, he clasped Lokki's hand in a firm grip. 'Well met, my brother,' he said, 'I am Uthor Algrimson of Karak Kadrin, and this,' he added, gesturing towards his companion, a dwarf bearing an eye patch and carrying a strange looking crossbow, 'is Rorek Flinteye of Zhufbar.'

'We are in your debt,' Lokki said, nodding his appreciation.

'You are of the royal clan of Karak Izor,' said Uthor, noting the gilded earring that Lokki wore. It was a statement, not a question.

Lokki nodded.

'Then it seems the rumours of the urk gathering in the mountains must be true, if royal clans are taking an interest,' Uthor remarked. 'The greenskins are bold indeed to venture all the way to Black Water.'

'You too have been summoned to Karak Varn?' Lokki asked, inferring it from Uthor's comment.

'Indeed,' he said, 'and we would be honoured to travel at your side, noble thane.'

'Yes, yes. Enough talk,' growled Halgar, wrinkling his nose as he surveyed the carnage. 'These urk are starting to stink.'

HALGAR MUTTERED WORDS of remembrance over the cairn tombs of the skeletal remains of Lord Kadrin of Karak Varn and his followers. The dwarfs had carried the bones reverently from the battlefield of the narrow ravine to the western ridge in the shadow of Karak Varn. They were well equipped, as was prudent for long journeys, carrying short shovels and picks, and buried the remains deep so they would not be disturbed. As the longbeard conducted the brief ceremony, the other three dwarfs stood silently around him with their heads bowed as a mark of deep respect. Below them, and in the distance, the oily smoke rising from a burning pyre, on which the orcs smouldered, stained the air.

'May Gazul guide you to the Halls of the Ancestors,' Halgar whispered, invoking the name of the Lord of Underearth. Making the rune of Valaya – goddess of protection – over his chest, the longbeard got to his feet and the four dwarfs moved away in silence.

After a time, Uthor spoke.

'You are certain it was the body of Kadrin Redmane?' He regarded the talisman of his distant kinsdwarf thoughtfully as he slowly traced the rune markings with his finger. Lokki had given him the heirloom immediately after he had explained how he and Halgar had come across the old battle site, the dead dwarfs with the ore chests and the subsequent ambush by the orcs. As he was a relation of Redmane it was only right that he have it.

'I cannot be certain, but the bones we found bore that talisman and they were old, as if he had been dead for some time.'

'Was there a hammer amongst the remains?' Uthor asked.

'None that we discovered,' Lokki replied.

Uthor sighed lamentably.

'Dreng tromm, then I am doubly saddened. Lord Kadrin's rune hammer was presented to him many years ago, when he was in his youth, by the then High King, Morgrim Blackbeard,' Uthor said. 'If my ancestor is dead then it means the hammer is lost, either to the urk or the Black Water,' he added, tucking the heirloom back under his armour. 'We had best make haste,' he said grimly, 'this does not bode well for Karak Varn.'

CHAPTER TWO

IT WAS WITH some relief that Gromrund and Hakem finally reached the gate to Karak Varn. The hammerer's mood had grown steadily more belligerent the longer they travelled together and the prince of Barak Varr feared the two of them might have come to blows. His tunic was freshly tailored and he would not have it soiled in a brawl, nor would he be received into the hold of Karak Varn in such a state of disrepair.

'Behold,' said Gromrund. It was the first time he had spoken in over an hour. 'The southern gate of Karak Varn.' The hammerer seemed to straighten as he said it, and was made impossibly tall by the mighty warhelm that sat upon his brow, the two great horns spiralling from it almost touching the roof of the tunnel. The helmet incorporated a half mask, too, that concealed much of the hammerer's face, but still his moods were easy to discern.

The gate was impressive. Tall and wide, it was set into a vaulted antechamber that ended the narrow tunnel. Etched with gilded spiral designs and elaborate cross-hatching, it was the height of the fully helmeted hammerer five times over. With the intricate gold framing and knot work the past histories of the karak were described in painstaking mosaic. Truly, it was a stunning piece of craft and a testament to the dwarfs' mastery of metal, displayed ever proudly, for what was merely a side entrance into the hold. To Hakem, it was little more than an ornate door, plain and austere – nothing like the bejewelled entryways of Barak Varr.

'There is something wrong here,' Hakem said suddenly, his mood darkening quickly.

'If you remark of the lustre of the gilded gates of Barak Varr, once more...' Gromrund warned, brandishing his great hammer meaningfully.

'No, it's not that.' The seriousness in Hakem's tone demanded attention as he gripped his rune hammer.

'Yes, I see it,' Gromrund said, facing the southern gate, gripping his hammer haft a little tighter.

'Where are the guards?'

GROMRUND LED THE way through the gate. Deciding against hailing for it to be opened or even knocking, the dwarfs had to push hard against it to force an opening. Worryingly, it was neither locked nor barred. Once inside, a long and lofty hall stretched before them. It was lined with stone statues; thanes and kings of Karak Varn and lit by flickering braziers mounted in sconces. One of the statues was toppled over. Its fall had shattered the terracotta slabs beneath and removed its head. Rubble was strewn all about. On the left wall, a huge tapestry depicting a great battle fought against the elves during the War of Vengeance was torn. Shreds of material hung down like strips of flayed skin.

'This was not the welcome I had envisaged,' Hakem said humourlessly, gaze ever watchful in the deepening shadows of the hall. 'Where are our clan brothers?'

'Karak Varn is invaded,' Gromrund hissed, fear edging his voice. 'These halls should be the dominion of Kadrin Redmane, lord of this hold.'

'Yet, they seem abandoned.' Hakem finished for him, saying what the hammerer was thinking.

'Indeed,' Gromrund concurred, noting the absence of any dwarfs at the south entrance, even dead ones.

'Is it possible that Redmane and his kin merely moved on, following another seam of ore? It is the way of our people,' Hakem reasoned, stepping carefully, every footfall a clattering din in the abject silence.

The two dwarfs advanced slowly and cautiously, and spoke in low tones. Something was desperately wrong here. Both knew that this was no dwarf migration; no pursuit of a more promising vein of ore. Some terrible fate had befallen the karak. It appeared empty – in a place where guards at least should be present – utterly bereft of life; even the hammer falls of the forges, usually an ever present and reassuring clamour, were silent.

The long hall soon gave way to another area of the hold, perhaps a merchant quarter – it was wide and dark, shadows cast from the illuminated entryway suggesting another hall with associated galleries and antechambers. Unlit braziers, growing cold, were set in the walls and the detritus of trade lay all about: ruined casks, broken carts and broad barrels, wrecked wooden stalls and racks.

'I thought the hold had been resettled,' Hakem remarked, biting his tongue about the great merchant halls of Barak Varr. 'If it was recently contested, where are the signs of battle? What in the name of Grungni happened here?'

'I know not,' Gromrund breathed. 'Karak Varn was wrested back from the rat-kin and the grobi years ago. The entire upper deeps were conquered by dawi, though much of the lower levels are ruined and flooded still from the Time of Woes.'

'It is as I read it,' agreed Hakem. 'Though this place looks dead, as if...'

'Hsst!' Gromrund motioned for quiet, raising a clenched fist. With the same hand he pointed towards a runty-looking figure, swathed in shadows and crouched with its back to them, in the middle of the hall.

With unspoken understanding, Hakem ranged wide of the figure, moving silently to catch him at his flank. Gromrund headed straight ahead, low and quiet as he stalked his prey.

As the hammerer drew close, he saw more of his prey's appearance. Its clothes were ragged; coarse and filth-stained garments, the stink of which rankled at his nostrils. Gromrund could not keep the sneer of contempt from his face – if it was a grobi swine his hammer would crack its wretched skull, though as he got closer he realised it was too big for a mere goblin. The creature wore a helmet upon its head, too, dented and tarnished. Doubtless, the foul greenskin, whatever its breed, had stolen it from some noble dwarf's corpse.

Anger swelled in Gromrund's breast and a red rage overlaid his vision, before he saw Hakem ready to strike at the creature's flank.

'Turn, filth!' Gromrund bellowed, all thoughts of caution gone. He wanted to see the fear in the green-skin's eyes before he smote it. 'Turn and feel the wrath of Karak Hirn!'

The runt-like shadow figure seemed to leap up in sudden shock and whirled around to face the hammerer.

'Hold!' it cried in Khazalid. Gromrund's hammer stalled a few inches from stoving its skull in. Hakem, frozen momentarily, held his rune hammer aloft and ready to strike. 'Hold!'

It was no goblin. The bedraggled swine before them was a dwarf. Gromrund, now facing him, recognised the dwarf's garb as belonging to that of the Grey Mountains. Known as 'Grey dwarfs', they were the poorer cousins of the Worlds Edge Mountains, the Black Mountains and the Vaults. The hammerer then noticed a large pack behind the dwarf, who held up his hands plaintively. Some of the contents had spilled out: spoons, a silver ancestor idol and even a dented firkin were amongst the booty. It was unlikely that these trinkets were the Grey dwarf's belongings.

Gromrund's lip curled up with distaste as he saw the scattered treasure, but he lowered his hammer.

The Grey dwarf exhaled in relief, shaking slightly at almost being sent to his ancestors prematurely, and nodded his thanks.

'I didn't hear you approach,' he said, voice quivering a little as he extended a grubby hand. 'Drimbold Grum,' he offered, 'of Karak Norn, in the Grey–'

'Doubtless you were too intent on whatever it was you were doing,' Gromrund grumbled, staring from Drimbold's hand to the bulging pack. 'And I already know of your heritage, dawi,' the hammerer growled, keeping his hands firmly at his side, 'and of your name. The Grums are well recorded in the Tallhelm Clan's Book of Grudges. One hundred years ago, you supplied us with a stable of shoddy lode ponies, weak of back and bowel. Recompense for which is yet to be made by the reckoners,' he added through gritted teeth.

'Ah, no, that was the Sournose Grum's,' said the Grey dwarf, 'I am one of the Sour*tooth* Grums,' he added, smiling.

Gromrund glowered.

Drimbold lowered his hand and his eyes, and quickly set about replacing the items that had spilled from his pack.

'He smells worse than a narwangli,' hissed Hakem behind his hand, not entirely convinced the Grey dwarf hadn't soiled himself when they'd surprised him.

Gromrund ignored him.

'What do you know of the fate of Kadrin Redmane and his kin?' the hammerer demanded, once Drimbold had turned back around to face them and was on his feet. Even the dwarf's mail was rusted and ill kept, and his beard was infested with gibil.

'I do not know, my kinsdwarf. I only just arrived myself. I was *adjusting* the items in my pack when you found me. I noticed one of the straps was loose,' he added by way of explanation.

'Indeed,' muttered Gromrund, not bothering to disguise his suspicion.

'Has Karak Norn made a pledge to Karak Varn, also, in ridding the Black Mountains of the urk tribes gathered there?' Hakem asked, wrinkling his nose at the Grey dwarf's stink.

'Precisely that,' Drimbold confirmed brightly.

'Then, Grum or no, you had best come with us,' Gromrund returned. 'Perhaps the Grey dwarfs have something to contribute if they are willing to send an emissary across the mountains. Besides, I have an ill feeling about this place,' the hammerer added, looking around the large hall of the merchant's quarter again, before returning his gaze to Drimbold. 'It smells foul.'

With that, the hammerer stalked off into the gloom, Hakem following at his side. Whatever differences were felt by the Karak Hirn and Barak Varr dwarf, they were nothing compared to the mutual distaste they held for a resident of the Grey Mountains. They were poor dwarfs, scratching a living off rocks, without the breeding or heritage of the other holds. Still, a dawi he was and if part of the war council they should travel together. In any event, it was far better that a stern eye was kept upon him, lest he get into trouble and bring it down on all their heads.

'Where are we going?' Drimbold asked, adjusting his cumbersome pack, an eye on the way he had come.

'To the audience chamber,' Gromrund replied, 'where the rest of the war council are due to assemble.'

'What if they're gone, too?' Drimbold asked again.

'Then we wait,' Gromrund snarled, turning briefly to set his steely countenance upon the Grey dwarf, 'for as long as it takes!'

In truth, Gromrund did not know what else *to* do. His role here was merely to hear of Lord Redmane's grievances and commit what forces to staunching the growing grobi hordes that he was permitted. With Redmane absent, and his hold deserted he was slightly lost and getting steadily more annoyed.

'An ufdi and a wanaz,' he muttered, bemoaning his travelling companions as he followed the runic markers that would lead them to the audience chamber, 'why Valaya, do you test me so?'

THE GREAT GATE of Karak Varn loomed large and imposing – two immense slabs of stone, bound with steel and gold set into the very mountainside.

'Tis quite a sight,' breathed Lokki, arching his head properly to survey the gate's majesty.

'Aye lad, an eye opener you might say,' Halgar agreed.

'Indeed,' said Uthor.

Rorek nodded sagely, supping on his pipe.

The four dwarfs were standing on a short, but wide, road fashioned from stone tiles of ruddy terracotta and grey granite that led up to the massive gate. The walkway, a preamble to the majesty of the entrance proper, was decorated with square spiral devices and inset by a band of runes on either edge. Shallow stone steps met the short road and ended in a wide plateau of smoothed rock, similarly inscribed with gold intaglio.

The main gate itself was a full two hundred feet at its highest point and framed by a stout arch of fashioned bronze, inlaid with intricate copper filigree. A cross-hammers device encompassed both sides of the gate, the stone haft of each inset with large gemstones. Judging by the crude scratch marks around the jewels, efforts had been made to remove them but to no avail. On either side of the gate was a symbolic rendering of a dwarf face, each wearing helmets, but one with an eye patch, the other bearing horns, and forged from bronze. At the gate's apex was a carved stone anvil.

At each end of the immense structure there stood an eighty-foot statue, set proudly upon a rounded stone dais, banded with runic script. On the left there was Grungni, clad in long mail, a forge hammer in his hand. On the right, the imposing figure of Grimnir, war-like with his noble crest standing sternly from his shaven skull, the mighty axes forged by his brother god gripped in both hands. Other, smaller statues gave way to the ancestor gods – kings and thanes of Karak Varn all – set in mighty alcoves carved into the mountain rock. Harsh weathering had worn the statues down, some were even toppled over.

'Praise Grungni for his skill and wisdom that we humble dawi might fashion such beauty,' Uthor breathed reverently.

'For his hand guides all things, and is felt in the hammer blow of every forge,' Rorek completed the litany.

Uthor clapped the engineer heartily on the shoulder then turned towards Lokki, his expression serious.

'We had best keep word of their liege-lord's death to ourselves until we are admitted,' the dwarf suggested.

Lokki nodded. 'Agreed,' he said and cast his gaze up to an empty parapet carved out of the rock and above the gate itself. It was a watch station, yet strangely there were no quarrellers in evidence to garrison it. Still, Lokki noted the crossbow slits and murder holes warily.

'Ho there!' he bellowed. 'The emissaries of Izor, Kadrin and Zhufbar seek an audience with the lord of Karak Varn.' The last part nearly stuck in the thane's throat, given his foreknowledge of Kadrin Redmane's demise. It was likely, given the condition of the bones they'd found, that the dwarfs of the hold already knew of it, but then a successor would have been chosen, or at the very least a warden appointed to act in Red-mane's stead. In either case, it did not explain the fact that there were no guards at the main gate.

'Fellow dawi beseech admittance and the hospitality of Karak Varn,' Lokki cried again. He was met by silence.

Though it was only late afternoon the sun was dipping in the sky, thick black clouds, pregnant with rain, smothering it. From the north, a fierce wind was blowing, its howling chorus tearing through the peaks.

'The weather bodes ill,' grumbled Halgar, casting a look behind him at the deepening shadows.

Uthor stepped forward and hammered on the door with his fist. It only made a dull thud. 'Teeth of Grimnir,' he swore, 'this is hopeless! How are we to attend a council of war if we are unable to enter the very hold at which the council is to take place?'

'I fear we may already be too late, Uthor, son of Algrim,' said Lokki. 'But still we must try to get inside. Perhaps if we were to take the Ungdrin road, there is an entryway a few leagues east, and approach through the southern gate?' he wondered.

'A journey of two weeks at the very least and we have no way of knowing that the entryway is still open to us,' said Halgar, wincing as he sat down upon a rock. The spear wound was still a little raw but the tenacious dwarf had refused any treatment. 'It'll take more than an urk blade to finish me off, lad!' he'd bellowed to Lokki, when the thane had expressed his concern. The longbeard mastered the pain quickly and took out a small clay pipe from within his beard. He stuffed it with weed from a pouch on his belt and lit it with a small flint and steel device. Taking a long draw, he blew out a large smoke ring and added, 'The hour grows late and soon grobi will swarm this mountainside. They are curs, and would likely shoot us in the back from behind a rock,' he spat, taking another pull on his pipe.

'Two weeks is too long,' said Uthor with uncharacteristic urgency. 'I would gladly fight an army of grobi should circumstances require it, but we need to get inside now and find out what fate has befallen our kinsdwarfs.'

'There might be another way,' said Rorek from the back of the group, chewing the end of his pipe as he eyed the lofty watch station a further twenty feet above the two hundred foot gate. He paced forward then stopped a short distance from the entranceway. Raising his left hand in front of him – his right still holding the pipe as he supped on it – he stuck up his thumb and pointed his forefinger. Looking down the extended finger, squinting slightly with his good eye, he mumbled something and took three paces backwards. Then he unslung his crossbow from around his side and detached the metal box attachment filled with quarrels. With the others rapt in silent incredulity, he hung the metal box back onto his tool belt and replaced it with another, except this one harboured a coiled up rope with a hook at one end.

Rorek then crouched down on one knee and aimed the crossbow, complete with new attachment, towards the watch station parapet. Squinting slightly, he flipped up a metal catch on the crossbow's stock – it was a small steel ring with a cross in it. Trapping the crossbow in his right armpit and against his shoulder, he tucked the pipe back in his belt, stuck the thumb of his

left hand in his mouth and raised it up to catch the
wind. Satisfied, he aimed down the steel cross and
fired.

There was the sudden crack and twang of a heavy
spring as the hook exploded from the end of the crossbow, followed by the whirring of rope unwinding from
a metal pulley as it was carried with the hook, flying
upwards and then arcing in the direction of the parapet. Each of the four dwarfs followed it, mesmerised.
The hook sailed over the parapet and into the open
watch station, followed by the clang of steel against
stone. Rorek wound the crank at the end of the stock
furiously, steel scraping stone above them until the
hook caught and the rope pulled taut.

'Grungni's steel tongs,' said the engineer.

'May they ever bend the elements of the earth to his
will,' Uthor finished for him. 'What now?' he asked;
slightly dumbfounded.

If any guards were present above the gate, they would
have come to investigate by now. It seemed the dwarfs
had no choice.

'Now I climb,' Rorek returned, setting the crossbow
against a rock as he strapped a set of shallow spikes to
his boots. 'Look after these for me,' he added, shrugging
off his weapon's belt and pack. He then proceeded to
walk forward slowly, all the time steadily winding up
the slack from the rope. Once he reached the gate wall,
he attached a small clasp on the crossbow's stock to his
tool belt, and placed a spiked boot against the mountain rock. He wound a little farther, and when he was
certain the rope supported his weight, placed a second
boot against the rock. Now suspended above the
ground, he wound the crank slowly and carefully, one

steady step after another as he climbed up the sheer wall.

'Impetuous youth,' Halgar mumbled from his seat on the rock, puffing smoke rings agitatedly. 'Beardlings,' he muttered, despite Rorek's gnarled leather skin and broad beard making him at least a hundred, 'no respect for tradition.'

It took Rorek almost an hour to climb the two hundred and twenty feet to reach the edge of the parapet. By the time he did, the sun had all but faded in the sky as the engineer scrambled over it. Rorek gave a short wave to indicate his success and then disappeared from view. All the dwarfs could do now was wait for Rorek to try and open the gate.

'I HAVE TRAVELLED far to reach the hold of my kinsdwarf,' Uthor remarked, 'but to venture from the Vaults, across Black Fire Pass no less, that is indeed a perilous journey and Redmane, to my understanding, was not your clan brother.'

The dwarfs had set up camp outside the gate upon the roadway, far enough from the edge of the mountains to ensure they were not surprised by a grobi ambush or unknowingly preyed upon by some other beast. Like the rest of their kin, they had little need for shelter, hardy enough to weather even the harshest conditions, though the lack of a roof, together with several tons of rock, above their heads was a little unsettling.

Uthor sat facing Lokki. Both dwarfs had their weapons laid in front of them, their hands locked around stout tankards, and were seated on their shields. They had made a small fire, surrounded by a thick belt of stones. If they were to attract the attention of grobi, they would do so with or without the flames in their midst. Besides, greenskins hated fire, as did many other denizens of the night – it would be a useful weapon, if it came to it.

The dwarfs were arranged so each could look over the shoulder of the other at the high crags into which the main gate of Karak Varn was wedged, should any threat present itself.

'Halgar and I...' Lokki began, looking towards his venerable mentor. Halgar was nearby, and sat unmoving on the rock, his eyes fixed forward, unblinking. His hands were sat upon his lap, restfully. Uthor followed Lokki's gaze and saw the statuesque longbeard for himself.

'He bears many scars,' he said, noting the lack of fingers on Halgar's right hand.

'He lost them long ago, but won't speak of how. At least he never has to me,' Lokki told him.

'Is he… all right?' said Uthor, a hint of concern in his voice as he continued to regard the still form of Halgar.

'He's sleeping,' Lokki explained with a thin smile.

'With his eyes open?'

'Grobi will as sure as kill you in your bed as on the battlefield, he always taught me,' said Lokki.

'Truly, the wise have much to teach us.' Uthor nodded his deepest respect in the direction of the slumbering longbeard.

'Halgar and I,' Lokki tried again, once he had Uthor's attention, 'are here on a debt of honour,' he explained. 'Almost nine hundred years ago, during the War of Vengeance, Kromkaz Vargasson, my ancestor and grandsire of Halgar, was ambushed on the way to Oeragor by a band of elf rangers.'

At the mention of elves, Uthor hawked a great gobbet of phlegm into the fire where it sizzled briefly.

'The elves were swift and cunning,' Lokki continued, the glow of the fire casting his face in increasing shadows with the gradual onset of night. 'Four of Kromkaz's kin lay dead before a shield was raised, an axe drawn, and yet still more fell,' Lokki went on, repeating by rote the tale that Halgar had taught him. 'Hiding behind their bows, they herded Kromkaz and his warriors into a narrow defile and my ancestor would surely have died – he and his warriors – were it not for miners from Karak Varn. They emerged from a hidden tunnel, part of the Ungdrin road, at the ridge from where the elves had Kromkaz pinned. The miners, dwarfs of the Copperhand clan, fell upon the elves, chasing them from their hiding places. His foes revealed, Kromkaz ordered his warriors to attack and the elves were crushed. Kromkaz reached Oeragor that day. They fought alongside the Copperhand clan and witnessed Morgrim, cousin of Snorri, son of the High King, slay the elf lord Imladrik,' Lokki said, and the reflected glare of the fire made his eyes seem as if they were ablaze. 'We come to honour that debt, to repay the dwarfs of the Copperhand clan and the hold of Karak Varn.'

Uthor nodded solemnly, wiping a tear from his eye as he did so.

'Great deeds,' he said, his voice slightly choked, 'great and noble deeds.'

'Ho there!' the distant voice of Rorek broke the reverie.

The engineer was nowhere to be seen. Lokki and Uthor got to their feet, and took up their weapons and armour.

Halgar blinked once and was awake, the old dwarf standing up as if he'd never been asleep.

Uthor kicked out the fire and went over to stand expectantly beside Lokki and Halgar, outside the great gates.

'About time,' Uthor muttered. Halgar's low grumblings were indiscernible, though Uthor thought he caught the word 'wazzock'.

'What are you doing stood over there?' came the engineer's voice again, echoing throughout the canyon.

This time all three turned in the direction of the sound. Still there was nothing. With Lokki leading them, the three dwarfs moved away from the great gate, cautiously, and towards where Rorek's voice was coming from. Negotiating their way around the right-hand side of the gate, to where one of the long galleries of statues was arrayed, they saw Rorek's head about fifty feet up and poking over a shallow lip of stone. Such was the ingenious geology – part natural, part dwarf-made – of the stone overhang that were it not for the fact that his voice had guided them and that his head was sticking out, the engineer would have been invisible.

'Take this,' he hollered from above and shortly afterwards a trail of rope came down to them.

One by one, the trio of dwarfs climbed up a stark, flat face of rock that got them to a short ledge from where Rorek's seemingly disembodied head was watching them keenly.

When they found the engineer, he was sat inside a narrow, dank-looking tunnel. Only a dwarf, and one that was being particularly observant, would have been able to detect the opening. Stretched over the narrow ledge, Rorek was holding up an ironbound grate, thickly latticed and stained in brown and yellowish hues that were visible even in the fading light. A trail of darkly stained water, long since dried up, fed away from the opening into a shallow rut in the ledge and was carried in long streaks down a section of the rock face, away from the statues.

'I have found our entrance,' the engineer said proudly.

'Wazzock!' bawled Halgar, cresting the ledge. 'You have found the tunnel to the latrine.'

Uthor wrinkled his nose when he noticed the concealed pit far beneath the grate.

Unperturbed, Rorek crept back from the ledge, retreating back into the tunnel to allow the others to pass. 'I could not operate the mechanism to open the great gate, try as I might,' he explained, 'and this was the only other way in. I've disarmed any traps but you'll have to duck, though.'

Lokki went in first, pausing for a moment at the mention of traps, but traversing the short ledge quickly. Halgar followed, grunting and muttering all the while. Uthor brought up the rear, gathering the engineer's rope up after him and giving it back to Rorek, along with the rest of the engineer's possessions.

The latrine grate slammed shut in their wake. Rorek bolted it shut from the inside, before ramming down a heavy looking second gate. Three clockwise turns of a stylised, bronze ancestor face wrought into the wall completed the ritual and was accompanied by the dull retort of more, hidden, locks. 'Just a short crawl to the outer gateway hall,' the engineer said and started off down the narrow tunnel. It was disgusting, a long dark yellow stain ran down the middle of it and the walls of the tight space were encrusted with dried filth. The stink of it was palpable.

'I have smelled urk less foul,' Halgar grumbled again as the dwarfs set off after Rorek.

TRUE TO ROREK'S word, the dwarfs emerged from another iron grate into the outer gateway hall. It was a fairly spartan room, but vast, designed to accommodate huge throngs of dwarfs as they entered from the main gate. Any nobles, craft guild masters or other notable dignitaries could then be received by the lord of the hold in the audience chamber that resided at the bottom of a lengthy stairway connecting it to the outer gateway hall.

'This is how I found it,' said the engineer. The chamber was deserted and barren save for a dwarf helmet resting forlornly on its side in the centre of the room. 'Not mine,' Rorek added.

'Draw your weapons,' Halgar growled, glancing first to the gate on the left and then to the gate on the right – beyond them were the barracks, where a throng's warriors could be housed temporarily. Lastly, his gaze fell to the gate at the far wall, that which led to the stairway.

Axe in hand, shield raised, Lokki said, 'We head for the audience chamber and make oaths to Grungni that we are not too late.'

Beyond the next gate the long stairway wended down into the darkness, great columns of stone carved with clan symbols and runes punctuating it. Though lit by hulking iron braziers set at regular intervals, the shadows cast upon the stairway were long and could hide any number of lurking dangers.

The dwarfs moved swiftly and in single file, two watching the left, and two the right, until they reached the entrance to the audience chamber.

'Someone has been here before us,' Lokki hissed, standing on one side of the double gate that was slightly ajar. Uthor quickly took up a position on the opposite side, axe in hand. Halgar and Rorek waited pensively behind them, ready to charge in.

'Make ready,' said Lokki.

Uthor nodded.

The two dwarfs thrust the door open and charged into the audience chamber, weapons drawn and bellowing war cries. When they saw the dwarf wearing the massive warhelm sitting at a long oval table, the merchant thane bedecked in fine velvet and the dishevelled looking creature huddled in the corner, counting silver spoons into a burgeoning pack, they stopped abruptly and were lost for words.

'How LONG HAVE you been waiting here?' Lokki asked.

The dwarfs were seated around the wood table, carved of mountain oak and inlaid with intricate runic designs rendered in gold. Introductions had been made and it had been quickly established that they were all there for the same purpose: to attend a council of war at the behest of Kadrin Redmane, to discuss the best way to rid the nearby mountains of the gathering greenskin tribes.

'Three weeks, is as near as I can reckon,' said Gromrund, his eyes fierce behind the faceplate of his warhelm. He was the only dwarf not to have divested himself of his helmet – a fact Lokki was wise enough not to press.

'And you have seen no one in that time?' Uthor chipped in, leaning back in his stool as he lit up his pipe.

'I ventured a look up the great stair and even explored two of the clan halls, but there was no one. I returned to the audience chamber and waited as I was bidden,' Gromrund explained. 'I had hoped to be received by Lord Redmane,' he added.

Uthor flashed a glance at Lokki, who then turned to the hammerer.

'Kadrin Redmane is dead, slain by urk, may he sit at the table of his ancestors,' he said grimly. 'Halgar and I found his remains on the Old Dwarf Road at the edge of Black Water. The four of us buried him and his companions in the earth, under the shadow of the karak.'

'Remains?' said the hammerer. 'How can you be sure it was Kadrin Redmane?'

'He wore this talisman,' Uthor told him, holding it aloft in the light cast by the torches in the room.

'Dreng tromm,' Gromrund muttered, bowing his head, momentarily lost in his thoughts. 'Then we are too late,' he said, grimly meeting Lokki's gaze.

'Many years too–'

'Quiet!' Halgar cut Lokki off before he could speak.

The sudden outburst spooked Drimbold, who dropped a gilded comb that he was using to preen the gibil from out of his beard.

Hakem's expression showed that he recognised it, but before he could take it up with the Grey dwarf, Halgar was on his feet and stalking to the back of the room. He edged towards a stone statue of Grungni set upon a large octagonal base, axe in hand. Lokki followed him, knowing by now to always trust the longbeard's instincts. Rorek waited just behind him and readied his crossbow. Uthor went the other way around the table, Gromrund right at his back.

'What is that stench,' the hammerer whispered, sniffing at the air.

'It matters not,' Uthor snapped, drawing his axe, 'make ready.'

Hakem followed them, the Barak Varr dwarf stealing a reproachful glance at Drimbold who waited pensively at the table, clutching his pack.

Halgar stopped at the statue and listened intently. He motioned to Lokki. The thane came forward and examined the statue. Looking down, he saw something.

'Rorek,' he hissed, beckoning the engineer, who quickly joined him, shouldering his crossbow, as Halgar stepped to the side.

Rorek followed Lokki's gaze to the octagonal base and noticed a strange configuration of carvings, slightly outset from the rest. Crouching down, the engineer carefully ran his fingers over the stone, seeking out any imperfections. He pulled a piece of the design out, a perfectly round dwarf head effigy and rotated it. When he pushed the head back into place, there was a grinding sound and the dull scrap of a sliding bolt of stone, then a small crack appeared at the lip of the octagonal base.

'Help me lift it,' Rorek said, getting his fingers beneath the lip. Lokki did likewise, catching on quickly to what the engineer wanted him to do. Halgar stood poised with Uthor, whilst Gromrund and Hakem had gathered torches and held them at the ready to be thrust at whatever lurked beneath them.

'Heave!' Lokki cried and the two of them lifted off part of the octagonal slab, revealing a small, darkened chamber within, below the statue itself, with several tunnels leading off from it. Inside, blinking back the glare of the torches was a dwarf, a thick, leather-bound book clasped to his chest.

'Ralkan,' he mumbled, half-crazed, trying to ward off the bright light with his hand, 'Ralkan Geltberg,' he repeated, louder and with greater lucidity. The dwarf's eyes were pleading as he added, 'last survivor of Karak Varn.'

CHAPTER THREE

SKREEKIT WRUNG HIS paws together, and fought the urge to squirt the musk of fear. Beneath filth-caked robes, daubed in the bloody symbols of Clan Skryre, the skaven's fur was moist with sweat. A furtive glance at another agent, a warlock of low breeding, drowning in his own blood from a dagger thrust in his lung, and he found his voice at last.

'Three hundred warp tokens, four cohorts of warriors for protection against Clan Moulder and a hundred slaves is our price, yes. Make deal, quick-quick,' Skreekit blathered.

STANDING BEFORE THE warlock, in a dank chamber edged in filth, dirty straw, and other signs of skaven habitation, was Thratch Sourpaw. He called it his 'scheming room' but in truth it was merely one of the many antechambers appended to the subterranean warren of the skaven. The black-furred warlord of Clan Rictus sneered his dissatis-faction, looking at Skreekit down his long snout and revealing an old, but horrific, wound on his neck. Coarse, brown stitching was still embedded in his flesh, made vis-ible by the pink scar tissue. Thratch's cold reddish eyes picked out something behind the nervous warlock, who had just soiled his robes further.

Thratch watched as something detached itself from the cavern wall at the agent's back, a layer of swiftly moving shadow, silent and at one with the darkness. There was the sound of metal tearing flesh and blood exploded from the warlock's mouth, spraying the dirt-encrusted stones in front of him with crimson, a jagged blade punching through his chest. The knife was with-drawn savagely and Skreekit slumped forward. Sheer terror twisted his face, lying in a puddle of his own filth and viscera, blood bubbles bursting on his froth-drenched muzzle as poison ravaged his innards.

Thratch was one of the many warlords of Clan Rictus as well as dwarf slayer, goblin killer and conqueror of Karak Varn. Clad in thick metal armour, wreathed in a fine patina of rust, stray black tufts of his fur eking out beneath the pauldrons and vambraces, he looked for-midable. The warlord knew this and played on it as he approached the last of the three warlocks that had come to make deals with him.

'Now,' the warlord said, signalling for his assassin, Kill-Klaw, to emerge fully from the shadows, certain there would be no attempt on his life. The Clan Eshin adept obeyed dutifully and lingered at the warlock's side, just enough so the skaven was aware of his pres-ence, just enough so the warlock couldn't see him.

'You build device for me, yes-yes.' Thrath pointed a claw towards a crude design he had scratched on the wall with the spike he had instead of a paw – the three warlocks had winced as he had done it. 'Your promise-price,' he demanded.

The last representative of Clan Skryre gulped audibly before he answered – a half glance at the lurking assassin.

'*One* hundred warp tokens, *two* cohorts of warriors and... *fifty* slaves,' he ventured.

Thrath loomed close, hot breath making the agent's eyes water.

'Accepted, yes,' he hissed, a long and terrible grin wrinkling his features.

'WHAT HAPPENED HERE, brother?' Lokki asked, his tone soothing.

Ralkan sat in front of him, still. He was fairly diminutive, even by dwarf standards, and the great tome he clutched to his breast only made him seem smaller still.

'Red eyes,' he murmured, 'red eyes in the dark... everywhere.'

The crazed dwarf wore the scholarly robes of a lore-keeper, one of the few chosen to chronicle and remember all the great events of a hold – its deeds, its heroes, its grudges. A talisman bearing the rune of Valaya hung around his neck – it seemed the goddess of protection had heeded his pledges. He wore a series of belts and straps over his scribe's attire, Lokki assumed they were designed to secure the book should the lorekeeper require the use of his arms. The dwarf's beard was dishevelled, wretched with dirt and encrusted filth as were his skin and nails. He looked

wasted and thin, like he could do with a good meal
inside of him. How long he had been there, hiding
within a warren of tunnels, scrabbling in the dark,
Lokki could only guess. Rorek was in the secret chamber beneath the statue of Grungni at that very moment,
trying to ascertain how far the tunnels went and how
many there were. Of the others, Uthor and Halgar were
with Lokki, while Gromrund and Hakem stood guard
at each of the entranceways. Drimbold sat sullenly in
the corner, occasionally glancing at the way out of the
audience chamber, before returning to his thoughts.

'Bah,' snarled Halgar, the old dwarf getting to his feet.
'He has said nothing else since we dragged him from
his hole.' The longbeard walked away to go glare at
Drimbold, the end of his pipe flaring to life as he lit it.

Lokki watched him go, then turned back to Ralkan
and reached for the book he had pinioned to his chest.
The lorekeeper seemed reluctant to part with it, but,
with some gentle urging from Uthor accompanied by
several dried strips of meat, released it.

'Tis the Karak Varn Book of Remembering,' Uthor
said solemnly.

Lokki opened it, thumbing carefully through the
thick parchment pages. Names, in their hundreds of
thousands were etched within, names of all the dwarfs
of Karak Varn that had lived and died: their clans, their
deeds and how they met their end.

Lokki skipped ahead to the last of the entries and
read aloud.

'*Marbad Hammerfell, journeyman ironsmith, fell to a
skaven blade in his back. Fyngal Fykasson, stonecutter, died
by drinking water from a tainted well. Gurthang
Copperhand, miner, inhaled deadly skaven gas.*' He

lingered on this last one and mouthed a silent oath to Valaya. 'There are hundreds like this,' he said, 'killed by the rat-kin, stabbed in the back with spears and daggers, poisoned in their sleep!'

Uthor clenched his fists until his knuckles cracked. He was breathing loud and heavily, his face was flushed a deep red.

Before he could say or do anything, Rorek emerged from the secret chamber beneath the statue of Grungni.

'As far as I can tell, there are several tunnels,' he began, 'extending far into the hold and across many deeps. But they are narrow; I doubt any of us could get through them.'

'Little wonder he is so filthy,' Lokki remarked with a short glance at the Ralkan. The lorekeeper, having devoured the meat given to him by Uthor, was staring aimlessly.

'I found markings scratched onto the wall in the chamber immediately below...' said Rorek, arresting Lokki's attention. For the first time the thane noticed that Ralkan had a small rock pick tucked into his belt.

'...made by some tool or other,' Rorek continued. 'If they equate to years, he has been here for a while.' The engineer's expression was grim as he regarded Lokki.

'How did this doom befall Karak Varn?' Lokki asked the lorekeeper again. 'How long have you been in hiding?'

Ralkan's lips moved soundlessly. There was desperation in his eyes as he met the thane's gaze.

'Red eyes...' he sobbed at last, tears flowing down his face, making pale streaks in the grime. 'Red eyes, everywhere.'

* * *

'IT IS SIMPLE,' Uthor said firmly, on his feet and pacing the length of the audience chamber, 'we find the hold's book of grudges – that will tell us all we need to know.'

'And risk alerting whatever sacked this hold to our presence?' Gromrund countered. 'It is reckless folly.'

Uthor rounded on the hammerer, who was sat on one of the stools, an imposing sight in his warhelm and full armour. 'The hammerers of Karak Hirn are obviously of less sterner stock than those of Kadrin,' he snarled.

Gromrund shot to his feet, thumping his hand down so hard upon the table that it shook, spilling ale with his vehemence, much to the annoyance of the other dwarfs.

'The brethren of Horn Hold are ever bold, and not lacking in courage,' he bellowed. 'I would not sit here and have their name–'

'Quiet fool,' hissed Halgar, reproachfully, 'lest you have forgotten your own desire for caution at rousing the denizens of this place.'

The entire dwarf throng were once again arrayed around the table – all except Ralkan who had retreated to a corner and was mumbling quietly. Some smoked pipeweed, others nursed tankards forlornly – ale supplies were running low. This was despite the fact that Rorek had discovered a hidden vault inside the room that contained several reserves of beer, doubtless left there in preparation for the council. The assembled dwarfs were locked in a long and hard debate, not to be rushed into rash action without due and proper consideration, about what they should do. All except Drimbold who was eyeing the finery of Hakem's merchant attire, before averting his attentions to Halgar as something else caught his interest.

'I say we venture into the deeps,' said Uthor, eyeing Gromrund as the dwarf sat back down, clearly disgruntled and chewing his beard in agitation. He switched his gaze to Lokki, knowing as a thane of a royal clan and with his venerable companion, it was his favour he needed to sway. 'It is our duty to discover the fate of our kinsdwarfs and avenge them! What do we, sons of Grungni all, have to fear from ratmen?' he added, top lip curling in a derisive sneer. 'We can scare those cowards away.'

Lokki remained thoughtful throughout Uthor's impassioned rhetoric.

'How are we to find the kron?' asked Hakem, using a second beard comb to preen himself. 'I for one have no desire to scramble around in the dark, looking for something that might not even be there.'

'Indeed,' Gromrund chipped in, suddenly emboldened again. 'Even the ufdi sees the madness in what you are suggesting.'

If Hakem thought anything about the slight, he did not show it.

'The lorekeeper can guide us,' Uthor said simply, addressing the group again. 'But he is *zaki*,' Rorek whispered, casting a furtive glance at Ralkan before he twirled his finger around his temple.

Uthor turned to the lorekeeper. 'Can you guide us?' he asked. 'Can you take us to the dammaz kron of Karak Varn?'

There was a flash of lucidity in Ralkan's eyes and a moment's silence before he nodded.

Uthor looked again at Lokki. 'There you have it, the lorekeeper is our guide.'

Lokki returned Uthor's gaze, and was careful not to look to Halgar for guidance. This was something he would have to decide for himself. As member of a royal clan, be that of the Vaults or nay, hereditarily he had the highest status, despite the fact that both Halgar and Gromrund had longer beards. He was the leader.

'We head into the lower deeps,' he said, ignoring the grunting protestations of the hammerer, 'and retrieve the dammaz kron. The fate of Karak Varn must be known and these facts presented to the High King.'

'It is settled then,' said Uthor, with no small measure of satisfaction.

'It is settled.' Halgar spoke his approval.

'I have one question,' Drimbold piped up, beer froth coating his beard as he supped from his own weather-beaten tankard. 'Wise grey beard, why do you have an arrow sticking out of your chest?'

Halgar scowled.

THE DWARFS TRAVELLED down a long and narrow tunnel. They had passed numerous hallways, clan chambers, armouries and galleries during that time. So far, no more dwarfs of Karak Varn – not even skeletons – save for Ralkan, were found in the creeping dark of the deep. All that remained, it seemed, were the last vestiges of a toppled kingdom, its reclaimed glory wrecked by calamity, its once proud stature rendered to rubble. Dust lay thick in the air and it was tainted with the bitterness of regret and defeat.

The dwarfs had discovered, during Ralkan's more lucid moments – which were becoming ever more frequent – that the dammaz kron, the book of grudges, was in the King's Chambers located in the second deep.

Much of the hold, even the upper levels, was in a state of utter ruination – fallen columns and statues, collapsed ceilings and gaping chasms all in evidence – and the dwarfs had been forced to take a fairly circuitous route. The narrow tunnel, fraught with rubble and jutting rocks where the walls had split, was merely part of that route.

Uthor strode alongside Ralkan, who was at the head of the group, the lorekeeper leading the way. Often he stopped suddenly, causing a clash of armoured bodies and muffled swearing behind him, pausing to regard his surroundings and then set off again without a word.

'Like I said, zaki,' Rorek, immediately behind them, had whispered in Uthor's ear. 'Are you sure he knows where he's going?'

Gromrund walked beside the engineer and wore an expression like brooding thunder. The hammerer had been silent throughout the trek, positively bristling at the will of the 'council' going against him. He gripped his great hammer tightly, glowering behind the mask of his helmet as he focused meaningfully on the back of Uthor's head.

Behind them was Hakem and Drimbold, a bizarre pairing of wealth and poverty. Hakem cast frequent, sideways glances at the Grey dwarf, who stooped occasionally to pick something up and add it to his pack. The merchant-thane took great pains to ensure the strings of his purse were tight and his possessions securely fastened. Drimbold paid no heed to his discomfort and smiled back at Hakem broadly, using a silver fork, encrusted with jewels – Grungni only knew where he had appropriated it from – to pick strips of goat meat from his blackened teeth.

Lokki and Halgar brought up the rear, taking care to watch the route the dwarfs had taken, lest anything be following them.

'What do you think of the son of Algrim?' Lokki asked, keeping his voice low.

Halgar thought on it a moment, scrutinizing Uthor carefully and considering his answer before he spoke. 'He is a hazkal, to be sure. But he fights as if the very blood of Grimnir flows in his veins.' The longbeard blinked twice and rubbed his eyes with the back of his hand. 'And he bears a heavy burden, I know not what.'

'Are you all right, old one?' Lokki asked the longbeard. Halgar had been rubbing his eyes intermittently for the last hour, gnarled fingers kneading out whatever fatigue ailed them.

'An itch, is all,' he growled, 'Damn grobi stink is everywhere.' The longbeard stopped rubbing and stalked on a little harder, making it clear the conversation was at an end.

Halgar was old, so old that Lokki's father, the King of Karak Izor, had urged the longbeard not to take the road with Lokki, that one of his hammerers could accompany him instead. Halgar had snarled his derision at the stoutness of hammerers in 'these times' and more placidly had said he wanted to 'stretch his legs.' The king had relented, unwilling to go against the wishes of one of the oldest of the clan. Besides, there was the debt of Halgar's grandsire to consider and the king would never oppose the pursuit of a pledge of honour. But throughout their journey to Karak Varn, Halgar had been prone to dark and reflective moods. Lokki had often woken in the night, after quaffing too much ale and needing to empty his bladder, to find the

longbeard staring off into the dark as if looking at
something just beyond his field of vision, just beyond
his reach. It was as if he sensed an end was coming and
he had no desire to wither and atrophy in the hold,
scribing of his last days in some tome or scroll. He
wanted to die with an axe in his hand and dwarf
armour on his back. Lokki hoped his own end could be
so glorious.

After that, Lokki fell into silence, remaining watchful
of the dark.

THE LONG STAIRWAY stretched down into the waiting
blackness of the second deep. Much like that which led
to the audience chamber at the great gate, it was broad
and illuminated by gigantic iron braziers wrought into
the fearsome image of dragons and other creatures of
ancient legend. The flames cast dancing shadows on
the walls, throwing ephemeral slashes of light onto
finely carved mosaics fashioned into the rocks. Each
one was broken up by thick stone pillars, marked by
rune bands of the royal clan of Karak Varn.

'Here, does High King Gotrek Starbreaker slay the elf
king and take his petty crown,' intoned Halgar, pointing to one of the mosaics. On it, Gotrek Starbreaker
was depicted in refulgent, golden armour, his axe
drenched with blood. An elf corpse lay at his feet, the
Phoenix Crown held aloft in the High King's hand and
presented to a mighty throng of dwarfs arrayed about
him.

'Lo, does the Bulvar Troll-beater, three-times grand-
son of Jorvar who did flee at Oeragor, face the grobi
hordes, and reap a doom worthy of the sagas of old,' he
said wistfully. Bulvar was a slayer, and bore a massive

crest of red hair upon an otherwise shaven head. Half his body was painted to resemble a skeleton – an affectation common among the cult and indicative of the slayers' death oath – the other half was scribed with swirling tattoos and runic wards of Grimnir. Bulvar was alone, surrounded by orcs, goblins, trolls and wyverns. His last stand was made upon a great host of greenskin carcasses, the twin axes in his hands slaying goblins for all eternity.

'And there,' added the longbeard, 'King Snaggi Ironhandson, son of Thorgil, who was sired by Hraddi, atop his oathstone at the Bryndal Vale after the sixth siege of Tor Alessi.' The noble figure of the dwarf king stood upon a stout, flat rock with the rune of his clan carved onto it, his warriors with shields locked around him as they faced off against a host of elves with levelled spears. 'Great was Snaggi's sacrifice that day,' said Halgar, his expression faraway as he became lost in remembrance and the expedition moved onward.

At last the dwarfs negotiated the stairway, taking care to avoid numerous pitfalls that bled away into the dark nothing of the underdeep far below.

From there they passed through a great, wooden door that only yielded when Lokki, Uthor, Gromrund and Hakem heaved on the mighty iron ring bolted to it, and into a feast hall – its hearth cold and long extinguished. A guild hall followed, of the Ironfinger miners, if the runic rubrics lining the walls were any proof, and then a long, vaulted gallery, until the dwarfs were before another great gate.

Standing almost fifty feet tall, it was decorated with a final mosaic – rendered in copper, bronze and gold – surrounded by a gilded, jewel-encrusted arch. There were voids in the arch where some of the gemstones had been prized loose and stolen. Such defilement brought about ambivalent feelings of sorrow and rage in the on-looking dwarfs.

'Ulfgan...' Halgar struck a sombre note, barely a choked murmur, as if his voice held the burden of ages, '...the last king of Karak Varn.'

The mosaic was cracked, some of the gemstones set in it missing, each empty socket like a wound in stone.

'It is the King's Chamber,' he breathed.

'IT IS NO USE,' stated Gromrund. 'The gate is barred, and no locksmith can grant us entry. We have no choice but to turn back.'

The dwarfs had been outside the gate to the King's Chamber for almost an hour. A thick, steel bar lay across it on both sides that would only be opened by means of a great iron key – that which was carried only by the hold's gatekeeper and chief of the hammerer guards, or by the king himself. Since the dwarfs had neither, their quest to retrieve the Karak Varn Book of Grudges had stalled.

Rorek worked slowly and painstakingly at the lock hole, ignoring Gromrund's nay saying and derogation.

Uthor, stood patiently by the engineer's side, would not be baited into another argument.

'I am in agreement with Gromrund,' said Hakem, deliberately keeping his distance from Drimbold, who was lurking at the edge of the gallery in the shadows, doubtless looking for more trinkets to further burden his weighty pack. 'There is no more we can do here.'

The hammerer looked around the throng for further supporters but found none.

Halgar's eyes were far away as he regarded the King's Gate. Lokki seemed intent on thoughts of his own as he watched intermittently between the engineer cycling through his many tools and the darkness that lay behind them. Uthor was predictably tight lipped, and maintained a certain grip on his axe haft.

Again, it seems the ufdi is the only one willing to side with me, thought Gromrund, with some annoyance.

'Hakem may be right,' Lokki said at last.

Hakem! Hakem the ufdi! You mean Gromrund Tallhelm, son of Kromrund, who fought at the steppes of Karak Dron is right, thought the hammerer with growing ire.

'Though it galls me, there is no way past the King's Gate without the key and I will not take up arms against it.'

Uthor bristled, looking like he was about to protest, when he was interrupted by the voice of Drimbold.

'I've found something,' said the Grey dwarf, stepping out of the shadows, 'What's this?' He pointed out a concealed rune marking set in the stone and glowing dully in the gloom.

Halgar snapped out of his thoughts and stalked over to investigate, grumbling beneath his breath.

'Stand aside, wanaz!' he bawled at Drimbold, scowling. The Grey dwarf ducked quickly out of the furious longbeard's path, allowing Halgar to get up close to the rune, which was set just above head height into the rock itself.

'*Dringorak*,' Halgar said, tracing the rune with his finger, rather than reading it. 'Cunning Road. It is a rhun of disguise.'

'I thought only rhunki could detect such things,' said Gromrund, eyeing the Grey dwarf suspiciously.

'Aye,' Halgar replied, 'but this one has lost much of its potency. Doubtless from the grobi filth and rat-vermin infesting these once great halls,' he snarled, hawking a gobbet of thick phlegm onto the ground. 'Still, 'tis remarkable that you saw it.' Halgar glared at Drimbold.

'Just luck,' said the Grey dwarf, diffidently.

The longbeard turned his attention back to the rune and carefully felt the rock beneath, then drew a rune of passage in the dust and grit. He waited a moment and then used his gnarled fingers to find the edges of a door. Halgar opened it carefully.

'A tunnel lies beyond,' he said.

Lokki looked at Ralkan, but the lorekeeper was *elsewhere*.

'Bring him with us,' he said to Hakem. 'We enter the tunnel.'

THE TUNNEL WAS short and narrow, the dwarfs emerging quickly through a great, cold hearth and into the King's Chamber.

'A secret door,' remarked Uthor as he stepped out into a large room.

It might once have been splendid, but decay had visited itself upon it without restraint. It was also painfully clear that the dwarfs were not the first to have walked this chamber since the fall of the karak. Dried grobi dung smeared the walls and the desolation of shattered statues, torn tapestries and even the defilement of a small shrine to Valaya lay all about.

'Where are our enemies?' said Gromrund in low tones, gripping his great hammer.

'The hold is vast, hammerer,' said Lokki. 'If we are fortunate, they will not show themselves at all.'

There were three other ways leading off from the
room, besides the barred King's Gate. All were open,
their doors shattered or archways collapsed in on
themselves. It was here that the current denizens of
Karak Varn had gained entry and egress. It was a
sorry sight. The king's bed was painstakingly carved
from stout wutroth and in a state of disrepair. His
brooding-seat had been upended – one of the arms
ripped off. But there was no sign of the book of
grudges or indeed, a lectern or mantle that might
once have held it.

The dwarfs had gathered in the centre of the room,
wary of the darkness that persisted beyond the three
open doorways, enraged at the despoliation.

Drimbold was the last of them and, as he joined the
throng, began surreptitiously poking about the room,
aghast at the finery on display. Rummaging around a
rack of kingly robes, weighed down by dust, Drimbold
heard a low 'thunk', followed by the scraping retort of
a hidden mechanism, beneath the floor. The Grey
dwarf lifted his hand from where he'd been supporting
himself on the wall and noticed a small stone
depressed into the stonework, behind the robes. It
would have been easy to miss, and avoided altogether,
had the dwarf's palm not pressed upon it in such a way
and with sufficient force.

Six pairs of accusing dwarf eyes fixed upon Drimbold, but quickly turned towards the back of the room,
where the king's bed resided. The once-magnificent
artefact swivelled to the side on a concealed stone dais.
In its wake another door was revealed. It too slid to one
side with the grinding protests of stone against stone.
Beyond it lay a vault, the flickering luminescence of

glowstones set into the walls striking great mounds of coins and gemstones casting shadowy penumbra.

'Thindrongol,' said Lokki, stepping forward into the threshold of the room. It was one of the many secret vaults of the dwarfs used to hide treasure, ale or important artefacts from invading enemies. Given the fate that had befallen Karak Varn it seemed a prudent measure to take. The rest of the throng quickly gathered by Lokki's side and gaped in wonder.

Uthor had lit a torch and, stepping inside, used it to better light the room. Flickering half-light revealed something else, hidden at first in the wan illumination.

There at the back of the long vault was a gilded throne, and sat upon it a dwarf skeleton. Strands of thick, dust-clogged spider web wreathed it, cloaking the entire room. The gruesome thing wore kingly robes, now moth-eaten and age-worn. On its head rested a crown, its lustre only slightly dulled by time, a few ragged hairs poking beneath from the bleached yellow skull. A few errant tufts of beard remained too, and in the skeleton's bony grasp, fingers still clad in tarnished rings, there was a rune axe – unblunted and its glory undimmed.

'King Ulfgan,' uttered Halgar, standing beside Uthor, and bowed his head.

They all did, even Drimbold, and observed a sombre moment of respectful silence. Ralkan bowed deeply, going down on one knee and weeping.

Lokki gripped the lorekeeper's shoulder and looked back up. 'May he walk with the ancestors, his tankard ever full, his seat at Grungni's table,' he said solemnly.

'For his wisdom is great and his craft everlasting,' Uthor, Gromrund, Hakem and Rorek replied in unison.

Halgar nodded his approval.

Off to the king's right hand, several feet away, there stood an unadorned iron lectern. In its cradle sat a thick book, its parchment pages old and worn, the leather of its binding cracked.

'We have found the dammaz kron,' Lokki intoned softly.

THE DWARFS HAD brought several more torches into the hidden vault, lit from Uthor's, and set them in wall sconces to augment the light of the glowstones. The illumination had revealed a counting table in one corner, a large pair of iron scales upon it. Oddly, though there wasn't much gold or many precious jewels in the treasure vault; it felt bare as if some of it was missing. Hakem had reasoned that it could not have been stolen by grobi or skaven – why would they have resealed the room?

It was easy to imagine a lorekeeper scribing dutifully at the lectern as his lord dictated a raft of wrongs perpetrated against their hold and clans, but it was now Uthor who stood before it. As Redmane's descendant, it was deemed he should be the one to read from the kron. With tentative fingers, the other dwarfs standing patiently before him as if he were about to deliver some sermon or lecture, Uthor turned to the first page. The Khazalid script was scribed in dark, brownish blood – the blood of Ulfgan – as were all books of grudges. By the blood of kings were the oaths within them sworn, and the misdeeds of others recorded for all time. Reading quickly to himself, Uthor skipped ahead – with due reverence – until he reached the final few pages.

'*Let it be known that on this day, Ogrik Craghand and Ergan Granitefist of the miner's guild were slain as a pall of poison gas did infest the southern mines. The foul cloud did then boil up the southern shaft and kill many more dawi. Their names will be remembered,*' he read, skipping ahead further.

'*Our lord Kadrin Redmane has not returned. Incensed at a spate of urk attacks on the road, he was to lead a shipment of gromril to High King Skorri Morgrimson personally. No word has reached the karak of his fate, or that of his expedition. As if to compound this dark turn of events, a horde of grobi did attack the first deep and slay many dawi. Skaven gather in the lower deeps and we cannot contain them,*' Uthor continued, looking up briefly to regard the grim faces of his kinsdwarfs.

'It goes on,' he said, reaching the final entries. '*The third deep falls, grobi and skaven attack in vast numbers and we cannot hold them. There are few of us left. Thane Skardrin makes his last stand at the Hall of Redmane… He will be remembered.*

'*A beast is awoke in the underdeep. Rhunki Ranakson, apprentice to Lord Kadrin, does venture into the fifth deep in search of it but does not return. We cannot prevail against it. It is our doom.*'

'That is the end of it,' Uthor breathed, slowly closing the book of grudges.

Silence descended, charged with anger and sorrow, each dwarf lost in his own thoughts at the account of the last days.

A raucous clattering broke the moment abruptly. The throng turned as one to see Drimbold, the rune axe of Ulfgan in his grubby hands, a pile of spilled coins and gemstones sprayed at his feet.

'Must you touch everything?' Gromrund raged, incensed at the Grey dwarf's curiosity.

'This is a weapon of kings,' said Drimbold in response, without hint of trickery or subterfuge this time. 'This axe is your birthright,' he added, turning to Uthor. 'It should not fester in this tomb, for the grobi to defile and plunder.' He pulled the axe carefully from the dead king's skeletal grasp and held it out for Uthor to take.

The scowls of the dwarfs lessened, though Halgar muttered something about 'desecration' and the 'slayer oath'.

Uthor approached Drimbold, the others parting to let him through. His gaze never left the mighty weapon, the runes on the blade still glowed dully; magical marks of cutting and cleaving inscribed long ago. The long haft was wrought in knots of gold and studded with emeralds. A talisman, engraved with the rune of Ulfgan's clan and bearing the face of one of his ancestors, was bound beneath the blade by a thick strap of leather. The axe was the most beautiful thing he had ever seen.

'It is wondrous,' he breathed, reaching out, almost fearful to touch it. As his hands grasped the tightly bound leather grip and he felt the weight of it for the first time, the head of Ulfgan slumped to one side. The dwarfs turned to witness the old king's shoulders slump and cave. The spine split, ribs cracked and the entire skeleton fell in on itself, crumbling into a mass of bone.

'And so passes Ulfgan,' said Halgar, 'last king of Karak Varn.'

A sudden scratching sound filled the air.

'What is tha–' Hakem began.

Halgar hissed for silence, closing his eyes to better hear the noise.

The scratching was getting steadily louder and the sound of squeaking accompanied it; a shrill and discordant chorus of hundreds of voices converging on the dwarfs.

'We are discovered,' said Halgar, unslinging his axe and shield. 'The skaven come!'

The other dwarfs quickly followed suit, steel scraping leather.

'Into the King's Chamber,' bellowed Lokki. 'We must not be trapped in here!'

The throng piled back into the King's Chamber, Ralkan taking up the dammaz kron after strapping the book of remembering to his back by means of his many belts. Rorek was the last out of the vault, shutting the door once the others were clear, the king's bed swivelling back into place to leave the room looking just as it had when they'd first entered.

The dwarfs closed together, shields locked and faced in three directions, towards each of the open doorways.

'Make ready,' Lokki shouted above the now deafening screech of the skaven.

Countless pairs of tiny red eyes glinted menacingly in the dark void beyond all three of the doorways and the skaven surged into the room like a pestilential tide of fur and fangs.

'Grimnir!' Lokki cried, invoking the name of the warrior god as skaven steel clashed with dwarf iron.

The first wave of skaven crashed against the sturdy shield wall and was thrown back, broken. Lokki, Halgar, Uthor and Hakem all dug in their heels, bracing themselves against the swell. Skaven bodies were everywhere, their foul sewer stench assailing the dwarfs' nostrils.

The shield-bearing dwarfs were formed in a locked triangle formation, with Lokki at its apex. Uthor guarded his left; Halgar his right. Hakem stood next to Halgar, while Gromrund, whose great hammer precluded the use of a shield, protected their backs.

Behind the shield wall was Rorek, his crossbow unhitched. Drimbold was next to him, his duty to protect the lorekeeper at his side.

Shrieking war cries and curses, the skaven – foul parodies of giant rats walking on two legs – regrouped and charged again, stabbing with spears and cruel daggers.

Lokki bore the brunt and felt a great dent punched into his shield. His brother dwarfs steadied him, their interlocked shields a nigh on impenetrable wall of metal.

'Heave!' cried Halgar.

Boots scraped against stone, and the dwarfs pushed back together. The skaven were repulsed and the dwarfs broke formation for but a moment to swing axes and hammers. A skaven fell dead for every blow. A flurry of crossbow bolts flew above their heads, even Rorek could not miss at this range and with the foe packed so tightly, and more of the rat-kin squealed.

The King's Chamber was filling rapidly with the rat-men, scurrying in a seemingly endless deluge from the open doorways.

At the back of the dwarfs' shield arc, Gromrund roared, splitting skulls with every stroke of his great hammer. Blood flecked onto his armour and the face plate of his warhelm but he gave it no heed. He swung left and right, corded muscles in his arms and neck bulging as he exerted himself.

'We are surrounded!' he cried to the others, smashing a black-furred skaven in the snout with an eruption of blood and yellowed fangs.

Lokki heard the hammerer's warning and knew they could not hold out. His axe was slick with skaven blood, his armour and shield badly dented. 'They are endless,' he breathed to Halgar, thumping a ratman to the ground with the flat of his blade before severing its neck with the edge of his shield.

'They are doomed!' laughed the longbeard, grinning wildly as he hacked a skaven from groin to chest. His axe blade jarred in the ratman's sternum and he had to step from the protection cordon of the shield wall as he used his boot to free it. A spear thrust flew in and took Halgar in the arm; the dwarf bellowed in rage.

Hakem turned, smashing the spear haft in two with his rune hammer before he stove the rat's head in. He closed tighter, until the longbeard regained his position.

Halgar roared, redoubling his efforts.

Uthor rent armour, flesh and bone as if it were nothing. Wherever the axe of Ulfgan fell a skaven died. A hulking brute of a ratman waded in towards him, brandishing a heavy looking halberd. Before the creature could swing, it was cut in twain down the middle, viscera spilling onto the ground in a sanguine soup.

The skaven were thinning, but Lokki knew the dwarfs could not battle forever, despite the protestations of Halgar.

'We cannot win this fight,' he said, and saw the way to the hearth and the dringorak was relatively clear. 'Break and make for the hearth,' he cried.

'Aye,' Gromrund replied, followed by the squealing retort of another felled skaven.

No one countermanded Lokki's order, not Uthor or Halgar. They all saw the wisdom in his actions. He led and they followed.

The dwarfs retreated into their shield wall, crushing closer, until they were almost arranged in a circle. The skaven surged against them, pressing hard and screeching fervently.

When the swell became almost unbearable, Lokki bellowed. 'With all your strength… Now!'

The dwarfs pushed as one, Gromrund, Drimbold and even Ralkan lending their weight and the skaven were smashed back. Without pausing to take advantage of those skaven prone or stunned, the dwarfs broke, the shield wall dismantling as they ran for the hearth. The few skaven stood in their way were hacked and hewn aside as Uthor took the lead, carving a red ruin in their feeble ranks.

The dwarfs barrelled into the hearth and into the dringorak. They negotiated the tunnel quickly and emerged into the vaulted gallery outside the great gate of the King's Chamber. With no time to seal their route off they ran headlong up the long hall, the enraged squeaking of the skaven close behind them.

Rorek paused a moment, part way down the gallery and fired a fusillade of crossbow bolts at the pursuing skaven as they poured from the hidden doorway. Most of his shots missed, but two of the ratmen fell with quarrels in their necks and bodies.

'Come on,' Lokki urged, tugging on the engineer's arm. The thane had been the last to leave the King's Chamber, ensuring everyone had made their escape.

Rorek shouldered his crossbow and gave chase as the others pounded onwards.

Ahead, a horde of skaven spilled out of hidden crevices in the walls, scurrying quickly to form a blockade.

Unrestrained by the formation of a shield wall, the dwarfs struck the skaven picket line in force and the killing began in earnest.

In an orgy of blood and screeching death, the ratmen were scattered with the dwarfs barely stalled in their stride.

Through the long gallery they went, back the way they had come across the guild hall, the feast hall and through the wooden gate, skaven harrying them without respite.

'You expect me to flee the length of the hold!' Halgar bawled to Lokki as they forged up the long stair that led from the second deep.

'I thought you trekked all the way to Karak Ungor,' Lokki gibed, grinning broadly.

'In my youth!' Halgar replied, snarling.

Lokki laughed aloud and the dwarfs drove on: negotiating the dilapidated tunnel and through manifold rooms, passageways and halls until they reached the audience chamber, hands on their knees and breathing hard. The scratching, squeaking retort of the skaven echoed after them.

'They are persistent bastards,' Uthor said, begrudgingly between breaths.

'We must make for the outer gateway hall,' said Lokki, readying himself for flight once more as he regarded the throng. 'Wait–' he added. 'Where is Drimbold?'

Drimbold was nowhere to be seen. In the frantic race through the deep, Lokki had lost sight of many of his

companions – the Grey dwarf could easily have fallen
without his notice.

'Does anyone know of his fate?' he demanded
quickly, acutely aware of the rising din of the skaven as
they closed on them.

The shaking of heads met his steely gaze. The thane's
expression lapsed briefly into sorrow and then hard-
ened.

'He was a greedy wanaz,' said Gromrund, 'but it is no
way for a dawi to die, fleeing through shadow.'

The stink of skaven grew abysmally strong as their
screeching became ear-piercingly loud.

'Onward,' said Lokki, 'or we shall all share his fate.'

The dwarfs hurried from the audience chamber and
were halfway up the second stairway that led to the
outer gateway hall when the skaven reached them. The
ratmen flung spears and crude knives, and pelted the
dwarfs with stones launched from slings. The throng
stopped and raised shields to ward off the missiles as
the first of the skaven overtook them.

The dwarfs hacked left and right, fighting a running
battle as they pounded up the last half of the stairs. The
throng had almost reached the archway to the outer
gateway hall. Uthor was carving a path through the
skaven who had got in front of them, Gromrund and
Hakem defending the lorekeeper, striking down any
ratmen who got too close. As Hakem smashed one of
the skaven warriors into the floor with the flat of his
shield, another got past him and advanced upon
Ralkan.

Red, beady eyes gleaming maliciously, the ratman
brandished a long knife and made to stab the lorekeeper in the heart. Months of waiting in the darkness,

cooped up in the dank tunnels, every noise sending shivers of dread down his spine welled up in Ralkan and he snapped. Bellowing a battle-cry that resounded around the stairway he smashed the creature aside with the book of grudges itself. The skaven crumpled under the furious blow but was then battered down by the book again as the lorekeeper bludgeoned it, all of his pent up fury and anguish vented in a few seconds of bloody battery. In the end, Hakem hurried him on, the skaven a smear of red paste on the ground.

'Feel better?' said the Barak Varr dwarf.

'Yes,' Ralkan replied. His face and beard were flecked with blood, the book of grudges drenched in gore.

'Good, because there are more...'

LOKKI BEHEADED A skaven warrior, before impaling another on the great spike at the top of his axe blade. Halgar was at his side, battling furiously, the two dwarfs fighting the rearguard as always. Looking down at the massing horde, Lokki thought he saw something nearby – nothing more than a fleeting scrap of shadow – dart into the darkness at the edge of the stair. He wondered on it no further, his attention diverted to a diminutive skaven, wearing robes daubed in wretched symbols and bedecked in foul charms. In its greying paw it clutched a bizarre, arcane-looking device. It was like a staff but almost mechanical in nature. The creature raised the staff high and devoured a chunk of glowing rock, swallowing it labouredly, throat bulging.

A strange charge suddenly filled the air as Lokki's beard spiked.

'Sorcery,' he breathed, making the rune of Valaya in the air.

Greenish lightning arced from the skaven's staff, zigzagging wildly until it struck the stairway roof, earthing into the stone. There was a low rumble and a tremor rippled across the ground, great chunks of masonry plunging downward, shattering as they struck the stair.

Halgar staggered and nearly fell.

Lokki looked up. A great slab of granite dislodged itself from above and was plummeting down about to crush the longbeard.

Lokki smashed him aside, rolling furiously as the massive rock missed him by inches. It splattered several skaven and began rolling slowly down the stair. It granted the dwarfs a brief reprieve as the skaven wailed, fleeing in all directions.

Wiping a swathe of sweat from his face, Lokki got up and helped Halgar to his feet. The thane didn't see the scrap of shadow creep up behind him. At first he didn't feel the blade sink into his back.

'That was close, lad, Grungni be–' Halgar stopped as he saw Lokki's wide eyes and the blood seeping from his mouth.

The longbeard was paralysed as a skaven thing bound in black cloth – its eyes blindfolded with a filthy, reddish rag – snarled from beneath a long hood revealing a stump of flesh for a tongue. It emerged slowly, tauntingly from behind the thane and ripped out its dark-stained dagger.

Lokki lurched, spitting blood and fell backwards down the stair, his armour clattering.

Disbelief then rage filled Halgar and he roared.

His anguished cry was crushed by the screeching retort of another bolt of lightning surging from the robed skaven's staff. The eldritch energy exploded against the archway, which shuddered and started to collapse completely. The violent quake that accompanied it threw Halgar down as the skaven assassin bled away into the darkness, Lokki lost from view.

A sound like pealing thunder echoed menacingly above him and Halgar prepared to meet his doom with grief in his heart.

HAKEM CRUSHED A skaven skull, his rune hammer exacting a fearsome tally, and looked back from the threshold of the outer gateway hall to see Lokki fall. He watched as a black scrap of shadow seemed to withdraw from the dwarf and shaded his eyes as harsh, green light flared below in the stairway tunnel. He staggered, but kept his feet as the archway to the outer gateway hall started to crumble, Halgar beneath it.

Hakem raced back through the arch, and hauled the longbeard backwards with all his might.

'Nooo!' Halgar bellowed, as the archway and part of the roof collapsed downward, smashing into the stair and crushing any skaven in its path. The route down to the audience hall was blocked. The dwarfs had become separated from the ratman hordes.

RIVULETS OF DUST and grit flowed readily from the ceiling cracks and the small chunks of dislocated rock that crashed down to the ground added to the imagined peril that the outer gateway hall was about to cave-in.

Eventually though, the tremors subsided and only dust motes remained, clinging to the air like a thick fog.

Uthor coughed in the dust-clogged atmosphere and beheld the huge slabs of granite that effectively sealed off the route to the first deep. He knew that Lokki's body was behind it. In the end, just ahead of Hakem, he had witnessed their leader fall. He watched the other dwarfs stunned by their own grief, silently regarding the mass of fallen stone. Drimbold too was lost it seemed, to Grungni only knew what fate. They had the book of grudges, but at what price?

'Old one,' said Uthor, his voice low and reverent. 'We must not linger here.'

Halgar had his hand on the wall of stone. He bowed his head and listened carefully. Muttering something under his breath – it sounded like a short pledge – he turned and looked Uthor in the eye. His face was like chiselled stone for all the emotion it betrayed.

'Let it be known,' he said aloud for all the throng to hear, 'on this day did Lokki, son of Kragg, thane of the royal clan of Karak Izor fall in battle, stabbed in the back by skaven. May Grungni take him to his breast. He will be remembered.'

'He will be remembered,' the other dwarfs uttered.

'The skaven still gather at the other side of the rock fall,' said Halgar, stalking toward the great gate. 'They will seek a way to get through to us,' he added, turning to Uthor. 'You are right, son of Algrim. We should not linger.'

'I think we might not have to traverse the latrine tunnels to escape the hold,' Rorek said, his back to the others as he examined the great gate, its antediluvian mechanism wreathed in a fine white patina of dust. 'The five of us may be able to open the gate from inside.'

* * *

'PUSH!' ROREK CRIED and the dwarfs heaved with all their collective might. The engineer had disengaged the massive locking teeth on the gate by means of six circular cranks. With the aid of Uthor, Hakem and Halgar he then released the three huge, metal braces barring it. It was then just a matter of opening the gate itself. Two large, thick chains hung from the ceiling. As each was dragged downward, by means of an immense circular reel set flat into the stone – ten broad handles on each – a series of interlocking cogs and pulleys would go to work, hitching each gate, inch by laborious inch, along an arc carved into the rock. Slowly, but surely the gateway would open. The throng only needed to work one gate – that would be enough to allow them egress – but with only six dwarfs, instead of ten, gathering in one of the chains it was extremely hard going.

'Enough!' shouted Rorek again. The left-hand gate was open a shallow crack – just three feet wide but enough for them all to squeeze through. Hazy light was spilling onto the open courtyard.

'Follow me,' said Uthor, taking the lead.

As he emerged into the harsh, late afternoon sunlight of the outer world, he covered his eyes against the glare. When he saw what lay beyond, he quickly lowered his hand and bellowed, 'Grobi!'

A small horde of orcs and goblins gathered in the crags outside Karak Varn. They appeared to be making camp – sat around crude fires and the debased totems of their heathen gods – eating, squabbling and sleeping.

The first orc died with Uthor's flung axe in its chest. The beast stared down stupidly at the ruin of its torso – at first stupefied – then it let out a low gurgle and slumped dead.

A goblin fell, its skull crushed by Hakem, before it could let out a warning. A third, then a fourth was killed by Halgar, holding his axe two-handed, meting out death with silent determination.

Gromrund killed another, smashing an orc in the back, brutally collapsing its spine and crushing its neck.

Rorek put his crossbow to work and pitched several goblins off their feet, their torsos pinioned by tightly bunched quarrels.

Before the greenskins even realised what was happening, eight of their number were dead. The thirty or so that still lived roared and snorted in anger, frantically taking up weapons. A host of snarling green faces all turned in the direction of the onrushing dwarfs, drawing up into a ramshackle picket line of bristling spears and curved blades.

'Charge through them!' Uthor cried, wrenching his thrown axe free of the orc carcass, before sheathing it and drawing the blade of Ulfgan. The dwarf of Kadrin surged into the masses, the undeniable spike of the throng's attack. Gromrund and Halgar were at his heels. Hakem followed with Rorek, the two of them keeping the lorekeeper safe as he was carried along by the charge.

A flurry of arrows came at the dwarfs as they ran, the hooded goblins loosing short bows and screeching madly. Uthor took one in his pauldron, two more struck his shield but he did not slow, ducking an overhead cleaver swipe and, as he rose, hacking off his attacker's arm.

In the end, it was over quickly. The dwarfs smashed through the camp like an irresistible hammer, leaving the greenskins bloodied and bewildered in their wake. They didn't stop running until they could no longer hear the bestial calls and cries of the orcs and goblins. They weren't followed. Foolishly, they had left a way in to the karak and doubtless the greenskins were exploiting that mistake.

THE DWARFS HAD made camp in an enclosed crag, a fitful fire at the centre. There were only two ways in and out, Gromrund stood ready at one, hammer held across his chest; Hakem was at the other, watching the road ahead.

Night was drawing in, the last vestiges of sunlight bleeding blood red as they slowly vanished into the horizon. Uthor warmed his hands by the fire. None of them had spoken since the battle with the greenskins.

'We make for Karaz-a-Karak,' Uthor muttered darkly across the crackling embers of the fires.

'It is a fair march from here,' said Rorek, smoking his pipe. 'At least two days over rough terrain and our rations are few – the ale has all but run dry.'

'Then we had best tighten our belts,' said Uthor.

'Hsst!' The warning came from Gromrund. 'Someone approaches,' he hissed, just loud enough for the others to hear. The dwarf crouched low, adopting a stalking position. He held his great hammer in one hand, the other raised in a gesture for the rest to wait.

'It is Drimbold,' he said aloud in surprise. 'The Grey dwarf lives!'

Drimbold walked into the camp, his face cut and his already worn attire ripped in several places. Even his pack appeared lighter. The dwarf quickly explained to the others how he had become separated from them, the skaven blocking his path. He had taken another tunnel and wandered in the dark until he'd luckily found another way out – a secret door in the mountain that led to the Old Dwarf Road. He'd watched the dwarfs fight through the orc camp at the gate, but had been too far away to do anything. After that he'd followed their trail, until it led them here.

'I am lucky to be alive,' he confessed, 'by the favour of Grungni.'

He smiled broadly, reunited with his erstwhile companions, and then said, 'Where is Lokki?'

'He is dead,' said Halgar, before any of the others could speak, 'slain by skaven treachery.' The longbeard's expression was like steel. There was but one thing concerning him now, Uthor could see it in his eyes. Vengeance. And he meant to exact it.

Uthor got to his feet and regarded his kinsdwarfs.

'A great wrong has been done this day,' he uttered, with fire in his eyes. 'But it is one among many. One that began with the death of my kin, Kadrin Redmane and now Lokki, too, rests in a stony tomb. Karak Varn lies in ruins; its once great glory rendered to nought.'

Many of the dwarfs began pulling at their beards and growling in anger.

'It cannot stand!' Uthor bellowed, watching the grim faces of his companions alight with the flame of vengeance, the dwarf's rhetoric emboldening.

'It *will* not stand,' he added solemnly. 'I Uthor, son of Algrim, lord-regent to the clan of Dunnagal do hereby swear an oath to reclaim Karak Varn in the name of Kadrin Redmane, Lokki Kraggson and all of the dwarfs that gave their lives to defend it.'

'Aye!' cried the dwarfs in unison.

Only Halgar kept his silence.

'Until the end,' said the longbeard, holding out his open palm.

Uthor met his stony gaze and laid his hand on top of Halgar's. 'Until the end,' he said.

The others followed. The oath was sworn. They would go to Karaz-a-Karak and return with an army. Karak Varn would be retaken or they would die trying.

FROM ATOP A lonely crag overlooking the camp a dwarf sat in solitude. The faint flare of a pipe briefly lit his battle-scarred face, his nose pierced by a line of three gold rings, a chain attached to the opposite nostril running to his ear. A huge crest surged from his forehead, appearing like a spike as he was silhouetted against the night.

'Until the end,' he muttered, crushing the smouldering pipeweed with his thumb and leaping down off the rocky promontory into the darkness below.

LOKKI AWOKE, NOT in the halls of his ancestors, his place made ready at Grungni's table; but coughing and spluttering amidst the ruination of the long stair. He was alive; a terrible, searing pain in his back where the knife had gone in reminded him of that fact. He'd lost his helmet somewhere – there was a large gash on his forehead, the blood was still slick and filled his nose with a copper-like scent.

Rubble lay all about and the air was thick with dust and grit, his once dark brown beard was wretched with it. A brazier still burned from a sconce attached to a nearby wall. Its flickering aura cast long, sharp shadows. The skaven were gone, as were their dead. They must have thought him slain, else he would be dead too.

Lokki tried to look around and found he couldn't move. A huge slab of granite crushed his legs. With some effort he heaved himself up onto his elbows and pressed both his hands against the rock but it wouldn't yield. He slumped back down again, gasping for breath. He was weak; the blade that had stabbed him must've been coated in poison. Dwarfs were a resilient race though, and could survive all but the most potent venoms – at least for a time.

Mustering his strength Lokki glanced around, hoping to find something he could use to lever the slab off his legs. His axe lay just beyond his reach. He tried desperately, gloved fingers clawing, to touch it but it was too far.

A stench wafted over him on a weak-willed breeze emanating from some unseen source. He knew it well. It was the cloying, rank and musty odour of skaven. The reeking stink was overpowering; Lokki felt bile rising in his throat and his eyes water. Then he heard something, the tiny sound of claws scraping stone.

'Poor little dwarf-thing,' said a horrible, rasping voice.

A skaven, clad in thick rust-ridden armour, with black and matted fur, loomed over Lokki. The creature gave a half snarl, half smile revealing yellowed fangs. Lokki noticed a scar beneath its filthy snout; the stitches were still evident in the pinkish flesh. On the fingers of its right paw the ratman wore a golden ring; a rune marked it out as treasure stolen from the vaults of Karak Varn. The other ended in a vicious-looking spike. A crude helmet sat on its head, two small ears poking through roughly sheared holes. Lokki had fought enough rat-kin to realise this was one of their clan leaders – a warlord.

'This is skaven territory, yes-yes,' hissed the creature. Lokki fought the urge to wretch against its foetid breath as it crouched down close, beady little eyes scrutinizing, mocking.

'Neither dwarf-thing nor green-thing rule here now. Here, Thratch is king. Thratch will kill, quick-quick, any who set foot in his kingdom, yes. Dwarf hold is mine!' he snarled, slashing a deep wound in Lokki's cheek with a filthy spike.

Lokki grimaced and spat a thick gobbet of blood into the skaven warlord's face. 'Karak Varn belongs to the dawi,' he growled, defiantly.

Wiping the dwarf's blood away with the back of his remaining paw, Thratch stood up, a feral grin splitting his features. Lokki watched as the creature slowly backed away into the darkness, and at exactly the same time another skaven emerged from it as if the shadow were an extension of his very being.

It was clad in black rags, its eyes blindfolded, its gait slightly stooped as it crept towards Lokki menacingly.

'Tried to cut my throat, Kill-Klaw did yes...' hissed the warlord, who was lost from view. 'Took his eyes, took his tongue – but Kill-Klaw not need them to stab-stab, quick-quick. Now Thratch is master, and he bids Kill-Klaw... stab... stab... slow... slow.'

The blind skaven assassin loomed over Lokki, dagger in hand. For the first time, the dwarf noticed it wore a necklace of severed ears strung around his neck. Kill-Klaw screeched – a terrible sound, emanating from the very gut – and darkness engulfed Lokki utterly. Agonised screams ripped from the dwarf's mouth, echoing

through the ancient halls of Karak Varn and into the
uncaring blackness, as Kill-Klaw went to work.

CHAPTER FOUR

BLOODY BUT UNBOWED, Fangrak trudged through the winding goblin tunnels of the Black Mountains and thought of how he might avoid a grisly demise. The orc chieftain was accompanied by a band of his warriors; the greenskins – orcs and goblins both – that had survived the attack by the dwarfs at the gate.

Twice now, he had been defeated. After the massacre in the foothills at the edge of Black Water he had gathered more warriors. He knew the dwarfs were headed for the old city, but he hadn't bargained on how long they would be down there. Two days he had waited, his patience thinning with every hour. Even choking the odd goblin hadn't alleviated his boredom. They'd erected totems, made offerings to Gork and Mork out of dung, and lit fungus pyres – the thick fumes cloying and potent. A stupor had descended from the heady fug exuded by the smouldering pyres, and the dwarfs had surprised them as the greenskins had awaited their return outside the gate of the hold. All of this he would have to explain to Skartooth.

The long tunnel opened out into a wide cavern. Daubed upon the walls in dung and fungus paint were the markings of the orc gods. Fires were scattered throughout the vast room beneath the mountain, goblins clad in thick black robes hunkering together and stealing malicious glances at Fangrak as he passed them by. Some hissed and snarled at him as he went, navigating the clutter discarded by the greenskins and the ubiquitous filth that pervaded everything. Fangrak wasn't scared of any of them, orc or goblin. He growled back, brandishing his flail meaningfully. The brutal weapon was slick with greenskin gore – he'd had to take his wrath out on someone before they returned...

At last, Fangrak reached the end of the chamber. Flickering torches clasped in crude iron sconces threw slashes of light on scattered bones that lay in abundance there. Orc, dwarf and skaven were all picked clean, even the marrow sucked dry by Skartooth's 'pet'. The beast was ever hungry and it was unwise to let him starve for too long.

Ungul was the first thing that Fangrak noticed as he approached the seat of his warlord with shoulders slumped, his defeated warriors in tow. The troll languished on a cot of straw and flayed skin – brown and coarse like leather, and curled at the edges. Chewing on a blood-stained, meaty rib bone, the beast grunted at the orc chieftain, the chains that shackled it to the ground rattling agitatedly.

Fangrak kept far enough away from Ungul so that it couldn't reach for him with its long, gangling arms, relieved as the beast went back to chewing at the bone. The orc chieftain bowed down on one knee before his warlord.

Skartooth was sat upon his 'throne', as the goblin warlord liked to call it. Wrought from bone, divested of flesh and meat by Ungul, the 'throne' took on a macabre aspect. A skull rack served as a back rest, crested by the heads of dwarfs and skaven, and any greenskins who displeased the agitated goblin. Rib, thigh and shin bones fashioned the seat, while the arms, legs and feet were made from an assortment of other parts, each surmounted by more skulls. Skartooth liked skulls; he had one on top of his great black hood, a mere rat skull – else the towering peak would collapse into his eyes. Around his neck he wore an iron collar, infested with spikes. It was a grotesque talisman. As Fangrak stooped he imagined tightening it around the goblin warlord's neck, until his eyes burst from his tiny head and his thin tongue lolled from his simpering little mouth. The orc chieftain allowed himself a grin at that, careful to conceal it from Skartooth as the warlord spoke.

'So, you is back then,' sneered the goblin, enveloped in his voluminous black robes, stained with the symbol of the blood fist – his tribe. ''Ave you killed them stinking stunties yet?'

'No,' growled Fangrak, keeping his head bowed.

'Useless filth!' Skartooth spat, lobbing a handful of rotten meat he'd been playing with, rather than eating, straight at Fangrak. The wretched meat struck the orc chief in the head, knocking his helmet askew. Fangrak went to right it without thinking.

'Leave it,' Skartooth screeched, getting to his feet and
yanking hard on Ungul's chain. The troll, who had
been busying himself picking scabs from his stony
flesh, grunted in annoyance, but the goblin warlord
held the creature's gaze and it became placid.

'You want to feel the insides of Ungul, do ya?' Skartooth snarled.

Fangrak looked up at the goblin warlord, but
betrayed no emotion.

Skartooth took a step forward. Fangrak could see the
goblin's dung staining the furs laid out on the seat of
his throne.

'You want to get in 'is belly where 'is juices will melt
ya away to nuthin', eh? You worthless scum, you dung-
eating swine.'

Fangrak responded levelly, his voice deep and
unmoved.

'We ave found a way through the gate.'

Skartooth halted in his menacing tirade to listen
intently.

'But there's a rock fall in the way,' Fangrak said
calmly. 'I reckon we can get in, but I'll need a few lads
to clear it.'

Skartooth looked Fangrak in the eye, scrutinizing
him carefully to try and detect if he was lying. Satisfied,
the goblin warlord sat back down.

'You'll ave what you need,' he whined, squeakily. 'But
Ungul is still 'ungry and I've peaked 'is appetite.'

Fangrak got back to his feet and pointed to one of his
warriors. It was Ograk – he'd been the lookout at the
gate, sprawled on a rock, snoring loudly when the
dwarfs had attacked.

'Oi!' said Fangrak, gesturing Ograk towards him,
'Come ere.'

Ograk pointed dumbly to his chest, to make sure it was him that his chieftain meant. Fangrak nodded once, very slowly. The orc shuffled forward, one eye on Ungul, who was licking his lips.

Fangrak got up close, eye-to-eye with Ograk, then took a knife slowly and quietly from a sheath at his thick waist and slit the backs of Ograk's legs with two fiercely powerful swipes. The orc howled in pain and rage, collapsing to his knees. He ripped his cleaver from its sheath, spitting fury, but Fangrak swatted it from his grasp with a heavy backhand blow.

'You'll not be needin' that,' he said, grabbing Ograk by the scruff of the neck and growling in his ears, 'and you'll not be runnin' away, iver.' With a grunt of effort, Fangrak hurled Ograk into the reach of the troll. Ograk screamed as Ungul battered him down with a meaty fist, the splintering retort of bone echoing around the cavern.

'Are we done?' he said to Skartooth, belligerently.

'Go clear that rock fall,' Skartooth said, 'or it'll be you in its belly next time.'

Fangrak turned, snarling harsh, clipped commands at his warriors before going off into the cave to press-gang others for his work crews. In his wake, he heard the wet tearing sound of rending flesh and the dull crunch of slowly mashed bone. He didn't stay long enough to hear the sucking of juices or the swallowing of innards; he was hungry enough as it was.

UTHOR LED THE procession of dwarfs as they approached the Great Hall of Everpeak, Seat of the High Kings, behind Bromgar, one of the High King's hammerers and bearer of the key to the King's

Chamber. It was a great honour indeed and Bromgar bore it with stoic fortitude and irresolute dourness.

The gatekeeper had met them at the mighty entrance to the hold – an impregnable bastion of flat stone that defied the ravages of the ages. He'd been waiting there as they'd approached from the Everpeak road – a lone dwarf made seemingly insignificant before the edifice of rock and iron.

The dwarfs of Everpeak had been expecting them.

A series of secret watchtowers set into the highest crags offered a view of many miles and were a ready early warning of approach. Quarrellers had stood at sombre guard from a final pair of watchtowers, flanking the outer gate. They were wrought with massive statues of the ancestors and the High Kings of old, the imposing sentinels glaring down at all-comers. The venerable image of Gotrek Starbreaker was amongst them, holding aloft the Phoenix Crown of the elves, a trophy won at Tor Alessi and which still resided in Everpeak as a reminder of the dwarfen victory.

At the loftiest upper wall the glint of armoured warriors could just be seen, patrolling diligently. The gate itself was a colossal structure. Some four hundred feet tall, its zenith seemingly disappeared into sky and cloud. So solid, so formidable was the great gate to Karaz-a-Karak it was as if it was carved from the very mountainside itself. Valaya's rune was inscribed upon it in massive script, a sure sign of the protection of hearth and hold.

They had been granted entry mainly due to Halgar's presence and the fact that they bore dire news and the Karak Varn Book of Grudges as proof of it. Bromgar had turned then, rapping five times with his ancient runic hammer on the immense barrier of stone and tracing a symbol with a gauntleted hand. Uthor had stared, enrapt, as a thin silver seam appeared and a portal no larger than four feet tall opened and allowed them all admittance.

'Ever since High King Morgrim Blackbeard ordered them shut during the Time of Woes, the great gates to Everpeak have not been opened,' the gatekeeper had said dourly, by way of explanation.

Having been received by an honour guard of Bromgar's hammerers in the audience chamber, the dwarfs now walked down a vast gallery, flanked by the royal warriors in silent vigil, their great hammers held unmoving at their armoured shoulders.

NEVER HAD UTHOR witnessed such beauty and such immensity. The audience hall rose up into a vast and vaulted roof, banded by gold and bronze arcs. Columns of stone, so thick and massive it would take a dwarf several minutes to walk around them, surged into that roof, resplendent with the bejewelled images of kings and ancestors. A mighty bridge, a thousand beard-spans across and covered in a mosaic representing the past deeds of Everpeak, stretched across a gaping chasm that fell away into the heart of the world. It led to a broad gallery lined by a veritable army of gold statues, each one a perfect rendition of the royal ancestors of the hold. So wondrous was Karaz-a-Karak that even Hakem was stunned into abject silence.

Of their company, only six now remained for an audience with the High King himself. Rorek had parted ways with the throng at the edge of Black Water. He would take the long road back to Zhufbar, taking care to avoid the greenskins lurking in the mountains and petition his king to grant troops for the mission into Karak Varn and the reclamation of the hold. Lokki, of course, had fallen. It was a bitter blow, felt by all, but none so keenly as Halgar who had said little since they'd made their oaths.

After a bewildering journey, they stood at last before the doorway to the Great Hall, resplendent with runes, etched in gold and gromril and bedecked with a host of jewels. Uthor quailed within, humbled to be at such a place. It even banished the dark spectre that haunted the edges of his mind – the memories back at Karak Kadrin – if only for a moment.

Horns bellowed throughout Karaz-a-Karak, their notes deep and resonant, heralding the arrival of the visitors to the king's court. The great stone doors opened slowly, grinding with the weight of ages. Another hallway stretched before the dwarfs, so long and wide it could have held several small over-ground settlements. Its vaulted ceiling seemed to disappear into an endless firmament of stars as an infinite array of sapphires and diamonds sparkled high above. Light cast from huge iron braziers, forged into the dour faces of high kings and ancestors, inlaid with huge fist-sized rubies, created the glittering vista and made it seem as if the hold was open to the very heavens.

The awesome planetarium made Uthor feel insignificant, as did the hundreds of beautifully carved columns stretching away in the shadows, much further than he could see. They were etched with the deeds and histories of the clans of Everpeak. Bare rock was visible on some, where a clan's line had been wiped out. Even now, high up in the lofty space, artisans were at work dutifully engraving with chisel and pick.

Like the thick tongue of some immense beast of myth, a mile-long red carpet swept down the centre of the massive hall. As the dwarfs made their way along it, treading down the mighty crimson causeway in awestruck silence, Uthor noticed the great deeds of his forebears etched onto the walls. These vistas were much, much larger than those of Karak Varn, over a hundred feet tall: the ancestor gods, Grungni and Valaya teaching their children the ways of stone and steel; mighty Grimnir slaying the dark denizens of the world and his long trek into the unknown north; the coronation of Gotrek Starbreaker and finally the great deeds of High King Morgrim Blackbeard and his son, the current lord of Everpeak, Skorri Morgrimson. Uthor wiped away a tear at their magnificence.

At the edge of a vast circular dais of stone, Bromgar bade the dwarfs stop. Around the far side, the ancient faces of the Karaz-a-Karak council of elders regarded them. Every one of them sat upon a seat of stone, the high backs decorated with ancestor badges wrought of bronze, copper and gold. Each seat bore its own particular device to reflect the status and position of the incumbent. A gruff-looking dwarf, his long black beard flecked with metal shavings, bound in plain iron ingots and with tan skin that shone like oil, could only have been the king's master engineer; his chair was decorated with tongs crossed with a hefty wrench. The high priestess of Valaya, a wise old matriarch wearing long purple robes was seated in a chair that bore the image of a great dwarfen hearth, the rune of the ancestor goddess above it. There were others too; the head victualer

had a tankard, the longbeards of the warrior brother-
hoods bore axes and hammers, and the chief
lorekeeper an open book.

In the centre of this venerable gathering, atop a set of
black marble steps and sat upon a further dais was the
High King himself, Skorri Morgrimson.

He wore a doublet of white and royal blue, edged in
silver thread over a broad, slab-like chest. Thick and
rugged, his black beard – the namesake of his father –
was bound up in ingots of gold. Dappled with grey
hair, it hinted at his age and wisdom. Thick, heavily
muscled arms, banded with rings of bronze, copper
and gold, and inscribed with swirling tattoos were
folded across his chest. On one arm, the various
devices of the ancestors were depicted; on the other, a
rampant red dragon, its coiling serpentine tail made
into a runic spiral.

THE SEAT OF the High King broke the semi-circle of
elders into two smaller, but equal, arcs and was altogether more grandiose.

Backed with a bronze motif of a hammer striking an
anvil, the face of Grungni wrought above it in a trian-
gular apex of gold, the Throne of Power was a mighty
symbol of Karaz-a-Karak and all the dwarf people. It
bore the Rune of Azamar, forged by Grungni and the
only one of its kind, and was said to be all but inde-
structible. For if the rune's power was ever broken, it
was believed that it would signal the doom of the
dwarfs and an end to all things.

Stood just behind the king, two at either side, their
gromril armour resplendent in the light from the
roaring braziers, were Skorri's throne bearers. During

times of war, and at the king's command, they would bear the mighty throne of power into battle, with the High King sat upon it reading from the Great Book of Grudges. They were the finest of all Karaz-a-Karak's warriors. Uthor would have bowed to them alone and yet here they all were before the High King himself!

'Noble Bromgar, whom do you bring before this council?' asked the high priestess of Valaya.

'Venerable lady,' said Bromgar, bowing deeply. 'An expedition from Karak Varn seeks the wisdom and the ear of the council of Everpeak on a matter of dire import.'

'Then let them step forward,' the priestess replied, observing the custom of the High King's court.

As one, the dwarf throng stepped into the circle as Bromgar stepped back into the shadows, his immediate duty done.

'Lord Redmane is the master of Karak Varn,' said the High King. The dwarfs were almost twenty feet away, such was the size of the circle, and yet the king's voice came across loud and resonant to all. 'A grudge is scribed in his name in the Dammaz Kron,' the king continued, 'for failing to deliver a shipment of gromril as was his oath. What have you to say on this matter? Who speaks for you?' snarled the king, glowering at each of the dwarfs in turn. Only for Halgar did he hold back his ire.

Uthor stepped forward from the throng.

'*Gnollengrom*,' he said, bowing down on one knee and removing his winged helmet, cradling it under his arm, to observe due deference. 'I do, sire – Uthor Algrimson of Karak Kadrin.'

'Then be heard Uthor, son of Algrim,' boomed the voice of the king, brow beetling beneath the golden dragon crown of karaz sat upon his head.

'I bring dire news,' Uthor began. 'Kadrin Redmane, my ancestor and lord of Karak Varn, is dead.'

A ripple of shock and despair from across the council greeted this stark revelation. Only the High King remained stoic, shifting in his seat and leaning forward to rest his chin on one fist. His eyes regarded Uthor intently and bade him continue.

'Slain by urk at the edge of Black Water; his talisman is proof of this fell deed.' Uthor held it aloft for all to see. Grim faces, etched with grief, looked back at him.

Uthor gestured to the rest of his companions. 'We ventured deep into his hold and found it abandoned, overrun by skaven.'

The High King scowled at that. Uthor went on.

'Through death and blood we recovered the book of grudges,' said Uthor and Ralkan came forward, head bowed low, the Karak Varn Book of Grudges held before him on his outstretched arms. It was still spattered in skaven blood from when he had used it as a bludgeon.

'Ralkan Geltberg, last survivor of Karak Varn.' There were tears in the lorekeeper's eyes as he said it.

'It tells a sorry tale indeed,' Uthor interjected. His face fell as he returned to a dark memory. 'One of our party... Lokki, son of Kragg, royal thane of Karak Izor, died retrieving it.'

Halgar straightened; the mention of his charge's name still felt like a raw wound to the longbeard.

'Venerable Halgar Halfhand of the Copperhand clan was his kinsdwarf,' Uthor explained.

Halgar came forward now, removing his helm and bowing in the time-honoured fashion, but with his fist across his chest as was the custom in years gone by.

High King Skorri nodded his respect to the longbeard.

'Fell deeds to be sure,' he said. 'The great holds fall and our enemies grow ever bold. This slight will not be forgiven and will be forever etched in the great kron.'

'Noble King Morgrimson,' Uthor said boldly, the entire assembly shocked by his impertinence at speaking before being asked to. 'We seek vengeance for our kinsdwarfs and the means to take back the hold of Karak Varn from the wretched rat-kin. Each of us has sworn an oath in blood!'

Incensed at this act of disrespect, Bromgar stepped forward but a glance from the High King stayed the gatekeeper's hand.

Passion blazed in Uthor's eyes so bright and powerful that none could have helped but be moved by it. Skorri Morgrimson was no exception.

'Your cause is noble,' said the High King, levelly, 'and no oath is ever to be taken lightly, but I cannot help you in this deed if it is the might of my warriors you beseech. There are precious few to spare; our kin have been ever dwindling against the attacks of the grobi and their kind. There are other, more pressing matters that demand the strength of Karaz-a-Karak. Alas, the plight of Karak Varn is dire, but one that will have to wait.'

'My king,' said a voice from the council below. It was a female dwarf, one of the attendants of the high priest of Valaya. She had been shrouded in the shadow of the matriarch and Uthor had not noticed her before. Long, golden plaits cascaded from her head and a round stubby nose sat between eyes of azure. She wore a purple sash over simple brown robes, but also bore a talisman bearing the rune of the royal clan.

The High King turned to her, incredulous at the interruption.

Many of the longbeards on the council grumbled loudly about the impetuousness of youth and their lack of respect. Even the matriarch turned to scowl at her attendant.

'My king,' she repeated, determined to be heard, 'with Karak Varn in ruins, surely Everpeak must act.'

The High King fixed the maiden with his gimlet gaze and, noting the courage in her eyes, breathed deeply.

'With war to the north beckoning and the retaking of Karak Ungor, I can spare but a handful of warriors to this cause, my clan daughter,' said the High King, content to relent and indulge her for now, before turning to regard Uthor once more. 'Sixty warriors is my pledge and that is a generous offer.'

'My liege,' the attendant continued, 'I must protest–'

The High King cut her off.

'Sixty warriors and no more,' he roared. 'And I will hear no more of it Emelda Skorrisdottir. The High King of Everpeak has spoken!' The High King's glowering gaze went to Uthor and the others, ignoring his clan daughter's indignation.

'Take these dwarfs back to the audience chamber,' he growled. 'There they shall await my warriors, but I warn them…' the High King stared at Uthor sternly, '…this is a foolhardy mission and one that I do not condone; they would fail it at their peril. Now…' he said, leaning back in his throne, breathing in deeply as he puffed up his mighty chest, 'Dismissed!'

CHAPTER FIVE

'HE IS RECKLESS,' growled Gromrund, 'a reckless fool,' he said. 'Sixty dwarfs to retake a hold full of skaven... It is madness.'

Three months they'd been at Everpeak as the warriors were gathered and prepared. Careful note had been taken of the cost of weapons and armour afforded to the clans and made in the reckoner's log, so that it might be levelled against the coffers of Karak Kadrin, Norn, Hirn, Izor and Barak Varr. With everything in order, at last they had made for Karak Varn once more. The throng was bolstered by forty warriors of the Firehand, Stonebreaker and Furrowbrow clans, and a coterie of twenty ironbreakers led by the ironbeard Thundin, son of Bardin, and the king's emissary in the mission to reclaim the karak. He walked alongside Uthor, clad in thick gromril, his ironbreakers keeping

measured step behind him. Thundin was possessed of
a warlike spirit and had been eager to join the throng
to recapture Karak Varn. His helmet device, a miniature
hammer striking an anvil, rocked up and down vigorously in time with the great wings on Uthor's warhelm
as the dwarfs forged on in search of glory.

'Doubtless he will add Gunbad next to his list of con-
quests,' Gromrund grumbled, as they were led west
along the Silver Road.

Mount Gunbad was a pale shadow on the northern
horizon and the dwarfs were keen to avoid it on their
journey back to Karak Varn. The great and prosperous
gold mine there had fallen over three hundred years
ago, sacked by grobi, and no attempt had yet been
made to retake it – at least none that was in any part
successful. The richest mine in all of the Worlds Edge
Mountains and the sole repository of *brynduraz*, the
rare 'brightstone' sought by miners and kings with
equal fervour, and it was lost to the greenskins.

'And what of his plan?' the hammerer continued, 'We
know nothing of that.'

'You would not renege on your oath?' said Hakem, who
had been travelling with Gromrund since Everpeak. Ill-
suited as they were, Gromrund at least felt he had an ally
in the ufdi, despite his garish sensibilities and boastful-
ness. In truth, since Karaz-a-Karak, the dwarf had said
little of the 'wealth and glory of Barak Varr,' and it meant
the hammerer could stomach his presence.

'I am no unbaraki,' hissed Gromrund, keeping his
voice low as he said the word. To be an 'oathbreaker'
was the worst insult to any dwarf and to even say it in
company was frowned upon. 'But I seek neither personal glory, nor to settle my own account before I stand

in front of the gates to the Halls of the Ancestors… It is for Lokki we do this deed,' Gromrund added solemnly with a glance at Halgar.

The longbeard walked alone, a few feet away. No one spoke to him, none dared for he wore a scowl the likes of which might be forever ingrained onto his face and a deep burden that fell like an eclipsing moon across his eyes.

'For Lokki then,' said Hakem – he too was looking at Halgar – full of honourable bluster. 'By the Honnakin Hammer it is sworn.'

'For Lokki,' murmured Gromrund, as the throng left the Silver Road, following a tributary of Black Water and, once they'd reached that great pool of jet, back to the hold once more.

Drimbold walked amongst the throng of warriors from Everpeak, with Ralkan beside him. The Grey dwarf didn't know what had happened to the lorekeeper. He never fought in the final battle to escape the karak; he had long since taken his leave by then. But though he was no longer the shell he had been, he didn't carry much in the way of gold either, so Drimbold wasn't interested either way.

Reclamation, that's what he was doing and he was determined to return to Karak Varn so he could continue his endeavours, but he'd rather do so with a band of stout warriors than by himself, although alone he could probably enter undetected as he had done previously. For now though, other thoughts occupied his mind.

For several days the Grey dwarf had kept a close watch on two of the travelling throng, intent on their wares. Both were nobles of Everpeak, a beardling and his older cousin if Drimbold's memory served, and possessed of a desire to honour their clan by retaking Karak Varn. *In a way*, he thought, *we are all reclamators really.*

As they trod amongst their kinsdwarfs Drimbold eyed the ringed fingers of the elder dwarf, the bands of polished bronze bent around his warhelm and vambraces. Drimbold's eyes widened as he caught the flash of something bright and shiny around the beardling's waist. It took but a moment for the Grey dwarf to realise what it was.

Gold no less! These Everpeak dwarfs are rich indeed, thought Drimbold. He picked up his pace, just a few steps behind them and reminded himself of something very important: on the road, there's always a chance that things will get dropped.

UTHOR TURNED AND gave the signal for the throng to leave the Silver Road at last. The tributary that would lead them to Black Water beckoned, and though the terrain would be fraught with crags, clawing bracken and scree underfoot it was the most expedient way to Karak Varn en masse.

A warhorn resonated down the short marching line of the dwarfs, five abreast, and the column wended north-east following Uthor's lead, Thundin and the ironbreakers in tow. It wasn't long before the shadow of Karak Varn loomed large once more, though they faced a different aspect to that which Uthor had confronted on their first foray to the hold. But it was another sight – an altogether more welcome one – that caught his attention this time.

* * *

'BEHOLD,' SAID ROREK to the thong of dwarfs gathered around him, 'Alfdreng – Slayer of Elves!'

A stout, wooden stone thrower sat behind the engineer lashed to a heavy-looking cart hauled by three lode ponies. Thick metal plates were bolted to its carriage and they in turn attached it to an iron-plated circular platform inset into the base of the cart itself. A crank, wide enough for two dwarfs to work it, was driven into a second plate next to the circular platform and a supply of expertly carved rocks sat in a woven basket at the end of the cart. Each stone bore runic slogans and diatribes directed at the race of elves. During the War of Vengeance, the stone throwers the dwarfs had used to bring down the walls of Tor Alessi had been renamed grudge throwers as the practice of inscribing the ammunition they flung came about, reflecting the deep-seated fury the dwarfs felt against their once-allies during those days.

There were mumbles of approval as the engineer paraded the ancient grudge thrower before the warriors of Karaz-a-Karak and his erstwhile companions. The dwarf had also brought with him no less than two-hundred warriors from Zhufbar, a pledge from the king. The Bronzehammer, Sootbeards, Ironfinger and Flintheart clans all plumped up their chests and twiddled their moustaches and beards as they regarded the appreciative gestures of their Everpeak kinsdwarf.

'Only an engineer would bring a machine to a tunnel fight,' muttered Gromrund to anyone who was listening. 'We dwarfs have been fighting battles without such contrivances for thousands of years; I fail to see how it would advantage us to do so now.

'Elf slayer you say,' Gromrund bellowed.

Rorek nodded proudly, one foot rested on the side of the cart and striking a dynamic pose.

'We go to kill grobi and rat-kin, not elves,' the hammerer grumbled.

'Bah,' said Rorek, taking a long draw on his pipe, 'it will crush grobi and ratman as well enough as elf. So speaks Rorek of Zhufbar,' he added, laughing, backed up by a chorus of cheers from his kinsdwarfs.

THE GREENSKINS ATTACKED quickly and without warning, descending down the steep-sided ravine like a bestial tide. Night goblins, hooded and cloaked, poured from hidden mountain burrows and sent black-fletched arrows into the dwarf throng. Three warriors fell in the first volley, before the dwarfs had shields readied. Hulking orcs, led by their black-skinned brethren, surged forward cleavers upraised, spears outstretched, and crashed into a hastily prepared shield wall of Karaz-a-Karak clan warriors. A horde of trolls, lashed and goaded into battle by a cruel orc beastmaster, fell among the ironbreakers at the head of the group, stamping and goring. A belt of foul-smelling stomach acid wretched from one, engulfing one of the veteran ironbreakers, his stout armour no proof against the foul stuff.

In a few, brutally short moments the dwarf army was embattled.

'Gather together!' Uthor bellowed, shielded from the trolls for now by Thundin and his ironbreakers. A nearby warrior, his kinsdwarfs fighting hard against the pressing orc horde, heard the order and blew a long, hard note on his warhorn. A second note from farther up the line responded and the throng began to form up in a thick wedge of steel and iron. Beset to the front and on one flank, it was slow going and some dwarfs got left behind as they fought.

Goblin wolfriders, howling and hooting as they scampered into view from behind a dense cluster of crags on their lupine steeds, harried the rear of the dwarf column, shooting short bows and making daring lightning raids on the stragglers.

FROM ATOP A viewing tower fixed to the side of the cart, Rorek bellowed furious orders to his crew below. Two dwarfs pumped the crank frantically and Alfdreng was rotated on the circular platform to face the hordes spilling forth from the ravine sides like malicious ants.

'Brace!' he cried and six metal clamps with broad teeth at the ends swung down from the cart and dug deep into the ground, securing it firmly. The lode ponies snorted and kicked in agitation but Rorek gave them no heed.

'Hoist!' he bellowed and the giant throwing arm of the grudge thrower was wound back on a stout wooden spindle. The wutroth of which the arm was carved, bent and creaked under the strain; Rorek felt it tense even in the watchtower.

'Load!'

A heavy boulder was rolled into the throwing basket, by two sweating crewmen, its grudge runes angled to face the enemy.

Through his good eye, the engineer fixed his gaze on the rampaging night goblins and a wave of orcs about to hit the dwarf column. The tension of the throwing arm persisted, resonating throughout the wooden structure.

'Wait…' he said.

The hordes were thickening into a densely packed mob, goblins and orcs taking up positions with short bows.

'Wait…'

The greenskins halted at a rocky ridge and began to draw back their bow strings.

'Fire!' yelled Rorek.

A belt of air whipped past him and a dark shadow became a blot in the darkening sky before the boulder crashed into the dead centre of the ridge, crushing orc and goblin alike. With the sound of wrenching stone, the ridge collapsed, and several more of the greenskins were buried.

A terrible aim with a crossbow he might be, but the engineer was a deadeye with any machinery.

A cheer went up from the crewmen and the Zhufbar dwarfs surrounding the war engine protectively, but Rorek had no time to celebrate as he eyed more greenskins.

'Five degrees to the left,' he bellowed. 'Crank!'

SHOULDER TO SHOULDER with warriors from the Firehand clan, Gromrund and Hakem fought a mob of spear-armed urk. A dense forest of sharpened stone tips thrust at them as the orcs pressed. One Firehand dwarf fell, gurgling blood as a spear pierced his mail gorget.

Hakem smashed one haft in two and parried another away with his shield, a third struck his pauldron and he recoiled but quickly righted himself to fend off a death-blow aimed at his neck.

Without the room to swing his great hammer, Gromrund used the weapon like a battering ram making pummelling drives with the hammer head. Wood splintered and bones cracked before his weighty blows but more orcs came on. Nearby, he could hear the battle-dirge of Halgar above the din of clashing steel.

UTHOR STOOD WITH Thundin, his axe carving through troll hide as if it were nothing. Every wound left a searing mark, hissing as it struck the hideously pale grey flesh. Trolls were known for their miraculous ability to regenerate from even the most heinous of injuries. Even now, one of the gruesome beasts recovered from a host of axe wounds inflicted by three of Thundin's ironbreakers. One was battered into the dirt by the creature; a second swatted into his kinsdwarfs before the veterans came at the troll again and proceeded to dismember it. Wherever the blade of Ulfgan fell skin did not re-knit or bones reset; where it fell was death and it was the reason the dwarfs were winning.

'You fight with the fire of Grimnir; may his axe be ever sharp,' Thundin said as he ducked a vicious sweep of a troll club and moved in to open its bloated gut. The beast recoiled in pain, bellowing in fury. The iron-beard rushed passed it, armour clanking, having created the opening he needed.

Between blows, Uthor watched as Thundin came face-to-face with the orc beastmaster. The snarling creature sent out its barbed whip hoping to tear chunks off the ironbeard, but Thundin caught the lash around his armoured wrist and yanked the orc towards him. The beastmaster was nearly barrelled over. Thundin beheaded it, a gout of crimson gore erupting from its ruined neck as it fell. With the rest of the ironbreakers pressing and Uthor's axe blade carving ruination, the trolls broke, their long, gangly legs taking them back into the hills.

'It seems I am not the only one,' Uthor replied, having fought his way to Thundin's side.

The ironbeard followed his gaze to the two nobles from Everpeak.

They fought like slayers at the head of the Stonebreaker clan, hewing greenskins with controlled fury. Several goblins had already lost heart and were scampering away from their flashing axe blades.

All across the line the dwarfs fought. Some had fallen and their names would not be forgotten, recorded in Ralkan's book of remembering, which the lorekeeper still carried, strapped onto his back. Though they were tightly packed, and the orcs assailed them on two sides, the greenskin dead were ten-fold that of the dwarfs. They piled in great stinking heaps, the brethren who still possessed the will to fight clambering over the rotting corpses. With a stout row of mountain crags at their backs, and shields locked to the front and sides, the dwarf formation was virtually impenetrable. The greenskins would not break it.

We will win this fight, Uthor thought.

An ululating war cry broke suddenly above the roaring battle-din, echoing through the narrow pass. Uthor's gaze swept west to the crags at the dwarfs' backs.

'Valaya's golden cups,' he breathed.

'May they be ever bountiful,' Thundin concluded, having followed Uthor's gaze.

A second horde of greenskins, vastly outnumbering the first, barrelled down the opposite slope howling like daemons.

Uthor saw the chieftain Lokki had fought at Black Water riding a snorting, thick-hided boar. He was surrounded by a guard of stoutly armoured orc warriors, also riding boars who were much bigger and darker-skinned than the rest. One carried a ragged banner adorned with skulls and black chains, the symbol of a clenched and bloodied greenskin fist daubed upon it. The glint of massive spear-tips twinkled in the moonlight like ragged stars and Uthor realised the greenskins had brought machineries of their own.

ROREK SAW THE goblin bolt throwers, ramshackle war engines hammered together with crude greenskin craft and carrying a massive spear of thick, black iron. Too late, he bellowed, 'Turn!'

The whipping retort of six bolt throwers loosing in quick succession found Rorek's ears on the fitful breeze. The sound of splintering wood followed quickly and the engineer gaped in horror as he realised he was crashing to the ground, one of the watchtower's supports brutally severed. Another bolt pierced the throwing arm of Alfdreng just as it was being frantically rotated into position and its arm tautened. A crewman was flung into the air screaming as the wutroth snapped and flipped backwards. A second dwarf was killed by the rope wound on the spindle as it lashed out and garrotted him.

Three more bolts buried themselves in the Zhufbar ranks, piercing armour as if it were parchment, pinioning three and four dwarfs at a time.

NIGHT WAS NEAR as the orcs from the western slope fell upon them, the sun dipping beneath the mountain peak, washing the sky with blood. It fell swiftly as the dwarfs fought, the last diffuse vestiges of day giving way to twilight and then dusk. The orcs became primeval in it, the false light casting them in an eldritch aspect.

The orcs and goblins swarmed, Rorek was lost from sight and many of the Zhufbar dwarfs would now be dining in the Halls of the Ancestors – this was not how Uthor had envisaged his glorious return journey to Karak Varn.

With the onset of darkness the greenskins became further emboldened, until a discordant note rang out, resonating around the high peaks.

The greenskins at the back of the western horde were turning, their screams rending the air. An urk in the fighting ranks noticed it too and turned for but a moment. Uthor cut it down contemptuously. He was about to press his attack when the front rankers started to waver and fall back, distracted by the events unfolding behind them. Then Uthor saw them, a band of at least thirty slayers, axes sweeping left and right, their blazing orange crests like a raging firewall even in the darkness. The orcs quailed before them and trapped between two determined foes their will broke. The chieftain's guttural cry split the air again, but this time it was to signal retreat. Dwarfs on both sides redoubled their efforts until both the east and west greenskin hordes were repulsed and the few that remained were cut down.

Uthor wiped a swathe of orc blood from his face and beard, chest heaving painfully so that his voice was barely a whisper. 'Thank Grungni.'

* * *

'Borri, son of Sven,' the beardling replied gruffly and over-deep. Uthor suspected the dwarf was compensating for his youth. The beardling wore a full face helmet, metal eyebrows and a beard fashioned into the design all supplemented by a long studded nose guard. Although the shadows cast by the mighty helm shrouded Borri's eyes they flashed with fire and pride.

Small wonder he fought with such vigour, thought Uthor at the steel in the beardling's expression.

With the battle over, the dwarfs were gathering up the wounded and burying their dead. A careful watch was maintained by the slayers, with whom Halgar had much to say, throughout. An early count by Ralkan estimated that the throng had lost almost sixty, the slain mostly amongst the Zhufbar clans, and around another thirty grievously wounded. They'd found Rorek amidst a pile of wooden wreckage, inconsolable at the destruction of Alfdreng but otherwise alive and not badly injured. Gromrund, Hakem and Drimbold had all survived the battle, too.

While the dwarfs made ready, Uthor felt it was his duty to recognise the efforts of his warriors and speak with the mysterious group of slayers whose timely intervention had turned the tide. He resolved to get to them later.

'Barely fifty winters, eh?' Uthor said, 'and yet you fought like a hammerer.'

Borri nodded deeply.

'As did you,' Uthor added to Borri's older cousin, Dunrik of the Bardrakk clan.

This dwarf had clearly seen much of battle, Uthor realised immediately. A patchwork of scars littered his face and his beard was long and black, banded with grudge badges. He wore a number of small throwing axes around a stout, leather belt and shouldered a huge axe with a deadly looking spike on one end. It was much like Lokki's. Incredibly, given their efforts, both had emerged from the fight almost completely unscathed.

'Son of Algrim,' growled the voice of Halgar.

Uthor turned to face the venerable longbeard and bowed his head as always.

'Meet our ally, Azgar Grobkul.' Halgar stepped to one side, allowing Azgar to come forward.

The slayer's bare chest bore numerous tattoos and wards of Grimnir. A spiked crest of flame-red hair jutted from his skull that was otherwise bald, barring a long mane of hair that extended all the way down his muscled back. Across his broad, slab-like shoulders, Azgar wore a troll-skin pelt, stitched together by sinew. A belt around his thick waist was cinctured by goblin bones and adorned with a macabre array of grisly trophies. The call to arms he had issued in the throng's defence was made by a wyvern horn he slung across his body on a strap of leather and he gripped a broad-bladed axe – a chain linking it to his wrist by means of a vambrace – in one meaty fist.

'*Tromm*,' the slayer muttered, his voice like scraping gravel as he met Uthor's gaze steadily.

The slayer's eyes were like dark pits, exacerbated by the tattooed black band across them but Uthor knew them, and knew them well.

'It is ever the burden of those who take the slayer oath to seek an honourable death in battle, in the hope to atone for their past dishonour,' Uthor replied, his expression tense.

'Perhaps I will meet it in the halls of Karak Varn,' said Azgar, dourly. 'It seems a worthy death.'

Uthor's fists were clenched. 'Perhaps,' he muttered, relaxing, 'Grimnir willing.' Uthor nodded once more to Halgar and then stalked away to find Thundin.

'He bears a dark burden, lad,' said Halgar, momentarily lost in his own thoughts, 'think nothing of it.'

'Indeed,' said Azgar, a noble cadence to his voice despite his wild appearance. 'Indeed he does.'

The slayer watched Uthor walking away. His face betrayed no emotion.

ACT TWO
OATH AND HONOUR

CHAPTER SIX

THE DWARF THRONG reached the outer gate of Karak Varn in confident mood. The greenskins had been put to flight and, though only some two hundred or so strong, the army was now bolstered by a band of ferocious slayers. It also seemed word of the orcs' defeat had spread, for no such creature opposed them as they made camp in the long shadow of the mountain.

The dwarfs gathered in small groups, heavy armour clanking noisily as they came to a halt and took in the impressive sight of the hold. Mutterings of wonderment and dour lamentations could be heard on the silent breeze that such a jewel in the crown of the Karaz Ankor could have fallen into depredation. Others, those older members of the clan who had seen greater glories, merely sighed in relief that the first part of the journey, at least, was over.

Strangely, the orcs had closed and barred the great gates left open in Uthor and his companions' flight several months ago, and so, with a day passed since the battle in the ravine and night approaching once more, the dwarfs pitched tents. They were large, communal structures that were used to house some twenty or so dwarfs at a time. Standards of bronze, copper and steel were staked in the ground at the encampments of each individual clan to indicate who lodged there. Warriors removed weapons and helmets as they huddled together, looking for casks of ale to moisten parched throats, and shake the grit from their boots. It had been a long march through the mountains. Tonight they would rest, before making their initial excursion into the karak come the morning.

'THERE IS BUT one sure way to secure the hold,' stated Gromrund, 'we clear one deep at a time and seal all ways in and out.'

'There is little time for that, hammerer,' Uthor argued.

Several of the dwarfs gathered in the largest of the tents, a broad but squat affair made of toughened leather and supported by stout metal poles. So low was the roof that Gromrund's warhelm would occasionally scrape the ceiling. There were a few muttered comments between dwarfs as to why the hammerer did not remove it, but as of yet no one had asked him. No guide ropes were required to keep the tents up, such was the ingenuity of the design, and each took on the bulky and robust appearance of rock. A shallow flume was cut into the roof and through it the smoky vapours of a modest fire billowed. Red meat on a trio of spits dripped fat and oil into the flames, making them sizzle and hiss sporadically. A large, flat table had been erected and each of the assembled war council sat on small rocks around it, drinking from tankards and firkins, and smoking pipes.

'According to the lorekeeper,' Uthor said, gesturing to Ralkan who sat quietly and supped at his ale, 'there is a great hall in the third deep, big enough to accommodate our forces. It is defensible and a fitting place to stage our reconquest.'

Uthor switched his attention to the rest of the gathered dwarfs. Halgar, Thundin, Rorek and Hakem all sat around the table, watching and listening to the two dwarfs debating.

'We get to it and secure a bridgehead,' Uthor continued. 'From there we can launch further attacks into the hold, striking deep at the skaven warrens, and reclaim Karak Varn for good!' He thumped his fist down on the table – the assembled throng wary of such outbursts, astutely raised their tankards a moment before – for emphasis.

'Delving so deep without knowing the dangers ahead and behind us is folly.' Gromrund would not be dissuaded. 'Have you forgotten the battle in the King's Chamber and how quickly we were surrounded?'

'We were but a party of eight back then.' Uthor stole a glance at Halgar. Yes, eight old one, he thought, when Lokki was still alive. 'Now we are many.' A fire glinted in Uthor's eyes at that remark.

'I maintain we will stand a better chance if we take the deeps one at a time. We have Thundin's ironbreakers to consider, far better employed as tunnel fighters than holding a single massive chamber, and let's not forget the Grim Brotherhood–'

'The slayers will do as they will, but they seek to die in this mission,' Uthor snapped, a bellicose demeanour possessing him suddenly. 'I for one do not want to be honoured posthumously, hammerer.'

Gromrund snorted his breath through his nostrils, and what part of his face that was visible behind his warhelm's face plate flushed red.

'A vote then,' the hammerer growled, through clenched teeth, slamming down his ale to the rapid upraising of tankards around the tent. He held up a coin that shimmered in the firelight. On one side was an ancestor head; the other bore a hammer. 'Heads, we clear the deeps one by one–'

'–or hammers, we head for the Great Hall and make our stand there,' Uthor concluded.

Gromrund slammed his coin down first, head facing upward.

'Venerable Halgar,' said Uthor, matching the hammerer but with his coin, hammer upturned, 'yours is the next vote.'

Halgar snorted derisively, grumbling at some unknown slight and set his coin down upon the table, but left his hand over it to conceal his decision.

'The vote is secret, as it was in the old days,' he snarled, 'until all parties have made their choice.'

Hakem nodded, placing his coin down and covering it. In turn the process repeated, until each and every dwarf present had placed his voting coin.

'Let us see, then, who has the support of this council,' Uthor intoned, eyeing the table with the concealed coins upon it eagerly.

As one, the assembled dwarfs revealed their decisions.

* * *

GROMRUND LEFT THE tent muttering heatedly under his breath and went off in search of his own lodgings for the night. Drimbold, who was sitting a short distance from the tent, watched him as he ladled a stew over a low fire. Gromrund stalked right through the Grey dwarf's encampment, tripping on the stones surrounding the fire and accidentally kicking over a steaming pot of kuri.

'Be mindful!' Drimbold said as his meal was unceremoniously splattered over the ground.

Gromrund barely broke his stride as he snarled, 'Be mindful yourself, Grey dwarf.'

'Grumbaki,' Drimbold muttered. If the hammerer heard him, he did not show it. Must be that warhelm clogging up his ears, he thought with a wry smile. Looking down at his spoilt food he scowled but then dipped his finger into a portion of the kuri he'd made with troll flesh, before putting it in his mouth. He chewed the cured flesh for a moment, the fire putting paid to any regenerative qualities the meat might have once possessed, then sucked at the juices, grinding the added dirt and grit in his teeth. 'Still good,' he said to himself and dipped his finger in the spilled stew again.

Drimbold ate with a small group of Zhufbar dwarf miners of the Sootbeard clan, sitting around a fitful fire. Not all of the dwarfs were sleeping in tents tonight and, as none had wished to share with him on account of the fact that several personal items from around the camp had already gone missing with a fairly strong suspicion as to who the culprit was, he was amongst those unlucky few. The Grey dwarf didn't mind, and neither, it seemed, did the Sootbeards, one particularly enthusiastic and slightly boss-eyed dwarf by the name of

Thalgrim regaling them with tales of how he could 'talk' to rocks and the subtleties of gold. The latter subject interested Drimbold greatly, but Thalgrim was currently entrenched in matters of geology, so the Grey dwarf paid little attention to the conversation and instead contemplated his evening beneath the stars.

In truth, Drimbold was as at home looking up at the sky as he was beneath the earth at Karak Norn. He came from a family of kruti and had worked the overground farms of his hold since birth. His father had taught him much of fending for oneself in the wild and the art of kulgur was one such lesson.

Chewing on a particularly tough piece of troll flesh, Drimbold noticed another fire, higher up, on a flat rock set apart from the closely pitched tents. He could see the slayer, Azgar, up there in the light of a flickering fire sitting with his Grim Brotherhood as they were known. They ate, drank and smoked in silence, their gazes seemingly lost in remembrance at whatever fell deed had meant they'd had to take up the slayer oath.

Bored of watching the slayers, Drimbold decided to observe the Everpeak nobles instead. They were close by, just north of his encampment and farthest from the gate. Typically aloof, they sat in their own company and spoke in low tones so that none could hear them. Both wore short cloaks, etched with gilded trim, and finely wrought armour. Even their cutlery looked like it was made from silver. He had yet to catch a second glimpse of the belt the beardling wore around his waist, but he was certain it was valuable. They even possessed their own tent, which had an ornate lantern hanging from the apex of its entrance. The Grey dwarf watched as the beardling retired for the night and his cousin dragged the rock he was sitting on over by the entrance flap, sat back down and lit up a pipe. Drimbold had seen it earlier, as they were setting up camp. It was made of ivory and banded with copper. The Grey dwarf was wondering what other objects of worth they might own when the conversation with the Zhufbar miners turned to gold again and his attention went back to Thalgrim.

UTHOR SAT ALONE outside one of the dwarfen tents in darkness, deliberately apart from the fires of his kinsdwarfs, and found some solace in it. He stared into the distance, absently polishing his shield. The night formed shapes before his eyes, the long shadows cast by the flickering light of faraway fires resolving themselves into a familiar vista in his mind's eye...

The trading mission at Zhufbar had gone well and Uthor was full of boastful pride as he entered his clan's halls at Karak Kadrin in search of his father to tell him the good news. His hauteur was abruptly quashed, however, when he saw the grave expression of Igrik, his father's longest-serving retainer.

'My noble thane,' uttered Igrik. 'I bear grim tidings.'

As the retainer spoke, Uthor realised that something fell indeed had transpired in his absence.

'This way,' Igrik bade him and the two headed down for his father's chambers.

Uthor could not help notice the dark expressions of his kinsdwarfs as he passed them in the clan hall and by the time he reached the door to Lord Algrim's rooms, the two warriors stood outside wearing grim faces, his heart was thumping so loudly in his chest he thought he might spit it from his mouth.

The doors opened slowly and there was Uthor's father lying on his bed, a deathly pallor infecting his usually ruddy complexion.

Uthor went to him quickly, uncertainty gnawing at him at whatever fell deeds had transpired in his absence. Igrik stepped inside after him and closed the doors quietly.

'My lord, what has happened here?' Uthor asked, placing a hand upon his father's brow that was damp with a fever-ish sweat.

Algrim did not answer. His eyes were closed and his breathing fitful.

Uthor whirled around to face Igrik. 'Who did this?' he demanded, anger rising.

'He was poisoned by rat-kin,' Igrik explained dourly. 'A small group of their black clad assassins entered through the Cragbound Gate and attacked your father and his warriors as they toured the lower clan holdings. We killed three of their number once the alarm was raised but not before they slew four of our warriors and got to your father.

'As Algrim's oldest son, you are to act as lord-regent of the clan in his stead.'

Uthor was incensed, his gaze fixed to the floor as he tried to master his rage. His mind reeled at this trespass – there would be a reckoning! Then a thought occurred to him and he looked up.

'The Cragbound Gate,' he said, seeing the wound to Igrik's face for the first time, partially hidden by his thick beard, 'it is guarded at all times. How did the assassins get by the door warden?'

Igrik's face darkened further. 'I'm afraid there is more...'

Uthor's reverie was broken by the hacking cough of Halgar. The longbeard also sat alone on a shallow ridge overlooking the camp, and despite hawking most of his guts up drew deeply of his pipe and rubbed his eyes with his knuckles. The venerable dwarf had insisted he take first watch, and who was there to argue with him.

Uthor's thoughts returned to his past. He gritted his teeth as he recalled his hatred for the one that put his father on his deathbed. 'Never forgive, never forget,' he muttered and went back to staring down the darkness.

FROM A HIGH promontory, away from where dwarfish eyes might find them, Skartooth watched his enemies in the deep valley below, a malicious sneer crawling across his thin features. Greenskins needed no fires to see and so the warlord waited in the thickest shadows, weapon sheathed should an errant shaft of moonlight catch on his blade and give his position away. A small bodyguard of orcs and goblins was arrayed around him, including the troll, Ungul, and his chieftain, Fangrak.

'We could kill 'em in their sleep,' growled the orc chieftain, nursing the stump of his missing ear as he peered downward at the resting dwarfs.

'No, we wait,' said Skartooth.

'But they is 'elpless,' Fangrak replied.

'The timin' ain't right,' Skartooth countered, backing away from the ridge, not wanting to be discovered.

'You zoggin' what?' Fangrak's face screwed up into a scowl as he regarded his warlord.

'You urd and if you don't want to lose that other ear you'll shut your meat-ole,' he screeched.

'Hur, hur, meat-ole,' Ungul parodied, the troll's hulking shoulders shrugging up and down as he laughed.

'We wait until the stunties get inside…' Skartooth added, striking Ungul hard on the nose with the flat of his small sword to stop him laughing. The troll rubbed the sore extremity but fell silent, glowering for a moment.

'We wait,' Skartooth began again, 'and then we attack from secret tunnels only greenskins know about,' he added, his mouth splitting into a wicked grin.

'Oi!' squeaked the goblin warlord, remembering something.

Fangrak was already trudging away and turned to face Skartooth.

'Oose clearin' that rubble?'

'Gozrag's doin' it; must be almost finished,' Fangrak replied. Realisation dawned as he looked back down at the dwarfs encamped below.

'Aw zog...'

THUNDIN STEPPED BEFORE the great gates of Karak Varn, morning sun cresting the pinnacle of the mountain, and pulled a thick iron key attached to a chain around his neck from beneath his gromril armour. The iron-beard, and emissary to the High King himself, was standing at the head of the assembled dwarfs who had mustered in their clans, fully armoured and bearing weapons ready.

With the other dwarfs looking on, Thundin placed the key into a hitherto concealed depression in the stone surface of one of the gates and it glowed dully. The dwarf muttered his gratitude to Grungni and with a broad, gauntleted hand turned the rune-key three times counter-clockwise. Beyond the gate from inside the hold, there came a dull metallic 'thunk' as the locking teeth barring the door were released. Thundin turned the key again, this time clockwise but only once, and the scraping, clanking retort of the chains gathering on their reels could be heard faintly. Thundin stepped back and the great gates began to open.

'We could have used one of those earlier,' griped Rorek, standing at Uthor's side a few feet behind Thundin. The other dwarfs from the initial expedition into the hold were nearby. 'My back still aches from the climb.'

'Or from when the war machine collapsed on top of you,' Uthor replied, smirking beneath his beard.

Rorek looked crestfallen as he remembered back to the collection of timber, screws and shredded rope that was Alfdreng. He was still trying to devise a way that he could break the news of its destruction to his engineer guildmasters back at the hold. They would not be pleased.

'I'm sorry my friend,' said Uthor, with a broad smile. ''Tis a key from the High King, forged by his rhunki. Only his gatekeeper or a trusted emissary may bear one. Your efforts were just as effective though, engineer,' he added, 'but far more entertaining.' He laughed, slapping Rorek heartily on the back.

The thane of Karak Kadrin was clearly in ebullient mood after his dark turn towards the end of the war council. Ever since the battle in the ravine, Uthor's demeanour had been changeable. The engineer was baffled by it. With the loss of his war machine, shouldn't he be the one in the doldrums? He had little time to ponder on it as with the way laid open, the dwarf throng started to muster inside. It was a sombre ceremony, punctuated by the din of clanking armour and scraping boots. A grim resolve welled up in the throng as they followed Thundin, a charged silence that was filled with determination and a desire for vengeance against the despoilers of Karak Varn.

'URK!' SHOUTED ONE of the Grim Brotherhood. The slayers were the first to enter the hold and, once through the great gate, barrelled past their comrades to set about a band of around thirty orcs labouring in the outer gateway hall. The greenskins looked dumbfounded as the slayers charged, midway through hauling rocks away to the sides of the chamber in crude-looking wooden carts and bearing picks and shovels.

An orc overseer, uncoiling a barbed whip, could only gurgle a warning as Dunrik's throwing axe thudded into its neck. A second spinning blade struck the greenskin's body as it clutched ineffectually at its violently haemorrhaging jugular vein.

A troll, whom the overseer had been goading to lift a large boulder out of their path when the dwarfs attacked, stared stupidity at its dead keeper then roared at the oncoming slayers. It tried to crush Azgar beneath a chunk of fallen masonry from the cave-in but he dodged the blow and weaved around behind the beast. Looking under the rock, the troll was dismayed to discover no sticky stain where the dwarf had been and was dimly wondering what had become of its next meal when Azgar leapt onto its back, wrapping his axe-chain around the creature's neck. The troll flapped around, trying to dislodge the clinging slayer, crushing several orcs in its anguished throes. Azgar's muscles bunched and thick veins bulged on his neck and forehead as he strained against the creature. Eventually though, as the rest of the Grim Brotherhood butchered what was left of the orcs, the troll sank to its knees and a fat, purpling tongue lolled from its sagging mouth.

'You're mine,' the slayer snarled between clenched teeth.

With a final, violent twist of the chain, the beast fell prostrate into the dirt and was still. Quickly on his feet, Azgar caught a flaming torch thrown to him by Dunrik and set the troll ablaze.

Several dwarfs muttered appreciatively at the display of incredible prowess. Even Halgar nodded his approval of the way Azgar had slain the beast.

By the end, it was a massacre. Dismembered orc corpses lay everywhere, splayed in their own pooling blood.

Dunrik approached the dead overseer and wrenched his axes free in turn, spitting on the carcass as he did it. He gave a last hateful look at the barbed whip half-uncoiled at the orc's waist and turned to find Uthor in front of him.

'Well fought,' he said. The other dwarfs barely had time to draw their axes before it was over. Only Dunrik had shed orc blood with the slayers.

'It was a runk,' he replied bitterly, as if dissatisfied with the carnage and walked away to stand by his younger cousin.

Uthor's gaze met that of Azgar but he said nothing.

One of the Zhufbar miners, a lodefinder by the name of Thalgrim, if Uthor's memory served, broke the charged silence.

'Shoddy work,' he muttered, observing the crude braces the orcs had rammed in place to support the roof, though much of the rubble had been shifted and a gap made that was wide enough for the dwarf throng to traverse, 'shoddy work indeed.' Thalgrim smoothed the walls, feeling for the subtle gradations in the rock face. 'Ah yes,' he muttered again. 'I see.'

A bemused glance passed between Uthor and Rorek before the miner turned.

'We should move swiftly, the walls are bearing much of the weight and in their dilapidated condition are unlikely to hold for long.'

'I agree,' said Rorek, appraising the braces himself. 'Umgak.'

'That,' added Thalgrim, 'and the rocks told me so.'

Rorek flashed a worried glance at Uthor, mouthing the word 'Bozdok' and tapping his temple.

Mercy of Valaya, the dwarf thought to himself, as if one zaki wasn't already enough.

THRATCH WAS PLEASED. Before him stood his pumping engine, a ramshackle edifice wrought by the science and sorcery of Clan Skryre, that even in its latter stages of construction was easily worth the meagre price he had paid for it.

The vast device was located in one of the lowest deeps of the dwarf hold, where the worst of the flooding was, held together by a raft of crudely welded scaffolding and thick bolts. Three immense wheels, driven by giant rats and skaven slaves, provided energy to the four large pistons that worked the pump itself. Even now as the Clan Skryre warlocks urged the wheel runners to greater efforts with sparking blasts from their arcane staves, green lightning crackled between two coiled conductor-prongs that spiked from the top of the infernal machine like some twisted tuning fork.

As the warlord watched, standing upon a metal viewing platform, nervously eyeing the vast body of water below him and taking an involuntary step back, a streak of errant lightning wracked one of the wheels, immolating the slaves within and setting the wheel on fire. Clan Skryre acolytes wearing hooded goggles and bizarre, protruding muzzle-bags over their faces, scurried in and pumped a billowing cloud of gas over the fire. A few slaves from the adjacent wheel were caught in the dense yellow fug and fell, choking to their knees. Syrupy blood bubbled from their mouths as their lifeless bodies smashed around the impetus-driven spinning wheel, but the fire was quickly extinguished.

Thratch scowled, wrinkling his nose against the stink of singed fur.

'Ready-ready very soon,' a representative of Clan Skryre squeaked, cowering before the warlord. 'Humble Flikrit will make fix-fix,' it blathered.

Thratch turned his venomous gaze on him and was about to mete out some form of humiliating punishment, when a shudder ran up the viewing platform. The skaven warlord thrashed about as he lost his balance and fell. The skaven's eyes were wide as he landed just a few inches from the platform's edge near what would have been a deep plunge into the water below had he fallen any further. Thratch squealed and hauled himself quickly to his feet, scampering backwards. He almost collided with a skaven warrior, whose bounding approach had very nearly pitched Thratch off the side of the platform. The ratman was lightly armoured and slight – one of Thratch's scurries, a message-bearer.

'Speak. Quick, quick,' the warlord snarled, recovering his composure.

As the scurrier whispered into Thratch's ear, the war-lord's scowl grew deeper. 'You have done well, yes-yes,' said Thratch when the skaven was finished. The scurrier nodded vigorously and risked a nervous smile.

Thratch turned to the warlock still cowering behind him. 'Strap him to the wheel, yes…'

The scurrier's face fell and he turned to flee, but two burly stormvermin, Thratch's personal guard when Kill-Klaw was not around, blocked his escape.

'And no more mistakes,' snarled the warlord, 'or Thratch will have you fix-fix.'

'DIBNA THE INSCRUTABLE,' Rorek said to the throng as they paused at the threshold to a mighty guild hall. Like much of the hold, it was illuminated by eternally blazing braziers. They were filled with a special fuel created in collaboration by the Engineers' and Runesmiths' Guilds that could last for centuries. Uthor had heard of such things spoken of only in whispers by the guilders of Karak Kadrin, and knew the precise ingredients of the fuel, as well as the rituals that took place to invoke its flame, were closely guarded secrets.

An immense stone statue stood before the dwarfs, venerating one such guildmaster, though Dibna was an engineer of Karak Varn. It was erected, column-like in the centre of the vast chamber, carved to represent Dibna holding up the walls and roof with his back and arms, dour-faced as he bore the tremendous burden stoically.

'This has been added recently,' Thalgrim added, noting the hue and coarseness of the rock from which Dibna was wrought. He approached the statue cautiously, bidding the others to wait. Once he'd reached it, the miner carefully ran his hand across the stone, sniffing it and tasting a patch of dust and grit picked up by his thumb.

'Fifty years, no more,' he said, wandering off into the shadows.

'Where are you going, lodefinder?' Uthor, waiting at the head of the throng behind Rorek, hissed loudly as Thalgrim disappeared briefly behind the statue before reappearing through the gloom several minutes later in the glow of a brazier. He was standing at the back of the room, something else obviously having caught his eye.

'There's a lift shaft here, too,' said the lodefinder. He was looking through a small portal made in the rock, delineated by gilt runic carvings that flashed in the brazier flame. 'It goes deep.' His voice carried over to the dwarfs as it echoed.

'Perhaps we could use it to get to the Great Hall,' muttered Uthor.

Halgar stood next to him.

'With no way of knowing where it leads, I wouldn't risk it lad,' the longbeard replied.

Uthor acceded to Halgar's wisdom with a silent nod.

Rorek was surveying the roof. He eyed it suspiciously, noting the dark streaks running down the walls. 'The statue shores up the chamber,' said the engineer, 'Lord Redmane must have commissioned it as a temporary measure to prevent the Black Water flooding the upper deeps.' He turned to Uthor, several ranks of dwarf warriors standing patiently behind him. 'We can pass through, but must tread with the utmost caution,' he warned them.

* * *

'THIS WAS HERE before even Ulfgan's reign,' Halgar muttered, tracing his gnarled fingers across the mosaic reverently.

The dwarfs had been travelling for over a day, traversing Dibna's guild hall without incident, through long vaulted tunnels and numerous halls and were already at the second deep with still no sign of opposition.

Uthor had planned it that way, instructing Ralkan to take them down seldom trodden paths least likely to be infested by skaven and to the Great Hall in the third deep. On no less than three occasions though, the lorekeeper had led them to dead ends or cave-ins, his recollection of the hold growing increasingly unreliable the farther the dwarfs delved. Often Ralkan would stop completely, and peer around, perplexity etched on his face as if he had never been in the tunnel or chamber in which the throng was standing. Strangely, a word from Drimbold in the lorekeeper's ear and they were on their way again. The Grey dwarf merely said he was 'urging the lorekeeper to concentrate' when asked what he'd said to Ralkan.

Another day from their goal, according to Ralkan, and Uthor had decided to make camp in a huge hall of deeds – the entire throng, almost two hundred dwarfs strong, barely took up a quarter of it such was the immensity of the room. Mosaics, like those upon the long stairway to the King's Chamber, were etched onto the walls and he and Halgar regarded one as most of the other dwarfs were setting up camp.

'From before the War of Vengeance then?' Uthor asked.

The image was that of a huge dragon, a beast of the elder ages. Red scales like incandescent flame covered its massive body and a yellow, barrel-ribbed chest bulged as it spewed a plume of black fire from its flaring nostrils.

'Galdrakk,' Halgar murmured beneath his breath.

Uthor's look was questioning.

'Galdrakk the Red. It was a creature of the ancient world, old beyond reckoning,' the longbeard said, deigning to elucidate no further.

Uthor was reminded of the dire words in the dammaz kron, '*A beast is awoke in the underdeep...*'

A dwarf hero, wearing archaic armour, was depicted warding off the conflagration with an upraised shield. A host of dwarf dead lay around him, rendered as charred skeletons.

'*...it is our doom.*'

A second image showed the hero and a group of his kinsdwarfs sealing the dragon in the bowels of the earth, a great rock fall entrapping it for all time.

'It stirs the blood to think of such deeds,' said Uthor proudly.

'And yet it reminds me of our faded glories,' muttered Halgar with resignation. 'I will take the first watch,' he added after a momentary silence.

'As you wish, old–' Uthor began after a moment, but stopped when he realised the longbeard was already walking slowly away.

'YOU'D THINK HE would remove that grobi arrow,' said Drimbold to Thalgrim.

The two dwarfs were taking second watch, sat outside one of the two grand doorways into the hall of deeds, and to pass the time were observing their comrades.

'Perhaps he cannot,' Thalgrim replied, 'if the tip is close to his heart.'

Halgar was laid on his back, the snapped black arrow shaft protruding upwards. Apparently the longbeard was asleep, but his eyes were wide open.

'How does he do that?' Drimbold asked.

'My uncle Bolgrim used to walk in his sleep,' offered Thalgrim. 'Once he excavated an entire mine shaft whilst slumbering.'

Drimbold looked back at his companion incredulously. The lodefinder shrugged in response. His face was illuminated in the blue-grey glow of a brightstone; a fabled piece of brynduraz hewn from the mines of Gunbad. Several chunks of it were set throughout the hall; though the dwarfs could see quite well in the dark, a little additional light never hurt.

Uthor had forbidden the lighting of fires, and ordered the few torches set in sconces around the chamber to be doused as they slept. They would impair the dwarfs' otherwise excellent night vision and they needed every advantage they could get against the rat-kin. The stink of smoke or cooking food might also attract the skaven and he wanted to fight them on his terms only, once they had reached the Great Hall. No cooking also meant the dwarfs were reduced to eating only stone bread and dried rations. Thalgrim fed a hunk of the granite-based victual into his mouth and crunched it loudly.

Drimbold had no taste for it – he'd been on stone bread for the last two days having consumed all of his other rations – and made a face. Then he watched as Thalgrim reached underneath his miner's pot helmet, a clump of stubbed out candles affixed to it by their waxy emissions, and produced what looked like a piece of moulding fungus.

'What is *that*?' The pungent aroma made the Grey dwarf's beard bristle, but it wasn't entirely unpleasant.

'Lucky chuf,' Thalgrim explained. The ancient piece of cheese in the lodefinder's hand looked half-eaten.

'I've only needed to use it once,' he said, taking a long, deep whiff. 'I was trapped for three weeks in a shaft made by the Tinderback miners;.. Weak-willed and thin-boned that lot, much like their tunnels.'

Drimbold licked his lips.

Thalgrim saw the gesture and put the chuf back under his helmet, eyeing the Grey dwarf warily.

'Perhaps you should get some sleep,' he said. 'I can manage here.'

It wasn't a request.

Drimbold was about to protest when he noticed the stout miner's mattock, one end fashioned into a pick, at Thalgrim's side. He nodded instead, and dragging his pack with him – now burgeoning with loot once more – went off to find a suitable alcove out of the lodefinder's eyeshot.

Drimbold sat down against one of the massive columns that lined the edge of the hall of deeds. So massive was it that he was shielded from Thalgrim's view. Satisfied, he went back to surveying the slumbering throng.

Almost everyone was asleep. Dwarfs were lined top to toe, despite the fact they had the room to spread out – gregariousness and brotherhood amongst their own kin was ingrained since the time of the ancestors. One or two were still awake, smoking, supping or talking quietly. The majority of the Grim Brotherhood looked comatose, having swigged enough beer to kill several mountain oxen. It seemed the slayers had a nose for alcohol and had discovered another hidden ale store in the deep. 'Brew stops', as they were sometimes known, were not uncommon – the holds were vast and should a dwarf be forced to undertake a long journey, he would have need of such libations. Of course some were merely secret stores left by forgetful and aging brewmasters.

Azgar was the only one of the Grim Brotherhood still up. He was sitting at the perimeter of the camp, axe in hand as he stared at the outer darkness. The tattoos on his body seemed to glow in the light cast by the ring of brightstones nearby, giving the slayer an unreal quality. Drimbold recognised some as wards of Grimnir, he'd also heard the slayer mention that he bore one for each and every monster he had ever slain. The Grey dwarf suppressed a shudder – Azgar was nearly covered head to foot. Drimbold looked away, in case the slayer caught his eye.

Reverberant snoring emanated from the prone form of Gromrund through his mighty warhelm that the hammerer – for reasons unknown to the rest of the throng – still wore, his head propped up on a rock. He was divested of his other armour, which sat next to him in careful and meticulous order.

Hakem was close by – it seemed the two had reached some kind of understanding – laid with his hands across his chest, one clamped over his gold purse. The ufdi wore beard-irons clasped over his finely preened braids and softened his sleep with a small velvet pillow. Rather unnervingly, the merchant-thane had one eye open and was looking directly at Drimbold! The Grey dwarf quickly averted his gaze again.

Deciding he was finished observing, he began to settle down for what was left of the night. His eyelids felt
heavy and were sloping shut when a shallow cry
snapped him awake. He reached for his hand axe
instinctively, but relaxed when he realised it was Dunrik, waking from some night terror. Borri was quickly at
his cousin's side, a few other dwarfs who had been disturbed by the sudden commotion grumbling as they
got back to their own business.

The beardling was whispering something to Dunrik,
so low and soothing that Drimbold could barely hear
it. His interest was piqued when he caught something
about a 'lady' and 'a secret'.

Was Borri marrying into money and he didn't want
the others to know? Drimbold then wondered if the
dwarf had joined the mission to Karak Varn to secure
part of his bride's dowry. The thought made his blood
run cold. It meant that Borri was a salvager, just like
him!

CHAPTER SEVEN

'THE GREAT HALL should be just ahead,' Ralkan announced.

The two hundred-strong throng had reached as far down as the third deep, eschewing the use of scouts as the lorekeeper was the only one who knew where they were going and he couldn't be risked sent ahead with only a small bodyguard. Should they be slain or the rest of the army cut off from them they would surely meet with calamity. Strength in numbers: that was the dwarf way. The dwarfs need not have worried, for they had got this far without encountering any resistance. That very fact unnerved Halgar who peered anxiously into every shadow, stopping and raising his axe in readiness at any incongruous sound or tenuous sign of danger.

'Can't you feel it?' he hissed to Uthor, as the throng marched though what must once have been a mighty feast hall, its hospitality long since eroded.

'Feel what, venerable one?' Uthor asked, genuinely curious.

'Eyes watching us…' uttered the longbeard, squinting at the darkness clinging to the edges of the hall, '…in the blackness.'

Uthor followed Halgar's gaze but could feel or see nothing.

'If they are,' he said assuredly, 'then we will put them out, one by one.' Uthor gave a bullish smile at the thought, but the longbeard seemed not to notice and continued his paranoid vigil.

The throng left the feast hall and proceeded down a short, but broad passageway. As they rounded a corner, Ralkan leading them, the lorekeeper said, 'Just beyond this bend and across the gallery of kings, there lies the Great Hall…'

Peering through a wide arch as he joined a dumb-struck Ralkan at the threshold to the room, Uthor saw a massive, open plaza stretch away from them. Immense stone statues of the kings of Karak Varn lined both flanking walls, though some were diminished by time and bore evidence of dilapidation. Magnificent though the statues were, it was the gaping chasm rent into the cracked and crumbling flagstones that got his attention. Like a vast and jagged maw torn in the very earth, it filled the entire width of the room, exuding thick trails of smoke, and blocked the dwarfs' progress.

'IT'S DEEP,' MUTTERED Halgar, 'all the way down to the mountain's core. Likely a wound made when Karak

Varn was wracked by earthquakes and the Black Water first flooded its halls, so the legends hold to be true.'

Uthor and Rorek stood beside the longbeard and peered over the edge of the chasm. Darkness reigned below; only a hazy, indistinct glowing line in all the blackness dispelled the myth that the tear in the earth had no end and yawned into eternity.

Uthor imagined a great reservoir of lava at the nadir of the gaping pit: bubbling and spitting, venting great geysers of steam, chunks of molten rock dissolving in its heat and carried by a thick syrupy current. Briefly his mind wandered to what else might lurk in that abyss, kept warm beside the cauldron of liquid fire. He dismissed the thought quickly, unwilling to countenance such a thing.

'We have to find a way across this,' he said instead. 'Is that strong enough to bear our weight?'

Uthor pointed towards a wide, but ramshackle, bridge spanning the mighty gorge. It was crudely made, seemingly bolted together without design or care. Such slipshod construction was anathema to the dwarfs, especially an engineer.

'Umgak,' Rorek muttered. The engineer was crouched down next to the bridge, which was little more than a roped affair with narrow struts of weather-beaten wood. He turned to Uthor. 'Not of dawi manufacture,' he added, much louder. 'Likely it was made by grobi or rat-kin.' The engineer curled his lip in distaste.

'We should find another way,' Gromrund stated grimly, having joined the dwarfs at the precipice of the chasm. 'I do not trust the craft of neither greenskin nor skaven, and I have no wish to fall, honourless, to my doom.'

Uthor chewed it over. Crossing the bridge was not without risk.

'We cannot go back,' he said after a momentary silence. 'And I doubt the lorekeeper could even *recommend* an alternative route, let alone lead us to it.' He gestured to Ralkan, who was stood off to one side of the throng with Borri and Dunrik, muttering incessantly.

'I don't understand...' he garbled. 'I don't remember this being here.' The words spewed from his mouth repeatedly like a mantra, his gaze lost and faraway.

'It's all right,' Borri said, trying to soothe the addled dwarf but without success.

'I will not trust my fate to a grobi bridge,' Gromrund asserted, planting the pommel of his great hammer into the ground as if that was an end to the discussion. 'This is folly,' he added, 'and I am not the only one who thinks it so.'

Uthor moved his glowering gaze from the hammerer and swept it over the throng waiting behind him.

The warriors mustered close together, banners resplendent with their ancestral badges touching. Dour faced clan leaders stood at the forefront; ironbreakers, their grim faced masks unreadable, were alongside. Slightly removed from them were the slayers – wild-eyed and bellicose of demeanour. There were dissenting voices, Uthor heard them grumbling to each other.

'We have come this far,' he said, addressing the throng, 'and endured much. The names etched in the book of remembering are testament to that,' he added, pointing to Ralkan, who wore the tome on his back. 'I would not be thwarted by a lowly bridge and have

those names besmirched; the honour of their deeds–
Nay! Their *sacrifice*, be for nought.'

Silence descended at Uthor's impassioned rhetoric.
Several shame-faced dwarfs looked back at him; others
couldn't meet his fiery gaze and looked down at their
boots instead.

Uthor stood there for a moment, basking in this victory and then turned to scowl at Gromrund, the
hammerer almost livid.

'We take the bridge,' Uthor stated.

Rorek was getting to his feet, fairly oblivious to the
tension and the speech. The engineer took a good, long
look at the bridge and sucked his teeth.

'I'll need to test it.'

RorEK yanKeD on one of the guide ropes, attached to a
broad metal stake rammed into the rock and earth, and
the entire bridge shuddered. But it held.

He was aware of the charged silence around him as
he took his first faltering step onto the bridge itself. The
engineer felt for the rope around his waist to make sure
it was still there. He daren't look back to see if Thundin
and Uthor were still holding onto it. The rope was his.
At least he knew *that* would hold.

After what seemed like an hour, Rorek had reached
the middle of the bridge. It creaked menacingly with
every step and swayed slightly with the warm air cur-
rents emanating from below. As far down as it was, the
dwarf could still feel the heat from the subterranean
lava stream; smell its sulphur stink faintly in his nostrils. Some of the wooden struts were placed far apart,
or were simply missing, and the engineer needed to
concentrate hard on his feet to prevent any mishap. He

stared downward and swallowed as the abyss stared back.

Having got this far and with a hand on each guide rope, Rorek was growing more confident and progressed steadily. Relieved, he reached the other side at last and waved the others on.

'No more than four at a time,' he called back to the throng, 'and watch your step, the way is perilous.'

Thundin's expression darkened as he turned to Uthor, who was gathering up the rope.

'This is going to take a while.'

UTHOR HAD POSTED lookouts at the entrance to the gallery of kings, and at the edge of the chasm to watch the exit to the vast plaza. Whilst they crossed the bridge the dwarfs would be vulnerable. He did not want to be caught unawares by skaven saboteurs lying in wait for them on the other side, or ready to spring out and cut the ramshackle structure from under them as they were crossing en masse.

Steadily, in groups of four, the throng made its way across the bridge. The dwarfs crossed without incident and soon there were many more warriors on the far side than the near. Uthor instructed the guards at the edge of the chasm to cross. It left him, Halgar and two miners from the Sootbeard clan, Furgil and Norri, who'd been stationed at the gallery entrance. As he called them over Uthor noticed a straggler, hunting around the statues on their side of the chasm.

'You too, Grey dwarf.'

Drimbold looked up from his rummaging, having detached himself from the main throng long ago to explore the vast room, and started to wander over.

Uthor turned to face Halgar.

'I will guard the way,' he said.

The longbeard grumbled and went to step onto the bridge, but missed the guide rope, clawing air as he fought to snatch it. The bridge swayed violently with his displaced weight.

'Venerable one!' Uthor cried, reaching out for Halgar's arm. The longbeard found the guide rope at last and smacked Uthor's hand away.

'I can cross well enough unaided,' he snarled and started to tramp gingerly away, feeling for the rope with his hands, rather than looking for it with his eyes.

Uthor turned back to Drimbold, who was getting ready to set foot on the bridge, the Sootbeards waiting behind him.

'I will follow the great beard,' he whispered, with a glance at Halgar who had already reached the halfway point. 'Wait until he is safely across before you proceed.'

Uthor hurried on after the longbeard, but in his haste misjudged his footing and trapped his boot between two struts. He swore out loud and by the time he'd freed it, Halgar was on the other side, rudely refusing any offers of help and bustling past the clan dwarfs in his way.

Nearly two-thirds of the way across and with his boot now loose, Uthor made to move on, aware that the rope bridge was creaking ominously. He glanced back. Drimbold was at about the halfway point, his massive pack thumping up and down on his back with every step. Furgil and Norri were a short way behind him.

There came a sudden, tearing sound and Uthor's eyes widened as he saw the rope tied to the nearside stake begin to fray. It coiled apart seemingly in slow motion, the thin strands unravelling inexorably as he watched. Already, the bridge was beginning to sag to one side as the shredding rope yielded to the tension put upon it.

'Move,' he cried, waving the dwarfs on urgently even as a violent shudder passed through the bridge. 'It will not hold!'

Uthor heaved the Grey dwarf past him, nigh-on pushing him. He looked back to the Sootbeards, urging them on. They moved quickly, determination in their eyes.

The rope snapped.

The sudden feeling of the world giving way beneath him filled Uthor's senses. His vision blurred as the crumbling bridge below and the vaulted ceiling of the gallery merged as one. Smoke-drenched darkness came rushing towards him. His breath pounded in his chest and he thought of his hold, the lofty, cloud-wreathed peaks he would never see again; of his quest unfulfilled and the shame it would bring to his clan; of his father lying on his deathbed, as he faded away bereft of glory and unavenged; of Lokki, slain with a skaven knife in his back. Uthor wanted to cry out, to shout his anger at the ancestors, to defy them, but he did not. Instead, he felt the coarse brush of twined hemp against his fingers and grabbed it tightly.

A bizarre sensation of weightlessness passed quickly and Uthor was slammed into the side of the chasm, his shield and weapons – mercifully well-secured – clanking as they struck rock. The dwarf's shoulder blades were nearly yanked from their sockets as the weight of his armour pulled at him. White heat blazed up his arms and a dizzying fog obscured his vision. For but a moment, he lost purchase and the rope burned through his grasp, tendrils of smoke spiralling from his leather gauntlet. Uthor roared, biting back the pain as he gripped the rope hard to arrest his descent, one-handed, the other arm flailing about as he spun and thrashed. At last it was over and a hot line of pain gnawed at his arm, back and head. Through the dense aural fug of resonating metal in his ears from his helmet, the dwarf heard shouting.

'Uthor!' the voices cried.

'Uthor!' they said again.

Uthor looked up through a haze of dark specks, a spike of pain flaring in his neck and saw Rorek. The engineer had a rope around his waist and was peering over the edge of the chasm.

'Here,' Uthor said groggily. He didn't recognise the sound of his own voice.

'He lives!' He heard Rorek say. The dwarf's vision kept coming in and out of focus. When it returned, Uthor noticed Drimbold being hauled up the dangling bridge by Gromrund and Dunrik. The Grey dwarf clung to his pack, trinkets spilling out of it as his rescuers heaved. The lost treasure shimmered in the torch light – Uthor's world was darkening – they looked like falling stars...

'HE IS SLIPPING,' said Rorek urgently, turning to Thundin and Hakem who were holding the rope with feet braced. 'Lower me down...'

Rorek watched as Uthor drifted into unconsciousness... and let go of the rope. Before the engineer could cry out a half-naked dwarf barrelled past him out of the corner of his eye.

* * *

AZGAR WAS LEAPING through the air, a pledge to Grimnir on his lips as he swung his axe-chain rapidly in a wide circle. Over the edge of the chasm he went, through a faint wall of heat and plunged into the endless abyss. He turned his body in mid-flight, releasing the axe-chain and flinging it upwards in the direction he had just come. He watched for a moment to see the heavy blade arc over the lip of the gaping gorge and then wrapped both hands firmly around the chain. The links clattered and the chain pulled taut as the axe blade bit home above him.

Azgar felt the tension jar violently through his shoulders and back, but, grunting back the discomfort, he held on. The chasm wall rushed to meet him, promising to shatter his bones in a single crunching impact. Azgar absorbed the slamming force with his feet, bending his knees as solid stone made its presence felt. As he did, the slayer ran sideways like a mountain goat herder: nimble, light and assured. He reached out and caught Uthor's arm in one meaty fist. The slayer roared with the effort, thick cords of muscle standing out in his neck, arms and back. The chain lurched in his grasp for a moment and the two dwarfs fell a few feet. Azgar looked up in alarm as he imagined the axe blade churning a furrow in the flagstones above.

UTHOR OPENED HIS eyes, to see a wild-eyed slayer looking at him. Azgar's face was red. Veins stuck out on his forehead that was beaded with sweat.

'Hold on,' he snarled through gritted teeth.

Uthor looked down and saw the gaping blackness, a vague line of distant fire running through it. He gripped the slayer's arm with one hand and held onto the chain with the other, bracing his feet against the chasm wall.

AT THE CHASM'S edge, Rorek breathed a sigh of relief. He stepped back, untying the rope from around his waist. He checked to make sure Thundin and Hakem still gripped it and then tossed the end of the rope into the gorge.

'Coming down,' he bellowed.

Rorek took hold of the rope, wrapping it loosely around his wrist, just as it went taut. He felt the pull against his arms lessen as several more dwarfs joined him.

'Take the strain…' he cried. 'Now, heave!'

The dwarfs hauled as one, dragging the thick rope through their fingers, hand-over-hand in perfect unison.

'Heave!' Rorek bellowed, and they did again.

The command repeated several more times until two dwarf hands – one wearing a shredded leather gauntlet, the other hairy-knuckled and tanned – reached up over the edge of the precipice clawing rock with their fingers.

With Rorek and the others holding the rope firm, Gromrund and Dunrik reached down and hauled Uthor over the edge and onto solid earth once more. Two of the Grim Brotherhood grasped the thick wrist of Azgar and soon enough the slayer too was no longer imperilled.

Gasping for breath, Uthor regarded him sternly and gave a near-imperceptible nod of gratitude. Azgar reciprocated, dour-faced, and yanked his axe blade from where it had carved its way into the rock. After he'd gathered up the attached chain, ignoring the muttered admiration of a few of the clan dwarfs, he walked away from the chasm edge to be amongst his kin.

'Where are Furgil and Norri?' Uthor asked of Rorek, looking around once Azgar was out of eyeshot.

The engineer's face darkened, as did the faces of those dwarfs stood around him.

Drimbold was amongst them, sat clutching his pack. The Grey dwarf's expression was distraught.

'They fell,' he breathed.

'They fell,' echoed Halgar, stalking through the throng, dwarfs barrelling quickly out of the grizzled longbeard's way. 'They died without honour,' he snarled at Drimbold. Halgar's ire was palpable as he eyed the bulging pack the Grey dwarf clung to.

'The bridge it was–' Drimbold began.

'Overburdened,' said the longbeard.

'I thought it would–'

'You do not get to speak,' Halgar raged. 'The bodies of our kin were smashed on rock, immolated in the river of fire. Forever they will wander the catacombs of the Halls of the Ancestors, bodiless and with deeds unreckoned. Your greed has condemned them to that fate. You should throw yourself off into the underdeep...' the longbeard growled. 'Half-dwarf, I name thee!' he bellowed for all the throng to hear.

Shocked silence followed the declamation.

Halgar stormed off, grumbling heatedly as he went.

Several amongst the throng muttered in the wake of the insult he had levelled against Drimbold. To be so besmirched... especially by a venerable longbeard, it was a heavy burden indeed. A host of accusatory faces gazed down at the Grey dwarf. Drimbold did not meet their gaze but, instead, held onto his pack tightly like it was a shield.

Uthor watched the Grey dwarf thoughtfully, his head still thundering from his fall. He saw the borrowed helmet, the tarnished armour, the blunted hand axe: these were not the trappings of a warrior.

'You were not summoned to the war council, were you, Drimbold?' said Uthor.

'No.' Drimbold's voice was barely a whisper, shoulders slumped and mournful.

'You know this place too well.' Uthor's eyes narrowed. 'All the times you have guided our guide, you knew which way to go, didn't you? When we thought you lost to the rat-kin as we fled for our lives, you escaped another way.'

Drimbold's face fell further still as the weight of his leader's discovery struck him like a physical blow. The Grey dwarf exhaled deeply, his shame could be no greater, and then spoke.

'When Gromrund and Hakem found me, I had been looting from the hold for months,' he admitted. 'There is a cave – I have hidden it well – not far from the karak, where the treasure lies. I knew there were dangers, of the grobi and the rat-kin, and I took steps to avoid them.' Drimbold's voice grew more impassioned. 'Karak Varn was lost and its treasures laid bare for any greenskin to steal or defile. My clan and hold are poor–' he explained fervently, 'far better that the lost riches be in the hands of the dawi, so I sought to reclaim them.' The look in Drimbold's eyes was one of defiance. It faded quickly, replaced by remorse.

'You knew of Kadrin's death and the fall of the hold, yet you said nothing?' Uthor said, clearly exasperated.

'And likely he is a Sournose Grum and not a Sour-tooth as he alleged,' snarled Gromrund, the hammerer having bustled his way forward upon hearing his name mentioned.

Uthor fixed him with a reproachful glance.

Gromrund scowled back and stood his ground.

'My clan knew of the prosperity being enjoyed by Lord Kadrin,' Drimbold continued, 'so I ventured to the hold in the hope of panning some of the ore from the edges of Black Water. I did not think the Karak Varn dwarfs would miss it.'

Uthor's expression darkened at that admission, but Drimbold went on, regardless.

'I discovered the skeletons by the Old Dwarf Road, just as you did,' he said shamefully. 'And yes, I am one of the Sournose Grums.'

He could not meet the thane of Karak Kadrin's gimlet gaze any longer, nor the fierce anger of the hammerer, and lowered his eyes.

With the throng looking on, Uthor regarded the Grey dwarf in stony silence.

'Yours is a heavy burden,' he uttered prophetically. 'Furgil Sootbeard and Norri Sootbeard,' he added, 'may they be remembered…

'We've lingered here long enough,' Uthor said after a moment, addressing the throng. 'Make ready, we muster out for the Great Hall at once.'

The throng was forming up into organised ranks, gathering at the exit and waiting for Uthor as he strode purposefully to the front to meet Ralkan.

Rorek followed in his stead.

'With no bridge to speak of,' said the engineer, 'how are we to go back?'

When Uthor turned to him he was smiling darkly. 'There will be no turning back.'

CHAPTER EIGHT

Hoisted up on Ungul's back in a crudely woven basket, Skartooth looked over the goblin runners hurrying ahead of the greenskin horde as they tramped through the narrow tunnel. The roof was low and, on more than one occasion, the warlord had thumped the troll hard with the pommel of his sword after his head had struck a jutting rock.

Fangrak trudged alongside, the chieftain's thick hob-nailed boots crunching gravel underfoot. A great mob of orcs followed close behind him, shoulders hunched in the tight confines of the tunnel. Behind that there came yet more goblins. Wreathed in their black, hooded cloaks, they were little more than scurrying shadows in the gloom.

Skartooth had almost gathered the entire tribe for his 'cunnin' plan'.

'You is sure this is the way?' moaned Fangrak, again, snarling at an orc bumping into him.

'Ow many times ave you gotta be told?' whined Skartooth. 'These is gobbo tunnels and I knows 'em like the back of my 'and.' Sneering, the goblin warlord showed Fangrak his puny claw for emphasis. A look of surprise briefly crossed his weaselling face as he saw something there as if for the first time, before he continued. 'All that snotling rutting must ave addled your brain,' Skartooth said with a malicious grin.

'Hur, hur, ruttin',' droned Ungul.

Skartooth started laughing uncontrollably in the basket, spittle flicking from his tiny, wicked mouth. The hilarity stopped abruptly when he almost fell out, for which he struck Ungul viciously across the back of the neck. The troll turned to snarl at him, but when it met Skartooth's gaze, fell quiet and acquiesced.

'You leave the thinkin' to me,' warned Skartooth, his attention back on Fangrak.

Fangrak clenched his fists. No one spoke to him like that. When Skartooth looked away again, bawling at the goblin runners, he rested one meaty claw on the hilt of a broad dagger at his waist. Ungul glared at him as he did it, regarding the chieftain hungrily. Fangrak let it go – if it weren't for that beast... He was averting his gaze when he saw an ephemeral glow emanating from some symbols etched onto the spiked collar Skartooth wore around his neck. They looked like shamanic glyphs...

AFTER CROSSING THE chasm, the throng had been forced to take yet another detour. The main gate leading into the Great Hall was blocked by rubble; so massive was the ruination that even with the clan of miners they had, it still would have taken several days to get through. Another gallery had brought them to this point, the Wide Western Way. The tunnel was aptly named. Such was its girth that the throng could have marched fifty dwarfs across in four long lines, gazing up at its thick, vaulted arches in the light of the smouldering brazier-pans chained above. They did not. The long tunnel's state of dilapidation prevented it, with its broken pillars and sunken floors. Instead they strode in a column no more than four shields wide and in deep ranks; ever watchful of the pooling shadows that stretched from walls they could not fully see.

Naturally Uthor took the advance party, though even he was forced to concede the head of the column – that went to the Sootbeards. Though expansive, the Wide Western Way was fraught with pit falls and rock-strewn in places. It would be easy to slip in the gloom and never be seen again. The miners were ensuring the passage was clear and safe. There'd already been too many lost needlessly to the creeping dark.

Thalgrim was amongst them, overseeing their endeavours. It was painstaking work. Uthor had instructed that the throng stay together and in formation, lest anything be lurking in the darkened recesses of the tunnel. It meant excavating the scattered rock falls that impeded the dwarfs' path, and quickly. He paused a moment, his miner's mattock over one shoulder and lifted his pot helmet a little to wipe away a swathe of sweat.

'Mercy of Valaya, may her cups be ever lustrous, what is that stench?' said Rorek, wrinkling his nose. He looked back to Uthor for support, but the thane seemed lost in another of his dark moods.

The engineer was in the advance party, too, his structural expertise invaluable as they made progress down the Wide Western Way.

'Nothing,' said Thalgrim, sitting his helmet back down on his head quickly.

The pungent aroma still clung to the air and Rorek gagged.

'A pocket of gas, perhaps – nothing to worry about,' the lodefinder assured him.

Rorek mouthed the word 'gas' to Uthor, who looked askance at the lodefinder with some concern.

'Shouldn't we make certain?' he ventured.

'No, no. It's probably just some cave spores we've disturbed. Foul smelling, perhaps but certainly harmless, my brother.' Thalgrim was about to busy himself with something, thus avoiding further questioning, when he saw that the passageway narrowed ahead. The two walls on either side arced in dramatically in a cordon of around six shield widths. Bereft of brazier-pans, it was also miserably dark.

'Call a halt,' he bellowed, as the Sootbeards started to gather in the sudden bottle-neck.

'DO YOU THINK this route will finally lead us to the Great Hall?' Hakem asked.

Dunrik shrugged, seemingly distracted as he kept one eye on his cousin walking just ahead of him.

The Everpeak noble had offered little by way of conversation, despite the hour that they had been traversing the Wide Western Way, which Ralkan claimed would get them to their destination.

The lorekeeper travelled with them for now, in the middle of the column, staying out of the way of the miners' excavations. The last thing the dwarfs needed was their guide crushed beneath a slab of fallen rock or lost to the underdeep, in spite of his occasional befuddlement.

'I have my doubts,' whispered the Barak Varr dwarf conspiratorially, careful not to raise his voice so that Ralkan could hear him.

Still Dunrik gave him nothing.

The column was slowing. The armour of the ironbreakers, who were a few ranks in front, clattered as they started to bunch up. Thundin raised his gauntleted hand in a gesture for the throng to stop.

The message went down the line, a hand raised every ten ranks or so, until it reached Azgar and his slayers who were guarding the rear. Halgar had joined them, the longbeard preferring their silent, fatalistic company to that of the rest of his kin.

Hakem tried to look ahead to see what the delay was, but all he got was a small sea of bobbing dwarf heads.

'Perhaps it is another wrong turn?' the merchant thane offered.

It seemed Dunrik had no opinion on the matter.

Hakem was a gregarious dwarf by his very nature. He liked to talk, to boast and regale people with tales, and was not prone to long bouts of brooding like some of his kin. As a trader, his livelihood and the prosperity of his clan depended on the bonds he could forge, but despite his best efforts Dunrik was proving tight-lipped.

He was not the only one, either. Since the tragedy on the bridge, Drimbold had become like an outcast. He travelled in the column, much like the rest, but he kept his eyes down and his mouth shut. At least it meant Hakem didn't need to keep such a hawk-like watch over his purse and belongings. It was small recompense for the grief he felt in his heart.

The merchant thane brought his attention back to Dunrik. It was clear that he too had his own travails.

'I heard your screams when we last made camp,' said Hakem, his tone abruptly serious. 'Your scars go deeper than the flesh, don't they? I have seen their like before...'

Dunrik didn't bite.

Hakem persisted, anyway.

'...from the barbed whips of a grobi slave master.'

Dunrik twisted sharply to face him, his expression fiery.

Borri overheard and was turning around, about to intervene, when Dunrik's fierce gaze stopped him.

'I mean no disrespect,' Hakem said calmly, noting that Borri had continued on his way, albeit slightly uncomfortably. Gromrund, who walked on the other side of Dunrik, shifted a little in his armour, too.

'My great, great grandfather was captured by grobi for a short time, taken whilst driving a caravan to one of the old elgi settlements before the War of Vengeance,' Hakem went on. 'The greenskins ambushed them and slew many of our warriors. They turned the wagons into cages for our kin and were taking them, my three-times grandsire included, to their lair when a party of rangers found them.

'Three days my kin had been on the road before they were rescued and in that time the grobi had visited much pain and suffering upon them.'

Gromrund, having heard the entire recounted tale, turned to regard Hakem with newfound respect but stayed quiet.

'His face and body were scarred much like yours,' Hakem said to Dunrik, 'he showed me just before he passed on into the Halls of the Ancestors.'

Dunrik's anger drained away and a look of resignation passed across his face.

'I was held at Iron Rock,' he said, voice low and full of bitterness, 'taken whilst patrolling the Varag Kadrin.' Dunrik breathed deep as if recalling a dark memory.

'Of the twenty-three of my kin brought there in chains, only I escaped the urk fortress alive.' Dunrik was silent for a beat as he revisited the stinking dungeon, heard again the tortured screams of his brethren, felt anew the savage beatings of his vindictive captors.

'I did not do so unscathed,' he added, not just referring to his lasting physical injuries.

The Everpeak noble's face was wretched with the greenskin's 'attentions'. A long, jagged line ran from forehead to chin; some of Dunrik's beard was left patchy in its path. Weals of still reddened flesh pockmarked the right side of his face, burns left by the brander's iron, and he was missing three teeth.

Gromrund, who had respectfully remained silent throughout the exchange, could not help but be moved by such tales of honourable forbearance and grievous loss, gripped the dwarf's shoulder. As he did, he caught sight of where Dunrik's left ear had been almost chewed off – a wound kept mostly hidden by his helmet.

'Dreng tromm,' the hammerer muttered.

'Dreng tromm,' echoed Hakem.

Dunrik stayed silent.

Hakem, suddenly aware they had fallen into solemn lamentation, and slightly regretful of his questioning, sought to quickly lighten the mood.

'Tell me,' he said to Dunrik, eyes brightening, 'have you ever seen a more magnificent hammer than this?'

'A fine weapon,' Dunrik remarked.

'Indeed, it garners that reaction often,' Hakem replied, a little perturbed as he noted the smirk on Gromrund's face just visible below his massive warhelm.

'It is the Honakinn Hammer,' he explained, aware of Gromrund's sudden interest, 'and I bear it proudly as an ancient symbol of my clan. As heir to the fortune of my father, merchant lord of Barak Varr, it is my great honour to carry it into battle. Make no mistake, this is a very serious undertaking,' Hakem told them, indicating the thick leather strap that bound the weapon to his wrist. 'This cord has never been cut, for if it ever was and the hammer was lost, the prosperity of my clan and my line would be lost along with it.'

'A noble undertaking,' said Dunrik solemnly.

'Indeed,' Gromrund muttered reluctantly.

'Certainly, the fall of the Honaks would dull the lustre of the hold,' Hakem went on. 'Tell me, Everpeak dwarf, have you ever seen the wonder that is the Sea Gate?'

Gromrund grumbled loudly. 'Whether you have or have not, you are about to be regaled of its splendour,' he barked. 'I have no stomach for it,' he added gruffly and stormed off, shouldering his way further up the column to find out what was causing the delay.

* * *

'Put your backs into it,' Thalgrim chided, standing atop a flat stone so he could see his miners working at the door impeding their path.

The stone barrier sat right at the end of the bottle-necked section of the tunnel and Thalgrim assumed the Great Hall was beyond it, this lesser door a secondary way into the room. The lodefinder realised now that the Wide Western Way was narrowed by design, to make it easier to defend should it be invaded. A wise strategy and one he applauded, only not right now.

Most of the throng were grouped together in the narrow defile, shoulders touching, with a wall at either flank. The stone door being pushed by the Sootbeards wasn't particularly tall or broad, but it was obviously thick and heavy. Rorek, with Uthor at his shoulder, had already released a series of stone bolts by carefully manipulating the door's ingenious locking mechanism. Much of its resistance came from the fact that it hadn't been opened in many years, but eventually the door yielded to the miners' exertions, and ground open noisily.

'At last,' breathed Uthor, finding the closeness of his kinsdwarfs around him and the enveloping darkness disconcerting. 'This tunnel is the perfect place for an ambush.'

Thundin saw a strange globe-like object fly overhead then heard the gurgled warning of his kinsdwarfs before he saw the billowing cloud of yellowish gas. Bordak, one of his fellow ironbreakers fell back clutching his throat as bloody foam bubbled down his face and beard.

They were wedged in the bottle-neck of the Wide Western Way, many other dwarfs of the throng having already moved through the stone door and into the Great Hall beyond it. Thundin and his ironbreakers were trapped with the rest, shoulder-to-shoulder with their kinsdwarfs and strangely vulnerable.

'Gas!' cried the ironbeard. The acrid taste of the noxious fumes was upon his tongue before he could clamp his mouth shut. He watched as three more filth-stained globes soared out of the darkness and into the packed ranks of the dwarfs. He was powerless to intervene as they shattered on raised shields and unsuspecting helmets, disgorging their foul contents amongst the throng.

The dwarfs retreated instinctively, and those that remained on the near side of the door were herded back into the bottle-neck.

Thundin caught a snatched view of the Great Hall through the small portal and massing bodies. He could only guess at its immensity as the others, seemingly so far away and oblivious to the attack, gathered inside.

'Back into the Wide Western Way,' he bellowed, risking another mouthful of the gas, his voice croaking as the virulent poison wracked his throat and insides. Head reeling, he felt the press of warriors at his back moving steadily out of the bottle-neck. He vaguely saw the opening through his blurring vision when two concealed alcoves opened up on either side of him. Ratmen wearing strange, sacking hoods tied at the neck with a filtered muzzle and dirt smeared-goggles, poured out brandishing knives.

One came at him with vicious abandon, cackling with malevolent glee as all around Thundin his ironbreakers died, their armour no defence against the invasive poison.

Choking on his own blood, Thundin smashed aside the skaven's dagger thrust with his shield and hacked off its head with his axe. A loud crack echoed inside his helmet as he caught a flash of fire in the darkness and the whiff of burning. Another ironbreaker fell, a smoking wound in his chest plate.

Thundin was slowing now. He couldn't breathe, tasted blood in his mouth and felt it trickle from his nose and ears. He clutched at his throat, dropping his shield to claw at the metal gorget around his neck. An immense flare of green and incandescent flame surged from an alcove further up the bottle-neck to his left. Thundin was blinded for a moment. In his disorientation he thought he heard screams, as if he were listening to them from the bottom of a deep, dark well. Through the mucus and blood in his nostrils, he caught the stench of burning flesh. The ironbeard wanted to retch but couldn't. He slumped to his knees, his armour heavy and removed his helmet. The effort to hold his breath with it on was suffocating. As he gazed bleary-eyed at the carnage of dead dwarfs all around, something large loomed over him. Thundin's nerveless fingers let the axe slip from his grasp.

'Valaya,' he croaked with his final breath as the beast crushed him.

Dunrik rolled; the lumbering rat beast tore into the ground with its claws in the dwarf's wake as he desperately tried to reach Thundin who lay prone in a rapidly expanding miasma of sulphurous fog. Trapped in the bottle-neck, the fighting was fierce and close. All around him his brothers fought hammer and axe against a seemingly endless tide of skaven.

The creature before him had come with the rat-kin, lumbering out of the shadows like some cruel experiment. It was huge and grotesquely muscled; a horrific fusion of ogre and skaven. Its body was wrapped in thick, pus-soaked bandages and ravaged by sores and overly distended muscle growth. Dagger-like claws extended from fingers encrusted with dirt and dwarf blood. Blinded, the beast tracked the dwarf by smell alone and with lethal efficiency. The rat ogre sniffed for his prey and came at the Everpeak dwarf again, its savage backswing sending a hooded skaven screaming backwards into the melee.

Dunrik ducked the swiping arm of the rat ogre, its claws digging four deep furrows into the bottle-neck wall. The dwarf came forward quickly, beneath the creature's guard and rammed the spike of his axe into its frothing jaw, so hard that it punched straight through and came out of the rat ogre's skull. Dunrik ripped the axe free, with a roar of defiance, gore and brain matter showering from the gaping wound. In its death throes the beast came on still. It was about to lunge for Dunrik with the last of its fading strength when Hakem, who was also trapped with the skaven attackers, shattered its wrist with a blow from the Honakinn Hammer. The weapon's runes glowed dully as the merchant thane fought, a second blow crumpling what was left of the rat ogre's skull.

Dunrik nodded a hasty thanks and then pointed to the door to the Great Hall. Nearly half the throng had already filed through, but the tail end was being ravaged by poison gas as they struggled to turn and fight the skaven massing behind them, realising slowly they were under attack.

Hakem nodded his understanding and the two dwarfs ran to the stone door, covering the short distance quickly. They held their breath in unison as they plunged into the cloud of poison gas eking through it. A few dwarfs of the Firehand clan were battling furiously against a horde of hooded skaven at the threshold to the room. Borri, having been pushed further down the bottle-neck in the press of the fighting, was amongst them just beyond the door arch and inside the Great Hall itself.

He met the gaze of Dunrik across the open doorway, hacking down one of the ratmen with his axe. Borri's eyes were pleading when he realised what Dunrik was about to do.

Anguish crushing him, Dunrik heaved against the stone door with Hakem at his side and a few of the Firehand dwarfs, the rest of the clan warriors forming a hastily arranged shield wall to protect them. The door yielded quickly this time and scraped shut with a thudding echo of stone on stone, the thick bolts sliding into hidden recesses automatically. Dunrik looked down at the locking mechanism and smashed it. There would be no opening it.

'Magnificent...' Uthor gazed in wonderment at the Great Hall of Karak Varn. As leader of the throng, he was the first through and was vaguely aware of the others amassing in his wake.

By far the biggest chamber they had been in yet, the Great Hall was supported by a veritable forest of symmetrically arranged columns that stretched down its full length. At one end of the mighty room there was an immense hearth fashioned to resemble the ancestor

god, Grungni, his wide open mouth giving life to the
flames that must have once blazed in it. Statues lined
the walls, interposed with bronze brazier pans made
into the image of the engineers who had fashioned
them, immortalising the dwarfs for all time, their outstretched hands cupping the dormant coals within.
Shadows hugged the walls and pooled thickly around
each of the columns. The Great Hall was gloomy,
despite the firelight. There were stone tables throughout. The king's resided at the top of a rectangular
plateau – broad stairs leading up to it – and overlooked
the rest.

'Here, it begins,' Uthor murmured beneath his
breath, privately congratulating himself. 'Here, we take
it all back.'

'Dunrik!'

Uthor heard Borri's cry from the front of the throng
before the thunderous, booming retort of the stone
door to the Great Hall slamming shut, and was arrested
from his brief moment of vainglory.

Skaven infested the doorway behind him, cut off
from the rest of the horde, and tendrils of gas evapo-
rated around it. Several dwarfs littered the floor of the
Great Hall, spitting blood and snot.

'Turn!' he bellowed. 'Turn, we are under attack!'

AZGAR THROTTLED THE skaven warrior with one hand,
right in the thick of the fighting at the edge of the
bottle-neck and the broader section of the Wide
Western Way, trying to battle a way out for his kin. The
ratman's eyes burst with the sheer pressure exerted by
the muscle-bound slayer, coating the inside of its
goggles in sticky crimson. Discarding the creature like

an unwanted rag, Azgar freed up his hand to disembowel a second onrushing skaven with a brutal upswing of his chained axe.

The fighting was close; so close he smelled the sweat of his brothers around him, tasted blood on the air, and heard their deathsongs in his ears. The sound of killing became a macabre chorus to the doleful dirge as ratmen funnelled into the churning blades of the Grim Brotherhood, held in the bottle-neck and unable to get out. From the Wide Western Way the skaven came at them in their droves, hemming the dwarfs in.

Azgar cursed loudly as one of his tattooed kinsdwarfs was dragged silently to his doom by a vicious swarm of rats. No way for a slayer to meet his end, he thought bitterly, hoping that his own death would be more glorious.

A muted scream and a wash of hot fluid splashing against the side of Azgar's face got his attention – the stink of copper filled his nostrils and the slayer realised it was blood. He turned and looked up as a gargantuan rat ogre loomed over him, the beast casting aside two wet hunks of armoured flesh that had once been a dwarf warrior.

Metal plates, ravaged by rust, were fused to the monster's body like scales and it wore a cone-like helmet with a perforated grille at the muzzle – but hinged so that it could still bite – and two holes for its malevolent, red eyes. It swung a gore-splattered ball and chain that had been bolted to its wrist; a serrated boar spear was grafted to the other in place of a hand.

Azgar's flesh burned. He noticed the tattoos of Grimnir blazing brightly on his body and then the glowing, black-green rock studding the rat ogre's torso from between the cracks in its scale-armour.

Roaring a challenge, spittle frothing from beneath its helmet, the beast loped forward, with ball and chain swinging.

Azgar smiled, gripping his axe as he fixed the hulking mutant in his sights.

'Come on,' he said. 'Come to me.'

'OPEN THE DOOR,' Uthor demanded. 'I will not leave them to be massacred.'

The half of the throng inside the Great Hall of Karak Varn had slain the meagre few skaven that had got through before Dunrik and Hakem had shut out the rest.

The throng waited in pensive silence behind the thane of Karak Kadrin, listening to the muted sounds of battle, dulled by thick stone, through the closed entry door.

'The locking mechanism is ruined, I cannot release it,' said Rorek, one of those to have made it through, crouching by the doorway and replacing his tools in his belt.

'Can it be broken down?' Uthor asked desperately, switching his attention to the lodefinder, Thalgrim, all of the Sootbeard miners having made it into the Great Hall.

'Given several days…' said Thalgrim, rubbing his chin. 'Perhaps.'

'We must get through,' urged Borri, a slightly high-pitched, hysterical tone to his voice. 'My cousin is on the other side. I saw the rat-kin hordes through the fog, they couldn't possible prevail against such numbers. We must get to them.'

'We cannot!' Uthor snapped, enraged at himself more than the beardling. His face softened abruptly at the pain on Borri's face.

'I'm sorry, lad,' he said, placing his hand upon the young dwarf's shoulder and looking him in the eyes. 'Their names will be remembered.'

It was not supposed to be this way: desperate, divided... defeated. The thane felt his shoulders sagging as the burden of his oath exerted itself upon him. Had he been wrong? Was Gromrund right? Had he led them to folly? Aware of all eyes upon him, Uthor found inner steel and straightened up to address the throng.

'Secure the Great Hall, make barricades and set guards on every exit,' he ordered the clan leaders. 'We are but a hundred dwarfs,' he added, 'let them come in their thousands. They are but the rancid surf that breaks upon our rocks; each of us is a link in a suit of mail. Stay together, remain strong, and their blades will blunt and break against us.'

Chittering, squeaking laughter filled the massive room, coming from everywhere at once.

Uthor had heard it before.

Like miniature balefires, hundreds of eyes flashed in the outer darkness ringing the room – No, not hundreds... *thousands.*

Uthor gaped at the sheer size of the skaven horde closing in on them, rusted blades held ready in a vast sea of wretched, stinking fur. He *had* been wrong; this *was* folly.

'Valaya preserve us,' he breathed.

STONE SPLINTERED AS the ball and chain smashed against the ground. Azgar leapt back to avoid its deadly path and then ducked swiftly as the rat ogre swiped at him, the boar spear spitting sparks as it raked the wall. The beast swung again with the spiked ball. Azgar cut the chain in two with a blow from his axe and, stepping past the fierce swipe, reversed his cut to lop off the rat ogre's arm at the shoulder despite the armour plate. The creature howled in pain, the sound muffled and tinny through his cone-helm, and drove at Azgar with the boar spear, blood fountaining from its ruined stump. The slayer avoided the strike, which embedded deep into the flanking wall and held fast. The monstrosity heaved at the weapon impaled in the stone but couldn't free it.

Azgar regarded the rat ogre darkly as it struggled… and cleaved off the other arm. The beast fell back with the impetus of its own exertions. The slayer went to finish it but the rat ogre lashed out with its tail, taking Azgar's legs from under him. He hit the ground with bone jarring force and the slayer barely had time to get his bearings when a rust-brown blur came at him. Azgar reacted instinctively, holding onto the beast's jaws, one in each hand, a hair's breadth from biting off his face.

He shook with effort, every muscle straining as he fought to keep the rat ogre back. Saliva flicked his face and neck as the rat ogre's rotten meat breath washed over him. Digging deep, he summoned all the reserves of his strength and roared as he snapped the creature's jaws back, twisting metal and breaking bone. A howl of pain tore from the rat ogre's broken mouth. Azgar crawled out from under it, as the beast thrashed in fits of agony, gathering up the chain that was attached to his wrist and reaching for his axe.

'Chew on this,' he said and buried the blade in its tiny cranium.

* * *

MOST OF THE Firehands were dead, either suffocated or impaled by rat-kin spears, though the gas was all but dissipated. Dunrik risked a breath as he briefly surveyed the carnage.

The skaven assault had split the dwarfs still holed up in the bottle-neck into two. The ironbreakers were all dead. Of the advanced part of the force on Dunrik's side of the door only him, Hakem and a handful of clan warriors remained. If they could rejoin with the other forces further back down the Wide Western Way, they might be able to fight their way free.

Dunrik, his left eye blood-shot from ingesting some of the skaven gas, took an involuntary step back as two rat ogres lumbered into view, filling up the passageway. They demolished the feeble shield wall easily, one of the beasts biting off the head of a Firehand dwarf as he fled from it. All thoughts of escape disappeared from Dunrik's mind. He felt the stone door at his back, the closeness of the walls at either side, Hakem's tension as he raised his shield. There would be no escape.

HALGAR GASPED FOR breath through clenched teeth, making the most of a brief respite in the furious melee unfolding in the bottle-neck around him. He'd watched as the stone door was sealed, effectively trapping them with their enemies and was glad of it. At least he would go down fighting. The longbeard's arms and shoulders burned; the weight of his axe like a fallen tree in his gnarled hands. Blood – both rat-kin and dawi – splattered clothes, armour and skin. Halgar's vision blurred sporadically in time with a persistent throbbing in his skull; he put it down to when a skaven warrior had struck a lucky blow against his helmet – he would have to work out the dent later.

The longbeard tramped slowly through the carnage, past his battling kinsdwarfs as he tried to reach Drimbold. Having been near the back of the group, the Grey dwarf would never have reached the Great Hall, even if he'd tried. Instead, he had fought. Drimbold was a vague outline at times when Halgar's eyesight worsened, but he knew it was him – he could smell him. Ralkan was behind the Grey dwarf, clutching a borrowed hammer like his life depended on it. It did.

Out of the gloom, a hooded skaven came hurtling at the longbeard. Halgar sidestepped its attack, upending it with a smack of his axe haft against its ankles and then hacking the blade into the ratman's back to finish it. He shouldered a second rat-kin in the gut, using his armoured plate-mail like a battering ram and was rewarded with the crunch of bone. An elbow smash broke the skaven's skull wide open, blood and matter spilling freely. He felled a third with a hefty kick to the shins and then decapitated it with the edge of his shield to reach Drimbold's side.

'Stand firm!' he bellowed, cutting a savage diagonal blow against an onrushing skaven. More ratmen were pressing; their numbers seemingly endless. Even Azgar and his slayers were being slowly herded towards them.

'Fight until you've no breath–'

A massive ball of green and incandescent flame lit up the passageway, burning shadows into the walls and illuminating the conflict like some gruesome animation. Dwarfs fell screaming to the terrible conflagration – cloth, metal and hair melting before it.

'There!' cried Drimbold, fending off a rusty dagger with his hand axe. He pointed to a pair of hooded skaven lugging some kind of infernal weapon between them. One carried a bulbous cannon rigged with coiling pipes and a pull chain affixed to the fat copper nozzle. The other bore a large wooden barrel with bolted on plates that fed the cannon, bent-backed against the weight of whatever liquid was stored within.

A small band of dwarfs from the Stonebreaker clan charged toward the deadly arcane device, bellowing war cries.

The skaven gunner squeaked gleefully as he tugged at the pull chain, opening the nozzle. The Stonebreakers were immolated in a blazing inferno, their charred remains still smoking long after the flame had abated.

Halgar blinked back the after-image of the fiery destruction wrought by the skaven cannon.

'We must destroy it,' he snarled, as the nozzle swung in their direction.

The longbeard flung a throwing axe towards the weapon but missed, the blade 'thunking' harmlessly against the wall, before clattering to the ground. He stared down the gaping maw of the cannon, an indistinct circle of fathomless black, and closed his eyes.

The searing heat, the wash of flame didn't come. Skaven screaming filled his ears and Halgar opened his eyes to witness the bent-backed fuel carrier flapping at the barrel he carried. A hand axe was buried in its side and a volatile chemical mixture sprayed out eagerly. Patches of the ratman's fur burned and smoked where the fluid touched it – the stink of cooking skaven flesh was redolent on the breeze.

The gunner seemed oblivious to the screeching protestations of its partner and yanked backed on the firing chain with reckless abandon.

Halgar, Drimbold and all those dwarfs in the vicinity of the cannon were thrown back as an explosion wracked the tunnel, leaving a blackened scar on the ground fraught with tangled skaven corpses.

DUNRIK WAS SMASHED to the ground by a sudden, powerful shock wave. Dazed, he got to his feet, helping up Hakem and the few Firehand dwarfs that still lived.

Body parts littered the tunnel in steaming, fire-scorched chunks. The rat ogres were dead, engulfed in the fearsome explosion. Moreover, the way was clear to Halgar and the others. They'd have to run for it and close the short distance up the tunnel quickly. The skaven were already gathering their wits and regrouping to attack again.

'COME TOGETHER!' UTHOR cried in the Great Hall, his throng forming up in disciplined ranks around him, making a square shape with shields locked.

The skaven masses came from the shadows, spilling from their hiding places and concealed tunnels in a foetid, flea-infested swarm. They were on the dwarfs quickly, several warriors torn down before they had shields readied.

Uthor fended off a hail of missiles, before hacking down an emaciated ratman with his rune axe. More came at them in their droves, almost throwing themselves suicidally onto the dwarfs' blades and hammer heads. Blinking back a swath of foul-smelling skaven blood as it splashed against his face and helmet, Uthor saw these diminutive rats were nought but fodder, cast into the melee and urged on by the cruel whips of their masters. The skaven sought to tire them, wear them down until exhaustion took them and then death. Uthor raged against it and redoubled his efforts.

'Give no quarter,' he bellowed, turning left and right to bolster his warriors with his stirring rhetoric. 'Have no fear, for we are the sons of Grungni!' Uthor caught the eye of Borri, who fought furiously beside his kins-dwarfs, anger lending him vigour. Another hail of sharp stones and wicked throwing knives filled the air, flung from behind the skaven slave fodder. Uthor raised his shield to repel the missiles. When he looked back, he couldn't see Borri anymore.

DUNRIK AND HAKEM stood shoulder-to-shoulder with Halgar and the others in the bottle-neck. Azgar and what remained of the Grim Brotherhood backed up to join them, having aborted their attempts to break through the innumerable rat-kin hordes, and the trapped dwarf forces were finally reunited but being pressed into an ever diminishing circle.

Ralkan was at the centre of it, several stoutly armoured dwarf bodies between him and a vicious death at the claws of the skaven. The lorekeeper had abandoned his borrowed hammer – Drimbold wielded it now, in lieu of the weapon he'd thrown to destroy the rat-kin's fire cannon – and was frantically feeling the rock wall at the dwarfs' backs with his hands, muttering feverishly.

Dunrik watched the lorekeeper incredulously and caught Halgar's eye.

'His mind has finally given in to despair and terror,' said the longbeard, hacking down a skaven with his axe, before breaking the nose of another with his fist.

No matter how many the dwarfs killed, the numbers of the rat-kin did not dwindle and their vigour showed no sign of lessening.

'No way out,' growled Azgar cutting a ratman in half, 'and an endless horde to slay,' he added with no small amount of relish. 'It is a worthy death.'

Halgar nodded, battering a hooded skaven with his axe pommel.

'*There is my seat made ready,*' said the longbeard, his voice rising above the battle din so it might be heard by all of his kinsdwarfs. '*At the table of my ancestors it doth await me. Upon the rock are my deeds arrayed.*'

'*Lo do I see the line of kings,*' Dunrik said, joining in the sombre deathsong.

'*Lo do I see Grungni and Valaya,*' added Hakem, the words taught to him when he was but a beardling.

'*Tremble o' mountain.*' Azgar's distinctive timbre gave weight to the recitation.

'*Rage o' heart,*' said Drimbold, last of all. At least he would die with his kin, a hammer in his hand.

'*For hearth and hold, for oath and honour, for wrath and ruin – give fire to my voice and steel to my arm that I might be remembered!*' Halgar's voice was dominant as the entire dwarf throng rejoiced as one.

Only Ralkan did not sing. Instead, his fingers found the subtle permutations in the rock wall he'd been searching for. As he manipulated them carefully, a thin line ran rapidly up the length of the wall, across the roof and back down again spitting out dust as it went. A vein of light eked through it, shining faintly – a secret door, made in the elder ages, and Ralkan had found it.

* * *

GROMRUND CRUSHED ANOTHER skaven skull with his great hammer, but he was tiring. A boot to the groin and a pommel smash to its head as it doubled over put paid to another rat-kin, but the furred abominations seethed in the Great Hall. He had been one of the last to get through, not counting those unfortunates that had been poisoned to death by the gas or stabbed in the back by the rat cowards.

Bitterness filled the hammerer's heart as he fought. Uthor's plan had failed, and failed catastrophically. How the skaven had tracked them to this place in a domain as vast as Karak Varn, he didn't know. His only consolation was that he'd at least die with honour.

Through the curtailed view of his warhelm, Gromrund saw a savage blow come at him. Using his weapon defensively, he caught the attack against the haft of his great hammer. A huge skaven warrior confronted him, clad in thick, cured leather, studded with spikes. The creature's fur was the colour of coal. It wielded a brutal looking glaive, the blade dark and wet.

The ratman pressed, scraping the weapon against the wooden haft of Gromrund's hammer as a second blade thrust at him. Locked with the first skaven warrior, the hammerer was unable to defend himself. He did all he could, and twisted sharply, the second blade grazing against his armour, ripping out mail links and scattering them like silver coins. Gromrund staggered; managed to heave the first skaven back. He saw a blur of grey to the corner of his eye and felt an almighty blow against his head, the metal warhelm deafening him as it clanged loudly in his ears. Vision swimming, Gromrund went down on one knee, almost dropping his great hammer. He could smell blood. Through bleary eyes he saw the huge skaven cackle as it raised its glaive for the deathblow.

'I'm sorry, father,' he whispered and put up his hammer feebly.

The skaven fell; several black-shafted arrows pincushioned its swarthy body. The other turned, screeching maliciously towards some unseen threat.

Gromrund got to his feet and saw that a great many of the ratman had whirled around towards the source of the attack. He looked at the skaven corpse again – a momentary lull in the fighting, as the rules of engagement were seemingly re-established – it had been felled by grobi arrows.

Bestial war cries rent the air and Gromrund watched, open mouthed as hordes of greenskins streamed from unseen tunnels and unknown passageways. Black-garbed goblins, hooded and bearing short bows, loosed arrows into the packed rat-kin ranks; massive, brutish orcs smashed a thin line of slave fodder aside beneath hob-nailed boot and cleaver, whilst trolls were unleashed into the furred mass to gorge and crush and maim.

Where the skaven rushed to meet the greenskin horde their numbers thinned, and an avenue of escape presented itself. Across the melee in which dwarf, skaven and greenskin fought, Gromrund caught the attention of Uthor. The thane had seen the route too – it led to an oaken gate, stout enough to hold an army back if properly braced, but not so massive that it could not be opened and defended quickly.

'To the gate!' Gromrund heard Uthor cry, hoping that their embattled enemies would be too distracted to impede them.

'Go, now!' Gromrund added his voice to the thane's order.

Staying together, the dwarfs moved as quickly as they dared to the oaken gate. The way was diminishing all the time, as rat-kin began filling the gaps, struggling to fight them and the greenskins at once.

Building momentum, the throng adopted a spear-tip formation and drove a thick wedge into the skaven ranks, scattering them as they charged headlong through pressing bodies and the intermittent hail of arrows.

'They are the grobi from the ravine,' Gromrund shouted above the din to Uthor – the two dwarfs were shoulder-to-shoulder in the rush.

'I recognise the urk chieftain,' he added, catching glimpses through the frantic fighting.

'Lokki fought him at the edge of the Black Water,' Uthor offered, cutting down a skaven warrior who stood in his path, before battering another away with his shield.

'We were followed here,' the hammerer growled, shattering a ratman's spine and pummelling the hip of another with a wicked side swipe.

Anything further would have to wait. The gateway loomed.

The throng gathered into a semi-circle, arrayed around the gate at their back. Though fighting two foes at once, the rat-kin still came at them but the line was holding and the skaven were repelled by shield, hammer and axe.

As the battle became ever more furious, goblins and orcs found their way to the dwarfs' protective cordon. They too were repulsed with equal violent fervour.

* * *

ROREK WORKED DESPERATELY at the gate lock, wiping a wash of nervous sweat from his forehead. A shallow sounding click rewarded his efforts and, with help, he pulled the gate open. The depleted throng piled through quickly, barely half of those who'd made it into the Great Hall, but in good order. A thin line of shield bearers fought a desperate rearguard, allowing the majority of the dwarfs to pass through unhindered.

'Down!' Rorek cried and the rearguard squatted to the floor, shields upraised, as a host of quarrellers loosed a storm of crossbow bolts into the skaven harassing their kinsdwarfs. Rorek added his own rapid-firing fusillade and a score of ratmen were cut down. The short respite was enough time for the shield bearers to hurry through the doorway and those warriors positioned either side of it to slam the gate shut.

Thalgrim and two of the Sootbeards dragged a hefty bar across it before the dull hammering from the other side began as the skaven attempted to batter their way through. After that, Thalgrim took several thick, metal door spikes from a pouch on his belt and smacked them against the base of the door to wedge it shut. Rorek did the same and satisfied the way back was secure, at least for a time, the dwarfs fled.

'HELP ME PUSH!' the lorekeeper said, grunting as he threw himself against the wall. A few of the dwarfs turned and seeing the rectangle of light leant their own weight.

The secret door opened and Ralkan hurried through, eyes wide when he saw the plateau of stone basked in the white radiance coming from above. Through a long, natural funnel in the mountain the light of the upper world shone down, resolving itself in a hazy aura when it struck stone.

'The Diamond Shaft,' the lorekeeper breathed, in awestruck wonderment.

The plateau led to a set of descending steps and beyond that another plateau. From there a massively long stairwell dropped down into darkness and was lost from sight completely. On either side of the magnificent edifice of stone was a sheer drop into the underdeep, so cavernous and black that it might have been bottomless.

Overcoming his awe, Ralkan surged across the first plateau and was heading down the steps and onto the second, much larger, expanse of stone when the skaven came teeming through the secret door.

Most of the dwarf throng had followed the lorekeeper; the slayers and a few of the clan warriors mounting a fierce rearguard. The throbbing wave of rat-kin smashed against the rock of dwarf warriors and several of the foul creatures were pitched over the edge of the short stairway and fell screaming to their doom in the void below. But as the skaven numbers grew, the dwarfs were pushed back and slowly overrun. The fight came to a stalemate at the second plateau; the ratmen, despite their masses, unable to break the sons of Grungni, and the dwarfs refusing to give any more ground. Bodies, both skaven and dwarf, fell like fat rain into the hungry abyss surrounding them, the stone plateau, as mighty as it was, insufficient to hold them all. Rat-kin thronged on the stairs, bunched so close together that those in the middle were crushed and suffocated, while those on the edges were pushed off the edge into oblivion.

Rune-light illuminated Hakem's face as he struck relentlessly with the Honakinn Hammer, the weapon that was his birthright and a formidable relic of the craft of elder days. As he swung, the merchant thane sang the battle-dirge of his ancestors, the *Ever Blazing Beacon*. He smote his foes gloriously, punctuating every stanza with a hammer strike.

A sudden surge of skaven pushed forward into him and his kinsdwarfs. Hakem used his shield to crush a ratman's muzzle pitched another over the edge with a swift kick to the stomach. A third was smashed by the dwarf's hammer, its neck snapping back with an audible crack of bone. Hakem raised his rune weapon to smite a fourth but found he was pinned. The ratmen came on like a resurgent tide, literally thrown at him. Two dwarf warriors fell to their deaths in the charge. The merchant thane staggered, boots scraping stone underfoot; he felt the drag on his shield arm as it was crushed to his side. In the maelstrom of fur, flesh and steel a ratman bared its filthy fangs to bite at him. Hakem head-butted it and the creature's nose caved, before falling away into the mass. Bellowing, he freed his hammer.

'Feel the wrath of the Honakinn–'

There was the streak of tarnished steel in the gloom.

Pain seared up Hakem's arm, a dense ball of it throbbing at his wrist. He could no longer feel the weight of his rune hammer. Fear, so thick and palpable it made him almost retch, seized the dwarf and he looked over. In that brief moment of uncertainty, he thought of the shame he would bring to his family and his clan if his grip had failed him and the Honakinn Hammer was lost.

When Hakem saw the bloody stump of his wrist from where his hand had been cleaved off, he screamed.

DUNRIK SHOULDERED HIS way through the rat-kin mob, hacking frenziedly as he went. Hakem's agonised scream was still echoing in his ears as he ducked a blow aimed at his neck, the hooded skaven warrior killing one of its brethren behind the dwarf instead. With a grunt, Dunrik drove the spike atop his axe blade into the dumbfounded creature's chin. He kicked away the corpse and sketched a ragged figure eight with the blade, carving up a cluster of skaven who had sprung at him. Another launched itself over the melee, howling insanely, muzzle foaming and with daggers poised. Dunrik took it in flight on his shield – legs braced against the sudden impact – and using its momentum, propelled the snarling creature off the plateau and into the waiting darkness. He reached Hakem, intercepting a halberd blow aimed for the dwarf merchant's head. Dunrik trapped the weapon against the ground with his axe then stamped on the haft, shattering it. An uppercut with the edge of his shield ripped off the skaven's jaw and it fell in a mangled heap.

Hakem was clutching the bleeding stump of his wrist, his shield hanging limply on his arm by the leather straps as he scrabbled across the ground in search of his dismembered hand and hammer.

'Get to your feet, fool!' snarled Dunrik, fending off another hooded skaven – mercifully, it seemed they had exhausted their supply of poisoned globes.

'I must retrieve it,' the merchant thane wailed, crawling on his knees, heedless of the deadly battle around him.

Hakem's eyes widened suddenly. Dunrik followed his gaze and saw a dwarf hand, bedecked with jewelled rings and still gripping a rune hammer.

A tremor rippled through the plateau, felt even above the thudding resonance of shuffling feet. Deep rumbling, like thunder, came next and a cacophony of splitting stone swallowed up the battle din as if it were nothing but a morsel of sound. Terrified screams of dwarf and rat filled the air as the short stair collapsed, overburdened by the weight of armoured bodies and shaken loose by the exertions of combat.

The impromptu temblor shook Hakem's disembodied hand. It and the hammer pitched over the edge and plunged into the void. The merchant thane's anguished cries merged with the fading death screams of those on the short stair, and he raced forward about to go over the side after the ancient weapon.

'No!' Dunrik bellowed, battering a skaven aside as he reached out and grabbed Hakem's belt. 'Stand fast,' he cried, but Hakem was already on his way and the dwarf's momentum pulled Dunrik with him. The Everpeak dwarf slipped and Hakem was half over the lip on the plateau, staring down the throat of the abyss, when at last he arrested the merchant's flight and dragged him back.

'Idiot,' said Dunrik, leaning down to help Hakem up. 'No relic is worth an honourless death–' the dwarf stopped when he felt the first spear tip pierce his back. Snarling in rage, Dunrik was about to turn when a second split the links of his armour and drove into his side. He twisted to face his attackers; the snapped hafts of the spears still embedded in him were like ice blades of pain. Dunrik raised his axe, too slowly, as a third spear impaled his exposed chest. His shield arm went limp, a blow from a mace shattering his shoulder guard and bruising bone. The snarling visages of four skaven warriors, since divested of their hoods, regarded him.

Dunrik tried to bellow his defiance and ready his axe for one final swing, when one of the vermin lunged forward and sank a rusty dagger into his neck.

'Emelda...' the dwarf gurgled, and breathed his last.

HAKEM WATCHED IN horror as Dunrik died, snapped spear hafts still jutting from his body. The merchant thane was dazed and weak from blood loss. He still clutched his wrist feebly as the fully armoured Everpeak dwarf fell on top of him, smashing him into the ground. Hakem's head struck stone and he blacked out.

'HERE!' A VOICE cried. 'Quickly, he is alive.'

Drimbold heaved at the body of Dunrik crushing the merchant thane. Azgar arrived to help and the two of them lifted the dead Everpeak dwarf off Hakem.

'He's lost a lot of blood,' said Ralkan, waiting close by.

Azgar raised Hakem's arm carefully. 'He's lost a lot more than that,' he said, showing them the stump.

'Take this,' Halgar offered, the dwarfs all clustering around the wounded merchant. The longbeard held a flaming torch.

Azgar took it and smothered the flame into the stone, allowing the embers to burn with radiated heat.

'Brace yourself,' he told a bleary-eyed Hakem, still only partially conscious.

The merchant thane bellowed in agony as the slayer rammed the glowing torch into his wound, searing it shut. He tried to thrash about but Halgar held him down.

'Easy lad, easy,' he said, waiting for the nervous fits of pain to pass before he let Hakem go.

Ralkan came forward with several strips of cloth and started to bind the bloodied stump.

'Can you walk?' Azgar asked when the lorekeeper was finished.

Hakem staggered to his feet and, meeting the slayer's gaze, nodded slowly. He looked around him, his bearings returning, along with his memories. There was a gaping hole, some forty feet across, from the first plateau to the one on which he now stood with the rest of his kinsdwarfs. He could only assume that was why any of the slayers were left at all – unable to pursue their foes across such a chasm.

Bodies littered the broad expanse of stone; there were scarcely fifty dwarfs left from the hundred or so that must have got through the tunnel. Some of those that remained were throwing rat-kin corpses into the gaping drop on either side.

Hakem noticed the ashen-faced corpse of Dunrik last of all. He was laid on his back. An attempt had been made to wipe some of the blood from his armour and face. Someone had arranged his hands over his chest, as if in quiet repose – the spear heads still lodged in his body helped shatter the illusion. The other dwarf dead were laid down too, but with their cloaks covering their faces, hands made to clasp their hammers and axes, shields rested at their sides. There seemed so few, given those that had survived, but Hakem suspected many of the dawi had fallen into the darkness along with the skaven.

'We won,' said Azgar, bitterly when the merchant thane met his gimlet gaze.

Hakem thought of Dunrik, growing cold on the slab on stone, of the dawi falling to their deaths and of the Honakinn Hammer that shared their fate in the abyss.

'Did we?' he said.

FAR DOWN INTO the underdeep, beyond the barriers of even dwarfen curiosity, something stirred. Ancient memory, dark and ill-formed at first, flooded its mind as it woke from a long slumber. The scent of blood and steel filled its flaring nostrils, and it felt the subtle shift of stone down the cragged walls of its lofty cavern through its claws. The ground trembled as it shook away the dust of ages from its mighty body.

They had forgotten it. Thought it perished all these long years. But something had changed – it could feel it. The mountain had... *moved*. Through its slowly resolving vision it noticed the tiny bodies of lesser beings, fallen into its domain. It approached the shattered corpses and once it reached them it began to feed.

CHAPTER NINE

'I CAN RUN no further,' said Gromrund, puffing his cheeks and weighed down by his massive warhelm.

For almost an hour, Uthor's throng had fled through darkened tunnels, down stairways and shafts, with no knowledge of their destination, desperately trying to put as much distance between them and their foes. They gathered now in some nondescript gallery, not nearly as grandiose as some of their previous accommodations, or as large. Gromrund, for one, was glad of it – it meant less places for their enemies to hide and ambush them.

Uthor turned to regard the hammerer, noting that several other dwarfs were bent over with hands on knees, breathing hard.

'Very well,' he said at last. 'We rest for a moment, but then we must move on. It's possible that the others survived. If we can find a way through to reach them, we might–'

'We are defeated, Uthor son of Algrim,' Gromrund snapped. 'Barely fifty remain out of the two hundred with which we entered. The rat-kin number in the thousands – you know this – and there are the grobi to consider as well.'

'They may have worn each other down. If we were to take advantage of that…' Uthor didn't sound convincing.

'Your vainglory will kill us all!' Gromrund raged, squaring up to the thane, making his intentions clear.

'And your courage deserts you, Karak Hirn dwarf. Why is it that you never remove that warhelm of yours? Is it to hide your shame?' Uthor snarled.

A deathly hush filled the small gallery as the other dwarfs waited in the charged atmosphere, as the fight they all knew was coming slowly unfolded.

Gromrund bristled at the remark, Uthor near spitting the words at him. The hammerer clenched his fists.

'Never, in all the generations of Tallhelms has this helmet *ever* been removed,' he began levelly. 'Only upon my death shall it be prized from my cold skull and given to the next in my line,' he hissed through clenched teeth. 'It is tradition, and to go against it would disrespect the memory of my father, Kromrund Tallhelm, and besmirch the honour of my clan,' he concluded, beard bristling.

Uthor fell silent in an impotent rage.

'Our fallen brothers,' Gromrund continued darkly, now he had the thane of Karak Kadrin's attention, 'the needless death in pursuit of false honour… It ends now,' he promised. 'It is over, Uthor. You have brought enough shame to your clan.'

Uthor roared and right hooked the hammerer across the jaw. Gromrund staggered back, but like a prize-fighter, rolled on his booted heels and threw a punishing uppercut into Uthor's chin. The thane was knocked off his feet, but got up quickly and drew his axe.

Gromrund hefted his great hammer, leather gauntlets cracking as he tested his grip.

'I will show you the courage of Karak Hirn,' he promised, with violent intent.

'Come forward then,' Uthor replied, beckoning him. 'And I will knock that warhelm off your foolish head.'

'Enough!' A high-pitched voice rang out, shattering the violent mood. 'Stop this, now.'

Borri, the Everpeak beardling, rushed to stand between the two dwarfs. As he spoke, Gromrund was struck by the authority in the young dwarf's tone and despite his anger, lowered his hammer.

Similarly moved, Uthor did the same, staring non-plussed at a dwarf he thought was slain in the Great Hall.

'There has been enough death... enough.' Borri sagged, full with sorrow as his indignant fury was spent.

Uthor was incredulous.

'I saw you fall,' he ventured, stowing his axe. 'You could not have survived,' he added, appraising the near-pristine condition of the Everpeak noble's armour.

All eyes went to Borri at once.

The beardling opened his mouth to speak but Uthor was relentless.

'You barely have a scratch on you.' The thane regarded Borri suspiciously – his own armour was bent and broken in numerous places; even one of the wings on his helmet had several feathers torn out.

'I…' Borri began, taking a step back, suddenly aware of the attention fixed on him.

'It is not possible,' Uthor breathed and noticed the gilded cincture around the beardling's waist. He recognised one of the runes on it – he had seen it before… 'Let me see that belt,' he demanded, closing in on the young dwarf.

'Please, it is nothing…' Borri blathered, holding up his hands as if to ward off any further inquisition.

'And your voice,' Uthor said, eyes narrowing. 'It sounds different.'

Borri stepped back again, but quickly found he had nowhere to go.

'Show us what's on the belt, lad,' said Gromrund, directly behind Borri as he put his hand on the beardling's shoulder.

Borri sighed in resignation.

'There is something you should know, first,' he said, placing his hands against the sides of his helmet and lifting it slowly off his head.

ROREK CHIPPED AWAY at the chunk of rock with a small pick. The gallery wall at which he crouched, several feet away from where the rest of Uthor's throng congregated, felt cold to the touch and damp, so he worked carefully and with painstaking precision.

The engineer had noticed the runic rubric when the dwarfs had finally stopped, partly in the belief they were not followed by rat-kin or greenskins; partly from sheer exhaustion. Rorek was oblivious to the rest of his kinsdwarfs, and when his curiosity wasn't sated by merely examining the runes, partly obscured by calcified streaks of sediment, he had begun delicately excavating it. There was a message beneath, of that he was certain – perhaps it would provide some clue as to their location, or offer a way out. It was whilst digging out a particularly recalcitrant piece of rock, scrutinizing the markings he could discern beneath with the light of a candle, that the engineer became aware of a shadow looming over him.

'What are you doing, brother?' asked Thalgrim. The lodefinder was clearly as inquisitive as the engineer.

'There are rhuns beneath,' said Rorek gruffly, turning his attention back onto his work. 'They may indicate where we are.'

Thalgrim watched as Rorek chipped in vain at the hunk of rock obscuring the runic script beneath.

'Stand aside,' said the lodefinder, hefting his mattock and twisting it around in his hands to brandish the pick end.

Rorek paused in his endeavours, annoyed at the interruption. Looking back, he flung himself aside just in time as Thalgrim's pick smacked hard into the wall, the calcified rock crumbling under the impact.

Rorek was mortified at first, flat on his arse as he regarded the impetuous lodefinder; when he saw the broken rock and the intact symbol that it once concealed, he grinned.

'Well struck,' the engineer added, getting to his feet and clapping a hand on Thalgrim's back.

'Indeed,' said the lodefinder proudly, 'I mean no disrespect,' he went on, 'but though the engineers of Zhufbar fashion true marvels of ingenuity, it is the miners of the karak that know the vagaries of rock and stone best.'

Rorek nodded solemnly at that – there had ever been a strong accord between the guild of engineers and miners.

Full of pride, Thalgrim went to remove the pick from where it had embedded in the wall, but it wouldn't budge.

'Seems to be stuck,' he muttered beneath his breath, giving the haft of the mattock a tug. 'Release it,' said the lodefinder – Rorek couldn't be sure if he was talking to him or the rock wall – trying again. Still it didn't yield.

The engineer went to help and after testing their grip, the two of them heaved. There was the crunch of stone as the pick end of Thalgrim's weapon came loose, sending the two dwarfs sprawling to the ground. Another sound came swiftly afterwards, the wrenching retort of splitting stone as a large crack ran jaggedly up the wall and a thin trickle of murky water exuded from the hole made by the lodefinder's mattock.

'Grungni's girth…' Rorek muttered as the thin trickle became a steady stream.

'May it be ever broad and full,' Thalgrim added, watching the pool growing at their feet.

'Get up,' said Rorek as a thick chunk of stone fell away and water gushed out in its wake.

LONG, GOLDEN PLAITS cascaded down as Borri removed his helmet and a pair of piercing azure eyes regarded Uthor, from either side of a round, stubby nose.

Gasps and rumbles of amazement greeted the dwarf stood before them.

Uthor was aghast.

'Rinn!' hissed one of the Sootbeard dwarfs and promptly passed out.

Gromrund's hand fell from Borri's shoulder to hang limp at his side.

'By the Bearded Lady!' he heard another dwarf gasp.

Some of the dwarfs began smoothing down their blood and dirt-caked tunics, faces flushed a deep crimson as they went on to quickly preen their beards.

'I have not been entirely truthful,' said Borri with royal timbre, straightening up defiantly.

'I am Emelda Skorrisdottir...'. She parted the chain-mail of her armour, revealing a golden cincture so wondrously crafted and timelessly beautiful that some of the Sootbeard miners wept. Runes of protection were etched upon the magnificent belt around Emelda's waist, but one in particular caught Uthor's eye – the rune of High King Skorri Morgrimson. 'Clan daughter of the royal house of Karaz-a-Karak.'

'Rinn Tromm,' uttered Gromrund, bowing deeply on one knee. Still gaping, Uthor followed suit, the others then taking his lead.

'Arise!' Rorek cried, hurrying towards them with Thalgrim close behind him.

Uthor turned sharply towards the engineer, incensed at the interruption. The thane's anger drained away when he realised his knee was wet. When he saw the torrent of water flooding through the wall in the distance, he did as Rorek asked.

The gallery wall broke away as they were getting up.

'Run for it!' Uthor bellowed, herding the dwarfs down the long gallery.

The last of his throng were barrelling through as the foaming wave slammed into them, smashing the lagging dwarfs like dolls against the opposite wall. Those that weren't crushed to death were drowned soon after.

Uthor was blasted by a stinging spray, replete with grit and stone shards. He recoiled against the blow and ran, flashing a quick glance behind him as he fled, hell-bent on a large metal door at the end of the gallery.

As the massive wave crashed into the far gallery wall it demolished columns and archways in its fury. For a few seconds it swelled in the tight space, churning like the innards of some primordial beast, until it found a way through and raced after the dwarfs with gathering momentum.

'THE WAY IS long, indeed,' said Azgar, stood on a lower plateau, leaning on his axe as he looked down the wending stairway.

'The Endless Road,' offered Ralkan, enjoying one of his more lucid moments, 'with many winding turns that lead into the lower deeps. It was so named by the stonemaster who built it, Thogri Granitefist. May he be remembered.'

Azgar bowed his head in a brief moment of solemn remembrance.

Those who had escaped the tunnel battles with their lives had made an encampment a few plateaux down from the battle site, too tired and grief-stricken to move on immediately. After disposing of the skaven corpses they had left their slain brothers in quiet repose, unable to convey all the bodies. Only Dunrik went with them, carried on a makeshift hammock between Drimbold and Halgar. The longbeard wrinkled his nose constantly, complaining about the stink of the skaven rotting above them beyond the shattered stairway, the only bodies they couldn't reach to toss into the abyss. It seemed he had put his grievances towards the Grey dwarf aside for the time being, and was satisfied to let Drimbold lead them as they bore Dunrik to his final rest. As the Everpeak dwarf was of royal blood, it was only right and proper that he should be afforded a funeral and interred back into the earth so he might sit alongside his kin in the Halls of the Ancestors. For now, Dunrik was set down on the ground, all of his trappings strapped tightly to his body, so that when the funeral rites were enacted he would have them in the afterlife.

A sombre silence descended and Ralkan retreated away from the plateau's edge to sit alone.

Azgar was left in solitary contemplation as he regarded the abyssal gloom before him. Discernible by the ambient light cast from the Diamond Shaft, and filtered through the dust-heavy air, gargantuan dwarf faces glowered at him. They were the lords of the elder days of Karak Varn, hewn into the very rock face and made immortal in stone. As they looked upon the slayer, he found his mind wandering to the past and could no longer meet their stern gaze...

Azgar's head thundered like the great hammers of the lower forges. Each footstep was a physical blow, as if his skull were the metal pounded beneath the anvil.

It had been a mighty feast, though his recollection of it was dim. He recalled besting Hrunkar, the hold's brewmaster, at the ox-lifting and then of a drinking boast that the broad-girthed dwarf had accepted gleefully. To challenge a brewmaster to a quaffing contest, in retrospect, had been foolish.

Azgar had no time to ponder his misplaced confidence any further, the Cragbound Gate lay ahead and its current warden awaited him.

'Tromm,' said Torbad Magrikson, resting his axe over his shoulder and tapping out his pipe.

'Tromm,' Azgar managed, shuffling into position beside the gate as Torbad slowly walked away into the brazier-lit gloom.

An hour passed and Azgar felt the thrumming of hammers as engineers and metal smiths worked diligently at the forge, the resonance of their labours carrying through the very rock of the mountain. It was a soothing refrain rippling through his body as he leaned at the warden's post. Azgar's eyelids grew heavy and within moments he was asleep...

Desperate cries woke Azgar from slumber, that and the rush of booted feet.

'Thaggi!' shouted a dwarf voice.

Azgar opened his eyes blearily, suddenly aware that he was slumped in a heap against the wall. He was shaken roughly.

'Awake,' said Igrik angrily, standing before him. 'Thaggi, Lord Algrim has been poisoned!' he cried.

Azgar snapped to at that, heart thumping more loudly than any raging hangover ever could.

'Father?' he asked of the aging attendant, Igrik.

'Yes, your father,' he said, bitterly.

Then Azgar noticed something else: the wet footprints through the Cragbound Gate, its locks and bolts slipped silently. They were not made by dwarfen boots. They were long and thin with extended toes; they were the paw prints of skaven.

'Oh no...' breathed Azgar. 'What have I done?'

The scene shifted then in the slayer's mind's eye, resolving itself into the lustrous glory of the King's Court.

'Remove his armour,' ordered the king, his dour voice carrying despite the immensity of the mighty hall, 'and divest him of all trappings, save his axe.'

A four-strong throng of hammerers, their faces masked, moved in and solemnly took Azgar's armour, belts and clothes until he was stood naked before King Kazagrad of Karak Kadrin, his son Baragor looking on sternly at the right hand of his enthroned lord.

'Let him be shorn and his shame known,' Kazagrad decreed.

Four priests of Grimnir came forward from the surrounding gloom. They each bore two buckets, carried via a brace of wutroth across their backs, and bore shears. Setting the buckets down they began cutting off Azgar's hair until all that remained was a rough shock of it down the centre and his beard, the only thing preserving his dignity.

'You have undertaken the slayer oath to atone for deeds that are to remain unnamed,' intoned the king.

The priests brought forth broad buckets filled with thick, orange dye and began combing it through Azgar's hair.

'You are to seek your doom that you might die a glorious death...'

From another bucket the priests took handfuls of pig grease and congealed animal fat. With gnarled fingers, they worked it into Azgar's streak of hair until it was hard like a crest.

'Take up your axe and leave this place, and let your disgrace be remembered by all.'

The priests shrank back into the darkness. Without word, Azgar turned and, head bowed, began the long walk out of the hold. He had no desire to stay. His brother had been espied by the watchtowers returning to the karak. It was best that Azgar was not there when he discovered their father's fate.

* * *

THE INUNDATION RAMMED dully against the ironclad door with slow and thudding insistence.

Uthor's fleeing throng had made it through the gallery just in time, slamming the door in their wake when the last of them had got through. Those caught up in the waters were left for dead. It left a bitter canker in the survivors.

'It holds, for now,' said Rorek, noting that the door was at least watertight.

Exhausted, alongside the engineer, Uthor just nodded.

A great foundry stretched out before his sodden throng, who were huddled around the entrance to the chamber, having been battered and blasted throughout their desperate flight to the iron sanctuary.

Down a short set of steps the foundry opened into a vast plaza of stone, engraved with fifty-foot runes of forging and the furnace. Brightly burning braziers adorned the walls, doubtlessly lit by the hold's previous occupants, and punctuated the runic knots carved into them with perfect regularity.

Deep troughs of glowing coals smouldered and the light of the flickering embers illuminated racks of tools. Fuliginous chimneys were built at the ends of the troughs and rose up into the vaulted ceiling. Each of the stout, broad-based funnels was designed to lock the emanating forge heat and channel it into the roof space and the upper levels in order to keep them warm and dry. A raised stone walkway delineated the entire room and led to a wide, flat plinth with an archway wrought into the face of an ancient runelord overshadowing it. Through the venerable ancestor's mouth there was a mighty forgemaster's anvil, bathed in the fire-orange glow of brazier pans.

The foundry was divided into a central chamber and two wings, broken up by broad, square columns. On the left wing there was a vast array of armour suits, weapons and war machines; on the right wing, a long runway extended that ended in an octagonal platform.

A dais in the centre of it supported a statue of monumental proportions carved into the image of Grungni himself. The ancestor god's plaited beard went all the way to the base and in his hands he held forge tongs and a smithy's hammer. Beneath him there sat another brazier, raging with an eldritch blue-red flame that cast pooling shadows into the stone-worked face. Beyond this temple there was a sheer drop into a pit of fire, which burned so fiercely the coals within it were but a vague shadow in the emanating heat haze.

Great heavy pails were set above the vast pit by thick iron chains, ready to plunge into the fires and bring forth the precious rock to feed the forges.

'Magnificent,' said Thalgrim, tears in his eyes. Other than this laudation, the throng was stunned into silence.

They were arrested from their wonderment by the dull retort of 'thunking' metal against the iron door as the armoured dwarfs slain in the flood were butted against it by the swell of the water.

'We should move away from the door,' Uthor said darkly.

UTHOR'S THRONG SAT around the burning coal troughs of the foundry plaza, rubbing their hands and wringing out their beards in silent, grim contemplation. The heat warmed clothes, hair and hearts quickly but Uthor found no solace in their fiery depths as he drew deep of his pipe, lost in his thoughts.

'So is this how it is to end, then?'

Gromrund stood before the thane of Kadrin. The hammerer's armour was battered and broken in places. It was the first time Uthor had even noticed it since the fighting and their flight from the inundation.

'I need time to think,' the thane of Kadrin muttered, peering back into the flames.

Gromrund leaned in towards him, forcing the thane to look at him.

'You were so eager for your reckless glory but a few hours ago. Yet now you sit and do nothing,' he hissed, 'while all around your throng stagnates and festers like an old wound.'

Uthor maintained his silence.

'You have much to atone for already son of Algrim, do not add to the reckoner's tally further.' With that, the hammerer stalked away out of Uthor's sight.

After a moment, the thane of Kadrin looked up from the blazing coals and regarded his warriors as if for the first time since their defeat in the Great Hall. The wounded were many; some had lost limbs and eyes, a burden they would carry into the Halls of the Ancestors. Others wore bandages over deep wounds or displayed broad cuts openly, but not as the heroic ritual scars of combat; they wore them with the deep shame of the broken and beaten. The dwarfs sat together in their clans. Uthor noticed the large gaps in them, brave warriors all who would not know the feeling of their holds beneath their feet and above their heads ever again. He had condemned them to that fate. Unable to look further, Uthor averted his gaze.

'May I sit with you?' a voice asked. Emelda's eyes flashed in the firelight as she sat down, more perfect and beauteous than any jewel in Uthor's reckoning, her long plaits like streaks of gold.

'I am honoured,' said the thane, with a shallow nod. Her stealth was impressive; Uthor had not heard her coming.

The clan daughter's noble bearing was apparent in the way she held herself, proud and defiant. The other dwarfs would not sit with her, not because of any slight or ill feeling; rather that they were ashamed of their unkempt appearance and bashful in her presence as a lady and a royal consort. Since none would join Uthor, either, it meant that they were largely alone.

'You risked much to follow us here,' he said after a moment's silence, grateful of the distraction she provided.

'I believed in your quest,' Emelda replied. 'Too swiftly are the desolated holds left uncontested, for all the fell denizens of dark places to inhabit and despoil. There was honour in your plight and talk of such deeds that could not go unreckoned. Besides that, I have my reasons,' she added darkly.

'It was glory,' Uthor admitted after a moment, reminded of Gromrund's words as he stared into the fire.

'I do not understand.'

The thane gazed up into Emelda's eyes, his expression rueful.

'The promise of glory brought me to this place, not vengeance, and this folly has delivered us all to our doom. Cowering in the dark. Hunted like... like rats.' He curled his lip at that last remark and dipped his head again. It was a bitter irony; rats preyed upon by rats.

Emelda stayed silent. She had no words that would make right what had befallen them. The mood was grim; it chilled the bone despite the cloying heat in the air. Failure and dishonour hung like a palpable fug, and was felt by all.

'And what of Dunrik? Is he even your cousin?' Uthor asked.

Emelda felt her chest tighten at the mention of his name. She made a silent oath to Valaya that he had made it out of the tunnel alive, somehow.

'No,' she said, after a few moments. 'He was my guardian, sworn to protect me. Dunrik smuggled us into the escort from Everpeak,' she confessed.

'So you both defied the will of the High King, as I did.'

'Yes,' said Emelda, shame-faced.

Uthor laughed mirthlessly.

'Milady,' uttered Gromrund, clearing his throat as he appeared suddenly beside them, 'I am Gromrund, son of Kromrund, of the Tallhelm clan and hammerer to King Kurgaz of Karak Hirn.' The hammerer bowed deeply, ignoring Uthor. 'It would be my humble honour to serve as your protector and vouch safe-passage for you back to Everpeak.'

Emelda smiled benignly, full of royal presence.

Gromrund, meeting her gaze as he genuflected, reddened.

'You are noble, Gromrund, son of Kromrund, but I already have a bodyguard and we will be reunited soon,' she explained, unable to mask an edge of uncertainty in her tone. 'For now, Uthor son of Algrim will see to my safekeeping,' she said, gesturing in the thane of Kadrin's direction, 'but I will make certain to mention of your pledge to the High King.'

'As you wish, milady,' Gromrund said, a side glance at Uthor to make his displeasure known before he backed away in respectful silence.

GROMRUND STOOD ALONE at the anvil stripped of all his armour, barring his warhelm of course. With a forge-master's hammer in hand, he worked out the dents in his breastplate with careful and meticulous precision. He was glad of the solace that metalsmithing provided, especially after his recent rebuttal from the Lady Emelda. In truth, he was also working out the anger he felt towards Uthor, but was mindful not to let his ire spoil his re-crafting. The Tallhelms were all forgesmiths by trade, a source of much pride amongst the clan, despite their esteemed calling as royal body-guards.

Gromrund stopped a moment to check his labours, wiping the sweat from his face as he did so. Out of the corner of his eye, he caught sight of Uthor conversing with the Everpeak lady.

As he watched them, he noticed Uthor's face darken. Despite their grievances, and his earlier words, the hammerer took no pleasure in the thane's distress – though he still believed, as a hammerer, it should be he that saw to Emelda's well-being – an oath was an oath and each and every one of them had failed in that. As expedition leader though, the son of Algrim bore that shame most heavily.

The lady, Emelda, seemed to try and soothe him but to no avail.

A rinn! Gromrund thought as he looked at her. Posing as a beardling amongst the throng with not a dawi, save for her keeper, any the wiser – a truly shocking admission.

When she caught the hammerer's gaze, he averted his eyes to the anvil, bashful beneath her scrutiny.

Shocking indeed, he thought, toiling at his armour again, but not entirely unwelcome.

THALGRIM'S STOMACH GROWLED loudly. He went for the piece of chuf beneath his helmet, but stopped himself short. Perhaps it was that which attracted the skaven to them; perhaps he was the cause of the ambush in the tunnel, of so many dawi deaths…

'It was the Black Water,' said Rorek, sat across from the lodefinder, eyes ablaze in the light of burning coals.

The two of them were sitting with some of the Sootbeard dwarfs outside the great arch.

Rorek was tinkering with some spherical object he had fashioned from the materials in the forge. It helped keep his mind occupied.

Thalgrim returned a thoughtful expression, grateful of the distraction, as the engineer went on.

'Five hundred years ago, during the Time of Woes, a deluge from the great lake flooded the hold and ruined it,' said Rorek, carefully screwing a plate on the spiked ball of iron in his hands. 'I think, even in the upper deeps, there are pockets of trapped water. We released one when we split the gallery wall. It at least means the grobi and the rat-kin cannot follow this way.'

'It means we cannot escape the way we came, either,' Thalgrim countered, engrossed with the engineer's work. 'This entire hold groans under the weight of the

Black Water,' he added. 'I can feel it through the rock; the subtle vibrations caused by its movement are unmistakable.'

'Then we had best not linger,' muttered Rorek, looking up at the age-old cracks in the vaulted ceiling above them.

DRIMBOLD WOKE AWASH with sweat. A chill ran down his spine as the cries of Norri and Furgil, falling into the chasm as the rope bridge failed, echoed in his ears. Their faces were forever etched on his mind, contorted with sheer terror as they met their doom in the gorge, swallowed by fire. The Grey dwarf realised he was gripping his pack. The lustre of the treasure within had somehow dimmed. He released it quickly, as if stung. Some of the loot spilled out, clanking loudly against the stone plateau. The noise disturbed Halgar, who'd been rubbing his eyes. The longbeard scowled at Drimbold before returning to his dark thoughts.

The Grey dwarf cast his eyes around the forlorn throng, led now, it seemed, by Azgar.

Ralkan lay nearby him, twitching spasmodically, wracked by a fever dream about some unknown terror.

Hakem was awake, nursing the stump of his right hand, an ugly dark red stain emerging through the makeshift bandage. He was muttering. Drimbold heard the Honakinn Hammer mentioned several times. The merchant's boastful bluster was but a fading memory now. He looked pale and drawn, and not just from the amount of blood he had lost.

'It's time we made a move.' It was Azgar, at the top of the next descending stairway, his face an unreadable mask.

Without word, the dwarfs started to gather their belongings. When they finally left the plateau, only Drimbold's treasure-laden pack remained.

'I GROW WEARY of staring into the fathomless dark,' Hakem moaned, peering over the narrow ledge into a faintly rippling void below. It was the first time the dwarf had spoken since he'd lost his hammer and his hand.

The Endless Stair was above them now, its final plateau leading to a vast stone archway. From there, the dwarfs had found the narrow ledge. So narrow was it that Azgar's throng walked slowly in single file. On one side there was a sheer rock face that seemed to go on for miles in both directions; on the other side yet another deep chasm presented itself.

'This is the Ore Way, the threshold of the once great mines of Karak Varn,' Ralkan said wistfully, walking a few places behind Azgar who led the group with what remained of his Grim Brotherhood.

'I see nothing but darkness,' Hakem muttered bitterly, 'shifting below us like serpents.'

'It is not serpents,' Ralkan interjected, close to the merchant's position in the file. 'These are the flooded deeps.'

The shimmering in the darkness was water, so thick and murk-ridden it was like black ichor. Columns, leaning over and split in twain, languished in it, the stagnant dregs of the Black Water pooling where they broke the water's surface. The reek of wet stone clung to the damp air like a shroud.

'Look there,' he added, voice echoing as he pointed far out into the gloom-drenched cavern.

Hakem followed the lorekeeper's gesture to the wreckage of three lofty towers, wrought of wood and metal. Each tower had a massive pulley set at its apex, with the remnants of what once must have been a long chain. The links had been shattered long ago, but stout buckets clung tenaciously to one of the chain lengths. Hakem then realised the broken columns were supports for bridges that connected the towers to tracked lanes of stone that ran all the way across and down the empty gulf to the walkway they now traversed. One such lane still existed in part, its central support standing defiantly like an island in an ocean of tar.

'All dwarf holds began as mines,' Halgar remarked. 'These are from the Golden Age of the Karaz Ankor.' He and Drimbold took careful steps as they bore the body of Dunrik along the shallow pathway. The longbeard felt the wall with one hand as he went, making certain he was close to it at all times. One slip and all three would likely join the rest of their kin claimed by the abyss.

'Rich were the veins of ril, gorl and gromril,' the longbeard said wistfully. 'Such great days...' he added in a choked whisper.

Apparent that Halgar's reminiscences were at an end, some of the other dwarfs began talking amongst themselves as a slightly improved mood started to settle over the throng.

The longbeard paid them no heed as he allowed the surface of the rock face to pass beneath his hand, taking solace in the roughness and solidity of it against his leather-like skin. Then he heard, or rather felt, something that he did not expect.

Halgar stopped dead in his tracks.

'Stop,' he bellowed, though some of the dwarfs in the file had already bunched up and were bumping into each other with the longbeard's abrupt halt. Drimbold very nearly tripped and dropped Dunrik as he was pulled back.

'What is it?' Hakem called from behind Halgar.

'Be silent!' The longbeard said, admonishing him, before catching Drimbold's gaze.

'Set him down,' Halgar bade him, and they did, reverently. The old dwarf then turned back towards the rock face, placing both hands against it and pressing his ear as close as he could. The stone felt damp and chill against his face. A faint 'plinking' sound, dull and faraway, emanated through the rock.

'I hear nothing,' moaned Hakem.

'Save for the sound of your own voice, no doubt. Be still!' Halgar raged, ''Tis a pity it was not your tongue taken by the abyss,' he snarled, plunging the merchant thane into mournful quietude before listening intently.

The sound came again, muted but distinctly metallic.

'A hammer,' he snapped at a dwarf behind him, one of the Stonebreaker clan.

The clan dwarf returned a bemused look as he brought out a small mattock.

'Quickly now!' Halgar snatched the weapon and with his attention back on the rock face started to tap back.

GROMRUND KNEW HE must be a strange sight, wearing only his helmet and little else besides. It had grown so hot in the foundry that he had removed his outer garments as well as his armour and stood in nothing but boots and breeches as he toiled away at a vambrace. Slowly beating out a gouge from a skaven dagger,

Gromrund paused in his hammering to wring the sweat from his beard.

A dull 'thunk' got his attention. At first he looked down to make sure he wasn't still hammering, that the heat hadn't addled his brain and he'd just *thought* he'd ceased.

The noise came again, insistent and repetitive. He was too far away from the ironclad door for it to be anything beyond it in the flooded chamber. Still, he couldn't place it. Gromrund looked around and caught sight of Thalgrim sat by the arch, silently gripping his stomach.

'Lodefinder,' he called out to him.

Thalgrim looked over and the hammerer beckoned him.

The lodefinder was a little weary as he reached the sweating dwarf wearing nought but his boots, smalls and a massive warhelm.

'Listen,' said the hammerer urgently.

CHAPTER TEN

'IT'S COMING FROM the wall,' said the lodefinder, eyes brightening when he heard the sound. He rushed over, smoothing the wall with his hands to detect the subtle movements in the stone. 'There,' he said again, pinpointing the exact position from which the noise was emanating.

By now, Rorek, the Sootbeards and a number of other dwarfs had noticed the sudden commotion and were heading onto the anvil platform.

It was a welcome diversion. The throng had been waiting several hours for Uthor's decision on their next course of action. The thane was brooding when the flurry of movement began, drawing deep of his pipe and sitting in abject silence.

'*Grundlid*,' said Thalgrim, ear pressed against the wall. 'There's a message,' he added. 'We are sons of Grungni. It is them! Our brothers live!'

More and more dwarfs were gathering on the anvil platform as word of Thalgrim's discovery spread quickly.

'Where?' asked Uthor urgently, having fought his way through to the front of his throng.

Thalgrim looked back, nearly beside himself. 'I will find out,' he said, tapping back with meticulous precision using Grundlid, or Hammer-Tongue, the secret language of miners and prospectors. A series of careful scrapes and taps, with varying duration and intensity could convey a message. Most amongst the dwarfs knew its rudiments but only the most vaunted lodefinders were privy to its intricacies.

'The mines,' said Thalgrim, catching snatches of Grundlid as he responded with a long scrape of stone and three heavy raps, followed by a long, lighter one.

'We must get to them,' said Uthor.

'They are below us,' Thalgrim offered, between taps.

'The lodefinder and I will follow the message and bring them to the foundry. The rest of the throng will await our return, here.'

Gromrund stepped forward, about to protest but a look from Uthor silenced him. The thane of Karak Kadrin wanted to atone for his mistake, even if only in part.

'The less of us that venture from the safety of the foundry the better, and the less likely it will be that the skaven and whatever lurks in the dark will be aware of us. If the others still live, we two will find them.'

'We three.'

Emelda emerged through the pressing masses, the dwarfs respectfully allowing her passage. 'I'm coming with you.'

Now it was Uthor's turn to bite his tongue. The royal clan daughter's gimlet gaze told him all he needed to know of her reasons. Dunrik might be amongst them. She had to know.

'MAINTAIN A WATCH on all ways in and out.' Uthor addressed his throng as he, Thalgrim and Emelda stood before the only exit to the foundry that wasn't flooded on the other side. 'When we return, Thalgrim will provide a simple signal in Grundlid.'

Uthor went to walk forward when Gromrund stopped him.

'Grungni go with you,' said the hammerer, back in his armour again when he gripped the thane's shoulder.

'And you,' Uthor replied, unable to keep the surprise from his face.

The guards at the foundry door hauled away the locking bar and tugged on thick, iron chains attached to it. Screeching metal filled the air and a gaping black void of the unknown opened out before the three dwarfs, so dark and infinite it swallowed the light from the foundry whole.

'THIS WAY,' SAID Thalgrim, moving off quickly through a dilapidated corridor. 'Very close, now,' he added.

Uthor wasn't convinced that the lodefinder was talking to him or Emelda as the two of them ventured warily after Thalgrim. The path was treacherous, fraught with pit falls, sharp rocks and heavy debris. Dust motes fell eagerly from sloping ceilings with every step and Uthor dared not raise his voice above a whisper, lest the whole lot come crashing down on their heads.

'Slow down, zaki,' he hissed, struggling to keep pace. The thane cast a glance behind him and saw that Emelda was on his heels and showing no evidence of fatigue. When Uthor looked back, there was no sign of the lodefinder.

Grimnir's tattooed-arse, he thought angrily, the wattock has probably fallen to his death and left us lost in this labyrinth. The thane increased his pace, stumbled and nearly slipped but got his footing at the last moment, in the hope of catching sight of Thalgrim. He took another step and realised there was nothing beneath his foot. Scrambling for purchase, Uthor's hand gripped the wall but slipped on moisture slick stone. Flapping wildly, he was about to plunge headlong into a drop of sharp rocks when he felt his fall abruptly arrested.

Emelda, holding onto the thane's belt, hauled Uthor back onto solid ground.

'I hope this is the right way,' she said as Uthor flushed with embarrassment at being saved by a woman. The thane of Karak Kadrin looked back at the wall and noticed thin rivulets of water trickling down them and seeping into the porous rock at their feet.

'So do I, milady,' he said, striving to regain his composure.

Their eyes met for but a moment, before Uthor looked away abashedly.

'Not far.' The lodefinder's voice drifted on a shallow and foetid breeze to break the sudden silence.

Relief washed over Uthor, and not just because their guide was still alive. He emerged from the debris strewn corridor to find Thalgrim standing pensively before a triple forked archway. Each of the three roads were carved into the likeness of a dwarf face and led down still further – they had been steadily descending ever since leaving the foundry. The decline was shallow, but Uthor had felt it, even as he clambered over broken columns, stooped beneath fallen ceilings and crawled through shattered doorways.

'Which way?' Uthor asked, a little out of breath.

Thalgrim sniffed at the air, and felt the rock of each fork in turn.

'Down here,' he said, indicating the left passage. 'I can taste the ore seams, feel them in the rock. The mines are this way.'

'You are certain this is the way?' Uthor asked, unconvinced by the lodefinder's tone.

'Fairly,' he replied.

'And the other tunnels?'

Thalgrim looked Uthor in the eye.

'Our enemies.'

THE SHALLOW LEDGE ended in a narrow archway, through which a much wider and flatter platform opened out. It was a lodecarrier's waystation, one of several in Karak Varn, designed to service the many mines and act as barrack houses for the miners and lodewardens. Upturned ore carts and scattered tools littered the ground and smothered torches were cast aside like tinder. Whoever had been here had clearly left in a hurry.

'The Rockcutter Waystation,' said Ralkan as the dwarfs started filing into the room. 'We are in the eastern halls of the karak.'

'We will wait here,' Halgar decided, at the head of the group with Azgar and his slayers – one of the

Stonebreaker clan carried Dunrik's body, along with Drimbold, now. The old longbeard eyed the darkness wearily. In one corner of the modest chamber a broad shaft had been carved into the rock. A wrought-iron lift cage nestled within, battered and bent, the iron rusted and split, with a length of piled chain languishing nearby. A second shaft lay on the opposite side, leading down.

Ralkan approached it carefully. The lorekeeper stuck his head into the shaft and looked up and down.

'The rhun-markers are clear,' he said. 'It leads right down to the foundations of the hold.'

'And up?' Hakem remarked.

'Dibna's Drop,' Ralkan answered, looking back at the mauled merchant thane. 'The room we passed in the third deep is above.' Clearly, the long period of calm had improved the dwarf's lucidity.

'And that?' growled Halgar, pointing.

A third exit lay ahead in the form of a broken down doorway. Even in the gloom, it was possible to make out an ascending tunnel leading off from it. Besides Dibna's Drop, it was the only possible ingress to the waystation.

'I don't know,' Ralkan confessed, memory fogging once more.

The longbeard grumbled beneath his breath. The last message in Grundlid had been close. Their kinsdwarfs were on the way to them. He only hoped they would get there before something else did.

'Someone approaches,' Halgar hissed, gesturing toward the broken doorway. Shallow footsteps could be heard from beyond the threshold to the room, growing louder and with each passing moment. The dwarfs gathered together, the dull chorus of axes and hammers scraping free of their sheaths and cinctures filled the air.

'What if it is not dawi?' Hakem asked, shield lashed to his wounded arm, an axe held unfamiliarly in his remaining hand.

Halgar glanced at Azgar, glowering menacingly at the doorway in the gloom, before he replied.

'Then we cut them down.'

WHEN THALGRIM AND Uthor emerged from the tunnel they were met by a host of axe blades and hammer heads.

'Hold, dawi!' said Uthor, showing his palms.

'Son of Algrim.' Halgar stepped forward, stowing his axe and clasping the thane of Kadrin's forearm in what was an old greeting ritual.

'Gnollengrom.' Uthor reciprocated the gesture, and nodded in respect at being so honoured.

'So you're alive, after all,' the longbeard added, very nearly cracking a smile.

'As are you,' Uthor replied, throwing a dark glance towards Azgar as he noticed the slayer's presence for the first time.

'Round rump of Valaya!' Halgar blurted out suddenly when he saw Emelda emerge from behind Thalgrim, who was currently being slapped on the back and hugged by the Stonebreakers.

'There is much to be told,' Uthor said, by way of explanation. More gasps of shock greeted the revelation from the assembled dwarfs.

'Please,' Emelda said, stepping forward, her eyes bright and hopeful as she scanned Azgar's throng. 'Where is Dunrik?'

Halgar's face fell.

'Yes,' he said, with sorrow in his eyes, 'there is much to be told.'

'So few of you,' said Uthor as he sat around one of the coal troughs in the foundry. The way back to the iron sanctuary had been slow and trod with great care, but had passed without further incident. The returning dwarfs were met with heart-felt joy. The buoyant mood was short-lived however, when it was realised just how many had rejoined them. That, together with the maiming of Hakem and Dunrik's death, had conspired to create a grim, desolate atmosphere.

'We are fortunate to be alive at all,' said Halgar, breathing deeply as he savoured the aroma of the foundry, a chamber unsullied by skaven and redolent of ancient days. After that brief indulgence, the long-beard's face turned grim. 'The rat-kin were ready for us. They have been tracking us ever since we entered the hold...' Halgar looked deep into the coal fires, supping on his pipe. 'Such cunning! I have never seen the like in skaven.'

'How did Dunrik die?' Uthor asked, after a few moments of silence.

'Impaled by ratman spears – he died a noble death, protecting his kinsdwarfs.'

'May he be remembered,' Uthor uttered, his guilt was like an anvil trussed around his neck.

'Aye, may he be remembered,' Halgar added.

Emelda was divested of her armour and instead wore the plain purple robes of Valaya she had beneath her chain and platemail. The clan daughter had even removed the runic cincture – it glowed dully, nearby, in the reflected light of the vast forge pit.

She was alone at the forgemaster's platform in the foundry. Dunrik's cold body lay before her on the anvil. The rest of the reunited throng were sat below, most in hunched silence, contemplating their plight.

'Dunrik,' she whispered, placing her hand on the dwarf's clammy brow. His flesh was pale now; much like it had been when he'd escaped from Iron Rock. She had tended his wounds then as part of her training – for the priestesses of Valaya were battle-surgeons in times of war – and the bond between them had been forged. After that, he'd become her bodyguard and confidant – there was nothing Dunrik would not have done for her; he'd even defied the will of his king to get her to Karak Varn. How she wished to take that back: to be at Everpeak dreaming of glory and restoring the great days of the dawi to the Karaz Ankor, instead of preparing his corpse for interment.

'Are you ready, milady?' said a small voice.

Emelda turned to see Ralkan stood, head bowed, beneath the archway to the platform. She smeared away the tears on her face with the sleeves of her robes.

'Yes,' she said, mustering some resolve.

Silently, Ralkan walked forward. He carried pails of water, one in each hand, gathered from the vast cooling butts stood against the foundry walls. Setting the buckets down, he helped Emelda remove Dunrik's battered armour. The clan daughter wept as she struggled, with Ralkan's assistance, to pull some of the armour away from the embedded spear hafts. Beneath mail and plate, Dunrik's tunic and breeches were so badly sodden with blood that they had to be cut free. Emelda did this, careful so as not to pierce the dwarf's flesh or defile the body in any way. Next came the extraction of the embedded spear hafts. Each was like a wound against the clan daughter as she removed it.

Naked upon the anvil, Dunrik was washed head to foot and his beard combed. Emelda wrung blood soaked bundles of rags regularly and sent Ralkan back for fresh water on several occasions. After these ablutions Emelda stitched the spear wounds closed and redressed Dunrik tenderly with a borrowed tunic and breeches, uttering a pledge to Valaya as she did it. Ralkan had washed the original garments as best he could, but they were still wretched with blood and cut nigh-on to ribbons, so could not be salvaged.

Gromrund – working at one of the forge troughs below with Thalgrim operating the bellows – had repaired Dunrik's armour, and even given the shortness of time and the state of its degradation it still shone as if new. The hammerer brought it up the platform and left it there without a word.

Emelda dismissed Ralkan and clad Dunrik in his armour by herself. After a few moments, it was almost done and as she affixed the final clasps of Dunrik's left vambrace she went to retrieve the dwarf's helmet. Emelda paused before she placed it on him, setting it down on the anvil next to his head, and traced her finger down the scar the orcs of Iron Rock had given him long ago.

'Brave dawi,' she sobbed. 'I am so sorry.'

'WHAT IS THAT beardling doing?' snapped Halgar, suddenly.

Uthor was grateful of the distraction, so grim was his mood, and looked over to where Rorek – who was anything but a beardling – was tinkering with a globe-like object made of iron and copper. To one side of the engineer there sat a doused lantern. While Uthor watched, the Zhufbar dwarf picked it up and carefully poured the oil into a narrow spout fashioned into the globe. He then set the globe down and started to unravel a section of rope from that which was usually arrayed around his tool belt.

'I know not,' Uthor answered.

'Mark my words, he'll be for the Trouser Legs Ritual before long or maybe a cogging,' the longbeard grumbled.

Uthor was about to reply when Hakem approached them. His wound had been cleaned and redressed by Emelda in abject silence, before she had gone to tend to Dunrik.

'They are ready,' he uttered.

'HERE LIES DUNRIK, may Valaya protect him and Gazul guide his spirit to the Halls of the Ancestors,' Emelda declared, her voice choked.

She stood at the edge of the great fire pit beyond the statue of Grungni. Dunrik was before her, resting upon a cradle of iron. The Everpeak dwarf was fully armoured, the metal gleaming thanks to the efforts of Gromrund and Thalgrim, and wore his helmet. His shield lay by his side. Only his axe was missing. Emelda carried the ancient weapon as she invoked the funerary rites of Gazul, drawing the Lord of the Underearth's symbol – the great cave and entrance to the Halls of the Ancestors – upon the flat blade. Though Emelda was a priestess of Valaya, she was also learned in all the rites of the ancestor gods, even those lesser deities such as Gazul, son of Grungni.

'*Gazul Bar Baraz; Gazul Gand Baraz,*' she intoned, honouring the Lord of the Underearth, beseeching his promise to guide Dunrik to the Chamber of the Gate. The ritual conferred the dwarf's soul into his axe, and when it was buried in the earth Dunrik would pass from the chamber and be allowed to enter the Halls of the Ancestors proper. Only in times of dire need was such a measure undertaken. Since there was no tomb, no sanctuary for Dunrik's body, Emelda would not leave it in the foundry to be defiled. This was the only way he might know peace.

Inwardly, she pitied those others who had fallen, bereft of honour – left to wander the underdeep as shades and apparitions, ever restless. It was no fate for a dwarf to endure.

The rattling of chains attached to the makeshift bier arrested Emelda from her remembrances. It was time.

Sweating from the emanating heat haze, Thalgrim and Rorek pulled a chain, hand over hand, through one of the pulleys suspended above the pit of fire. Hakem and Drimbold pulled another, the merchant thane managing despite only having one hand. Each chain was split at the very end and branched off into two sections attached to the ends of the iron cradle. As the dwarfs heaved, Dunrik was lifted slowly off the ground. Once he had reached the zenith of the chamber, the chains were locked in place and a third chain dragged by Uthor pulled Dunrik high over the pit of fire. Now in place, and through means of ingenious dwarf engineering, he could be lowered slowly into the raging flames.

As Uthor did so, very slowly, Halgar stepped forward and Emelda, head bowed respectfully, retreated back.

The longbeard's expression was one of solemnity as he opened his mouth and sang a dour lamentation in a sombre baritone, all the while Dunrik getting closer to the forge fires.

In ancient days when darkness wracked the land,
'twas Grimnir ventured north with axe in hand.
To the blighted wastes he was so fated
to slay daemons, beasts and fell gods much hated.
Thunder spoke and tremors wracked the earth
Grimnir the Fearless fought for all his worth.
With the gods of ruin arisen all around,
with rhun and axe did Grimnir strike them down.
He closed the dreaded gate and sealed the darkness in
lest it curse the Karaz Ankor again.
Go now brave dawi, go if you are able
to Grungni's table – he is waiting.
In the Halls of the Ancestors with honour at your breast,
you will find your final rest.
Lo there is the line of kings arrayed,
your place among them is assured – they await you.
Go now brave dawi, the hammers ring your passing,
the throng amassing in the deep – your soul will Gazul keep.
Go now brave dawi, in glory you are wreathed,
unto the Halls of the Ancestors received.

As Halgar finished, Dunrik's body, already wreathed in flame, was plunged deep into the sea of coal and fire. In moments, he was consumed by it.

'So then does Dunrik, son of Frengar, thane of Everpeak and the Bardrakk clan pass into the Chamber of the Gate to await his ancestors,' said the longbeard.

'May he be remembered.'

'May he be remembered,' the throng responded in sombre unison, all except Emelda who kept her head bowed and stayed silent.

Ralkan, standing near to Halgar, inscribed Dunrik's name in the book of remembering, the massive tome held up for him by two dwarfs of the Stonebreaker clan.

As Halgar fell silent, Uthor stepped forward and turned to the gathered assembly. In his left hand he held a dagger. With a single, swift gesture he drew the blade across his palm, making a fist immediately afterwards, and then passed the dagger to Halgar, who wiped it clean. Uthor then waited for Ralkan to come forward. The lorekeeper carried a small receptacle and held it beneath the thane's cut hand. Uthor clenched his fist and allowed the blood to drip into the receptacle. When he was done, Emelda bound the wound as Ralkan went back to the book of remembering. The entire ritual was conducted in total silence.

'Let it be known,' uttered Uthor, Ralkan scribing the words in the thane of Kadrin's own blood into the tome in front of him, 'on this day did Dunrik of the Bardrakk clan fall in battle, slain by skaven treachery. Ten thousand rat-tails will avenge this deed and even then may it never be struck from the records of Karak Varn and Everpeak. So speaks Uthor, son of Algrim.'

Emelda raised her head and peered into the flames of the vast pit, the axe of Dunrik clutched firmly in her hands.

'AN OATH WAS made,' said Uthor, addressing the throng – less than half that which ventured from their holds to reclaim Karak Varn.

It had been several hours since Dunrik's interment and Uthor had spent that time consulting deeply with Thalgrim and Rorek. Halgar and Gromrund had been privy to their discussions too. Uthor had wanted Emelda to be present as well, but the clan daughter had retreated into herself following her kinsdwarf's passage to the Chamber of the Gate and was not to be disturbed. Once they were done, their decision made, Uthor had bade Gromrund to gather the throng together in readiness for his address.

Uthor was standing on the forgemaster's platform, beneath the arch, and all the dwarfs were arrayed below in their clans. The Bronzehammers, Sootbeards, Ironfingers and Flinthearts of Zhufbar, dark of expression, their numbers thinned by attrition. Alongside them were the Furrowbrows and the Stonebreakers of Everpeak, crestfallen and sullen. The latter bore the standard of the slain Firehands in dour remembrance. Gromrund stood amongst them, slightly to the front. The hammerer knew what was coming and was stern of face. At the back of the group was Azgar, surrounded by his fellow slayers. The Grim Brotherhood were as fierce and threatening as ever. Uthor paid them, and Azgar, no heed as he continued.

'An oath to reclaim Karak Varn in the name of Kadrin Redmane, my ancestor, and of Lokki Kraggson...'

The thane of Karak Kadrin looked over at Halgar, stood beside him, leaning on the pommel of his axe and scowling deeply at the warriors below.

'To wrest the hold from the vile filth that had infested it, the same wretches that took dawi territory, took their very lives in spite of our dominion of the mountain.'

There was muttered discord at that, as all around the throng chewed and pulled at their beards, spat in disgust and gnashed their teeth.

'We have failed in that oath.'

Sobbing and vociferous lamentation accompanied Uthor's remark. Some dwarfs began stamping their feet and drumming axe and hammer heads against their shields.

'And Karak Varn is lost to us.'

Shouting echoed from the back ranks, loud grumblings of discontent and dismay filled the chamber, threatening to turn riotous.

Uthor beckoned for silence.

'And yet,' he said, struggling above the residual din, 'and yet,' he said again as the foundry quietened at a glower from Halgar, 'we will have our vengeance.'

A great, war-like cheer erupted from the dwarfs below and the shield thumping began anew, together with the collective stamping of feet. The noise boomed like thunder, the throng abruptly ebullient and heedless of their enemies.

'If dawi cannot have the karak,' Uthor continued, 'then none shall!'

The thunder rose in great pealing waves, ardent voices adding to its power.

'As it was years ago, so it shall be again. The hold of Karak Varn will flood and all within shall perish.' The thane's gaze was as steel as he regarded his kin. 'So speaks Uthor, son of Algrim!'

From fatalism came defiance and the desire for vengeance. It was etched upon the face of every dwarf present as indelibly as if carved in stone.

'Sons of Grungni,' Uthor bellowed. 'Make ready. We go to war, again. For wrath and ruin!' he cried, the axe of Ulfgan held aloft like a rallying symbol.

'For wrath and ruin!' the booming thunder responded.

ACT THREE
WRATH AND RUIN

CHAPTER ELEVEN

Uthor stalked from the forgemaster's platform and down the stairs into the foundry plaza.

'Well spoken,' muttered Gromrund, the hammerer turning on his heel to walk alongside the thane. The still cheering throng parted like an iron sea to let them through.

'Aye it was,' Uthor replied, without arrogance then turned to look at the hammerer directly. 'Does this mean we see eye-to-eye at last, then?'

'You are not the only one who has much to atone for, son of Algrim,' came the terse response. 'If it is to be wrath and ruin, then so be it.'

Uthor smirked at that.

'Good enough,' he said then added, 'summon the clan leaders and gather the engineers. We know *what* we must do; now we must devise *how* it is to be done.'

* * *

'MAKE NO MISTAKE,' Uthor told them, 'most of us are likely to die in the enactment of this plan.'

The thane of Karak Kadrin sat upon a small wooden coal chest within a circle of his kinsdwarfs, next to the statue of Grungni. All of those who had first ventured into the hold were present – all except Lokki, of course. Thalgrim joined them, too, for the Sootbeards. As an expert in geology, his knowledge of the vagaries of rock and stone would be invaluable. Azgar took his place amongst the council as representative of the Grim Brotherhood – much to Uthor's chagrin – though if death was to be their fate then the slayer would have little qualms. The other clan leaders were present also, for the decisions the dwarf assembly was about to make would affect them all. Only Emelda was absent, still seeking solitude for her grief.

Further off into the plaza there was a flurry of activity as dwarfs sharpened axes, beat the dents from armour and made their final oaths to the ancestors. Strangely, the mood was not one of grim melancholy; rather it was jovial and comradely as if the spectre of some unknown doom had been lifted.

'Better to die with honour than festering in the uncertain dark, awaiting a long and drawn out demise,' growled Henkil of the Furrowbrows, supping on a long-necked pipe.

'Aye, let us meet our doom with axes to the fore,' said Bulrik – who represented the interests of the Ironfingers – brandishing his axe. The other lords and leaders muttered their approval of these remarks and stamped their booted feet in agreement.

'It is as well,' said Uthor as the bravado died down, 'for I do not expect to live out the rest of my days and neither should you.'

Grim resolution settled over the group. Only Halgar was unmoved, the old longbeard having seen and heard it all before.

'All we can hope for is to do our part and die well. Lorekeeper,' added Uthor, 'tell us all how.'

Ralkan, who had been silent up until now, shuffled forward on his own coal chest and, producing a thick wedge of chalk from within his robes, started to draw onto the flagstones.

'Karak Varn has ever stood beside the Black Water,' he explained, his frantic scribing seemingly irrelevant to his rhetoric. 'In the Golden Age it was a great boon to the hold, for the crater in which the lake's depths resided were thick with seams of ore and precious gromril.'

Ralkan looked up at that and observed the awe-struck expressions of his kin with satisfaction, their eyes alight with the lustre of great days past.

'It was during the reign of King Hraddi Ironhand that the Barduraz Varn was fashioned, a great sluice gate that when opened would yoke the strength of the Black Water to drive wheels that powered the forge hammers of the deeps and allow the prospectors of the hold to sift for minerals.

'Hraddi was a wily king and well aware of the dangers that such a gate presented, should it fail or it be opened too far,' the lorekeeper continued, his audience enrapt. 'He instructed his engineers to build a deep reservoir beneath the Barduraz Varn in which the water could flow and at the lip of this magnificent well he bade miners hew tunnels that would carry the water to an overflow in the form of a vast and heavy grate. Such was the ingenuity of Hraddi's engineers that the grate

would always open in the exact same increments as the
Barduraz Varn, so that no matter how wide the sluice
gate opened the hold would never flood.'

Throughout the explanation, Ralkan pointed to his
crude rendering – leastways, it was by dwarf standards
– of the gate, reservoir, tunnel and overflow grate.

'But was the gate not destroyed during the Time of
Woes?' Kaggi of the Flinthearts interrupted.

Ralkan regarded the clan leader in sudden befuddlement.

'I believe the gate is still intact,' Rorek interjected on the
lorekeeper's behalf. 'The flooding we have seen has been
isolated to certain chambers. Were the gate to be ruined
then the extent of the water would be much greater and
there are the records of the hold to consider–'

'Yes,' said Ralkan abruptly, remembering his place
again. 'My lord Kadrin did lead an expedition to the
Barduraz Varn and found it to be in working order,
though he did not linger. Much of the chamber was
inundated and the lower deeps – although many of the
skaven and grobi had been driven out – still held hidden dangers not so easily persuaded to leave.' The
lorekeeper suppressed a shudder as if in some fearful
remembrance.

'If we are to flood the hold,' Rorek continued, 'then
we must destroy the overflow mechanism.'

An uncomfortable undercurrent of shock and disap-
proval rippled through much of the assembly. To
deliberately set out to sabotage dwarfen craft was
almost unthinkable and something not to be undertaken lightly.

'*Dreng Tromm*,' said Henkil, 'that it should come to
this.'

'That is not all,' said Uthor. 'Once we have ruined the overflow, so that it stays shut, we must open the Barduraz Varn as far as it will go.'

'The rat-kin are not without wit,' said Hakem, sat across from the thane of Kadrin. The Barak Varr dwarf now wore a bronze hook, fashioned by Rorek and strapped onto the stump in place of his severed hand. 'Even if we are able to block the grate and open up the hold to the Black Water, they will flee before it into their tunnels and return once the flood has drained away.'

'Which is why we must start a second inundation, only from above,' Uthor replied, now looking to Thalgrim.

The lodefinder was busy scrutinising a small rock; the thane of Kadrin fancied he was even conversing with it. Thalgrim snapped upright when he realised the eyes of the council were upon him.

'Yes, above,' he said quickly. 'The temporary shoring we found in the third deep as made by Engineer Dibna can be brought down; it ruptures slightly even now. A shaft from that chamber leads all the way to the underdeep and to the overflow tunnel.'

'We must divide our throng into three *skorongs*,' Uthor said, picking up the slack. 'One will head for the Barduraz Varn; a second will go in the opposite direction, first to the overflow and then to Dibna's Chamber, thus starting the flood.'

'And what of our enemies?' asked Bulrik. 'They will not be gathered together. How are we to ensure they are all destroyed when the waters come?'

'If this plan is to succeed,' Uthor said, 'then we must draw the skaven to one place and channel the bulk of the rushing Black Water to it, ensnaring them until the flood can do its work. Like any rat trap,' he added, 'it requires bait. This is where the third skorong comes in, and theirs is a grim task indeed.' Uthor's face darkened. 'They will hold the rat-kin, here, in this very chamber.'

'And be drowned along with the skaven.' Bulrik finished for him.

'It is possible that some might survive, and any of us who do must take word of this to the High King with all haste. But, yes it is likely most will die.' Uthor's tone was sombre but firm.

'It will be a noble sacrifice.'

'How then are we to goad them?' asked Henkil. 'If the slaughter in the Wide Western Way taught us anything, save for the treachery of skaven' – a bout of spitting accompanied that remark – 'it is that their warlord has some intelligence. Likely they will not come of their own accord.'

'Halgar?' Uthor turned to the longbeard.

The venerable dwarf scratched at the grobi arrow stub embedded in his chest, before leaning forward.

'I have fought fiercer and wilier foes – that is for certain, but this vermin chief is not without base cunning,' he said, chewing on the end of his pipe. 'Like most creatures, even those wretches that prey upon us dawi in the dark and usurp our lands, the rat-kin nest. I can smell the stink of their lair even now, rotting below us like a rancid carcass,' Halgar added, sneering with disgust. 'In my younger days, I once came upon such a nest – I feel its canker crawling over my skin as I remember it. Litters of the foul things were all about, spewed from rat-kin birth mothers that were fattened on urk and dawi flesh. My brothers and I brought flame and retribution to the foul dwelling, slaying the birthing rats first of all. It drove the rat-kin into frenzy and they came upon us with such fervour that we fled back whence we came. Grokki, my clan brother, and I, realising we would not outrun the vermin, cut down the braces to the tunnel in which we were in and brought the weight of the mountain down upon us and our pursuers. Of my kin, I was the only one to survive. This,' he said, holding up his ruined hand, 'and the deaths of Grokki and the rest of my brothers upon my conscience, was my reward.'

The longbeard allowed for a moment of sombre silence, before he went on.

'Much like then we must find the filthy rat-kin nest and destroy all that lay within. That will bring them to us, mark my words on that.' With that the longbeard leant back, a heavy plume of pipe smoke issuing into the air around him.

'An expedition must venture from the foundry, once the other skorongs are under way,' Uthor said by way of further explanation. 'It will be small, designed to infiltrate past whatever guards the rat-kin will undoubtedly have in place and delve into the very heart of their nest. Rorek,' added Uthor, looking over to the engineer, 'has fashioned something that will get the ratmen's attention.'

The Zhufbar dwarf grinned, revealing white teeth in his ruddy beard.

'A fine plan,' Henkil concurred, 'but who is to do what?'

'Our most experienced warriors will be in the first two skorongs. The way will be perilous and should either fail then all our efforts will be for nought,' Uthor replied, 'Gromrund shall lead those heading for the overflow and Dibna's Chamber,' – the hammerer nodded his assent – 'together with Thalgrim, Hakem, Ralkan and no more than three warriors from the Sootbeard clan,' he said with a glance at Thalgrim to make sure he was paying attention.

'You, Henkil,' the thane continued, regarding the clan leader, 'will accompany Rorek, Bulrik, Halgar and I to the Barduraz Varn, which leaves the rest to hold the skaven at–'

'No lad,' said Halgar, his face illuminated briefly by his pipe embers before it was cast back into shadow. 'I am too old to be running around the underdeep. I will stay here. I like the smell of the soot and metal; it reminds me of the Copper Mountain,' he added. 'Besides, they will need my nose to find the rat-kin nest,' he said, tapping one of his nostrils.

'But venerable one…'

'I have spoken!' Halgar bellowed, but his expression soon softened, 'I have fought in many battles, more than I can recall; let this be my last, eh?'

Uthor's shoulders sagged. To be without Halgar as he ventured to the gate was almost unthinkable. 'Very well,' the thane said softly. 'Drimbold, you will join us to the gate.'

'I wish to stay here, too,' said the Grey dwarf, 'and fight alongside my kin.'

Halgar raised an eyebrow, but gave no other indication as to what he thought of Drimbold's pledge.

'Very well then,' Uthor said with a little consternation, 'Kaggi, you shall accompany us.'

Kaggi was about to nod but was interrupted.

'Kaggi should remain with his kin,' said a voice from outside the circle.

Uthor's temper was rising; it was quashed in an instant when Emelda moved into the light cast by the statue of Grungni, her armour resplendent before it. She had removed the face mask from her helmet and in her hand she held Dunrik's axe. '*We* shall take Halgar's place.'

Uthor did not have the will to protest. In truth, he welcomed Emelda's presence. Whenever she were near he felt the burden of his past, of his duty to his clan that he now knew he would fail, lift slightly. Her prowess, too, was unquestionable.

'Then please sit, milady, for this last part is crucial,' Uthor said and Emelda took her place amongst the circle, those dwarfs sitting next to her reddening about the cheeks and swiftly smoothing their beards.

Once order was restored, Uthor went on.

'None amongst the first two skorongs must release any flood waters until they hear Azgar's warhorn.' Uthor's jaw tightened only slightly at the mention of the name. 'Only then will we know the rat-kin are committed to the attack. After that, and by closing off tunnels, wells and door dams throughout the lower deeps as we go, the Black Water will be unleashed and channelled into the foundry.'

Uthor allowed a silence to descend as he regarded each and every dwarf in the circle in turn.

'Make your oaths,' he said, getting to his feet, 'in an hour we go to meet our destinies.'

THE THRONG MUSTERED together for one last time. Each and every clan dwarf was decked in their armour and brandished hammers and axes proudly.

At the foundry gate, Uthor and Gromrund, with their retinues, made ready to leave. Their paths would converge for a time, until they reached the triple forked road and then one would head eastward to the mines and the shaft that led to the underdeep, whilst the other would go westward, relying on Ralkan's prior instruction, to the Barduraz Varn.

'If memory serves, the route to both the gate and overflow should be fairly clear of obstruction, fifty years of rat-kin occupation not withstanding, of course.' Ralkan had said as the council were breaking up.

'Of course,' Uthor had replied with a wry glance at Gromrund, the thane noticing that other dwarfs in earshot made similar exchanges.

'YOU ARE CERTAIN its note will carry to the lower deeps?' Halgar asked as he watched the dwarfs slowly depart through the gate.

'The wyvern-horn will make itself heard, you can mark that – its note will carry,' Azgar answered deeply, with a furtive glance at Uthor. The thane of Kadrin was having a final private word with Drimbold. When he was done speaking into his ear, the Grey dwarf nodded and headed back to be amongst the other warriors.

'You fight with honour, slayer,' said the longbeard, watching him. 'But we all go to our deaths, now. Perhaps there might be some accord between you and your brother in this moment?'

A slight, near-imperceptible, tremor of shock registered in the slayer's eyes as he looked back at Halgar.

'I have known it from the first time I set eyes upon you,' the longbeard said. 'He even fights like you.'

Azgar considered Halgar's words before he spoke.

'I am sorry, venerable one. You are wise, but there can be no accord between us. I have seen to that.'

The slayer bowed deeply and took his leave.

'Aye,' Halgar said regretfully when he was gone, off to rejoin his Grim Brotherhood and make ready for the coming battle. Uthor, too, had now vanished into the dark, the foundry gate thundering shut in his wake. 'You're probably right.'

DRIMBOLD HEARD THE foundry gate slamming to and the thick bolts scraping across its metal surface as he headed for the weapon racks. The mattock he carried was chipped and battered, and he was unaccustomed to its weight. A stout hand axe, that was what he needed; even Halgar would condone him borrowing one.

Reaching the racks, he looked over to the longbeard who was wheezing badly and rubbing at the old wound in his chest. He only did it when no one else was watching, but Drimbold was skilled at secret observation and had seen him struggle often. The Grey dwarf remembered Uthor's words to him as he had left.

'I won't let you down,' he said to himself. Really, he had no choice. If this was to be the end, then honouring his pledge to Uthor was his last chance at redemption.

THRATCH WIPED THE flat of his blade on a skaven slave. The wretched creature was so emaciated that it nearly bent double with the warlord's heavy paw pressed on its back. Satisfied that his weapon was clean of goblin blood, despite the pathetic tufts of fur poking between the slave's patches of scar tissue, the warlord kicked the whimpering creature to the floor and stalked away to talk to his chieftain returning from the upper deeps.

'Most of the green-things are dead-dead, my lord,' Liskrit said, cowering slightly before his master, despite his well-armoured bulk.

'And the rest?' snarled Thratch, sheathing his sword as he paced over to the nearby door through which the dwarfs had made their escape.

The warlord had returned to the Great Hall with Kill-Klaw and the majority of his warriors once they had defeated the greenskins. Despite the victory, Thratch had lost many clanrats and almost all of his slaves. The few that did survive were shovelling dwarf and goblin corpses into crudely-made barrows to be taken below to the warrens to feed the birthing mothers.

When the nerve of the goblins finally broke – and Thratch knew it would – he'd sent a small cohort of elite stormvermin and slaves to harry them as far as the upper deeps. No creature, be it dwarf-thing or green-thing would usurp his domain – this was Thratch's territory now.

'They ran, quick-quick, yes.'

'Good,' said the warlord then screamed suddenly, 'No, no,' smacking the back of a warrior's head into the door as he probed at it with his spear.

'We don't go that way,' Thratch roared, noticing the thin trickles of water eking through the cracks with a slight prickling of fear. The skaven warrior's muzzle had been crushed into its brain with the impact and it did not answer. Suddenly aware of the fact, Thratch about turned and stalked back to his chieftain.

'You stay-stay, make sure the green-things do not return,' he commanded. 'I must check on Clan Skryre, yes,' he added, stalking off again. The progress on the pumping engine was going much slower than Thratch liked and he was debating which one of the Skryre acolytes to kill next when his chieftain spoke.

'Noble Lord Thratch,' said Liskrit, obsequiously.

'Yes-yes, what it is now?' Thratch whirled around, deciding whether or not to have Kill-Klaw gut the impudent chieftain now or wait until later while it slept.

'The dwarf-things... should we follow them?'

A vicious snarl crept across the warlord's snout, revealing glistening fangs, still slick with goblin blood.

'Dead-dead they are, yet they do not know it. Any that are left I will kill-kill or chase down into the dark for the fire-worm to eat.' The snarl twisted into a malicious grin and Thratch walked away, the creeping shadow of Kill-Klaw following silently behind him.

CHAPTER TWELVE

SKARTOOTH WAS DISPLEASED. His cunning attack against the skaven had been thwarted – largely by Fangrak's incompetence, he was sure – the dwarfs had escaped his wrath and his army, together with all his grand designs, was in tatters.

'Idiot!' the goblin warlord shrieked, pacing up and down the flat plateau of rock to which the remnants of the greenskins had fled. The path they had taken led them high into the mountains and three sides of the plateau fell away into a craggy gorge.

Several of the surviving orc tribes had already left, retreating silently into the mountains as Skartooth had led the flight to the lofty promontory. Only he, Fangrak and a meagre horde of other orcs and goblins remained. That and Ungul, of course. The pet troll was sat on its bony backside and paid little heed to the argument brewing between his master and Fangrak, too obsessed was it with watching the viscous drool dripping languidly from its maw and pooling on the ground in front of it.

'It was your plan to ambush the ratties and them stunties at the same time,' growled Fangrak, stood stock still as his warlord paced in front of him.

'There was nuthin' wrong with my plan,' squeaked Skartooth. 'You just didn't listen to my ordas, did ya?' he added, pointing his diminutive blade in the orc chieftain's direction.

'What ordas? "Get 'em"?' said Fangrak, building up to a roar. 'Is them your zoggin' ordas, eh?'

'I knew you were useless, you and your ole stinkin' lot,' snarled Skartooth. 'And now you've ruined everything... Everything!' he cried, apoplectic with rage, the veins in his forehead popping to the surface.

'I've 'ad enough of this,' Fangrak grumbled, turning away from the goblin warlord, 'I'm off.'

'Don't turn your back on me!' Skartooth shrieked, so high-pitched that Ungul waggled a finger in his ear to stop it ringing.

'Zog off,' said Fangrak, already walking away.

Skartooth roared, the goblin's anger getting the better of him as he launched himself at Fangrak, ready to plunge his sword beneath the orc's shoulder blades. But before he could strike the blow, Fangrak whirled around and grabbed Skartooth's scrawny arm in one meaty fist then quickly clamped his other hand around the goblin's neck. With a twist he snapped Skartooth's wrist and the sword tumbled from the goblin's nerveless grasp, clanging loudly as it hit the ground.

Fangrak drew Skartooth close as he started to squeeze his hand around the goblin's neck, slowly choking the life out of him.

Skartooth glanced over towards Ungul, fear in his eyes but the beast was quite far away and digging deep into its nostril at something that didn't want to be dislodged.

When he looked back at Fangrak, he realised that this had been the orc's plan all along. As that knowledge passed over his face, Fangrak smiled.

'What are you gonna do now?' he murmured sadistically, squeezing just a little tighter and taking great amusement in watching the blood vessels pop in Skartooth's ever widening eyes.

The goblin warlord soiled himself, a long streak of foul smelling dung streaming from his robes to spatter on the ground and Fangrak's leg.

'You filthy–' the orc chieftain began, slightly loosening his grip as he stooped to inspect the mess trickling down into his boot.

It was all the distraction Skartooth needed. The goblin wrenched himself free enough to bite down hard against Fangrak's hand. The orc chieftain howled in pain and threw Skartooth to the ground as if he'd gripped the wrong end of a branding iron. The goblin warlord scuttled backwards on all fours to the safety of Ungul's presence, the troll having suddenly blinked awake, as if for the first time.

'Kill 'im!' Skartooth squealed, his diminutive voice croaky after nearly being strangled by Fangrak.

Ungul didn't respond. It merely looked dully at Skartooth as if trying to remember something.

'What are you waitin' for? Kill 'im!' the goblin squealed again, smacking Ungul on the nose with his good hand.

The troll snarled at Skartooth, and the goblin warlord saw all the years of pain and mistreatment at his hands felt by Ungul anew.

'Oh no,' he breathed, reaching up to neck.

The collar was gone.

Fangrak had removed it.

''Ee 'ates you almost as much as I do,' said the orc chief, three of his warriors alongside him, awaiting the gruesome show.

Skartooth shuffled backwards as the troll stood up, its immense shadow engulfing him like an eclipse.

Ungul roared, beating its chest.

Skartooth back-pedalled as fast as he could but suddenly there was nothing beneath his feet and he fell off the promontory, screaming into the jagged gorge below.

Ungul bellowed in rage, watching the goblin disappear. The subject of its ire gone, it lumbered around and turned all of its anger on Fangrak.

'Aw zog,' said the orc chieftain, hunting around with his eyes to locate the collar. When Skartooth had bitten him he'd dropped it. His last memory of the artefact was of it rolling away across the plateau but now it was nowhere to be seen.

'Get it,' he snarled at his warriors, switching to his makeshift back-up plan. The orcs looked bemused at first, but when they realised Fangrak was serious they charged, roaring, at the troll.

Ungul roared back and vomited a searing spray of corrosive stomach acid all over the warriors, who screamed as the toxic liquid ate them up greedily.

Fangrak – seeing his minions turned to bubbling pools of greenish flesh and viscera – ran but Ungul reached out with its gangly limbs and seized him. The orc chieftain squealed as the troll pulled off both his arms and then went for the legs. As the troll sat down to feast, its anger sated for now, the rest of what was left of the horde fled, deep into the mountains.

THE FLICKERING TORCH flame illuminated the fearsome, scar-ravaged visage of Azgar as he led the warriors down the cramped passage.

'These are not dwarf made tunnels,' growled Halgar, two paces behind the slayer.

The longbeard ran his hand lightly along the walls, smearing away a thin veneer of slime and crusted filth. A trail of effluvia trickled languidly down the middle of the tunnel along the ground in a shallow and foul-smelling rut. Elsewhere, the skaven underway was littered with excreta and other detritus, and the dwarfs needed to traverse it with care lest they slip on clustered droppings or the rank remnants of a discarded rat-kin feast.

'How long have we been down here?' Drimbold piped up suddenly, trudging just behind Halgar.

'Too long,' the longbeard muttered. The twisting, turning route had led them deep into the earth. On several occasions the way had split, spiralling off into the silent gloom in myriad directions, some so obtuse that only one of the rat-kin could hope to travel them. Halgar knew that much of the skaven labyrinth inter-sected the paths of the Ungdrin road and even undermined and subsumed them in places. In his youth, he'd heard tales of huge, hairless mole rats that the skaven used to dig vast tracts into the rock and earth – whether or not such rumours held any truth the longbeard did not know. He had to suppress a shudder, though, when he wondered how long these tunnels had been here, unnoticed by Kadrin, Ulfgan and even their ancestors, balking at the thought of just how many were bored into the earth and exactly how deep they went.

Azgar was paying little heed to the conversation and was intent on the way forward when Halgar bade him pause a moment as he sniffed at the air. Wrinkling his nose he said, 'The wretched stench of the rat-kin is thickening,' he said. 'We are getting close.'

The slayer nodded and the dwarfs continued into the dark.

The dwarfs that remained in the foundry had waited for an hour before heading out. They too were destined for the triple forked road but preparations to meet and resist the skaven horde first had to be made. The delay would also allow Uthor and Gromrund, who had a much farther journey ahead of them, to get well under way. Azgar's expedition did not dawdle too long, however – in luring the skaven to them, it also meant their brothers en route to the Barduraz Varn and the overflow grate would be less likely to encounter much resistance.

The three dwarfs were not alone as they ventured toward the rat-kin warrens, three of the Grim Brotherhood and another dwarf by the name of Thorig, a warrior of Zhufbar who shouldered a heavy-looking satchel across his back, also accompanied them.

Halgar rubbed at his eyes as the dwarfs stopped in a sloped section of the labyrinthine tunnel network, a two-legged fork in front of them. Azgar brandished the torch light in front of it. His lip curled into a feral sneer as he recognised the foul script of the skaven scratched into the wall above each road. He turned to the long-beard and saw him kneading his eye sockets with his knuckles.

'Are you all right, old one?' asked the slayer.

'Yes,' Halgar snapped, 'this infernal flame is ruining my sight,' he complained, scratching at his chest wound again.

'I am not fond of it either,' Azgar agreed, 'but 'tis necessary,' he added, thumbing over his shoulder in the direction of Thorig, 'for what the engineer has planned.'

Halgar grumbled, his words indiscernible. He pointed to the left-hand opening of the fork, tasting the air as he did so. 'The stink is heaviest there,' he said more clearly, blinking several times before trudging onward. 'Are you coming?' he snarled back at the others.

'WE WILL NEED a rope,' cried Uthor above the raging din of the waterfall.

The dwarfs had been going steadily on a western course just as Ralkan had told them to. Already they had shut several door dams, which Rorek assured the thane of Kadrin would help channel the lower flood waters up to the foundry. They had also sealed a number of wellways, heaving large stones into their necks to act as stoppers. It was tough and time-consuming work but necessary. The road had led them downwards after that, the Barduraz Varn getting ever closer, to a sheer rock face and a sheet of shimmering, cascading water.

'Can we go around?' Emelda shouted, her voice dulled by the incredible noise of the thundering torrents.

'It is the only way into the flooded deeps and the Bar-duraz Varn,' Uthor replied, eyeing the rushing waterfall from the ledge where the dwarfs were standing. The ledge narrowed abruptly after that, where the waterfall began and had worn it down. Over the edge, the thunderous water fell away into a deep, dark chasm. Uthor imagined the vast expanse of the Black Water swelling far above them, its power evident even this far down and felt humbled.

Rorek unwound a rope from his tool belt, one of several, and brandished it in front of Uthor. 'This will hold. Dawi twine is not so easily broken,' he said, errant spray spitting at him and moistening his beard with jewels of water. He threw one end of the rope to Uthor, who caught it easily.

'Tie it around your waist and make the knot tight,' Rorek told him then turned to Emelda. 'You should do the same, milady.'

The dwarfs were moved into single file, first Uthor then Emelda followed by Rorek, Henkil and finally Bulrik. Slowly, with Uthor taking the lead, they worked their way towards the rushing waterfall.

As Uthor touched the narrowed ledge he instantly felt the slickness beneath his boots. It would be easy to slip and fall into the endless depths below, with a forest of razor sharp rocks at journey's end. The thane of Kadrin resolved not to look down. Instead, he dug around in a leather pouch Rorek had given to him and pulled out two broad spikes of iron. He put one in his mouth – the taste of metal was reassuring – and reached over to drive the other into the sheer rock. At first he faltered – unaccustomed to the battering force of the water, and recoiled – breathing hard, his beard, face and arm drenched. Then he gathered himself and tried again, taking an extra step as he did so.

Icy water smashed Uthor, robbing him of breath and setting his teeth chattering as he fought against the thunderous swell. Taking a small hammer from his belt, the thane drove the spike into the wall, where it held fast. Using the spike as a handhold, he eased himself further across the ledge and drove in another. Then came a third and a fourth, and Uthor reached the centre of the ledge, where a small crevice in the rock wall allowed him a moment's respite from the onrushing deluge.

Catching his breath, acutely aware that the others were following slowly in his wake, he was about to continue when he felt a sharp tug against the rope cinctured at his waist. The thane turned, his boots slipping on the drenched rock, and saw Emelda losing purchase on one of the spikes and falling backward. She was but an arm length away and Uthor quickly reached out to her, grabbing her by the wrist as she flailed, and heaved her towards him. The royal clan daughter thumped into Uthor's body with the momentum of her rescue and the two of them fell back against the narrow crevice in the rock wall, breathing hard.

'My thanks,' said Emelda, her long plaits dripping wet as she blinked away water droplets from her eyes. A smile starting to form in the corners of her mouth changed dramatically to a grimace as Uthor felt her pulled back again. He held her fast, gripping a wall spike with all his strength as he tried to see what was happening. Beyond the foaming, white veil of water blurred shadows presented themselves and dulled cries carried through the raging downpour.

* * *

ROREK WATCHED, POWERLESS, as Bulrik fell. The Ironfinger dwarf stumbled against a jutting rock and slipped. His death-scream was swallowed by the roar of the waterfall, his tumbling body lost from view in the churning mists.

Wisely, the dwarfs had left several feet of rope between each fastening around the waist but even so, Henkil only had a few seconds to un-tether himself or he too would be lost to the darkness. The leader of the Furrowbrows pulled frantically at the knot he had made. His clan were rope makers, he had boasted as much to Rorek before they had descended the stairway, and as such knew much of knot work, so much so that he had congratulated himself when he'd tied this particular binding, unthinking that he might have to untie it in haste.

Henkil's fingers slipped, the slack of the rope pulling taut and he looked up at the engineer when he realised all was lost. The Furrowbrow was yanked violently off the ledge to his doom, Bulrik an unwitting anchor. The rope started gathering again. Rorek was tugged forward at first, some of the slack piled at his boot, but then he stepped free of it. He pressed his back against the rock wall and braced his legs – no way could he bear the weight of two fully-armoured dawi. Like most of the throng, Rorek carried several throwing axes and with the trailing rope tightening before his very eyes, he pulled one free. With an oath to Grungni that his aim might this once be true he cast the blade, which span end over end scything through the water and smacking into the ledge, cutting the rope with no more time to spare. There it remained, firmly embedded, as the severed trail disappeared into the gloom following Bulrik and Henkil.

* * *

'Is it much farther?' groaned Hakem as he climbed down another few feet, through the cramped confines of Dibna's Drop.

The dwarfs had entered the shaft via the mines and were descending gradually to the underdeep and from there to the overflow tunnel – thanks to Thalgrim's rope, secured safely above – which resided a long way below. The going had been hard; much of the shaft was collapsed and in places, sharp rocks jutted out where adjoining tunnels had broken through the shaft wall like stone battering rams. Mercifully, the ancestors of Karak Varn had built a series of short ledges at intervals down the long shaft. Gromrund took advantage of this piece of engineering ingenuity gladly setting his boots onto the stone outcrop for a breather.

'Not sure. I think we are about halfway,' the hammerer reckoned, peering into the gloom below between his legs.

'In the halls of Barak Varr, gilded lifts allow passage up and down the deeps,' Hakem moaned, struggling to un-tether his hook from the rope as he too found one of the ledges.

'You must be feeling like your old self, again,' Gromrund remarked with a wry smile in the merchant thane's direction, 'to boast of your hold's magnificence. Or do you seek to outdo Halgar with your grumbling?' he added.

Hakem gave a half-hearted and ephemeral laugh. The loss of the Honakinn Hammer still dogged his thoughts. The memory of it vanishing into the darkness beyond his grasp and the subsequent death of Dunrik was like a sudden knife-blade in his heart and his expression darkened.

Gromrund saw it and averted his gaze upward to where Ralkan, Thalgrim and the three Sootbeards descended. Each of them found purchase on the ledges in short order; the relief of Ralkan though was almost palpable.

'How long can we rest?' gasped the lorekeeper, unused to such physical exertion, casting his gaze skyward and scarce believing he had come such a distance.

'Not long,' said Gromrund, 'a few minutes, no more.'

Thalgrim was in his element, as were his clan brothers. They chatted freely, taking the opportunity to eat what rations they had in their packs. One of the miners even dangled his feet over the edge, dropping a small piece of rock into the gloom. Thalgrim turned his ear towards it as it struck the bottom with a shallow and faraway 'plink'.

'One hundred and thirty-one feet,' said the lodefinder to the rest of the group, 'give or take a few inches.'

'There,' said Gromrund, looking back at Hakem. 'You have your answer.'

Hakem scowled.

'Definitely more like the longbeard,' Gromrund muttered beneath his breath.

THALGRIM LED THE rest of the way down Dibna's Drop. The darkness was particularly thick here it seemed and he and the rest of the Sootbeards lit candles stuck to their mining helmets to help light the way for the other dwarfs. There were no more stops and after what felt like several more hours to some, they reached the end of the shaft and the ancient rock of the underdeep.

The lodefinder landed with a dull splash, water coming up to his ankles and wetting the mail skirt of his armour. The underdeep was partially flooded. Tramping through the water to make way for the others he gazed in wonder at the vast subterranean halls at the lowest habitable levels of Karak Varn. Massive archways ran down the curved ceiling at precise intervals and stout columns, carved with runic script and the images of fabulous beasts, held the roof aloft. A fizzle of flame got his attention as the rest of the group made landfall. He realised it was his candle and craned his neck to regard the ceiling directly above. Liquid dripped intermittently from a shallow crack, an isolated pocket of flood water obviously trapped beyond it and trying to force its way through. Thalgrim was possessed by the sudden urge to hurry.

'Which way, lorekeeper?' he asked, turning back to the group, all of whom had now exited the mineshaft.

They were standing at a confluence of four tunnels, the crossroads stretching off into the distance seemingly without discerning features.

Ralkan regarded each avenue in turn, his brow furrowed as he tried to remember.

'I thought you knew how to get to the overflow,' said Hakem, with a furtive glance at Gromrund.

The lorekeeper scratched his head. Much of the tunnels were damaged: collapsed columns jutted from the water like miniature stone islands and some of the archway decoration had fallen away leaving them jagged as if gnawed upon. It was not how Ralkan remembered it, though he had seen the desolation before.

'We go north,' he said at last, pointing towards one of the tunnels.

'That way lies south,' said Thalgrim, his expression perplexed.

'South then,' replied the lorekeeper, a little uncertainly. 'Come on, the grate is not far,' he added and started tramping down the tunnel, the bottom of his robes water-logged.

'*South* it is,' muttered Hakem, exchanging a worried look with Gromrund as the dwarfs followed.

THE FOUL STINK of skaven was overpowering as they reached the entrance to the warrens; even Azgar and the others did not need the nose of the longbeard to smell it.

Halgar slowly and quietly pulled his axe from his belt as he approached the ratman chamber. Azgar was beside the longbeard and he turned to the slayer, first putting his finger to his lips and then showing the slayer his palm in a gesture to wait. The longbeard crept forward to the threshold of the room, his stealth incredible for a dwarf of his age and so armoured, and peered into it.

The skaven warren was made in a large, roughly-hewn cavern around three hundred beard lengths in each direction. Structurally, there were a number of raised stone platforms and Halgar also noticed the edge of several deep pits in the centre of the chamber. Rat-kin guards stood around them, wearing cracked, black-leather hauberks and carrying broad-bladed spears – they must be the birthing pens, where the bloated skaven females gorged upon the flesh of the dead and spawned litters of the mutated ratmen. The thought turned the longbeard's stomach and he gripped his axe haft for reassurance. Two more guards sat near the entrance, noses twitching but otherwise oblivious to Halgar's presence.

Slumbering slaves took up most of the rest of the floor space, heaped on top of one another in clots of fur and cloth, partially obscured by a low-lying, sulphurous fug. Halgar noticed it came from the birthing pens.

A languid, almost comatose, atmosphere persisted. Piles of excreta lay everywhere, along with bones and other debris. Urine stained the walls and sweat clung to the air, on top of the nostril-prickling stench of the sulphur fog. Halgar had seen enough and backtracked to his awaiting kinsdwarfs.

The longbeard beckoned Thorig forward and the Zhufbar dwarf did so quickly. Halgar nodded to him and Thorig unclasped the satchel he'd been carrying since they'd left the foundry. Delving deep, he produced a fist-sized ball of copper and iron. A faint seam was visible in the flickering torch light that ran across the ball's circumference, a hinge at one end and what appeared to be a spring-loaded catch at the other. A spout protruded from one hemisphere with a short length of twine sticking out of it.

Halgar took the ball in his hand and tipped it, the tinny sound of liquid sloshing inside could be heard very faintly. The longbeard raised an eyebrow at the Zhufbar dwarf.

'Zharrum,' whispered Thorig with a glint in his eyes. 'The mixture of soot and oil is particularly volatile when exposed to a flame,' he added, echoing the words of Rorek.

'Your clansdwarf will be for a quaffing,' Halgar grumbled quietly.

Thorig shrugged and passed a ball to each of the
other dwarfs. He then took the flaming brand proffered
by Azgar, crushing it into the ground until only glowing embers remained. The slayer then led them back to
warren entrance.

A shallow gurgling of blood and the two skaven at
the cavern entrance were dead with slit throats. Azgar
and Halgar laid their kills down almost in perfect unison and began the stealthy advance into the chamber.
The dwarfs trod in single file, Halgar at the front marking a path through the slumbering slaves. Should any
of them be disturbed and manage to raise the alarm
then the dwarfs would be quickly surrounded and
fighting for their very lives.

Azgar followed on after the longbeard, sweeping his
gaze left and right for any sign of movement, chained
axe held low in his grasp. So intent was he on what was
in front of him that he didn't see the rat tail flick
beneath his boot. The bulky slayer stepped on it and
the slave to whom it belonged would've screamed but
for Azgar reaching down like lightning, wrapping his
chain around the creature's neck and snapping it with
a vicious twist. Like before, he laid the body down carefully and the dwarfs moved on.

As they came close to the birthing pens and the
guards that protected them Halgar bade them
silently to spread out, using the shadows and the
soporific state of the rat-kin to creep up on them.
There were six guards in total; a pair for each of the
three pits and one each for Halgar, Azgar, Drimbold
and the Grim Brotherhood. Thorig stooped out of
sight, fearful that the embers of the torch would
rouse the skaven.

When they were all in position, Halgar rose up from a crouching stance and cut the first guard down. One of the Grim Brotherhood smothered the second with a meaty palm over the mouth and then broke its neck. Azgar and another of his slayers, looming out of the mist like ancient predators of the deep, dispatched the other two with equal and deadly swiftness. Drimbold and the third slayer finished the remaining guards, one with a well-flighted axe throw; the other with an axe spike to the throat. So silent was Drimbold that the other dwarfs didn't even see or hear him approach. The assassins shared a nod to acknowledge the task was done and crept over to the birthing pens.

Halgar peered into the deep pit and almost gagged.

Sat on its fat rump, its rolls of fat spilling over each other, was a vile skaven birth mother. The bloated female was mewling faintly with its scrawny legs spread wide in preparation for the expulsion of yet more skaven offspring. She was surrounded by bone carcasses: dwarf, goblin and even ratman were all in evidence. A host of diminutive rat-kin spawn suckled hungrily at a raft of small, pink teats sticking out of the birth mother's torso. Several of the spawn were dead and some of the stronger babies were devouring them, noisily.

In one corner of the pen there was a crude, iron brazier. Thick, billowing mist exuded from it as some foul-smelling skaven concoction was burned down within – doubtless, it was the source of the sulphur fog. Attached to the lip of the brazier cup was a thick tube. It ran all the way to a metal pipe that was affixed to the birthing mother's spittle-flecked muzzle. Judging by the inert nature of all the skaven in the chamber,

Halgar surmised that the gas was used to sedate the disgusting creatures for when they were birthing the rat-kin multitudes.

Skaven slaves were also present in the pits. They carried long wooden poles at the end of which were filthy-looking sponges. As the dwarfs watched, the slaves dolefully patted the birth mothers down with the sodden sponges, presumably in an effort to keep them cool throughout their exertions.

Halgar could barely contain his revulsion and as he sneered contemptuously one of the birth mothers looked up at him with her beady eyes and squeaked a frantic warning. All around the room, the skaven stirred.

Halgar roared and buried a throwing axe in the birth mother's skull, splitting it open like an over-ripened fruit. The skaven slaves screeched first in horror at the blood fountaining from the birth mother's ruined skull and then with rage as they saw her murderers above. They dropped their poles and drew rusty blades, rushing towards an earth ramp that would get them out of the pit.

Thorig had already sped from his hiding place and lit Azgar's zharrum with the torch's embers. The fuse burned down quickly and the slayer tossed the sphere into the pit where it exploded, the catch releasing on impact and spraying flaming liquid all over the slaves and the birth mother's corpse. The stink of burning fur and the wrenching scream of dying rat-kin filled the air as Drimbold threw in his zharrum too and the pit became a bowl of raging fire.

Halgar rushed over to the second pit, two of the Grim Brotherhood in tow. One of the slaves was coming off the end of the earth ramp, a wicked barbed spear in hand. The longbeard booted it in the groin and sent the creature back down again before he threw his zharrum in after it, engulfing the birthing pen in flame. The third and final pit was immolated shortly after, Thorig tossing two of the fire bombs into it before any of the skaven within could react. Through fire, thick with oily black smoke from burning body fat, the writhing shapes of the birth mothers and their slowly cooking offspring could be seen. The rancid stink of roasting rat meat brought tears to Halgar's eyes.

'Come on!' he bellowed. 'Our work is done. Back to the foundry.'

The dwarfs gathered together, cutting down slaves as they went. From the back of the chamber a cohort of previously unseen clanrats wielding spears and halberds had mustered. They squeaked ferociously and came at the dwarfs with muzzles frothing. Thorig threw a fire bomb into them and the sheet of flame reduced the first rank to flailing torches. But a second rank came on. A thrown spear passed Halgar's ear and 'thunked' into the wall behind him.

'Out! Out now!' he cried, rallying the charge once the dwarfs were reunited.

Azgar and the other slayers went first, cleaving a path through a welter of slaves that had sprung up in their path. Thorig was behind them and, with Drimbold at his side, the Zhufbar dwarf cast more fire bombs into the chamber at will, determined to raze the wretched nest to the ground. As he ran, he coaxed the embers of the torch into life and soon the brand was aflame. Halgar was the rearguard, backing away quickly as the clanrats closed on them, trampling any slaves in their way such was their fury.

Barrelling through their skaven assailants the dwarfs crossed the threshold of the massive cavern, now wreathed in fire as a mighty conflagration took hold, and out into the tunnel again. The clanrats were almost upon them when Thorig turned and thrust the flaming brand into the satchel. Casting the spent torch aside he whirled the burning satchel around his head like a sling and threw it, fire bombs and all, into the nest entrance. A huge wall of fire sprang up from where the satchel hit the ground, so dense and ferocious that the pursuing skaven came to an abrupt halt and became hazy silhouettes through it.

'Well done, lad,' said Halgar, coughing some of the smoke from his lungs and smacking Thorig on the back.

The Zhufbar dwarf nodded exhaustedly, and lifted his helmet to wipe a swathe of sweat from his forehead.

'But we must not linger,' the longbeard continued, eyeing the inferno that prevented the rat-kins' immediate pursuit. Even now, vaguely discernible through the blaze, slaves heaped great clods of dirt into the wall of fire in an effort to extinguish it. 'Destiny awaits us,' he added, grinning.

The dwarfs fled back whence they had came, Azgar to the fore retracing his steps flawlessly. Only the Grim Brotherhood remained. Drimbold noticed the warriors, standing solemnly before the raging fire wall, axes held in readiness.

'Come on,' the Grey dwarf cried at them, slowing his flight, 'the rat-kin will soon give chase!'

Azgar saw Drimbold falter and tracked back to drag him onward.

'But they will surely be slain,' the Grey dwarf said.

'As is their oath,' Azgar told him. 'They knew their part in this. Their sacrifice will stall the rat-kin long enough for us to make ready in the foundry.'

'They are your warriors; you have not even bid them farewell.'

'That is not our way,' Azgar replied. 'They go to meet with an honourable death.' The slayer's tone was almost longing. 'Soon they will be received in Grimnir's hall, to fight the endless battle,' he added, fixing Drimbold with his stony gaze. 'I envy them, Grey dwarf.'

'THIS IS NOT as the lorekeeper described it,' said Rorek, scratching his head.

'It bears the name of the brewmaster, though,' Uthor replied, pointing out a stone plaque in which the words 'Brondold's Hall – His Brew Will Be Remembered' were carved in Khazalid. 'This must be where Ralkan meant for us to go.'

'It more resembles a lake than any drinking hall I have ever seen,' added Emelda.

The three dwarfs were standing upon a stone-slabbed platform, which fell away at the edge into a vast expanse of turgid, greenish water, many hundred feet long. The murky lagoon of crud was still, like tarnished glass, the upper portions of columns protruding through it all the way to the high ceiling. Foamy deposits lapped around the pillars where they split the surface, and clustered at the edges of the walls. Braziers still flickered, just above the waterline, an incredible feat given that they must have been lit for over fifty years or more. They were a further example of the miracle fuel of the dwarf guildmasters. The light

illuminated massive bronze heads, belonging to submerged statues and depicting the ancient brewmasters
and lords of the hold, the tips of their beards dipping
into the rancid reservoir.

Save for the stone epithet dedicated to the long dead
brewmaster, numerous wooden barrels, kegs and steins
held fast in the stagnant, reeking water made it clear
this was indeed the drinking hall that Ralkan had
described.

'You will reach Brondold's Hall, arriving from the
northern portal,' the lorekeeper had said. 'Beneath the
south wall there is a trapdoor. Though bolted, it will
lead into the drainage tunnels below. Traverse this tunnel and you will emerge in the reservoir of the Barduraz
Varn.'

Uthor recalled the words dimly – Ralkan had said
nothing of a vast, un-crossable lake. Regarding the massive expanse of flood water, he noticed a dwarf skeleton
clinging to one piece of floating detritus like some
macabre buoy. It was the first time the throng had seen
any of their slain brethren in the entirety of the hold,
save for the remains of King Ulfgan. Uthor felt a tingle
of dread reaching up his spine as he watched the dead
dwarf, bobbing lightly in the rank water despite the
illusion of stillness, and was reminded of the recent
loss of Bulrik and Henkil. He tried to crush the memory quickly, but couldn't prevent his mind wandering
back to those frantic moments at the waterfall, the pal-
lid face of Rorek appearing through the spray with
news of the clan leaders' deaths.

The rest of the way down the narrow path had been
conducted in silent remembrance. So much death, and
so needless – I have brought this fate upon them. I

have brought it upon us all, Uthor thought darkly, averting his gaze to peer into the impenetrable murk. A raft of unseen terrors that might be harboured in the water's depths sprang unbidden into his mind. All dwarfs knew of the slumbering beasts that lay in the bowels of the Black Water, awaiting prey foolish enough to quest there.

'Let us quit this place with all haste,' said Emelda quietly at Uthor's shoulder. The thane of Kadrin turned to her and saw the concern for him etched upon her face.

'Yes,' Uthor agreed, his grim disposition diminishing before her countenance. 'But how are we to cross,' he added, moving away from the clan daughter to stand at the edge of a grand stairway that had once led down to the revelry of the hall but was now swallowed by a greenish mire. 'I can see no rafts.' Uthor crouched down and dipped one finger into the water, removing a thin piece of clouded film that overlaid the surface of the unnatural lagoon.

'We cannot swim it,' Emelda replied, gazing out across the stagnant plain, 'the distance is too long.'

'We would not get far in our armour, anyway,' Rorek piped up, 'even using the barrels for buoyancy.' The engineer was inspecting a statue that had collapsed on the stone platform, leastways the detached head and part of the torso had. Rapping it lightly with a small hammer from his tool belt, a dull gonging sound resonated around the chamber.

'Hollow,' Rorek muttered, scrutinizing the statue head further. The fall had made a clean break at the neck and he was able to peer inside its massive confines. 'Perhaps... Uthor,' he added suddenly, turning to the thane, 'we'll need those barrels after all.'

The engineer proffered a length of rope with a small metal grapnel attached. 'Have you ever been fishing?' he asked.

THE 'THWOMP' OF whirling rope cut through the air, followed by a snap as Uthor let fly. His aim was true but the barrel shattered under the impact of the grapnel... again.

'You are a warrior born, son of Algrim,' said Emelda, who'd been watching the thane's efforts for several swings, while Rorek busied himself with the statue head. She had no clue what the mercurial engineer was planning, but she felt certain it would not adhere to the strictures of the Engineers' Guild. 'Even fishing for barrels, you cannot resist the killing stroke.'

Uthor looked askance at Emelda, slightly ruffled and reddening at the cheeks. He was about to swing again when he stopped himself and turned to face the clan daughter.

'You think you can do better?' he asked, offering the rope and grapnel, now lathered in the water's stagnant residue.

Emelda smiled and took the rope and hook. She then walked over to the edge of the platform and tested the weight of them in her hands. Taking a step back, she swung the rope around swiftly in a wide arc with practiced ease, the clinging filth attached to it flicking outwards in a vile spray. Emelda then let fly. She noticed Uthor watch it as it landed just behind a barrel.

'A good effort,' said the thane, puffing up his chest slightly and trying to keep the grin from his face.

Emelda didn't take the bait; she merely gathered the rope slowly, allowing the grapnel to trail through the water and snag on the end of the barrel, after which she drew it in effortlessly. When the barrel bobbed against the edge of the platform she turned to Uthor.

'A defter touch was required,' she explained.

Uthor muttered gruffly to himself as he stooped to pick up the barrel and set it on the platform.

'Where did you learn that?' Uthor asked as Emelda cast out again and snagged another barrel.

'My father taught me,' she replied, dragging her catch through the murky water. 'Fishing in the mountain streams and lakes of Everpeak.'

'You mean the High King?'

'No,' said Emelda, bringing the barrel to the water's edge for Uthor to retrieve. 'The High King is not my father.'

'My apologies, milady, when I saw you in the court of Karaz-a-Karak, I thought–'

'My father is dead.' The rope sagged briefly in Emelda's grip and she looked at Uthor. 'He was the king's cousin. When he was killed, King Skorri took me on as his ward in recognition of an old debt between them.'

'Dreng tromm,' uttered Uthor, head slightly bowed in respect. 'May I ask, milady, how did he die?'

'He was inspecting our family's mine holdings and there was a tunnel collapse. We lost thirteen brave dawi that day. When the prospectors recovered their bodies they found that some of the braces had been gnawed upon and a second section of tunnel undermining the upper shaft.'

'Rat-kin,' Uthor assumed.

'Yes.' Emelda's expression was pained but also flushed with contained rage. 'So you see I not only came here to ensure that the great days of the Karaz Ankor return, but on a matter of personal grudgement also.'

Uthor fell silent and then took his leave when Emelda turned away. He went over to Rorek to find out what he wanted with the barrels. The whip and pull of the rope and grapnel followed in his wake as Emelda worked out her anger.

'Do you HAVE any beer skins?' Rorek asked intent on an inverted distilling funnel set into a metal frame.

'You seek to drink us a way across the lagoon?' Uthor countered, a bemused look on his face as he reached onto his belt. 'Here,' he added, 'though they dried up long ago.'

'Good,' Rorek replied, taking the skins Uthor offered without looking. 'No use in wasting grog,' he added, working meticulously.

'That is the last of them,' said Emelda, appearing behind Uthor with one more barrel. The thane avoided her gaze for the moment, the weight of her grief adding to his own. She set the barrel down. When she rested her hand upon his shoulder, Uthor felt his mood lighten instantly.

'We are almost ready,' said Rorek, interrupting the silent exchange as he got to his feet and revealed the contraption he'd been labouring over. The small funnel was set over a tiny fire that burned with a white-hot flame. Vaporous heat was visible emanating from a shallow, metal cup in which the fire was contained that fed into one of Uthor's beer skins affixed to the narrow spout of the funnel. Uthor's eyes widened as, in seconds, the leather skin inflated and became fat with heat vapour.

Satisfied, Rorek bent down and plucked the skin from the spout and stoppered it quickly. He then raised the skin to his ear.

Uthor was nonplussed and exchanged a worried glance with Emelda. 'Grungni's rump, tell me you are not trying to converse with that skin. I thought only the lodefinder was prone to such madness.'

'I am listening to hear if any air is escaping,' Rorek explained then lowered the skin to look at Uthor, again. 'It is not,' he added.

'Fascinating, I am certain,' Uthor stated, 'but how is this to get us across the lagoon?'

'Alone, it will not,' Rorek told them. 'We need this.' The engineer pointed to the bronze statue head. The Zhufbar dwarf had lashed all of the barrels, save the last, retrieved by Emelda, to the outside and had bored a hole through the very top of the statue's helmet, wide enough for a rope to pass through.

'Have you been eating frongol, engineer?' Uthor asked, staring at the giant bronze head.

'Stand aside,' Rorek growled, muttering beneath his breath as he tramped past the thane. Once he'd reached the platform's edge, he unslung his crossbow.

'You'd best not be pointing that thing anywhere near me,' Uthor warned him.

Rorek ignored the baiting and hunted around on his voluminous tool belt. Finding what he was looking for he attached it to the crossbow by means of its ingenious racking mechanism. After ratcheting the ammunition back, the engineer braced himself and took careful aim, flicking up the sighting ring with his thumb. He pumped the trigger and the crossbow loosed, sending a large, harpoon-like bolt into the roof with a rippling length of rope chasing after it. The thick, metal quarrel stuck fast with a shudder of stone, and three spiked prongs flicked out of a concealed compartment inside the shaft to latch onto the rock like a pincer. The rope was attached to the other end of the quarrel by means of a small pulley.

'Grapnel bolt,' Rorek explained with no small amount of boastful pride, gathering up the slack in his hands until the rope was taut. 'Here, take this,' he added, passing Uthor a section of rope before rushing over to tether the opposite end to the statue head.

'And what am I to do with this, engineer?'

'Pull,' came the laconic response.

Uthor did as he was told, Emelda joining in when she realised what Rorek intended. The engineer added his own brawn to the task and as they heaved the rope running through the pulley the statue head was slowly lifted upright and then off the ground.

'Keep going,' Rorek snarled through clenched teeth; the bronze head was monstrously heavy. As it rose higher, the weight of the statue swung itself out over the lagoon.

Satisfied with its elevation, Rorek shouted, 'Stop!' adding, 'hold it there,' as he let go of the rope before taking the trailing end piling behind Uthor and Emelda. He then tied it around the upper remains of the statue that still sat on the platform, until the rope was taut.

'Now,' Rorek said, 'release it, slowly.'

Uthor and Emelda did as they were asked. With a savage creak of metal as it tightened further at its anchor point, the statue head lurched down a few feet before it came to a halt. Rorek wiped a swathe of sweat from his forehead, and not from his earlier exertions.

'It holds,' he announced.

'I can see that, engineer,' said Uthor, 'what would you have us do now?'

'Now,' Rorek said, turning to face them both, 'we get wet.'

UTHOR TIED OFF a makeshift belt of inflated beer skins around his waist and chest as he prepared to walk down the grand stairway and into the wretched water.

'There is no honour in this garb,' he moaned. 'If I am slain and found like this by my ancestors there will be a reckoning against you and your clan, engineer.'

'Without them you will sink like a stone in your armour,' Rorek replied. 'And then where would your honour be?'

Uthor grumbled beneath his breath and started down the steps. Emelda awaited the outcome pensively behind him.

Ice blades stabbed into his legs as the thane of Kadrin waded into the water. Now up to his waist, the stagnant film sheathing the lagoon parted before him like clinging gossamer. At last he found the courage to plunge out into the open depths. Uthor felt the pull of his armour dragging him downward into the murk and for a moment he panicked, seeking the edge of the platform in an effort to heave himself up and out.

'Don't flap,' Rorek snapped at him, 'you will sink and drown.'

'Easy to say stood on dry land,' said Uthor, spluttering water. 'I have already had my dunkin' – dawi are not meant for water.' Taking a breath, spitting the turgid fluid from his mouth, Uthor managed to calm down and spread his arms wide as Rorek had instructed him. Pushing away slightly from the edge, incredibly he found he was afloat.

'By the beard of Grimnir, I can't believe that worked,' Uthor said, relieved and still spluttering – the beer skins only just putting his head and shoulders above the waterline.

'Neither can I,' Rorek muttered beneath his breath.

'Speak up,' growled Uthor, bobbing up and down slightly like a cork in soup, using his arms like oars to slowly position himself beneath the hollow statue head hanging above.

'I said, now milady can try.'

Uthor grumbled some more and fell silent as he waited for Emelda, similarly laden with inflated beer skins, to join him in the water.

Rorek came last of all, the engineer seeming as if he almost enjoyed the swim. All three positioned themselves beneath the shadow of the hanging statue head, staring up into its vast hollows. The engineer ferreted around in the water, reaching for something on his belt and eventually pulled out a throwing axe.

'Give that to me,' Uthor barked, 'you would as likely hit one of us.'

Flushed with embarrassment, Rorek passed the weapon to Uthor.

'You had best be right about this, engineer,' Uthor warned, holding the axe in one hand. 'Now you will see the killing stroke,' he boasted, winking at Emelda.

With a grunt, Uthor let fly. The throwing axe span through the air and sheared the tethered rope in two, sending the hollow statue head plummeting earthward. In the instant before the massive thing plunged into the water, the three dwarfs huddled together instinctively. Uthor noticed Rorek had his eyes closed and his fingers firmly crossed. 'Grungni's balls...' he muttered as the statue head crashed down.

'WAIT, I HEAR something,' Hakem hissed, edging up to the end of the tunnel before peering surreptitiously around the curved corner.

At the end of a short, wide corridor was the overflow grate. Two mighty hammerers fashioned from the very rock of the mountain stood sentinel before the massive gate that dominated the entire back wall of the tunnel. Their hammers were part of the actual mechanism that allowed the water through. At this moment they were clasped together – the Barduraz Varn was obviously still closed.

Huge cogs of iron with broad, fat teeth were bolted to the left facing wall and a bewildering array of inter-linking chains and conjoined pistons fed from them to the inner-workings of the grate itself.

Dwarfed by the immense structure was a small cohort of rat-kin, obviously sent to guard the grate from interference – a dozen clanrats and a pair of Clan Skryre engineers bearing another fire-spewing con-trivance, similar to that which had caused such havoc in the Wide Western Way.

Hakem rolled back around the curve to where the others were waiting.

'Twelve guards,' the Barak Varr dwarf reported, his demeanour increasingly taciturn and pugnacious since losing the Honakinn Hammer.

Gromrund cracked his knuckles and readied his great hammer, sloshing determinedly through the floodwa-ter. 'There is little time for it,' he said matter-of-factly, 'but needs must.'

Hakem stopped him.

'They also have sorcerous machinery of some sort.'

'Pah,' snorted Gromrund, marching past the merchant thane. 'Skaven engineering is cheap and unreliable. Doubtless, it will misfire before it can do any damage.'

Hakem blocked him again.

'Step aside, ufdi,' Gromrund snapped irritably, 'you will not soil your beard in this fight,' he added, though after the mining shaft the entire skorong was so lathered in soot it would be hard to notice either way.

'I have seen its effects with my own eyes,' Hakem warned, his gaze unwavering. 'And it is deadly. Armour, for one, is no proof against it. Burned to ash by the sorcerous fire of the skaven is not an honourable death.'

Gromrund backed down, planting his hammer head into the ground so he could lean on the haft.

'So then, ufdi, what are we to do? Wait here until the rat-kin die of boredom.'

'Lure them and thin their numbers.' Thalgrim's voice broke up the building tension.

Hakem and Gromrund turned to look at the lodefinder, who was grinning ferally. He lifted up his helmet and at once the dwarfs were assailed by a pungent, if not entirely unpleasant aroma.

'Lucky chuf,' Thalgrim explained, holding out the piece of moulding cheese in his hand.

Ralkan's eyes widened when he saw it, acutely aware of his groaning stomach.

'The skaven have a taste for it,' Thalgrim added, darkly, deciding not to mention his suspicions about the ambush. Plopping the remains of the chunk into his mouth, Thalgrim chewed for a moment then swallowed, savouring the taste.

Ralkan's shoulders sagged, his loudly rumbling belly seemingly inconsolable.

Gromrund was agog. 'Are you mad, lodefinder, you have just eaten our bait?'

'I did not want to waste it,' Thalgrim replied, licking his gums and teeth for any lingering traces of the ancient cheese. 'Besides, it is not wasted,' he added, breathing hard into the hammerer's face who gagged at once.

'Very well,' said Gromrund, putting up his hand to ward off any further emissions. 'Go and do what you must. You stay back, lorekeeper,' he said to Ralkan who was happy to oblige.

Thalgrim nodded, creeping stealthily to the end of the curved tunnel. Once he'd reached the end, he peered around once to see that the skaven guards were still there and then blew a breath, thickly redolent of chuf, towards them, hoping that the shallow breeze would carry it. He watched silently from the shadows, acutely aware of the other dwarfs behind him with weapons readied.

At first there was nothing. The skaven just chittered quietly to each other in their ear-wrenching tongue. But then the snout of one of the clanrats twitched and it sniffed at the air. Then another did the same, and another. There was a bout of frenetic squeaking and several of the rat-kin abandoned their posts to follow the cloying stink wafting towards them.

Thalgrim gave them another blast for good measure and then retreated around the corner.

'They come,' he whispered, unslinging his pick-mattock.

The dwarfs hugged the shadows, keeping to the very edge of the tunnel. The sound of padding, splashing feet carried on the cheese-tainted air towards them, getting closer with every second as their curious enemies approached.

Thalgrim held his breath when he saw the first clan-rat emerge from around the corner. Incredibly the creature's beady eyes were closed, using smell alone for guidance as it tracked the chuf's scent. Four of its flea-infested brethren followed, wielding a mixture of spears, blades and heavier-looking glaives.

Once they had all passed the threshold of the tunnel, the dwarfs attacked.

Thalgrim smashed the neck of one of the rats from behind, crushing its spine inward as it collapsed with a mewling cry. A second fell to Hakem's borrowed axe, the blade cutting a deep wound in the clanrat's belly through which its innards spilled. The creature looked dumbfounded at the dwarf as it tried to gather up its organs. One of the Sootbeards buried his pick in its forehead to silence it. Gromrund killed another two; one he choked with the wutroth haft of his great hammer, a second he bludgeoned with the hammer head. The last was cut high and low by the remaining Sootbeard dwarfs, its spear falling from nerveless fingers before it could retaliate.

'Tidy work,' muttered Gromrund, wiping a slick of expelled blood from his breastplate. 'That leaves seven, plus the war engine.'

'Let's take them now,' Thalgrim hissed urgently. 'They will only have time for one shot.'

The rat-kin had caught the scent of blood on the breeze and were squeaking at each other agitatedly, pointing towards the tunnel with clawed fingers.

'For Grimnir!' Gromrund bellowed, overwhelmed by battle-fever, and raced around the corner to meet his foes. The others followed – all except Ralkan, who awaited the outcome of the skirmish pensively – making their oaths as they went.

Screeching skaven levelled spears and blades as the dwarfs charged, before parting to allow the fire cannon through. A mighty whoosh of flame swallowed the cackling retort of the Clan Skryre engineers as they unleashed their war engine gleefully and lit up the tunnel in a blinding flare of angry green light. Thalgrim threw himself aside, flooring Gromrund in the process, but two of the Sootbeards were engulfed in the deadly conflagration and died screaming.

Rising from the floodwater, the hammerer parried a spear thrust with his hammer haft before stamping down on his assailant's shin, breaking it. He finished the clanrat with an overhead blow to the skull. Red ooze flowed thickly from the rat-kin's ruined head as it languished in the water.

Up-close, Hakem launched his shield like a discus at the fire cannon. The spinning weapon severed the first engineer's head and embedded in the chest of the second. So mauled, the pair fell back and splashed into the water in a rapidly spreading pool of their own fluids.

There was a gurgled cry as the last Sootbeard was impaled by a spear to the neck. A burly skaven shrugged the dwarf's corpse off the blade contemptuously before rounding on Thalgrim. The lodefinder ducked a savage swipe and came under the blow to ram the head of his mattock into the creature's chin. Dazed, the rat-kin staggered back but, blowing out a billowing

line of blood and snot, recovered its composure and
came at Thalgrim again. A blur of steel arrested its
charge, as the creature was smashed against the wall, a
thrown axe 'thunking' into its torso. The lodefinder
turned to see Hakem snarl as the rat-kin slumped down
and was still, and nodded his thanks. The merchant
thane nodded back, grimly.

The skaven were all dead. Gromrund finished the
last, crushing its skull with his boot as it tried to crawl
away through the flood water. He spat on the corpse
afterward and then turned to the others.

'They were still good deaths,' he remarked, regarding
the charred corpses of the two Sootbeards and the
floating, impaled body of the other.

'We must find a way to break the mechanism,' said
Hakem coldly, straight back to business. 'And I think I
know of such a way,' he added.

The other two dwarfs followed his gaze to the still
twitching Clan Skryre engineers and the volatile fire
cannon still strapped to their bodies.

'STEADY...' WARNED THALGRIM as he carefully lifted the
broad barrel of the skaven cannon where its volatile
mixture was held. 'Easy does it.'

'Filthy rat-kin, I doubt I will ever get the stink from
my beard and clothes,' moaned Hakem, carrying one of
the dead Clan Skryre engineers and having subse-
quently wrenched his shield free of its wretched corpse.

'Consider yourself lucky, merchant,' Gromrund countered, lugging the other corpse as he tried to arch his
neck away from the vile burden. 'Mine has no head!'

Between them, the three dwarfs heaved the bulky
skaven war engine and its mouldering crew to the

network of cogs and pistons that were the mechanism for the overflow. Ralkan – having been summoned once the fight was over – was with them, sat on a chunk of fallen rock as he held a burning brand aloft. The lorekeeper stayed back from the heavy lifting work, instead recording the names of the slain Sootbeards in the book of remembering that he rested on his lap.

'You are certain this will work,' grumbled Gromrund, on the verge of wedging the entire foul assembly into the grinding and massive cog teeth.

'Aye, I'm certain,' growled Thalgrim, a little put out by the hammerer's obvious lack of confidence. 'We Sootbeards have a close affinity with rock and stone, that much is true, but I also know something of engineering works, master hammerer,' the lodefinder added indignantly, before lumping the barrel and its various attached pipes and paraphernalia into the mechanism.

'Quickly, now,' Thalgrim said, edging backwards urgently. The cogs stalled for a moment, an ugly screeching noise emanating from the mechanism as it tried to chew flesh, bone and wood. 'It won't hold long,' he added, reaching out for Ralkan's torch as the other two dwarfs disappeared from beyond his eyeline. The lorekeeper had since packed away the book of remembering and he too was backing off.

Thalgrim grasped the brand and flung it, end over end, into the wrecked skaven cannon, which was even now haemorrhaging flammable liquid. As he threw the torch, Thalgrim turned and ran before diving into the shallow water. The others rapidly followed suit. The flame caught, igniting the chemicals in the barrel immediately, devouring the crude artifice and its crew hungrily.

Thunder cracked as the force of the massive explosion tore into the tunnel, amplified as it resonated off the stout walls, so powerful that it vibrated armour and teeth. Chunks of dislocated rock plummeted into the water in the aftermath, fire blossomed briefly and dust motes fell like a veil of shedding skin.

Thalgrim was the first to poke his head above the water and check that it was over.

'Clear,' he said, coughing back a cloud of dust and thick smoke.

'It is fortunate we are not dead!' barked Gromrund, after spitting out several mouthfuls of rank flood water. 'My ears still ring from the blast,' he added, waggling a finger in one.

'At least it worked,' said Hakem, without joy. The merchant thane was on his feet and surveying the carnage wrought upon the overflow mechanism.

'Dreng tromm,' Gromrund muttered, breathlessly as he went to stand beside him.

The stout dwarfen mechanism, that which had been built in the reign of Hraddi Ironhand, that which had withstood the wrath of the ages and even endured the Time of Woes, was ruined. A blackened scar overlaid a twisted mess of metal and broken stone. It was all that remained of the once great artifice of the engineers of Karak Varn.

Ralkan was beside himself and could not speak through tears of profound remorse. All of the dwarfs felt it; another small part of the Karaz Ankor meeting with ruination.

Is this how it is all to end, thought Gromrund? We dawi forced to lay waste to our own domains?

'It is sealed,' stated Hakem flatly, breaking the hammerer's solemn pondering. 'We had best move on,' he added, turning away from the gut-wrenching vista.

'Cold is the wind that blows through your house,' uttered Gromrund as the merchant thane walked away.

Hakem did not respond.

'How WILL WE know when we have reached our destination?' Uthor's voice was tinny and resonant within the close confines of the giant 'diving' helm, Rorek had constructed.

'It is simple,' the engineer remarked, even the muscles in his face straining as, together with his companions, he half lugged, half pushed the immense hollow helmet of bronze. 'We either reach the trapdoor at the south wall or we don't. The air will not last in here indefinitely,' he said.

At that Uthor looked down briefly at the water that had now reached his upper torso. It had been rising ever since the helm had crashed on top of them; its descent arrested by the numerous barrels that Rorek had assured them provided flotation. Despite that, though, the three dwarfs still needed to heave and push the helm forward, occasionally grinding its severed base against the flagstones beneath when the massive chunk of statue dipped.

Thanks to the Zhufbar dwarf's ingenuity, the dwarfs were able to traverse the murky depths of the lagoon through Brondold's Hall in what the engineer termed a 'submersible'. The thane of Kadrin had no clue to the word's meaning, nor had he any desire to discover it. All he knew was that a pocket of air was trapped in the upper reaches of the hollowed helm that allowed them to breath, whilst submerged far below the waterline.

'Your assurances provide much comfort, engineer,' Uthor growled.

'Speak less,' Rorek snapped abruptly. 'There is only a finite amount of air and the more we use, the less we will have,' he added, indicating the steadily rising waterline.

'Bah,' Uthor muttered. 'Dawi were not meant to be submerged in a tomb of bronze and iron.'

Emelda kept her mouth clamped shut throughout the exchange. Sweat peeled off her forehead in streaking lines that ran down her face. Not from exertion; she too was a warrior born and the equal of any male. No, it was from wide-eyed fear of being trapped here in the watery gloom, of her last breath being a mouthful of rank and foul-tasting water. There was no honour in it. As she worked, just that little bit harder than Uthor and Rorek, to get them to their destination, she surveyed the inner hollows of the diving helm nervously. Tiny fissures had already begun to appear in the aging bronze, and tiny rivulets of water ran weakly through the smallest of cracks. One of those cracks grew wider, even as she maintained her fearful vigil, so wide the water was nigh-on gushing. She opened her mouth to shout a warning but no sound came out at first. Desperately, and through a supreme effort of will, she found her voice.

'It is splitting!'

Rorek saw the danger instantly and redoubled his efforts. 'Heave,' he bellowed, the timbre of his voice thunderous and urgent inside the helm. 'The south wall cannot be far.'

Uthor grunted, shouldering as much of the burden as he could. A dull screeching sound, muffled by fathoms of flood water, came to the surface as the dwarfs leant their weight to one side of the helm and pitched it at an angle against the flagstones underfoot.

They panted and gasped with the intense effort. The water level rose, hitting their shoulders. In a few more seconds of frantic endeavour it had reached their necks.

'For all your worth!' Uthor cried smashing his body into the side of the giant helm, spluttering as the water came over his mouth and nose.

Muffled silence filled the statue helm as the last of the dwarfs' air was expended. Not only was it their lifeline, but it had also provided additional buoyancy. Without it, the three dwarfs took the full weight of the massive bronze helm.

Uthor felt as if leaden anchors had been attached to his ankles as he dragged one heavy foot in front of the other, his urgency suddenly blighted with agonising slowness. His lungs burned; there was little air left in his body. Then he felt the ground beneath his feet change subtly. Stamping down, something bent and yielded beneath him. He tried to peer through the gloomy water but all he saw was a cloud-filled murk. He raised Ulfgan's axe; it was like lifting a tree. The runes etched on the blade shone diffusely, like a submerged beacon, as he struck down towards his feet.

The ground broke away, broad spikes of it funnelled upward into the water-filled helm, and Uthor fell. Rorek and Emelda were lost to him in the clinging, green-tinged darkness. Something pulled at him, a forceful current propelling the dwarf to Valaya knew where. He barrelled and spun at first, smacking into unseen obstacles. Pain flared in his side as something sharp and jagged bit into him.

Fighting hard, Uthor got his bearings and started to swim, pumping legs and arms determinedly as the last of his air was used up. He was in a tunnel. So narrow and tight it could only be the one that Ralkan had spoken off. The way seemed long, black spots beginning to form in Uthor's hazy vision. Soon he too would be lost. His legs felt heavy, his arms seemed to hang limply at his sides and the sense of falling, falling deep into the abyssal gloom overwhelmed him...

Light flared, dim and washed out. Air rushed, unabated, into his body as Uthor was suddenly lifted free of oblivion, coughing and spluttering into renewed existence.

A figure stood over him, serene and benevolent, her arms outstretched and welcoming. Long, golden hair cascaded down her shoulders and a halo rimmed her head, her countenance refulgent in its reflected glory.

'Valaya...' Uthor breathed, bleary-eyed and slightly incoherent.

'Uthor,' said the figure. Strong arms shook the thane of Kadrin.

'Uthor.' The tone was urgent but low.

Emelda crouched over him, her face creased with concern.

Uthor came to senses, abruptly aware that Rorek supported his back. He'd lost his helmet somewhere along the way, his shield too – Thank Grimnir he still had his axe. Together, his two companions held him up, above the shallow water of a vast and expansive reservoir. Hraddi's reservoir, just as the lorekeeper had described. They had reached the site of the Barduraz Varn.

Uthor got to his feet and found the low-lying water came up to his knees.

'Keep down,' Emelda hissed, Rorek moving silently to her side, so low only the tips of his shoulders pierced the waterline.

Uthor did as he was told and crouched next to the clan daughter on the opposite side.

'We are not alone,' she hissed, pointing across the massive, flat reservoir.

Uthor followed her gesture. There, just beyond the edge of where the water ended in a rat-kin made platform of shovelled rock and earth, slaves toiled and hooded Clan Skryre overseers chattered. Thickly-armoured, black-furred skaven carrying curved swords and a number of their smaller brethren equipped with spears milled around in rough cohorts. Two other Skryre agents stood close by the bulkier skaven guards, drenched in filthy robes and carrying bizarre-looking staffs seemingly fashioned from a riot of crude skaven technology. Crackling energy played across spinning diodes and jutting forks. Uthor was reminded of the skaven sorcerer they had faced during their flight from Karak Varn all those months ago. He bit back the memory of Lokki's death during that dark retreat and re-focussed his attention.

Mercifully, the ratmen were intent on their labours and had not seen the dwarfs emerge from the underground river.

Uthor's eyes widened as they tracked further and took in a massive, infernal construction that dominated the back of the immense chamber. Huge, wooden wheels bolted together with crude strips of copper and iron were connected to the towering, ramshackle device. They ran rapid and wild with the frantic efforts of the slaves and giant rats imprisoned within.

Arcs of eldritch lightning flew across spiked prongs far above as the desperate slaves were urged to greater endeavour with the lash and crackling staves of the Skryre agents. All the while in the background, behind a raft of clumsy observation towers and platforms, great pistons thudded up and down in relentless unison and the water in which the device was sat, where the makeshift skaven embankment fell away, gradually drained.

'Valaya preserve us,' Uthor breathed. It was a huge pump; the rat-kin had devised a way to clear the flood waters from Karak Varn. His heart stammered when he perceived what was stood behind the wretched skaven contraption. It was the great sluice gate itself – the Barduraz Varn.

GROMRUND CURSED LOUDLY, striking his head for the seventh time as he and Thalgrim climbed up the narrow shaft of Dibna's Drop.

'You would find the going easier if you removed that warhelm, hammerer,' the voice of the lodefinder echoed down to Gromrund.

'I shall never remove it,' came the caustic response of the hammerer, the warhelm of his ancestors still ringing loudly in his ears. 'Some oaths were not meant to be broken,' he added in a murmur.

They'd left Hakem and Ralkan behind, waiting at the crossroads beneath the lofty shaft through which the two dwarfs now toiled. Ralkan was in no condition to climb, the book of remembering was a weighty burden to bear and with only one hand a climb upwards was too difficult for Hakem. Besides, as he'd muttered when Thalgrim and Gromrund had departed, someone needed to stay behind and guard the lorekeeper. The first part of the climb had been conducted via the lodefinder's rope, tied off at the mine shaft of the Rockcutter Waystation; the second meant scaling a length of thick chain hanging down from Dibna's Chamber, doubtless a remnant of when there had once been a lift cage.

Thalgrim went hand over hand, his pace quick and assured with the ready practice of repetition. The lodefinder seemed to bend and swing from the path of every jutting crag, every errant spike of rock, though the way upwards was largely clear of obstruction.

Gromrund found it harder going in his much heavier full plate, great hammer smacking against his back as he climbed. More than once he slipped, and each time he found his grip again. Thalgrim made no such mistakes and was soon far ahead of him in the soot-drenched darkness, the flame of his helmet candle flickering faintly above like a firefly.

When Gromrund at last reached the zenith of the shaft and Dibna's Chamber in the third deep, he found the lodefinder waiting with hands in tunic pockets and a smouldering pipe pinched between his lips.

'There,' he said, nodding in the direction of the stone statue of Dibna the Inscrutable, still just as they'd left it, bearing the weight of the room. 'A mattock blow to the left ankle, precisely three and three-eighths inches from the tip of Dibna's boot, will collapse the statue and give us enough time to climb back down.'

'And you know this, just by looking at it?' said Gromrund, a little breathlessly.

'Aye, I do,' Thalgrim replied, supping on his pipe. 'That and the rock–'

'Please, lad,' uttered Gromrund, 'don't say it.'

The lodefinder shrugged and test swung his mattock a few times before advancing forward carefully. 'Precision and a deftness of touch is the key,' he muttered.

Gromrund gripped his shoulder before he got any further.

'Wait,' snapped the hammerer.

'What is it? This deep is likely crawling with grobi and rat-kin by now, we should not linger.'

'I have not yet heard the wyvern-horn. We cannot release the waters until the slayer and the rest are ready.'

'Then I hope it is soon, for if the vermin come – and come they will – then we will have no choice but to act,' said Thalgrim.

'Then we had best hope they do not,' muttered Gromrund.

CHAPTER THIRTEEN

AZGAR EMERGED BACK into the foundry, Thorig at his heels with Drimbold and Halgar bringing up the rear.

'Close and bar the gate,' the longbeard growled, through rasping breaths. He was bent almost double, hands clamped to his knees and wheezing.

Drimbold went to his aid but recoiled before the venerable dwarf's bark.

'Leave me be, half-dwarf,' he snarled. 'I do not need the likes of you to help me stand and fight. I was fighting battles before some of your ancestors were beardlings.'

With a resounding clang, the gates to the foundry were shut and the bar slid across. Enraged skaven chittering emanating from beyond it was cut off abruptly as the way into the further deeps was sealed.

'Make ready,' bellowed Azgar, a half glance at Halgar to make certain he was still fit and able. The gnarled old longbeard was back upright and swinging his axe to work the cramps from his arm and shoulder.

Good enough, thought the slayer and marshalled the meagre dwarf forces that stood before him in four lines of iron and steel, axes and hammers ready, shields held to the fore.

Towards the barred gate the foundry plaza narrowed to such an extent it was possible to cover its breadth with twenty-five shields. Three further lines, similarly-armed, stood stoically behind it. If one dwarf fell, another would take his place. They were to hold the skaven as long as they could, defending solidly as only dwarfs knew how and infuriate the vermin hordes so they committed all their forces to the attack. Should the lines fail – and fail they would, Azgar knew – then the forgemaster's platform would be their egress and the site of their last stand, one worthy of a saga the slayer hoped.

'The rat-kin come,' Azgar said as he appraised the dwarfen ranks, 'and they are angered,' he added with a feral grin. A rousing cheer met his words.

Relentless thudding came from the foundry gate. Metal creaked and moaned against the determined assault and the bar bent outwards slightly with every blow.

'They will soon be upon us,' hissed Halgar to the slayer, who had taken up his position in the middle of the first line.

'Yes,' Azgar replied – a glint in his eye as he stood alongside the longbeard. His steely gaze never left the gate. When it shuddered and the bar began to split he tightened his grip on the haft of his axe. 'Let them come.'

Another crash and the gate shook hard. The dwarfs remained in silence, jaws locked and hearts racing in anticipation of the imminent battle. For most, if not all, it would likely be their last.

The gate was rocked again.

It was met with stony silence. The tension was almost unbearable.

'Shed blood with me,' Halgar cried out suddenly to the throng. 'Shed blood and be my brother. We are the sons of Grungni. Alone we are rocks; together we are as enduring as a mountain!'

'Aye!' came the response as almost a hundred dwarf voices responded in unison.

The gate shuddered for the last time and was ripped outwards, wrenched almost off its hinges. From the black void of the unknown came the skaven, squeaking and snarling in apoplectic rage.

'Quarrellers!' Halgar bellowed, and a host of crossbow-bearing dwarfs of the Flintheart clan came forward from the second rank, their clan leader Kaggi amongst them.

'Loose!' cried Kaggi and the snapping retort of flung quarrels filled the air. So densely packed, a rat-kin fell to every bolt but the skaven did not falter and the dead and dying were crushed. With no time for a second volley, the Flinthearts retreated behind the first rank shield wall to draw axes and hammers.

The furred skaven wave fell upon the throng without pause and engulfed it. Blades clashed, shields clanged and blood slicked the flagstones of the foundry plaza in torrents. The dwarfs reeled before the sudden,

furious onslaught. Many warriors fell clutching
grievous wounds, only to be stomped to death by the
relentless rat-kin masses driving forward. Other dwarfs,
the Flinthearts amongst them, fought hard to fill the
gaps in their shield wall but the skaven pressed with
unremitting wrath, their frenzy evident in their
foaming muzzles. Halgar was at the centre of it,
separated from Azgar somehow but with Drimbold
now at his side.

'Remember, King Snaggi Ironhandson at the Bryndal
Vale,' the longbeard bellowed as he fought. 'Remember
his oaths, my brothers, as I remember mine. Sing your
death songs loud, bellow your defiance to the deep, 'til
the sound echoes throughout the Halls of the Ancestors!' he said, hacking left and right, using his shield as
a bludgeon, his axe stitching a red haze in the air
around him. 'Join me now, brave dawi. Join me in
death!'

A rallying cry erupted from the dwarf ranks with all
the power and thunder of a landslide. Clan warriors
dug their heels in and repulsed the skaven horde with
all the steel they could muster. Halgar drove at the vermin with added purpose to let the other dawi see his
defiance. The stink of killing got into his nostrils and
he felt empowered. Perhaps it was infectious, even the
Grey dwarf seemed full with battle lust.

What Drimbold lacked in skill, he made up for with
effort. He guarded Halgar's side with such vehemence
that even the longbeard couldn't help but notice his
fervour.

A surge to the left of the skaven horde got Halgar's
attention as he cleaved another clanrat down. He felt it
ripple down the front rank. Following the source of the

tremor he saw the right dwarfen flank collapsing as the rat-kin scurried their way around the edges of the shield wall.

'Reinforce the flank,' the longbeard bellowed above the roar of combat. 'Don't let them get behind us.'

Kaggi saw the danger and, shouting commands, gathered his warriors to bolster the failing flank. As the brave clan leader led the way a spear flung by some unseen hand skewered him in the neck. Kaggi fell, clutching the wound, his lifeblood spilling eagerly. He was quickly lost to Halgar but the clan leader's warriors, enraged at Kaggi's death, pressed with fury and the line was re-strengthened again.

Halgar averted his gaze. The sorrow pricking at his heart turned to fury as he cut a black-furred skaven from groin to sternum.

'Uzkul!' cried the longbeard, wrenching his axe free in a swathe of dark blood.

'Uzkul!' echoed Drimbold, mashing a clanrat in the maw with the butt of his axe before finishing it with an overhand swipe to the head.

Still the rat-kin came on and Drimbold slipped and fell on the fluid-slick stone. A host of hate-filled skaven faces bore down on him but then recoiled before a swirling mass of steel.

Azgar wove amongst them, slightly ahead of the first rank and swinging his chained axe in a brutal, repeating arc. Limbs rained down upon the plaza floor as the grim-faced slayer was showered in blood.

Drimbold staggered up, two clan dwarfs helping him.

'Stay on your feet,' Halgar snarled, taking a moment to rub his eyes.

The Grey dwarf nodded dazedly. When he went to rejoin the fight he saw the skaven had gathered together and were backing off. The dwarf line, having weathered the first attack, did not press and a gap soon formed between the bitter foes.

'Nice of them to give us a breather, eh lad?' remarked the longbeard, wiping the blood slick from his axe and readjusting his shield.

'Why don't they come?' hissed Drimbold through gritted teeth. The tense lull was almost more than the Grey dwarf could take. Only when the lumbering shapes came slowly from the skaven ranks, bustling their smaller kin aside violently to reach the killing, did Drimbold understand why.

Huge rat ogres, ten-strong, bristling with muscle and raw, terrifying brawn bellowed challenges and beat their chests with slab-like claws. Confronted by these horrifying, freakish creations the dwarf line took an involuntary half step back.

Azgar, who had rejoined the line, saw it.

'Khazukan Kazakit-ha!' bellowed the slayer, invoking the ancient war cry of the dawi, and stepped forward a pace.

'Khazuk!' came the unified response from the throng who matched him.

'Khazuk!' they cried again and took a second pace.

'Khazuk!' came the final cry as the dwarfs stepped into the killing zone of the rat-kin ogres.

WITH JUST THEIR noses above the waterline, Uthor, Rorek and Emelda stalked across the shallow reservoir towards the guards lingering at the rock plateau. As they drew closer the three dwarfs fanned out at some unseen command.

Uthor's gaze was fixed upon three clanrats, leant on spears and bickering with one another at the base of one of the ramshackle observation platforms. Only a few feet away, the thane of Kadrin arose slowly and quietly from the water, his beard and tunic drenched. One of the clanrats turned just as Uthor raised his axe and balked when confronted by the thane's cold eyes.

That expression remained on the creature's cooling corpse after Uthor buried his rune axe into its forehead. Ripping the glittering blade free, he beheaded another and downed the third with a savage blow to the back after it turned to flee.

He looked over to his companions. Three more ratkin corpses lay at Emelda's feet in various states of mutilation. Rorek, too, had dealt with his guards. Two skaven pin cushioned with quarrels floated in the shallow water, exuding blood. With this outer ring of sentries dispatched, the trio of dwarfs grimly moved on.

Crouched low as they sneaked across the rock plateau, the dwarfs converged and reached the threshold of the skaven engine. Up close, the infernal machine gave off an almighty clamour that masked their booted footfalls and shook their armour. As they approached, one of the hooded Clan Skryre agents turned and squeaked a warning. Rorek stitched a line of crossbow bolts across its neck and torso as it went to raise its staff.

Alerted by the sound the black-furred skaven turned, together with their smaller clanrat brethren, and began herding the slaves towards the dwarfs. The rancid, emaciated creatures dropped barrows and sodden sacking filled with earth, and took up spades and picks, the fear of their masters overwhelming their terror of facing the well-armed dwarfs.

FLIKRIT WATCHED AS Gnawquell twitched and fell, a host of feathered shafts jutting from his body like spines. The Clan Skryre warlock grinned with glee at his fellow acolyte's demise. 'Favour finds the survivor,' that was his motto. You cannot be elevated in the eyes of the Thirteen if you're dead. When he noticed the three battle-hardened dwarf-things stalking towards him, ripping through his slaves like they were nothing, he readily squirted the musk of fear.

Mastering the terror that was threatening to loosen his bowels, Flikrit backed away. Delving into his robes he found a chunk of glowing warpstone and ate it up hungrily. The tainted rock tingled on his tongue: bitter, acrid, empowering. Fear ebbed away to faint, gnawing doubt as visions were visited upon the warlock. He raised his staff, full of warpstone-fuelled confidence and incanted quickly. A nimbus of raw energy played briefly around Flikrit's outstretched paw before he channelled it into his staff and unleashed an arcing bolt of lightning.

Green-black energy arrowed into the air, charging it with power and the redolence of sulphur, and split a slave before it earthed harmlessly away.

Flikrit snarled his displeasure and screeched again, thrusting his staff towards the marauding dwarf-things carving up his slaves; slaves paid for with his tokens! Lightning flashed and one of the dwarf-things was struck as the eldritch bolt exploded into the earth nearby, spewing razor chips of rock.

Flikrit cackled with glee, leaping up and down but scowled when he realised the dwarf-thing was alive and getting to its feet with the help of one of its kin. This new foe broke through the stormvermin ranks that were now bearing the full brunt of the dwarf-thing's fury with the slaves dead or running. It was beardless with long, golden fur hanging from beneath its helmet. Determined anger was etched on the beardless-thing's face and Flikrit squirted the musk of fear again as the effects of the warpstone chunk wore off. The warlock hunted around quickly for another hunk of the tainted substance and plopped it nervously into his mouth with quaking fingers. The dwarf-thing was almost upon him as he unleashed another lightning bolt.

Flikrit squeaked with relief and joy as his assailant was engulfed by a furious storm of warp energy. He closed his eyes against the flare of light, expecting to see a charred ruin when he opened them again.

Armour smoking, the dwarf-thing was alive! A faint glow emanated from a gilded belt around its waist. Having been brought to its knees, it got up in an even fouler rage than before, axe swinging meaningfully. Flikrit backed away, looking right and left for aid. Most of the stormvermin were dead. All of the Clan Rictus warriors were slain. He was alone.

Desperate for survival, the warlock dug his filthy paw deep into his robes and pulled out the last of his warp-stone. Three massive chunks went into his mouth. Flikrit swallowed loudly. Dark energy rushed into his body, setting his nerves on edge, like he was on fire. About to unleash a final bolt of terrifying power, Flikrit realised he *was* on fire. He tried to pat out the greenish flames in his smouldering fur but to no avail. Opening his mouth to scream, the warp-blaze ravaged him utterly, stripping fur and flesh, and rendering bones to ash.

EMELDA SHIELDED HER eyes from the skaven torch before her, lightning arcing wildly from its body and striking the roof of the chamber. The wretched sorcerer crumpled into a blackened heap of nothing as the deadly magic it had tried to unleash consumed it. The clan daughter's armour was still hot from the lightning blast and she smelled scorched hair before muttering an oath to Valaya. As the skaven magic dissipated, the runes at her cincture dulled and became dormant once more.

Slightly dazed she looked around at the carnage.

Rorek shot down a group of fleeing clanrats with his rapid-firing crossbow before rushing forward to finish a rat-kin slave crawling across the ground with the weapon's weighted butt.

Uthor dispatched the last of the burly black skaven, Ulfgan's axe flashing fiercely as it shredded armour and bone with ease.

They were victorious. The skaven were all dead. Only those trapped within the thunderously turning wheels remained, utterly oblivious to the battle and locked in a hellish, spinning nightmare.

But the destruction was not at an end. Even as Emelda stowed Dunrik's axe, slabs of rock broke away from the ceiling where the lightning had damaged it, plummeting into the pool of water surrounding the pumping engine. A massive chunk, one of the dilapidated archways of the vast chamber, crashed down onto one of the wheels that drove the pistons crushing it and the creatures within utterly.

'We must destroy that abomination,' bellowed Uthor as he fought the din of the engine, his steely gaze softening as it went from the skaven construction to Emelda.

'Are you…?'

'Valaya protects me,' she replied.

'We need only to open the Barduraz Varn,' said Rorek, the sporadic lightning generated by the two remaining wheels casting his face in ephemeral flashes. 'The flood waters will bring what is left down.'

'How are we to reach the gate?' asked Emelda.

'That stairway will take us to the opening mechanism,' Rorek answered pointing to a set of narrow, stone steps – partially obscured by the extremities of the pumping engine – leading to the huge bar of gold, copper and bronze that prevented the Barduraz Varn from opening.

Uthor at the lead, the three dwarfs rushed the steps quickly, taking them two at a time.

'Mind the wheel!' shouted Rorek above the incredible noise of the engine.

Part of the stairway brought the dwarfs perilously close to one of the whirring generator wheels. Uthor had to press his back against the stone to make sure he wasn't dragged off the steps and into it. Edging by slowly, he felt the whip and pull of the air as it was smashed against his face, thick with the stink of burning flesh. Through the blurring effect of the rapidly spinning wheel he caught snatches of the slaves labouring madly within. Their blood-shot eyes bulged with intense effort, panting for breath through froth-covered mouths, fur pressed down under a thick lather of sweat. The thane saw other shapes in the kaleidoscopic

vista, too, the remains of the wretched creatures that
couldn't maintain the pace or that fell, their broken
bodies bouncing up and down with the wheel's
momentum and slowly being smashed to pulp.

Traversing the deadly stretch of stairway, Uthor
finally reached the locking mechanism of the gate, the
way opening out into a simple stone platform with a
large wheel crank in the centre, riveted to the floor via
a broad, flat iron plate. The others were not far behind
when the thane of Kadrin took up a position at the
wheel crank. He pushed hard but it wouldn't yield, not
even a fraction.

'It's tough,' he yelled, 'lend your strength to it.'

'It can't be opened that way,' Rorek told him, arriving
on the platform just after Emelda. 'We must first release
the lock,' he added, pointing at the magnificent gold,
copper and bronze bar that spanned the entire width of
the gate.

'Here,' cried Emelda, stood before a shallow alcove in
the wall.

Upon closer inspection, Uthor noticed there was a
round metal recess in it with four square stubs of iron
sticking out.

'What now?' asked the thane of Kadrin, turning to his
engineer.

'It is rhun-sealed,' Rorek replied, scrutinizing the
indentation in the rock before he looked directly at
Uthor. 'We cannot open it without a key.'

STANDING ATOP THE great anvil, chained axe dripping
blood, Azgar surveyed the swell of the battle below.
Teeming rat-kin hordes thrashed against the thinning
dwarfen shield wall that had been pressed all the way

back to the forgemaster's platform. Death frenzy was seemingly upon the foul creatures, muzzles frothing as they squealed madly to get at the dawi through the great arch. An endless, undulating sea of furred bodies stretched beyond it as yet more ratmen piled into the foundry.

Azgar kept his hand on the wyvern-horn hunting through the thronging skaven with narrowed eyes. The dwarfs were but half the number they were at the start of the battle. They would not last much longer. Yet the slayer resisted the urge to blow the note that was to signal all of their deaths. He was waiting; waiting for something to show itself…

HALGAR WAS TIRING. He would not admit it to himself but his aching limbs, the fire in his back and shoulder, the thundering breaths in his chest told him so. He slashed open a rat-kin's throat, before breaking the snout of another with a savage punch. Three more of the vermin came on at him – the skaven seemed to surround them now – and he was forced back, defending a flurry of blows. For a moment his vision blurred and he misjudged a parry. The errant blow struck his thigh and the longbeard cried out.

Drimbold stepped in and hacked the cackling ratman down before it could take advantage.

Halgar nodded to the Grey dwarf, heaving more air into his lungs.

'Stay by me,' he barked, mustering what breath he could.

'You do not need to watch me,' Drimbold replied, slicing the ear off a slave fodder. 'I will stay in the fight.'

'No, lad, not because of that,' Halgar replied, his axe held uncertainly in his hand, 'because I'm going blind.'

'I will,' said Drimbold determinedly, taking up a position at the longbeard's back and fending off a reckless rat-kin spear lunge.

Halgar had gone past pain, surpassed exhaustion now. Raw hatred for his foes kept him going, made his axe blade swing and take more lives. The killing became almost ritualistic in the dense fug of battle and everything else; every sense, every feeling was swallowed by it. When the longbeard felt the rock at his back slip away, all of that changed. He looked over his shoulder to see Drimbold slumped on one knee, clutching his chest.

'To your feet!' he cried, cutting through the shoulder of a rat-kin slave. Drimbold wasn't listening or, at least, he couldn't hear the longbeard. The Grey dwarf cried out when a curved blade ran him through, punching out of his back, shearing his light armour easily. Halgar whirled, blinking back his blurring vision, or tears – he couldn't tell which – and cut Drimbold's attacker down.

'To me!' the longbeard cried, gathering the Grey dwarf up in his arms as he fell back, a cohort of clan warriors surrounding them both in a shield wall. Halgar dragged the Grey dwarf back bodily, a geyser of blood spitting from his chest, into the rear ranks and set him down.

'Uthor… told… me…' Drimbold gasped through blood-flecked lips – every word was a struggle. 'He said… I was to protect you…'

Halgar patted the Grey dwarf's shoulder, unable to speak as he regarded the dwarf's wounded body.

'I... failed,' Drimbold uttered with his dying breath, the light in his eyes fading to grey.

'No lad,' Halgar replied with tears in his eyes. 'No you haven't.'

The longbeard rested his gnarled hand over Drimbold's dead, staring eyes. When he took it away again they were closed. He then leant down. The words were choked as he whispered in Drimbold's ear.

'You are a half dwarf no longer.'

Halgar wiped the back of his hand over his eyes and stood up, brandishing his axe.

'Guard him well,' he ordered three shield-bearing warriors sternly, who nodded sombrely before arraying themselves around the Grey dwarf.

With that the longbeard stalked away, back to the front and back to the killing.

At long last, Azgar found what he was looking for. Across the skaven ranks he espied their warlord, squeaking orders and forcing his way to the front.

It was an unusual trait for a rat-kin leader, the slayer thought to himself, to throw itself into the fight. There could be no mistaking it, though. Decked in thick armour of tarnished metal, wielding a weighty-looking glaive and ragged cloak dragging in its wake, this was the opponent Azgar had been waiting for.

Now he knew the skaven were committed to the attack.

Bellicose glee in his heart, the slayer raised the wyvern-horn to his lips and, with his mighty chest bulging, blew out a long and powerful note.

CHAPTER FOURTEEN

THE WYVERN-HORN echoed throughout the hold, a reverberant and sonorous blast that carried through earth, stone and flood.

'There!' cried Gromrund, waiting inside Dibna's Chamber.

'I hear it,' Thalgrim replied, poised before the statue of the engineer. As the lodefinder lifted his pick-mattock he looked over his shoulder at the hammerer. 'Once this begins, there will be little time.'

Gromrund nodded his understanding. 'Make your strike well.'

Thalgrim let fly and met the statue with precise force.

'It is done,' he said, turning on his heel as a shallow crack emerged in the rock, running rapidly up Dibna's leg, across his torso, beyond his shoulder and up his outstretched arm until it finally reached the ceiling.

Gromrund watched the fissure's course slightly agog, small chips of rocks falling from its terminus at the ceiling.

'Flee, now!' Thalgrim urged, leaping into the shaft and disappearing from view.

Gromrund followed quickly, a final nervous glance behind him before he descended. Water was trickling through the ever-widening cracks and one of Dibna's fingers fell away, shattering as it struck the floor. Darkness beckoned the hammerer as he approached the shaft and raced into it.

GROMRUND HALF CLIMBED, half slid down the shaft. Wisps of smoke spiralled from his armoured gauntlets with the intense friction of his descent. There was a nervous moment when he switched from the thick chain dangling from Dibna's Drop to the lodefinder's rope but he made it without falling to his doom. A growing sense of urgency had started to overwhelm him, exacerbated by the speck of flame from Thalgrim's candles diminishing rapidly beneath him as the lodefinder made expedient progress.

'You'll get yourself killed at that pace,' Gromrund called down to him.

'As might you if you don't pick up yours,' came the distant, echoing response.

Gromrund intensified his efforts as much as he dared and, looking down again, swore he could make out a faint corona of washed-out light.

We will make it, thought the hammerer, as an almighty crash resonated above them, followed by a thunderous roar. Time was up.

Water fell like rain at first, droplets splashing harmlessly off Gromrund's armour. Then it became a torrent, growing more violent with each passing second. The hammerer slid now, almost free falling, determined to arrest his descent when he neared the bottom of the shaft. That plan was reduced to tatters when the full fury of the deluge above smashed into him, and he was forced to grip the rope tightly to avoid being ripped away from it and cast like tinder into the darkness.

Gromrund roared his defiance and tried to edge down an inch. He did but had to grip hard again as the icy cascade battered the hammerer remorselessly. Gromrund had his head down and the pounding water thumped against his neck, so hard he thought it might snap. Thalgrim was below him, he was sure of it. He could just make out the hazy figure of the lodefinder through the downpour. The shaft shuddered against the elemental onslaught, chunks of loose rock sent spiralling earthward. One smacked against Gromrund's warhelm, setting it askew. Another 'thunked' his pauldron armour and the hammerer nearly lost his grip, crying out in anguish.

Chilling heat blazed up his arm and back. Gromrund shut his eyes against the pain, it taking all of the hammerer's effort just to hold on. When he opened them again, he tried to gauge the distance to the ground – thirty, fifty feet, perhaps. If he dropped now he could survive. The decision was made for the hammerer when a great slab of stone sheared away from the shaft wall. Its jagged edge rammed the rope into the opposite side, cutting it loose. Gromrund fell and the hunk of rock fell after him.

* * *

PAIN SEARED UP his right leg and something cracked as
Gromrund struck the ground, spluttering as the gushing Black Water engulfed him. Underwater, his heavy
armour anchoring him, the hammerer's world grew
dim and quiet. Sound, light and feeling seemed to lose
all meaning as the icy deluge robbed him of his sense
and bearings. Memory reached out to Gromrund from
the past, the day when he had taken the warhelm of his
clan to continue the Tallhelm legacy.

Father…

*Kromrund Tallhelm lay before him in a gilded sarcopha-
gus carved from stone by the master masons of Karak Hirn.
Ashen-faced and in repose, his lord and father was no more.
Upon his breast there sat the mighty horned warhelm of the
clan, a prestigious symbol of their lineage and the oaths they
had made to serve King Kurgaz, founder of the Hornhold,
as his bodyguards.*

*As Gromrund reached out for the warhelm he felt himself
being pulled away and the sound of distant voices rushing
closer.*

Spitting and cursing, Gromrund emerged above the
flood water, cascading readily into the underdeep.

'Pull him clear!' he heard Thalgrim bellow and his
body was heaved away again.

Blinking back rivulets of water eking into his
warhelm and down his face, he recoiled, landing hard
on his rump, as a massive chunk of rock and debris
crashed down onto the confluence of the crossroads. A
few moments ago, he had been floundering in that
very spot. Looking around, Gromrund noticed his
companions were with him. Thalgrim and Hakem
helped the armoured hammerer to his feet. Getting up,
he saw that the flood water reached his lower torso.

'We cannot stay here,' Thalgrim cried above the crashing din of the waterfall, wading frantically in the only direction left to them, the rock fall having demolished and blocked off the other three.

Breathing heavily Ralkan slogged after the lodefinder, struggling in his drenched robes and dragging the book of remembering after him as if leading a lode pony. 'Farther ahead,' he gasped, 'I am sure there is a way upward.'

With no time to question or verify it, the dwarfs drove on.

Hakem and Gromrund laboured at the back – the two warriors wore the heaviest armour and were finding it hard going.

'Can you walk?' Hakem asked of the hammerer, supporting him beneath the shoulder.

'Aye,' Gromrund replied, but didn't refuse the merchant thane's help.

'You are limping badly,' Hakem told him, feeling the hammerer's laboured gait as the merchant thane bore his weight.

'Aye,' was Gromrund's reply.

'If we survive, you may need a stick.'

'There'll be no stick. The hammerers of the Tallhelm clan walk on two legs, not three!' Gromrund raged as the pair struggled on.

WADING THROUGH THE rapidly rising swell, the dwarfs made pitiful progress. Barely fifty feet from the crossroads and the water was already up to their shoulders.

Thalgrim gazed up at the lofty arches of the vaulted tunnel ceiling and realised they wouldn't make it like this.

'Remove your armour,' he cried to the others as a column behind them cracked and fell into the flood water, scattering debris. 'We will have to swim for it.' The lodefinder unbuckled his mail vest and let it plummet into the river surrounding them.

The other dwarfs followed suit, shrugging off chainmail, unclasping breastplates and greaves, divesting themselves of leather hauberks and vambraces. They shed the armour clumsily but quickly. Each piece was an heirloom, the loss of which was felt profoundly, and discarded with an oath to one of the Ancestor Gods that reparations would be made.

By the time it was done, the water had reached their chins.

'Your warhelm,' said Thalgrim, 'you must leave it behind – it will weigh you down.'

Gromrund folded his arms.

'The Tallhelm has never been removed in five generations of my clan, since before the Hornhold was founded. I will not break that tradition now.'

'You will drown,' Hakem reasoned, now wearing only his tunic and breeches. 'Leave it and come back to reclaim your honour.'

'Upon my death you may prize it from my head,' the hammerer snarled, still fully armoured.

The water rose again, up to the dwarfs' shoulders and getting deeper with each moment.

'Help me,' Hakem burbled, spitting mouthfuls of the Black Water as he tried to lift Gromrund. Thalgrim and Ralkan swam over to him, and hoisted the hammerer up from beneath his armpits.

'Leave me,' he roared, his head popping above the turbulent waterline with their combined efforts.

'Remove the warhelm!' Hakem begged him, staring the hammerer in the face as he said it.

'Never!' Gromrund raged back before his snarling visage softened. 'Go. Find your dooms and, if you're able, tell my king that I fought and died with honour.'

They could hold him no longer. The hammerer was like an anchor and dragged them all down with him.

Hakem felt his fingers slipping and watched as Gromrund – the hammerer had his arms folded still – fell away into the gloomy water, bubbles trailing from beneath his warhelm. The merchant thane, swimming hard, broke the surface of the now swelling river and drew great gulps of air into his lungs.

The current that surged through the underdeep was strong and carried the three dwarfs along by its will alone, smashing them into columns, plunging them beneath the water only for them to resurface desperately a moment later. Hakem was lost in it, lost in a maelstrom of spitting foam and churning water.

'Here!' he heard Thalgrim cry. Seeing something in the water, he reached out and grabbed it.

The lodefinder hauled him around the corner of a massive column, he and Ralkan crushed against it by the pressure of the flood. In his other hand he had his pick-mattock, lodged in the wall for grip. A brutal-looking gash was etched upon his forehead where it had been struck by a jutting stone.

'The rock is weak, here,' Thalgrim shouted over the thrashing surf. 'I can break through it.'

'Where will it lead us?' Hakem replied, looking to Ralkan.

The lorekeeper shook his head, just trying to hold on.

Though they had only been carried by the water for a few minutes, they could have travelled a great distance. There was no way of knowing where they were now.

'Does it matter?' cried the lodefinder. 'This path will end in our deaths.'

The water was getting steadily higher. There was only a few feet left before it engulfed the tunnel completely.

Hakem nodded.

'Hold on,' Thalgrim said and ripped his pick free. Using the column for support, he smashed the weapon, two-handed, into the bare rock. The wall crumbled and an opening was made wide enough for the dwarfs to pass through. Thalgrim went first, diving into the unknown, then Ralkan and finally Hakem.

First there was darkness then the sense of falling as the merchant thane struck the ground hard. He was rolling and skidding on his backside down a long and narrow tunnel, an undercurrent of rapidly rushing water beneath carrying him. So black were Hakem's surroundings and so disorientated was he, that all he could discern was that he was going down; down into the darkest depths of the hold.

'Is THERE NO other way,' Uthor cried, over the din of the thunderous skaven pumping engine.

'Rhun-seals are wrought by rhunki using rhun magic, as are the keys that unlock them. It is far beyond my skill. Without such a key we cannot release the bar and as long as the bar is engaged the Barduraz Varn will not open.'

As if to mock them, the echoing report of the wyvern-horn rang loudly through the chamber.

'We must release the Black Water now,' Uthor raged. 'In this deed at least, I *will* succeed.'

'We cannot,' Rorek told him. 'Besides the rhun-key, there is no other way.'

'Grimnir's hairy arse!' Uthor slumped down on his backside, Ulfgan's axe in his lap. 'The lorekeeper mentioned nothing of this. If we survive, I will personally see to it that his beard is shorn.' He gripped the haft of his axe as he thought about the retribution he would visit upon Ralkan. Regarding the glinting blade, the runes glowing faintly as he held the weapon in his grasp, something dawned on him.

'These rhun-keys,' said Uthor suddenly, getting to his feet. 'Who would bear such a thing?'

Rorek stared back at him, slightly dumbfounded. 'What does it matter?'

'Who would bear it? Answer me!'

'The rhunki that made it, of course,' Rorek blathered, unsure as to the reason for Uthor's sudden, urgent behaviour.

'Who else?' The thane of Kadrin was delving beneath his chainmail shirt.

'The king,' Rorek finished. 'The king of the hold.'

'Do you remember the King's Chamber?' Uthor asked the engineer.

'Of course, you bear noble Lord Ulfgan's axe to this day.'

'Yes, I do. But the axe was not all we salvaged from his private rooms.'

Realisation dawned on Rorek's face.

Emelda stood watching the entire display nonplussed.

'The talisman,' said the engineer.

Uthor found it beneath his armour, where he'd put it for safe keeping after fleeing the hold, and held it aloft.

Ulfgan's talisman – it bore the rune marking of the royal clan etched around the edge and in the centre was the badge of his ancestor, Hraddi. Flickering brazier light shone through two square holes in the eyes and a third in the mouth. Without looking, Uthor knew they would fit the mechanism perfectly. They had their key.

Uthor placed the arcane device into the recess in the wall, fixing the three holes in position over the iron studs. It clamped into place with a dull, metallic 'thunk'.

'Turn it,' said Rorek, standing just behind him and looking over the thane of Kadrin's shoulder. Emelda waited next to the engineer, silently apprehensive.

Uthor did as Rorek told him and turned the rune key once. Beyond the wall, he heard the sonorous retort of a hidden mechanism at work. Screeching metal filled the chamber, smothering even the sound of the chugging engine, as the mighty locking bar disengaged spitting out dust and stone chips. Hinged at one end, the huge bar split into two from a previously imperceptible join and fell away to clang thunderously into a thick bronze clamp on either side of the Barduraz Varn.

Moving away from the alcove, Uthor took his place at the huge wheel crank in the centre of the stone platform. His companions followed him, and together they turned the massive device that set yet more hidden feats of engineering in motion.

From below, a sudden onrush of water could be heard as the Barduraz Varn rose magnificently. Hauled up by a raft of iron chains, the great gate ascended vertically in slow and juddering increments, feeding gradually into a long and deep recess set into the chamber roof way above where the dwarfs stood on the stairway. Pushed past the point of no return, the gate would keep opening, its momentum as inexorable as the flood waters crashing through it, until it was fully released.

From their vantage point on the stone platform, Uthor gazed across the gradually deepening reservoir to another set of stone steps on the opposite side of the vast chamber. They led up to a thick, wooden door. With the destruction of Rorek's diving helm the way back was shut; this might be their only possible escape route.

'Head for that portal,' he cried, starting down the stone steps. 'Make haste,' he called back, 'the chamber will soon be flooded.'

The dwarfs negotiated the stairs quickly, slowing only slightly when they edged past the still whirring wheel. When they reached the bottom, the crude struts of the pumping engine were beginning to buckle under the sustained battering of the emerging Black Water. Several of the observation platforms had already been felled and swirled in the growing reservoir amongst the rotting debris of rat-kin corpses.

Slogging back across the carcass-ridden lagoon, making the most of the few islands of rock that had yet to be submerged, the dwarfs finally reached the second stairway, plunging waist deep into the water to get to it. Tramping up the stone steps was a great relief and once they had gained the upper platform and the threshold to the portal, they looked back.

The Barduraz Varn was a third of the way open and with smashing force the inundation unleashed by it

crushed the pumping engine utterly. Rat-kin slaves
mouthed silent screams as they were pummelled into
the thrashing depths, together with their wheeled pris-
ons that collapsed and split against the swelling water.
Like a fallen standard conceding defeat, the metal
prongs at the zenith of the engine were the last to
crumble. Arcs of lightning flared defiantly as a massive
wave engulfed the tower and it was dragged into the
depths. Flashes, stark and diffuse, raged for a moment
and were still as if the infernal engine had never
existed.

Having seen enough, Uthor turned away and made
for the wooden door.

HAKEM WAS FLAT on his back, his clothes sodden and
torn. Dazed, he got to his feet absently feeling a fat
bruise bulging on his head. Darkness surrounded the
merchant thane and an old, stagnant stench wafted
over to him on a warm and shallow breeze.

'Thalgrim,' he hissed, crouching down and scrambling around for his borrowed axe. It was nowhere to
be found. Patting down his body, he realised he still
had his beard-irons. Hakem looked at them for a long
moment then unhitched the irons from his belt and
dropped them to the ground.

'Here,' came the whispered reply of the lodefinder,
close by.

'Lorekeeper,' Hakem called quietly again, detecting
Thalgrim's vague outline just ahead.

'Am I dead, yet?' Ralkan answered.

Eyes adjusting to the gloom, Hakem made out the
prone form of the lorekeeper, flat on his back and languishing beneath a faintly trickling waterfall that fed

into a thin, downward wending stream. It seemed the rushing waters had been diverted at some point during their descent. Hakem wasn't about to question it.

'You're not dead,' he said, standing next to the exhausted lorekeeper. 'Now, get up,' he added, helping Ralkan to his feet.

Thalgrim joined them. Incredibly he still carried his pick though, try as he might, he couldn't light the clutch of candles gripped in his meaty fist.

'Water-logged,' the lodefinder explained unnecessarily.

Hakem ignored him. These were the lowest deeps, that much he was certain, and as a thane and bearer of the longest beard it was his duty to get them through it and somehow out of Karak Varn.

'What is this place?' he asked Ralkan.

The lorekeeper rubbed the water from his eyes and wrung out his beard, before peering intently at the surrounding gloom.

'We are at the lowest part of the underdeep,' he murmured, picking out age-worn runes and sigils carved into keystones.

The tunnel was wide but low. The three dwarfs were gathered where it flattened out to a level plain. Just beyond it the tunnel fell downward in a gradual slope. Other than that, the only other way was back up, over the lip of stone from which the dwarfs had been disgorged and a long, hard climb through the rapids.

'Is there a way out from here?'

Ralkan scratched his head and fell silent. It wasn't a good sign.

'I don't remember this place,' he admitted. 'I do not think I have ever been here... Yet...'

'Yet?'

'There is something familiar,' he said. 'This way,' the lorekeeper decided finally as he headed down the slope.

IT FELT LIKE they'd been wandering the tunnels for an hour, though Ralkan could not be sure – his judgement of the passage of time had been irrevocably damaged during his period of hidden isolation in the hold.

With each step that carried him further into the lower reaches of the underdeep a strange disquiet gnawed at him. Smothering it to the back of his mind for now, the lorekeeper led them on until they reached another crossroads.

The Barak Varr dwarf said something – Hakem, that was his name – Ralkan didn't hear what it was. His head was hurting. Nothing looked right.

East, he thought suddenly. East – that feels right, and took the left fork.

About halfway down the tunnel, the lorekeeper thought he heard something – faint, but it was definitely there. Vile squeaking drifted over to Ralkan on the weak breeze. Fifty years in the dark. Squeaking and scratching. Squeaking and scratching.

No – it wasn't right. Something boiled up inside the lorekeeper, something he'd buried. It slid, leaden in his gut, and icily up his spine until it dried his tongue to sand. Ralkan turned on his heel and fled.

'SKAVEN,' RALKAN HISSED as he rushed passed Hakem.

The Barak Varr dwarf looked ahead down the tunnel. His heart caught in his mouth when he saw the skulking shadows against the wall, stretching towards him.

Then came the squeaking, chittering sound of the rat-kin as the horde grew ever closer. Judging by the terrible cacophony, there must have been hundreds. Hakem's first thought was the flood waters might not reach them here; his second was he couldn't fight them and live. He gave chase after the lorekeeper with all haste, urging Thalgrim, who was dawdling in the tunnel, to follow him. The lodefinder was not far behind as Hakem fled by the crossroads and went after Ralkan, straight down the western fork.

'Lorekeeper,' bawled the merchant thane. 'Lorekeeper, slow down.'

In his frantic flight after Ralkan, Hakem raced through a myriad of tunnels. After a while, it became clear they had lost the skaven or that they had deliberately given up the pursuit. As he slowed, and a sense of creeping, ancient dread came over him, Hakem could understand why.

Ahead of him Ralkan was still running, though the lorekeeper was obviously exhausted now and had slowed down considerably. Hakem picked up his pace, trying to close the gap. He saw Ralkan look behind him, though the lorekeeper gave no indication he had seen the merchant thane. Then he slipped and fell to his knees. Ralkan was up swiftly and bundling himself around a corner was lost from sight.

Hakem hurried on. Sweat dappled his forehead and he noticed the air was getting warmer – his sodden clothes were gradually drying in it.

This tunnel is ancient, thought the merchant thane as he reached the corner, a sulphurous stench pricking at his nostrils, mixed with old fear. Hakem caught up to Ralkan at last. The lorekeeper's leather jerkin, the one he wore beneath his robes, was torn and he was feeling his way slowly along the wall.

'What is it?' Hakem asked, aware that Thalgrim had just reached them both.

Ralkan traced his fingers over a dust-shrouded symbol.

'Uzkul,' he muttered. He turned to the merchant thane, his face an ashen mask.

'Uzkul?' Thalgrim asked.

Ralkan nodded slowly.

Something was wrong, the lorekeeper was behaving more strangely than usual. Slightly on edge, Hakem looked past him and further down the tunnel. He saw a faint glow ahead.

'Perhaps it is an ancient hearth hall,' Ralkan offered, following the merchant thane's gaze. The lorekeeper's voice seemed far away as he said it, padding calmly down the tunnel and towards the light.

'You are sure this is the way?' Hakem asked as he followed, sharing a worried glance with Thalgrim alongside him. The sulphur stink was getting stronger with every step.

Ralkan didn't answer.

'Heed me, lorekeep–' the merchant thane began as he reached Ralkan, standing at the mouth of a huge cavern. The words stuck in Hakem's throat, gaping in awe as he was bathed in a golden aura.

'WE MUST TURN back,' said Rorek.

'There is no *back*,' Uthor replied, angrily.

Before them was a narrow stone bridge, spanning a deep gorge. A rushing spout of water surged violently across it, falling away into the dark recesses of the crevice beyond and below.

After they'd left the chamber of the Barduraz Varn, the dwarfs had sealed the door shut behind them. Making haste, for they knew the flood water would reach them soon enough, they had reached the bridge. Uthor had tried to cross, tied to Rorek and Emelda but the force of the spouting deluge had crushed him flat and nearly pitched the thane right over the edge. He'd crawled back, drenched and defeated with the rushing water battering him at every clawed inch.

'Then this is the end,' Emelda uttered with resignation. 'We cannot cross and we cannot retreat. I envy Azgar and the others,' she said, noting the tightening of Uthor's jaw at the mention of the slayer, 'at least they will die fighting.'

'I see something,' said Rorek, suddenly, squinting past the pounding water. The engineer pointed to the other side of the bridge and the mouth of another, small, portal. 'It's not possible,' he gasped.

From beyond the bridge, shrouded in darkness, a vaguely outlined figure hailed them. Any words were lost, swallowed by the roar of the thrashing water as the figure waved to them with an outstretched arm. Though mostly sketched in silhouette, the shape and size of the figure's warhelm was unmistakable.

'Gromrund?' breathed Uthor and suppressed a shudder, uncertain as to what he was actually seeing.

Gromrund's silhouette waved again and pointed down to the bridge.

Uthor followed the gesture but couldn't see anything past the rush of the water.

'I thought he was at the overflow grate in the opposite end of the hold,' Emelda whispered, clutching the talisman of Valaya around her neck for reassurance.

'He was,' Uthor replied darkly, searching through the pounding river for some sign of what Gromrund wanted them to find.

Then he saw the frayed edges of a rope. It was only a few feet away; Uthor could reach it at a stretch.

'Hold onto my ankles,' said the thane of Kadrin as he got down onto his stomach.

'What?' Rorek asked, still staring at the shadow beyond the bridge.

'Just do as I ask!' Uthor barked.

Rorek crouched down with Emelda beside him, and the two of them gripped Uthor's ankles as he crawled back across the bridge, the river battering him relentlessly.

Fingers numbing from the cold, Uthor reached out and gripped the rope.

'Pull me back,' he cried.

Dragged from out of the swell, Uthor clutched one end of the rope in his hand. On the other side of the bridge, Gromrund showed them the opposite end and beckoned for them to cross.

'Are you sure about this?' Rorek muttered, his voice a little tremulous as he eyed the dark portal and the shadow inside it.

'It is our only chance.' Uthor pulled the rope until it was taut. He saw Gromrund take the strain on the other end. With an oath to Valaya, he stepped bravely onto the bridge. At first he was battered to his knees but using the rope for support he got back to his feet and crossed, hand over hand, inch by painful inch. Rorek and Emelda followed.

It felt like hours but they reached the other side, collapsing into an exhausted heap on a small stone platform.

'My thanks, hammerer–' Uthor began but as he looked over to where Gromrund had been standing the rope fell slack. The Karak Hirn dwarf was gone.

AZGAR LEAPT FROM the forgemaster's anvil, clearing the last lines of dwarf defenders and landing amidst a clutch of rat-kin warriors who scattered before him. Before the vile creatures could close in again, the slayer swung his chained axe in a punishing circle, slicing meat and bone. Churning deeper into the fray, amidst a storm of severed limbs and shredded torsos, Azgar found his prey.

Shrieking a challenge the rat-kin warlord came on fearlessly, ducking the first swing of the chain as it stepped inside the killing arc and swatted away the second revolution of the deadly blade with the flat of its glaive. Pulling the weapon down, it made a powerful lunge that Azgar was hard pressed to dodge. The slayer twisted from the glaive's path, though it nicked the skin of his left side and drew blood.

Snarling exultantly, the warlord then licked the crimson droplets bejewelling its blade and surged at Azgar again. The slayer rolled beneath a wild, overhead swipe, gathering up his chain axe as he did so and gripping the haft to wield it conventionally. A vertical strike from the glaive followed, and the slayer dove forward to avoid it, gutting a black-furred skaven that got too close, before whirling on his heel and side swiping the overstretched warlord. The blow carved into the rat-kin's back, ripping off plates of armour. The warlord cried in pain, blocking a second blow with the haft of its glaive. Roaring back, Azgar struck again and again, until he sheared the glaive haft in half.

Staggering backward, the rat-kin warlord tossed the bladed end at the slayer, who smashed it aside with the flat of his axe. It slowed Azgar enough for the rat lord to draw its sword.

Slowly, the duelling warriors were afforded room to fight, neither skaven nor dwarf willing to step into the path of their whirling blades.

Azgar swung again, releasing a little chain for additional reach and surprise. The rat-kin warlord saw it coming and weaved out of the weapon's death arc. Rushing forward, the blurring steel flicking past its ear, the creature cut the slayer across the torso, using the momentum of the blow to carry it beyond the dwarf's reach.

Azgar felt wet blood between his fingers, clutching at the wound as he nearly fell to one knee. Screeching, high-pitched and sporadic, emanated from the rat-kin warlord's mouth in what the slayer could only assume was laughter. The dwarf stood and turned, the blood from his torso was already clotting, grinning contemptuously.

'Come on,' he growled, beckoning the skaven on, 'we're not done yet.'

HALGAR SAW THE slayer dive from the anvil but quickly lost him in the melee. There were no tactics, no scheme to the battle now. It was about dying and surviving, pure and simple. The remaining dwarfs, although few and surrounded by foes, fought as if the very spirit of Grimnir were with them. Halgar's heart swelled, belting out his deathsong with every blow and thrust of his axe. During the carnage he had lost his shield and wielded the weapon in two hands.

Cutting down a rat-kin slave, the longbeard screwed up his eyes again – the blurring was getting worse and dark patches lingered menacingly at the periphery of his vision. When Halgar opened them he saw something advancing toward him. Whether it was his failing eyesight or some brand of foul sorcery, he could not tell but it seemed as though it were a ragged blanket of drifting blackness. Shadows, as if drawn like moths to a lantern, mustered to it until the thing resolved itself in front of the longbeard. Out of the gathered darkness came a flash of metal. Halgar, acting on instinct, parried the dagger blow and took a step back as a second, blindingly fast swipe, cut through the air in front of him.

The longbeard bellowed defiantly, stomping towards his assailant and swinging his axe. Eyesight blurring badly now, Halgar missed by a foot.

The assassin recoiled, the old dwarf knew now it could only be such a creature, dodging the blade with effortless grace. Regrouping quickly it struck out again, severing the tendons in the longbeard's wrist. The axe clanged to the ground from Halgar's nerveless fingers. The second dagger punched into his chest and the longbeard suddenly found he could barely breathe.

Halgar fell onto his knees, trying in vain to staunch the blood flowing eagerly from his chest.

Drawing near, certain of its kill, the skaven assassin hissed with gleeful, undisguised malice. Ironically, it was blind and upon opening its mouth to gloat revealed it had no tongue, either. But something else caught the longbeard's attention, so close that even he could see it – the last thing he would ever see as his vision darkened completely. It was an ear, cut from the

head of some unfortunate victim. Embedded in the
lobe was a gilded earring that bore the rune of the royal
clan of Karak Izor. It had once belonged to Lokki.

Halgar roared, reaching out blindly to strangle the
creature that had killed his lord. He grasped air and felt
two dagger thrusts in his torso. Doubling over, one
hand supporting his weight lest he collapse, the longbeard tasted copper in his mouth as he spat out blood.
His nose twitched. He could smell Lokki's killer close
by. Halgar dropped his head submissively, knowing
that the creature would draw in to finish him. The
stench of it grew so pungent it must be upon him. Halgar reached across his body with his half hand, the
other no more use than a prop with the tendons
slashed, and gripped the grobi arrow embedded in his
chest. The air and scent shifted around him. This was it.

Halgar tore the arrow free, blocking the overhead
strike of the skaven assassin with his other arm, and
rammed it into the rat-kin's throat. He felt it flail; slash
weakly at his back and side. Strength failing, Halgar
held it there pushing the arrow tip even deeper. The
thrashing stopped and the skaven assassin slumped.
Halgar fell onto his back, life blood eking across the
foundry floor. Though he couldn't see, as the longbeard heard the onrush of flood water smashing into
the chamber and the shrieking terror of the drowning
rat-kin, he smiled.

'GRUNGNI'S HOARD,' HAKEM gasped. 'May its glittering
peaks reach the summit of the world.'

Gold: a shimmering, gilded sea of it stretched out in
front of the dwarfs who stood agog at the threshold to
the immense chamber. Illuminated by the natural light

of a narrow and lofty shaft far above, piles of the lustrous metal soared into its vaulted ceiling like mountains, touching the ends of dripping stalactites. Gems and jewels glittered like stars in the shining morass, together with copper-banded chests that jutted like wooden islands between refulgent straights. Ornate weapons: swords, axes, hammers and others of more elaborate artifice protruded from vast treasure mounds. So immense was the hoard that it was impossible to take it all in with a single look. The chamber itself was cavernous and appeared to tail off into an anteroom at the back that was lost from view.

Hakem could taste the gold on his tongue; its strong, metallic scent filled his nostrils. He had to fight the urge to run wildly into the room and immerse himself in it. But then he noticed something else amidst the hoard's lustrous mirage, skeletons picked clean, and fire-blackened armour and snapped blades. Great pools of heat-emanating sulphur confirmed Hakem's sudden suspicions and the creeping dread he had felt earlier returned. The chamber was inhabited.

Thalgrim mumbled something next to him. Hakem turned to find the lodefinder glassy-eyed and slack-jawed. A thin trail of drool came off his bottom lip and stretched all the way down to the floor.

'Gorl,' he garbled drunkenly.

'No,' the merchant thane cried, reaching out to grab him. But he was too late. Thalgrim stumbled madly into the chamber, burbling 'Gorl, gorl, gorl!' as he went.

Hakem went after him, despite every fibre of his being willing him not to. Ralkan followed in an entirely different delirium.

'Thalgrim,' Hakem hissed, stalling a few feet from the cavern mouth, not daring to raise his voice much above a whisper. 'Wait!'

The lodefinder was oblivious and, after diving amidst a mountainous pile of gold, went barrelling onward.

An inferno of roaring, black-red flame engulfed Thalgrim from an unseen source. The wave of heat emanating from it was incredible and felled Hakem to his knees. Ralkan collapsed into a heap before it, screwing his body up into a ball and whimpering. Hakem lost sight of Thalgrim in the fearsome blaze, shielding his eyes against its terrible glare. When he looked back, there was nothing left of the lodefinder except ash – he didn't even scream.

Survival instinct got Hakem to his feet. He rushed over to Ralkan and dragged him up by the scruff of his neck.

'On your feet,' the merchant thane snarled beneath his breath.

Ralkan obeyed as whatever fear seizing him drained his will.

Tremors shook the ground, sending coins and gems cascading from their lofty summits, so violent that Hakem struggled to stay standing.

From around the collapsing mounds of gold there emerged a beast so ancient and evil that many who lived had never seen its like.

'Drakk,' Hakem whispered, Ralkan murmuring next to him and gripping the merchant thane's tunic for dear life. Hakem felt his courage, his resolve and his reason stripping away as he beheld the snorting behemoth.

So massive was the dragon that its bulk pushed the mountainous treasure peaks aside, nearly filling the width of the immense chamber. Red scales that glistened like blood covered a brawny body fraught with scars. Its barrel-ribbed chest was broad and sickly yellow. Deep, black pools of hate served for eyes and regarded the dwarfs hungrily. Claws the length of swords three times over and half again as thick, scraped the ground as the creature sharpened them raucously. Raising its long, almost elegant, neck the dragon stretched its mighty, tattered wings and roared.

Mind-numbing terror gripped the dwarfs as they fought the backwash of dragon breath, rancid with the stink of sulphur and rotting meat. The beast made no attempt to advance. It merely snorted and hissed, tongue lathing the air as it tried to taste the fear of its prey.

Hakem gritted his teeth and forced his arm to move, prizing Ralkan's fingers off his tunic one-by-one. Released from the lorekeeper's grasp the merchant thane felt a sudden epiphany come over him, a surety of knowledge that let him bury his fear beneath something raw and primal.

'Go,' Hakem said calmly.

Rigid with fear, Ralkan responded with a murmur.

'Go,' he said again, more fiercely this time.

Eyes locked on the beast, the lorekeeper took a half step back.

'I have lost my honour,' Hakem uttered with absolutely certainty and took off his tunic. 'There is nothing left,' he continued, throwing down his belt. 'Perhaps if I die here, there will be some honour in that.' He tore off the hook that was strapped to his arm and unravelled the bandage – the wound was still bloody and seeped through it.

'Go, lorekeeper,' Hakem said, reaching down and taking up a hammer from amongst the scattered treasure. 'Recount my deeds that my name at least might live on.'

Ralkan took another fearful step.

'Flee you fool – now!' Hakem raged, shouting in the lorekeeper's face.

Ralkan found his will at last and fled.

'Now we are alone, you and I,' said the thane of Barak Varr, the frantic footfalls of the lorekeeper diminishing behind him as he allowed his blood-soaked bandage to fall to the ground. He bit into the stump of his wrist, reopening the wound and bringing fresh blood to the surface. Daubing it ritualistically over his bare chest in the arcane sigils of old, he muttered an oath to Grimnir.

The dragon sloped forward, baring its long and deadly fangs – its gaping maw could snap an ogre in two.

Hakem gripped the hammer.

'Come,' he said with grim finality. 'Face me and forge my legend.'

Rearing up on its haunches, the dragon snarled. There was the faintest trace of amusement in its eyes as it dove towards Hakem with bone-crushing force.

CHAPTER FIFTEEN

UTHOR HAD DESCENDED into a ravine of fire. Here in the very bowels of the underdeep the blood of the mountain itself ran in thick channels of lava. Blistering heat haze emanated from the syrupy magma rivers, gouts of liquid flame spitting sporadically to the surface. Igneous rock clusters swam the lava tributaries, shifting like miniature archipelagos, and ran as far as the eye could pierce dust and flame down a long and craggy catacomb.

Columns, carved from the rock in the earliest days of the world, supported a ridged and spiked roof that rose high into a billowing pall of grey-black smoke.

'I do not like the look of this path,' said Rorek, sweating profusely.

Stretching out in front of them was a long and wide road, wretched with cracks venting intermittent plumes of steam and sharp, jutting rocks.

'It is the only road we have left,' Uthor told him, exhaustedly. The thane of Kadrin was finding it hard to speak. Vapours of thick, repressive heat made legs and arms leaden and lungs burn. Carried on an arid, air-choked breeze that robbed breath and will, the effect was stifling.

'Then it is the way we must go.' Emelda mustered her resolve, swallowing back the taste of soot and ash on her tongue.

After the Barduraz Varn and the shallow bridge, the trio had rested for but a moment on the stone plateau, none of them wanting, or willing, to talk about the sudden appearance of Gromrund or what it meant for the hammerer. Gathering up their strength, they'd pressed on down shallow corridors bereft of light, going deeper and deeper into the hold aware that the flood waters might be just behind them.

At one point, Rorek had noticed a marker stone etched in runic script. 'The Lonely Road' it read – it was aptly named. They'd ploughed on in silence, finding no further signs, no indication of where they might be headed. Thunder roared above them constantly and small rock chips fell from the ceiling and scattered down the walls as the Black Water did its work. Then, at last, it caught them, a crushing wave of such fury that they'd fled before it. An ancient door of the underdeep had impeded their escape but together they'd released the elder portal and sealed it shut behind them with the last of Rorek's door spikes, descending into the magma caves at the very nadir of the karak.

Emelda took the first steps across the plateau, treading the most solid route through a cracking path rimmed with piles of hot, burning ash and cooling cinder. Uthor and Rorek followed tentatively behind her.

'Stay away from the edges,' she called from the front.

Uthor peered over the crumbling plateau periphery into deep pits of boiling lava, bubbling with submerged eruptions and gaseous emissions. When a section of rock broke off and fell away into it, only to be devoured instantly, he shrank back and stepped a little faster. All the while, the earth shook and the ceiling rattled, the sound of muted thunder emanating loudly through it.

'Watch out!' Uthor cried.

Emelda looked up and leapt aside as a dislodged spike of rock came crashing down and impaled into the hot earth where she had been standing. The clan daughter got to her feet, just as Uthor arrived, quickly dusting off a thin patina of scorching ash.

'Tromm,' she breathed, her face red and sweaty.

'Tromm,' Uthor returned.

'We had best not linger,' Emelda added, noting more errant chunks of stone impacting against the ground and shattering.

Uthor nodded and the three of them moved on hurriedly.

HAKEM WAS DEAD. Ralkan knew it in his heart, even if he didn't see him fall. Galdrakk the Red was a legend, a dark tale to scare beardlings to sleep or taunt a wazzock. The lorekeeper did not think for a moment that such a beast still existed. Yet he had seen it with his own eyes, even envisioned his own doom at its claws. Hakem had changed that doom and made it his own.

Ralkan cursed aloud, tripping and smashing his knee as he scrabbled in the darkened corridors, stumbling blindly, not knowing where he was but desperate for a way out. Honour was of little consequence to the lore-keeper now. He had to try and live or Hakem's noble sacrifice, his great deed would be for nought. That thought drove him and the certainty that once it was finished with Hakem, Galdrakk's appetite would not be sated and the beast would be coming for more...

THRATCH'S HEAD WAS spinning. He smelled damp fur and realised he was wet. Cold stone was hard and sharp against his back. Blurring memories filled his mind as he struggled to wake fully, of the battle with the dwarf-things, of the terrible thunder...

The painted dwarf-thing was fast, maybe faster than Thratch. No – that wasn't possible. No warrior, dwarf-thing, green-thing or skaven had ever bested him – even the assassins of Clan Eshin had failed in all their clumsy attempts to slay him. No, Thratch was king of his domain and no half-naked, furless dwarf-thing was going to change that.

Ducking instinctively, Thratch was forced to the task at hand and the raging dwarf-thing with his chain-cutter. More out of defensive self-preservation than any measure of sword skill the warlord swatted the shiny blade away, though he took pains to snarl his indifference at his enemy.

Thratch lunged, trying to gut the fat dwarf-thing like a stuck pig. The painted creature was fast but not fast enough and the warlord squealed inwardly with delight as he cut it, licking the shed dwarf blood from his blade. Frenzy filled his mind at the taste of it, the imminence of the kill intoxicating. Thratch would wear the dwarf-thing's head like a hat when he slew it.

The warlord drew down a wicked swipe to finish it but the painted dwarf-thing disappeared at the moment of victory. Searing pain flared in Thratch's back, dispelling his blood frenzy. Keen, skaven ears heard the split sections of plate hitting the ground as they were torn free. Silver flashed as the painted dwarf-thing came on.

Thratch blocked madly as the blows rained down – such fury! The glaive haft snapped under the barrage. Thratch threw the bladed end at his assailant desperately, fighting the urge to squirt the musk of fear and flee blindly. The skaven took a step back and came close to flight. No – he was master of this realm. Thratch had never fled; his strength was what marked him for greatness, it was the very thing that would get him noticed by the Council of the Thirteen and cement a vaunted position in the highest echelons of Skavenblight.

Thratch drew his sword. Rushing forward, he cut the dwarf-thing across the stomach. The skaven licked his muzzle – how succulent its entrails must taste. Another swipe, savage and unrelenting now – the dwarf-thing was tiring and Thratch could feel it. He shaped for another pass, the final blow, when the ground started shaking. Using his tail as a third leg, Thratch kept his feet.

Something didn't smell right. Thunder was rising; he could hear it distinctly getting closer. Thunder? Beneath the earth? Thratch turned. A mighty wave rose up before him, edged with white, frothing foam, thick with skaven and dwarf-thing bodies swept up in its watery maw. Thratch's fur stood on end, eyes widening in abject terror as he faced the pounding inundation. He pumped the musk of fear into the air around him as the remorseless wave crashed down...

Pain flared in Thratch's back from where the painted dwarf-thing had struck him. The skaven warlord

winced as he got shakily to his feet and wiped the
blood from his muzzle, trying to remember what had
happened after the wave hit. Memory was sparse, like
scratchings of meaning at the back of his mind. Darkness came first and then sound had fallen away as he
was carried off into the gloom.

Trying to piece together the time between then and
now, Thratch wandered wildly through the dwarfen
deeps, too dazed and incoherent to do anything else.
Scent, faint but distinct wafted over him on a hot
breeze. Thratch's nose twitched; the stinking aroma of
soot and iron was familiar. It was like acrid bile in his
throat – the hated stink of dwarf-things.

Thratch was angry as he followed the stench. His lair
was flooded, his engine was likely destroyed and his
army decimated. He still had his sword, though it was
chipped and a little bent, that was good. He'd need it
to exact his vengeance.

'THIS WAY,' UTHOR bellowed, treading carefully across a
rock path that fell away at one edge into a deep, undulating pool of liquid fire.

Emelda followed wearily. She had dispensed of her
armour – too heavy and hot to bear any longer.
Shimmering around her waist in the reflected glow of
the lava was the cincture, her only remaining protection. Rorek followed the clan daughter, some
distance behind as the trio passed the narrowing path
and came upon a wide tunnel that wended upward
but was fraught with shadowed alcoves and pits of
flame.

'Do you smell that?' asked the thane of Kadrin, let-
ting Emelda catch him up.

'I smell only ash and fire,' she replied, her expression haggard.

'Breathe deeply,' he told her.

Emelda closed her eyes and took a long and lingering breath. Beyond the scent of ash-laden, fire-scorched air was another smell – something much clearer and colder.

'The upper world,' she said, opening her eyes as tears were forming.

'And there,' added Uthor, pointing in the distance to a faint corona of light. 'The way out.'

'We have escaped…' said Emelda, her face alight with joy then twisting horribly in pain. The end of a rusted blade punched savagely through her chest as she spat a thick gobbet of blood into Uthor's soot-stained beard. Emelda sagged forward as the lustre of the runic cincture dimmed ever so slightly and the blade was wrenched free. The thane of Kadrin rushed to catch the clan daughter and saw past her falling form the visage of a burly skaven, wielding a bent and broken sword. The creature grinned maliciously and snarled at the dwarf.

Holding Emelda in his arms, Uthor was defenceless. He saw the blood-slicked blade poised for a second strike, one that would finish them both. Uthor let Emelda go and tried to unhitch his axe, knowing already it would be too late that, even so close to freedom, his death was assured.

Rorek bellowed a war cry, launching himself at the rat-kin with axe in hand. The creature turned, well aware of the engineer's presence, scraping its blade along the ground and flicking a cloud of burning ash and cinder into Rorek's good eye. Clutching his face and screaming, the dwarf's charge failed and he stumbled to the ground in a dishevelled heap.

Uthor was up, though his arms were leaden, and ready to fight. He stood protectively in front of Emelda who lay prone in the dirt. Rorek was off to his left, wailing in agony and rolling back and forth. Before him was the rat-kin lord, bloodied and breathing hard, its tiny eyes full with vengeful desire.

The skaven must have followed them, somehow got ahead and waited in one of the darkened alcoves to strike. There were so many hiding places, so many ways for unseen lurkers to attack and here, in the flattened plateau of the tunnel the creature had chosen to make its move.

Rocks were falling swiftly now and teeming lances of water came down from the ceiling in several places where the flood had found its way through. Steam hissed where they struck the ground and vaporised.

Uthor squared off against the rat-kin lord, side-stepping slowly, not daring to wipe the trail of sweat eking into his eyes.

'Come on then,' he gasped, the challenge unconvincing as he brandished Ulfgan's axe.

Chittering with glee, the skaven warlord was about to rush the dwarf when another figure stepped from the shadows and into his path.

'Go,' said Azgar, the slayer's muscle-bound back was a cross-hatch of cuts as he came between Uthor and the skaven, 'get the other two out,' he added. He too must have survived the floodwaters and followed the rat-kin lord to them. 'This one and I have unfinished business.' With that Azgar charged at the rat-kin and battered it back with a rain of savage blows.

Steel crashed in Uthor's ears, the rock fall a deep and resonant chorus to the cacophony as he went to Emelda.

She was pale as he cradled her in his arms, the light dying in her eyes.

'Leave me,' she begged through blood-spattered lips, her voice little better than a shallow rasp.

'We are close,' Uthor whispered, shielding her instinctively as a chunk of rock fell and shattered close by, showering him with cutting shards. 'Lean on me,' he pleaded, trying to get beneath her and use his shoulder as a crutch.

Emelda coughed as she exerted herself, spitting blood from her mouth.

'No,' she managed. 'No, I can't.'

Uthor set her down carefully.

'I go to my father now,' she rasped, clutching Uthor's hand. 'Tell the High King that I died with honour and take Dunrik to his rest.'

'Emelda...'

The clan daughter's hand fell away. Uthor clenched his eyes tightly shut, his grief overwhelming. Rage forced it down into the pit of his stomach and opened his eyes. He took the cincture from around Emelda's waist reverently and secured it around his own. He took the axe of Dunrik and strapped it to his back. Muttering an oath to Valaya and to Gazul, Uthor got to his feet and was about to go after the rat-kin when he heard Rorek, sobbing not far away.

Anger wilted as the thane of Kadrin's gaze fell upon the stricken engineer. For a moment he flitted from it to the duelling form of Azgar, his brother, as he battled the skaven warlord fiercely. The slayer's chain axe was

shattered and he wielded the broken end like a lash to
hold the darting rat-kin at bay. As Uthor watched, a
fiery column burst through the ground, flinging rock
and magma into the air. Another jet broke the surface,
then another and another. Azgar was all but lost
beyond the barrier of flame.

'I TOLD YOU we were not done, yet.' Azgar snarled at the
skaven warlord and charged.

Reeling against the barrage of blows, the rat-kin parried and countered furiously. At last, Azgar's frenetic
onslaught wavered and as the slayer unleashed a scything swing with his chain axe, the warlord weaved aside
and stamped its foot down upon the chain as it flew
past harmlessly. Having trapped the weapon, and without stalling, it brought its sword down two-handed,
shearing the chain in half.

Bladeless, Azgar fell back as it was the skaven's turn
to attack, using the length of chain that remained like
a whip to keep the creature at bay. Thick beads of sweat
trailed eagerly down the slayer's body, working their
way into the pronounced musculature as the two
fought on a narrow precipice. Lava bubbled below the
duelling warriors, exuding gaseous smoke and radiat-
ing intense heat.

Behind him, Azgar heard the raging eruption of
flame and magma as the chamber slowly started to dis-
integrate. If forced to back off much further, the slayer
would be consumed by it. Instead, he lashed out with
his chain one last time, smacking the skaven's blade
aside for but a moment and barged into the rat-kin
warlord. The rat-kin bit and clawed viciously, stabbing
with the spike of its left hand when it dropped its

sword as the slayer slowly crushed the creature's body. The blade fell into the lava pool and melted away. Heedless of the grievous wounds inflicted upon him, Azgar drove forward, lifting the skaven warlord up in a fierce bear hug. Claws digging into the ground, the rat-kin tried to arrest the slayer's determined drive but Azgar was not to be denied. He reached around to the creature's neck and, with his bare hands, tore out a raft of crude stitches. It squealed as he did it, the old wound opening readily as Azgar lifted his prey higher and up off the ground.

The edge of the precipice beckoned.

Azgar roared and flung himself and the rat-kin warlord over the edge...

A STRUGGLE, so indistinct that the details were lost, ensued through the shimmering heat haze as skaven and dwarf grappled. Then they fell, off the edge of the precipice to be swallowed by the lava pool.

'Brother...' Uthor muttered, and felt his grief two-fold.

With no time to mourn, the thane went to Rorek quickly, picking him up and hoisting the engineer onto his back with a grunt.

'I cannot see,' Rorek sobbed, rubbing at his freshly ruined eye.

'You will, my friend,' said Uthor, putting one foot in front of the other, just trying not to fall.

'Are we leaving now?' Rorek asked as he passed out.

'Yes,' Uthor replied. 'Yes, we're leaving.'

The chamber shook with all the natural fury of an earthquake as a beast, so old and terrible that Uthor felt the strength in his legs abandoning him, emerged into the wide tunnel behind the fire columns. Even through the flame Uthor recognised this creature as a dragon, the creature called Galdrakk the Red and enemy of his ancestors. With a powerful flap of its wings that staggered Uthor backwards, Galdrakk battered the fire down and launched through it. Lava hissed at its scaly hide but did nought but scorch it as the beast landed heavily on the other side.

Uthor found the strength to back away as the dragon regarded him hungrily. The foul creature's snout was broken and its right eye was crushed as if it had fought recently. The wounds served only to make its appearance all the more terrifying as it came on, one thought filling Uthor's mind as it did so.

We cannot make it…

An almighty wrenching of stone filled the air as a veritable avalanche of rock crashed down upon Galdrakk. The beast was so massive; it couldn't help but be struck. A spiked rock sheared into the soft membrane of its wing, and it roared in pain, followed by a heavy boulder that bashed its snout as others rebounded from its back, neck and forelimbs.

Uthor ran, head low as the ceiling crashed down, the thunderous cry of Galdrakk resonating in his wake. He kept running, not daring to look back, fearing that the beast might still be alive, that it might have gotten free and be on their heels. Uthor fled until, blinking, he emerged into the blazing day, a clear sky supporting an orb-like sun above him. Even then, he still ran, picking his way through mountainous crags, hastening past caves and negotiating patches of scrub and scattered scree until, gasping so hard for breath he thought his lungs might burst, he collapsed in a clearing encircled by rune-etched menhirs. Vision blurring, he recognised the sigil of Grungni and fell unconscious.

IT WAS A shrine to the ancestor gods. Runes for Grungni, Valaya, Grimnir and their lesser children were in evidence upon the foreboding menhirs that felt like the walls of some impenetrable citadel.

Uthor sat in front of a small fire as he read each and every one. He didn't know how long he had been out, but he and Rorek had not been bothered by beasts as they'd lain comatosed on the bare earth.

As far as Uthor could gather, they'd emerged far south of Karak Varn at a tributary of Skull River, which flowed quietly below them in a narrow, sloping defile. The deaths of his comrades weighed heavily upon him, but none more so than that of Emelda. For that and the failure of his oath, there would be a reckoning.

Rorek was stirring, and it arrested the thane of Kadrin from his melancholy thoughts.

'Where am I?' the engineer asked, blinking his fire-scarred eye, red-raw and blackened from the burning ash. 'I... I'm blind,' he said, trying to get to his feet as he started to panic.

Uthor laid a hand upon his shoulder.

'Rest easy, you are among friends.'

'Uthor...?'

'Yes, it's me.'

'Uthor, I cannot see.' The engineer's voice was edged with mild hysteria but he lay back down again.

'I know,' the thane of Kadrin replied, sorrowful as he regarded the milky white orb of Rorek's once good eye. The thane of Kadrin had hoped that the loss of sight might not be permanent but in the harsh daylight the wound looked grievous. He had brought this fate upon Rorek.

'I smell open air, grass and fresh water, and feel wind against my face. Where are we?' the engineer asked.

'Near Skull River, south-east of Karak Varn and, by my reckoning, a day's trek across the mountains to Everpeak,' Uthor told him.

'Are we escorting the Lady Emelda back to Karaz-a-Karak?' the engineer asked.

'No, Rorek. She fell.' Uthor couldn't keep the dark edge from his tone.

'Then are we the only survivors?'

'Yes, we are.'

A sound beyond the shrine circle broke the solemn silence. Uthor stood up, axe in hand.

'What is it?' Rorek was panicking again.

'Stay here,' Uthor hissed and stalked out of the circle, crouched low against the ground, using the long grasses and scattered rocks to cover his advance.

Something moved towards him in the shelter of an earthen overhang.

Uthor stooped to grasp a handful of gravel and cast it quickly ahead of him. Then he gripped his weapon in readiness and, ducking into the shadows, waited for his quarry to approach.

'By Grimnir,' he whispered through clenched teeth, 'I'll split your sides.'

Stone crunched as whatever had wandered across their camp tramped over the gravel noisily.

Roaring, Uthor sprang from his hiding place with his axe raised, ready to mete out death.

Ralkan recoiled from the sudden attack and fell back, the blade cutting air in his wake as Uthor swiped furiously.

'Lorekeeper!' said Uthor, lowering his blade and rushing to Ralkan's aid as he sat, dumped on his arse.

'Am I free?' Ralkan asked, fearfully. 'Am I alive?'

'Yes. Yes, you are free and alive.' Uthor extended his hand to help Ralkan to his feet.

'Uthor!' It was Rorek.

The thane of Kadrin turned, as he got Ralkan up, to see the engineer staggering toward him, axe in hand as he supported himself on a menhir. 'Is it grobi, rat-kin? Point me to them,' he growled, 'I can still shed greenskin blood.'

'Hold,' said Uthor, his voice jubilant. 'It is Ralkan. The lorekeeper lives!

'Tell me, Ralkan, do you have word of any of our other brothers?'

The lorekeeper's face darkened.

'Yes,' he said, simply.

THE WAY BACK to Everpeak was slow and laborious, Rorek's blindness making climbing of any significance impossible, and conducted in silent remembrance. In any case, Uthor wanted to avoid much of the mountain crags. They were fell places, rife with monsters and the three dwarfs were in no condition for a fight. Instead, they went southward, following the languid flow of Skull River, keeping to the shallows, and descended into a thick forest. Wolves hunted them under the false darkness of the tree canopy and more than once Uthor had been forced to take them off the trail and hide in the wide bole of some immense oak as he heard the chatter of goblins. It stuck in his craw to skulk in the shadows, but peril stalked their every step and if they were brought to the attention of even the most innocuous predator, their doom would be assured.

Karaz-a-Karak was a mighty and imposing shadow on a sun-bleached horizon when they finally reached it, the fiery orb red and bloody in a darkening sky that threatened the onset of night when the true dangers of the wild were made manifest.

Heavy of heart and of booted foot, the trio of dwarfs trudged down the gilded terracotta and grey stone runway that led to the formidable gate of the dwarfen capital. It had been many months since they'd left Everpeak. It would not be a happy reunion.

UTHOR HELD HIS head low. He was alone in the High King's Court, both Rorek and Ralkan were being tended by the priestesses of Valaya in a set of antechambers close by.

'Uthor, son of Algrim,' boomed the voice of Skorri Morgrimson, High King of Karaz-a-Karak. 'You have returned to us.'

'Yes, my king,' Uthor uttered with proper deference. The thane of Kadrin went down on one knee. Keeping his eyes on the ground, he dared not meet the High King's gaze.

'And the fate of Karak Varn?' the High King asked.

Uthor mustered his courage as he tried to find the words to relate his failure.

'Speak quickly,' the High King chafed. 'We march to Ungor this very night!'

Uthor looked up.

The High King was sitting upon the great Throne of Power and dressed in his full panoply of war. Clad in shimmering rune armour as forged by the venerable Skaldour in ages past, the dragon crown sat proudly on his beetling brow and with the axe of Grimnir clutched in one hand, Skorri Morgrimson was a truly fearsome sight. In the other hand, he held a quill, the end of which was dark with what appeared to be crimson ink. In front of the High King, upon a gilt and ornate cradle, was the Dammaz Kron. The Great Book of Grudges was open at a blank page.

The king's son, Furgil, stood behind him, also ready for war. The Council of Elders had been dismissed, only the High King's loremaster, his hammerer bodyguard, and Bromgar, the gatekeeper Uthor had met many months ago, were present.

'Karak Varn has fallen. Our expedition failed.' The words were like hot blades in Uthor's heart as he remained genuflect before his king.

'Survivors?' asked the High King, noting the presence of only the thane of Kadrin in his hold.

'Only the three of us that reached Everpeak.'

Skorri Morgrimson's face darkened at that admission.

'My lord,' said Uthor, his voice beginning to choke as he held out the runic cincture. 'There is something you do not know.'

The High King's eyes widened when he saw and recognised the cincture.

'No…' he breathed, tears welling in his eyes.

'My lord,' Uthor repeated, gathering his resolve. 'Emelda Skorrisdottir, clan daughter of the royal house of Karaz-a-Karak joined us in our quest but fell to the rat-kin hordes. She died with honour.'

'Dreng tromm,' the king muttered, pulling at his beard, tears streaming down his face. 'Dreng tromm.'

Bromgar approached Uthor and took the cincture from him to present solemnly to his king. Skorri

Morgrimson traced the blood-flecked runes upon its surface as if touching the face of Emelda herself.

'Take it away,' he whispered, averting his gaze from the bloodied artefact. Staring back down at Uthor, all semblances of grief and anguish drained away from the High King's face as it became as hard as stone.

'At least you can look me in the eye and say it,' the High King stated coldly. 'You are exiled,' he added simply, getting louder and more vengeful, 'cast out of the Karaz Ankor. You and the names of your companions will be etched in the Dammaz Kron in blood, never to be struck out – Never!' he raged, getting up out of his throne and snapping the quill in half in his clenched fist.

Uthor quailed before the High King's wrath but stayed his ground.

'Now leave this place, unbaraki. You are hereby expelled!'

Hammerers came from the wings and escorted Uthor away, who had to be helped to his feet, so great was the shame upon his shoulders.

THE NEXT MORNING as the great gates to Everpeak boomed shut in their wake, Uthor cast his gaze skyward. Flurries of snow were building amidst darkening cloud and a tinge of chilling frost pricked at the wild grasses. Autumn was ending and, in a few more weeks, winter would be setting in. Uthor thought of Skorri Morgrimson as the High King led his army to Karak Ungor, great marching columns of dawi intent on vengeance and retribution, standards reflecting the glimmer of the low lying sun, drums beating and horns blaring. There was a time when the thane of Kadrin would have relished being part of such a muster; now he could not wait to be as far away from it as possible.

'What do we do now?' said Rorek, guided by the vacant-looking Ralkan. The engineer had a blindfold over his eyes foregoing his patch, which now seemed surplus to his needs.

Ralkan no longer bore the book of remembering. It had been taken by the loremasters of Everpeak as a record of what had happened. Ralkan had done much to fill it with all the dwarfs' deeds in the time it had taken to the reach Karaz-a-Karak in the hope that the names of the slain would be remembered, if nothing else.

The three of them had been returned their weapons and other belongings, and even given provisions and fresh clothes before being summarily ejected from the hold. Only Dunrik's axe remained behind for the priests of Gazul to inter and set at least his spirit to rest in the Halls of the Ancestors.

Uthor kept an eye on the horizon as he replied.

'We go northward, to Karak Kadrin and the Shrine of Grimnir. There is but one more vow we must make, and I would make it there before my father if he still lives.'

With that the dwarfs trudged away from Everpeak lost in their thoughts. The wind was gathering in the north. A storm was coming.

EPILOGUE

SKARTOOTH AWOKE IN a deep gorge. His hood was torn, the rat skull ripped free and lost in his plummet over the edge of the plateau. Noises, like crunching bones and sucking meat, emanated from above. Dazed and bruised, sporting numerous small cuts and grazes, the goblin warlord struggled to his feet. Something dug into his bare foot that was swaddled with dirty, black bandages. Skartooth grimaced in pain when he saw it had drawn blood. He looked down ready to vent his diminutive wrath upon whatever rock or sharp stone had cut him. His mouth gaped open. Beneath his foot was the iron collar, the one that Fangrak had stolen!

Gathering the artefact quickly to his breast, Skartooth hurried away. The goblin was acutely aware of the deepening shadows in the nearby caves and though he disliked the blazing sun overhead he was nervous of

371

what things might dwell in those places. There was also the possibility of disaffected orcs and goblins to consider. Likely, they would not take kindly to Skartooth after their abject defeat, despite any protestations that the failure was all Fangrak's doing.

Skartooth took a wending trail down the gorge, picking through overhanging crags and avoiding the worst of the sun's glare. It didn't last long, something lurking in the gloom set his heart racing and his teeth on edge. He took his chances within a deep cave, its entrance so narrow that no beast of any great size could possibly reside there.

Leaving a cooling trail of piss in his wake as he failed to master his fear, Skartooth wandered into a large cavern. Shafts of hazy sunlight drifted down from a natural amphitheatre and illuminated a large patch of ground. Skartooth's heart was in his mouth again when he saw the bleached bones collected there.

Something stirred behind the goblin, something unseen as he'd wandered aimlessly into its lair. Hot breath lapped at the back of his neck. Skartooth turned slowly and came face to face with a massive, lizard-like creature with a thick, scaled head like a battering ram and broad, flat wings. Skartooth knew the creature's like: it was a wyvern. The shaman he'd stolen the iron collar from rode such a beast.

The wyvern hissed, baring its fangs. Skartooth soiled himself and backed away into the light, clambering over the bone nest, kicking skulls and rib bones loose as he fled. The wyvern followed. Skartooth noticed it only had one horn; the other had been shorn off at the nub. The beast snarled and flicked a rasping tail that ended in a savage-looking, poisonous barb. As it opened its mouth, preparing to devour the meagre morsel that was Skartooth, the goblin warlord held up his arms in a vain attempt to fend it off, eyes closed as he waited for the end.

At once the wyvern backed down and hissed its obeisance.

Skartooth opened his eyes, realising he wasn't languishing in the wyvern's gullet he saw that the creature had retreated. The collar glowed warmly in his outstretched hand. Skartooth brandished it experimentally in front of him.

'Bow to me,' he murmured tentatively.

The wyvern went down onto its knuckles and lowered its head submissively.

An evil grin spread across the goblin's face.

'Skartooth got a wyvern.'

ABOUT THE AUTHOR

Nick Kyme hails from Grimsby, a small town on the east coast of England. He moved to Nottingham in 2003 to work on *White Dwarf* magazine as a Layout Designer. Since then, he has made the switch to the Black Library's hallowed halls. His writing credits include several published short stories and the Necromunda novel *Back From The Dead*.

GLOSSARY

BARDURAZ VARN – Literally meaning 'stone river gate'.

BEARDLING – Young dwarfs, no more than fifty winters old, are known as beardlings, since beard length is an indicator of experience and wisdom.

BRYNDURAZ – Literally meaning 'brightstone'. Using the ancient secrets of dwarfen geology, this rare rock can be made to give off brilliant illumination and is used in many holds for just such a purpose. Once mined at Gunbad, the source of this exceptional and rare mineral was lost when the mines fell to goblins.

CHUF – A mouldy, extremely pungent, piece of cheese found beneath a miner's hat that is only ever eaten in emergencies.

COGGING – One of the punishments of the Engineers' Guild, believed to involve the placement of an exceptionally large cog around the recipient's neck and then, stripped naked, the incumbent would tour the entirety of the hold's workshops.

DAMMAZ KRON – Literally 'book of grudges', though the word has two meanings and can refer to the Great Book of Grudges, which resides in the dwarfen capital of Karaz-a-Karak and records all the wrongs and misdeeds ever perpetrated against the dwarf race, or it can also refer to a particular hold's book of grudges as each and every dwarf realm has one to record that hold's specific grievances.

DAWI – Literally meaning 'dwarfs'.

DEEPS – The levels into which dwarf holds are divided.

DRAKK – Literally meaning 'dragon'.

DRENG TROMM – Translates literally as 'slay beard'. It refers to a very serious lamentation during which a dwarf expresses his profound sorrow and desire to tear at his beard in shared remorse. The sentiment can also be conveyed more solemnly to indicate when something is a great shame or to acknowledge a profound loss or misdeed.

DRINGORAK – Literally translates as 'cunning road', often referring to a secret door or hidden door.

DUNKIN – Annual dwarf bathing ritual.

FRONGOL – Cave mushrooms, often used in stews.

GAZUL BAR BARAZ; GAZUL GAND BARAZ – Invocation of Gazul, Lord of the Underearth. Literally meaning, 'A bond to Gazul's gate' and 'Gazul help them find the gate'. It refers to the pledge made to Gazul that he might guide the dead to his gateway chamber where they will await judgement before entering the Halls of the Ancestors.

GNOLLENGROM – This greeting is a mark of respect afforded to a dwarf who has a longer and more spectacular beard. Commonly, it is a term used when in the company of longbeards or ancestors, but there are instances of it being used to address a dwarf of high station such as a king or runelord (who is likely to be a longbeard in any event).

GROBI – Meaning 'goblin'. The word grob, of which grobi is derived, also means green and can refer to greenskins in general.

GROMRIL – Also known as 'hammernought' or 'starmetal', gromril is the hardest substance in the known world and can only be fashioned by the craft of the dwarfs. The metal is incredibly rare and exceptionally valuable.

GOBLIN WARS – Period after the Time of Woes when goblins, orcs and other creatures attacked the dwarfs in their weakened state and sacked or took over many holds.

GORL – Especially soft gold that is yellow in colour.

GRUMBAKI – Literally meaning 'a grumbler' or 'whiner'.

GRUNDLID – Meaning 'hammer tongue', Grundlid is a secret language known in particular by miners and lodefinders. It consists of a series of taps or scrapes against rock and carried through to the listener to discern message and meaning.

THE HALLS OF THE ANCESTORS – These are the legendary feast halls where the ancestor gods, Grungni and Valaya sit for eternity. All dwarfs believe that, upon their death, they will pass on to the Halls of the Ancestors where they will feast with their ancestors forever more. Only if a dwarf's tomb is desecrated or some past deed undone will they be unable to enter the great halls, which is why the dwarfs view the sanctity of the dead with such seriousness.

HAZKAL – Impetuous youth or fiery young warrior dwarf. It is a word that also refers to recently brewed ale.

KARAZ ANKOR – The ancient realm of the dwarfs, encompassing all the holds of the Worlds Edge Mountains and beyond.

KHAZUKAN KAZAKIT-HA! – War cry of the dwarfs, literally meaning 'Look out, the dwarfs are on the warpath!'

KHAZUK – The shortened version of the war cry 'Khazukan Kazakit-ha!'

KRUTI – Derived from the word krut, which is an uncomfortable disease contracted from mountain goats and meaning 'one who suffers from krut'. It is also used to refer to goatherders and as such is regarded as an insult.

KULGUR – The art of cooking troll flesh.

KURI – A form of meat stew boiled up with whatever ingredients are to hand. Commonly used by travelling dwarfs when other food stuffs are in short supply. Troll meat is popular, occasionally spiced and flavoured wild berries.

NARWANGLI – An insult. A word used to describe a dung-collector or a dwarf that smells of dung, or anything else of an unsavoury nature.

QUAFFING – A punishment of the Engineers' Guild in which the incumbent must drink a copious amount of oil, meaning they will be unable to taste or enjoy ale or food for several weeks, even months.

RAT-KIN – Slang name for the skaven, a race of mutant ratmen that build their burrows and warrens beneath the earth and are constantly at war with the dwarfs.

RECKONERS – Those dwarfs charged with ensuing proper payment is levelled and paid for the grievances or other dwarfs. Each reckoner keeps a tally of deeds done and recompense made in his log or on stone tablets.

RHUN – Meaning 'rune', the symbols of the dwarfs that can be mundane or magical.

Rɪʟ – Brightly shining gold ore.

Rɪɴɴ – A dwarf woman or king's consort.

Rᴜɴᴋ – A massacre or overwhelming defeat.

Rʜᴜɴᴋɪ – Khazalid for 'runesmith'.

Sᴛᴏɴᴇ ʙʀᴇᴀᴅ – Granite like victual that forms part of the staple diet of the dwarfs. Such is its hardness and robust texture that only dwarfs have the constitution to consume it. Not unlike eating rock, but will never soil.

Sᴋᴏʀᴏɴɢ – A dwarf battle term referring to a small throng of twenty warriors.

Tʜɪɴᴅʀᴏɴɢᴏʟ – A hidden chamber where items of great value are kept, such as treasure or ale.

Tɪᴍᴇ ᴏꜰ Wᴏᴇs – Period in history when the Karaz Ankor was wracked by floods, earthquakes and eruptions devastating the dwarf realm so badly it would never recover.

Tromm – Meaning 'beard', but it is also a respectful greeting.

Tʀᴏᴜsᴇʀ Lᴇɢs Rɪᴛᴜᴀʟ – Ancient expulsion practice of the Engineers' Guild, the details of which are shrouded in secretive mystery.

Uꜰᴅɪ – This is a term used to describe any dwarf who labours over preening their beard. A vain dwarf, one who is over concerned with appearance and likely cannot be trusted to fight.

UMGAK – Meaning 'crudely made' or of 'shoddy craftsmanship'.

UNBARAKI – Literally meaning 'oathbreaker'. There is no greater insult that one dwarf can level against another and one not to be used lightly.

UNDERDEEP – The lowest and oldest levels of a hold. Few dwarfs venture here as they are often dilapidated and inhabited by dangerous monsters.

UNGDRIN – Also known as the Underway, the Ungdrin or Ungdrin Road is the massive network of subterranean tunnels wrought by the dwarfs in ages past to make travelling from one hold to another much easier and more expedient. As the ravages of orcs, goblins and skaven had taken their toll on the dwarf empire, much of the Ungdrin is in a state of disrepair or been made into the lair of monsters.

URK – Orc or enemy. This word also translates as 'coward' as all enemies of the dwarfs are considered as such.

UZKUL – Commonly meaning 'death', but can also be used to mean 'bones'. Often used as a warning to chambers where there are known dangers.

VALA-AZRILUNGOL – Ancient Khazalid name for Karak Eight Peaks, meaning 'Queen of the Silver Depths'. It was once the greatest and most vaunted of all the holds of the dwarf empire, greater even than Karaz-a-Karak but fell after over a century of bitter warfare against skaven and greenskins.

VARAG KADRIN – Mad Dog Pass, the route from the Worlds Edge Mountains to the Dark Lands and south of Karaz-a-Karak above Karag Dron.

VARN DRAZH – Khazalid for 'Black Water', the great lake-like expanse in the Worlds Edge Mountains wedged between the hold of Zhufbar to the north and Karak Varn to the south-east. Formed from the melt waters of the surrounding mountains and situated within a vast crater, history maintains that a meteor struck the point at which the Black Water resides and as such it is a source of the valuable meteoric-iron known as gromril.

WANAZ – The opposite of an ufdi, a wanaz is a dwarf that has an unkempt beard and is known to be disreputable. An insult.

WAR OF VENGEANCE – Period in history also referred to as the War of the Beard, when the dwarfs fought against the elves for dominion of the Old World. It was a devastating war in which none would truly emerge the victor, despite dwarfen boasts to the contrary.

WATTOCK – An insult meaning a down at heel or unsuccessful dwarf.

WAZZOCK – Foolish or gullible dwarfs, those who have been duped in matters of business, exchanging valuables for something of little or no worth, or who are easily parted from their gold in a doomed venture, are called wazzocks. Much like other dwarfish derogatory terms, this is regarded as an insult.

WUTROTH – Also known as 'ironbark' and 'stone trunk', this wood of dwarfen origin is incredibly rare and exceptionally strong but also very pliable.

ZAKI – The zaki is the dwarf that has lost his mind and wanders the mountains. Many dwarf hermits are often described thusly, as are those guilders who deviate from the strictures of their guild (quite a common occurrence amongst journeyman engineers).

ZHARRUM – Literally meaning 'fire drum'. Zharrum are metal spheres containing lamp oil or other combustibles and used like rudimentary bombs to spread fires quickly. In mining, they can be used on wooden supports to collapse tunnels.

ISBN: 978-1-84416-503-2

GRUDGELORE
Nick Kyme & Gav Thorpe

Presented as an artefact from the Warhammer World, *Grudgelore* contains a wealth of associated background about the dwarfs and in-character tales of heroism and desperate battles. It's a must-have for all Warhammer fans.